Karen Viggers was born in Melbourne, and grew up in the Dandenong Ranges riding horses and writing stories. She studied veterinary science at Melbourne University, and worked in mixed animal practice for seven years before completing a PhD at the Australian National University. Since then she has worked on a wide range of Australian native animals in many different wild places, including Antarctica. She lives in Canberra with her husband and two children. Her first novel, *The Stranding*, was published in 2008. You can find out more about Karen's books at www.karenviggers.com

The
Lightkeeper's
Wife

KAREN VIGGERS

ALLEN&UNWIN
SYDNEY • MELBOURNE • AUCKLAND • LONDON

Published by Allen & Unwin in 2011
This edition published in 2012

Allen & Unwin
83 Alexander Street
Crows Nest NSW 2065
Australia
Phone: (61 2) 8425 0100
Fax: (61 2) 9906 2218
Email: info@allenandunwin.com
Web: www.allenandunwin.com

Cataloguing-in-Publication details are available
from the National Library of Australia
www.trove.nla.gov.au

ISBN 978 1 74331 039 7

p. vii: Judith Wright extract from 'The Sitter's' from *A Human Pattern: Selected Poems*
(ETT Imprint, Sydney, 2010).

Text design by Emily O'Neill
Set in Adobe Garamond Pro by Bookhouse, Sydney
Printed and bound in Australia by the SOS Print + Media Group.

10 9 8 7 6 5

MIX
Paper from
responsible sources
FSC® C011217

The paper in this book is FSC® certified.
FSC® promotes environmentally responsible,
socially beneficial and economically viable
management of the world's forests.

For my grandma
Rhoda Emmy Vera Viggers
1912–2009

an inspirational and compassionate woman

My life was wide and wild,
and who can know my heart?
There in that golden jungle
I walk alone.

JUDITH WRIGHT
From *A Human Pattern: Selected Poems*

Prologue

She was in the kitchen when it came—a loud rap on the door that bounced down the hallway, off the floorboards, the hat stand, and ricocheted through the sliding doors into the kitchen. Wiping the table, she was in another world, remembering how it was to walk the wild beaches of Bruny Island.

The knock jolted her back to the present. It added fifty years to her body, reminded her she was old. She jerked in the middle of a circular sweep, sending a shower of crumbs to the floor. These days few people came to her house unexpected.

She retrieved her walking stick and shuffled down the hall. Through the frosted window she could see a silhouette—someone looking for a donation, no doubt. She twisted the locks and opened the door.

It was a hunched old man in a dark blue suit with a crooked tie. He had a craggy face and for a moment, she thought she knew him—from the bowls club, perhaps. Or Jan's church. Or maybe the opportunity shop. But at their age, everyone seemed similar. Only the details of their problems differed.

'Can I help you?' she asked.

He shifted, and something about the way he tilted his head and pawed at his hair halted her. She grasped the door and leaned there breathless, heart battering in her chest.

What was he doing, turning up where he wasn't welcome? And why had he come? Staring at her with those washed-out blue eyes that hadn't lost their intensity over the years. She dropped her stick and swung away.

'Mary.' His voice was a rasp. Old and worn out, like the rest of him. He extended a hand, and she was too shocked to push him away. Did he really think he could help her? One old spindle trying to prop up another. She glared at him and was once again aware of the panicked fluttering of her heart. It had never been this bad before. The doctor had said she must avoid shocks like this. Death was supposed to be the last surprise.

Uninvited, he put his hand on her shoulder and turned her into the house. She was too overwhelmed and appalled to protest. His proximity frightened her. He smelled of old age. Sour. The stale odour of clothes washed too infrequently. Pungent breath. He hadn't smelled like that the last time she saw him—then he had about him an aroma of nutmeg and cloves.

Following the direction of her nod, he guided her down the hallway. In the kitchen, he scraped out a chair and lowered her into it. Then he sat down opposite and studied her.

She wouldn't have recognised him if they had passed in the street. But then, who would look at *her* now and know she was Mary Mason? Of course, she'd never been pretty in the conventional white-skinned, delicate way. But she had been vibrant and colourful. Her body had been strong, firm and muscular. She'd been able to do things other girls couldn't, like lift hay bales and milk cows. She'd been alive in her skin. It was a feeling she missed every day. She slumped against the table, remembering her younger self. This man knew her from that time.

He was still watching her, his eyes trying to reach into her mind. But she held him out. Her thoughts were no longer his to inspect. Looking back, she cursed the past weakness that had led her to this moment. She, who had prided herself on being so strong.

'What do you want?' she asked, her mouth flattening.

He regarded her with expressionless eyes and brushed again at his thin grey hair—a gesture that took her back to the day she first met him. Now he unbuttoned his jacket, took out a white envelope and laid it on the table. Mary's heart began to tumble.

'What is it?' There was panic in her fingers, a tingling in her chest.

They both looked at the envelope, still partly covered by his leathery hand.

'You know what it is, Mary.' His voice was little more than a whisper. He leaned forward and stared at her. 'I want you to give it to him.'

She clawed at the edges of the table, trying to stand. 'I won't do it. It's best he doesn't know.'

The old man laughed hollowly. 'You choose the time, Mary. But you can't erase me. I exist. I could have made things much more difficult.'

He stood and pushed in his chair. The letter remained on the table.

'I'll throw it away,' she said. 'I'll burn it.'

A thin smile split his lips. 'But you won't, Mary. You've had things your way for so long. Now this is for me. It's something I need.'

He limped to the sliding doors and then glanced back. In spite of her fear, she was moved: in his look was embedded everything that had not been done, everything that had not been said.

This was it, then. The end of it.

'Goodbye, Mary.'

She listened to the uneven scrape of his feet moving down the hall.

'Don't make me do this,' she called.

But she heard the front door close with a bang, and she knew that he had gone.

PART I

Origins

1

For three days, the letter stayed on the table untouched. Every time Mary looked at it her heart thrashed like a wild bird in a cage. She bent her life around it, trying to avoid the kitchen, eating in the lounge room with a plate perched awkwardly on her lap, drinking tea hurriedly at the sink, and taking the phone out of the room whenever anyone rang. It was ridiculous and she knew it, but the handwriting on the front of the envelope made her nervous. God knows why she couldn't dispose of the thing; she ought to toss it in the bin or burn it in the fireplace, but she couldn't quite bring herself to do it.

She lived with a heightened sense of panic, sleeping fitfully. What if the letter bearer returned? She had to act. But what to do? The letter was a burden—the past and the future rolled into one. She became grumpy and irritable. This ought to be a time of peace, with Jack gone and her own health declining. But the letter was projecting her back into life. It insisted she take control.

On the third night, she found a feasible idea among her restless thoughts, and the next morning she shuffled into the study and riffled through a pile of papers on the desk, seeking the brochure someone had given her months ago. She'd been keeping it, waiting. The letter was the catalyst. It was time to go back. Her hand had been forced and she must address the past before she could decide what to do.

She found the brochure beneath an old electricity bill and called the number printed on it; then she opened the phone book on the kitchen bench and made another call. Afterwards, she pulled out a suitcase, folding into it neat stacks of underwear, poloneck sweaters, jumpers, woollen trousers, a coat, a thick scarf and a hat.

When her clothes were packed she went to fetch the letter. Her hand hovered over it and a wry smile twisted her face: she was behaving as if the letter might explode. And in a sense she supposed this was true. It had erupted into her life and could well blow apart what time she had left. Finally she picked it up, feeling the smooth texture of the paper with her thumb as she carried it to the bedroom and slipped it into a side pocket of the suitcase. Then she turned to the bookshelf and grasped an old photo album which she placed in the case on top of the clothes. Now she was ready.

In the quiet of the room, she gazed at the dark shadows that angled across the bed and lingered in the corners. She had lived here, in this old Hobart house, for twenty-five years, sharing her husband's retirement and decline—the terrible process of watching someone you love retreating from life.

Twenty-five years: a large portion of their lives together. Much had happened—ageing, a grandchild. Even so, she'd never really thought of Hobart as home. For her, it would always be Bruny Island. The light reflecting on the shifting water. The hollow voice of the wind. The lighthouse. The wide southern stretch of Cloudy Bay . . . It was right she should go there now, to the place she first met Jack, where she first came alive. And more than that; she owed it to Jack. On Bruny, she would remember him more clearly. Somehow, there she would reunite with him, relive the good times—those early days when the foundation of their love was shaped and their commitment was sealed.

She also owed it to herself to return. Time was running out, and there were old emotional wounds she needed to attend to before she died—matters neglected amid the soothing monotony of daily life. She needed to find peace and inner calm. To settle into self-acceptance. To grant herself release from guilt. Only on Bruny Island could she achieve these things.

And she must decide how to deal with the letter.

On Sunday morning, Mary sat on the couch in the lounge room. Half an hour ago, she had finished her final cup of tea then washed and dried the mug and replaced it in the cupboard. Now she was stiff after sitting still for so long, listening to the clock on the mantelpiece ticking into emptiness. Normally she'd be tuned in to ABC radio, the news and current affairs. But this morning she needed to sit quietly. There was too much ahead. Too much to contemplate. The clean air of Bruny was beckoning. The smell of wet trees. Salt on the wind. She wanted to be gone from here.

She heard a car pull up and the dull thud of a door closing. Jacinta at last.

Her granddaughter entered the room with the breeziness of the young, all brown eyes and smiles and long loose limbs. At twenty-five, physically, she was her mother all over again, although she'd hate to hear it. She bent for a hug and Mary clung to her, enjoying the feel of young wiriness, the tautness of unblemished skin. How sadly Mary had mourned the loss of her own youth, the decay to wrinkles and sagginess and waistline spread. Her strong wavy hair reduced to flimsy wisps. Over time, she'd learned to accept it and she'd embraced other things: simple pleasures, like bird calls, a good roast, familiar company, a favourite novel, the comfort of words unspoken but understood.

'Are you sure you're up to this, Nana?' Jacinta was regarding her assessingly. She'd always had an uncanny instinct for gauging Mary's physical and emotional health. It was part of what made their relationship special, and so different (thank goodness) from Mary's constant tussle with Jacinta's mother. With Jan there was always that particular tension belonging to interactions between mothers and daughters.

During her fortnightly visits, Jan had recently stepped up her comments about nursing homes; she'd even offered to organise a tour of suitable places that Mary might consider. But Mary would have none of it. She didn't want to die in a hospital bed with tubes sticking out of her like spaghetti. Nursing homes were expensive too. And she didn't want to be a burden on her children. She knew what it was to care for a dying person; she'd done it for Jack. Her family might not like it when they realised what she had chosen, but this option was better. It was *her* option. *Her* decision. She was doing this for herself.

'Of course I'm up to it,' she said quickly. 'This is my last chance.' She reached for her stick. 'Shall we get going, then?' She waved an arm towards her luggage near the door, attempting nonchalance, although this was difficult, knowing the letter was tucked inside. 'There's my case. And I've packed some things in the basket for a picnic.'

'A suitcase!' Jacinta laughed. 'We're only going for the day.'

They drove south out of Hobart in the sullen early light. The purple shadow of Mount Wellington loomed above them with caterpillars of mist clinging just below the summit. Low clouds sat close over the morning and it seemed the day was already weary. Through the dark cleft of the cutting, ravens picked at possum carcasses squashed on the wet road.

At the roundabout in Kingston, Jacinta glanced at her watch. 'Have you checked the ferry times?'

'There's one at nine thirty. We can get a cup of tea while we wait.'

'What about breakfast? Have you had any?'

'Yes, of course. I've been up since five.' It had taken her a long time to shower and get ready.

Jacinta groaned. 'I wish I could bounce out that early.'

Mary recalled the shrill of the alarm and the breathlessness that followed. 'I certainly didn't *bounce*,' she said.

Jacinta smiled. 'I didn't shower. I hope I don't smell.'

'Only of vegemite toast.'

'But vegemite smells awful.'

'I can think of worse.'

They laughed.

When Jacinta was small, Mary had cared for her while Jan was teaching. They'd had fun together, and she'd taken immense satisfaction in the task: after the lighthouse, it had provided her with a focus without which she'd have withered. Mary knew Jacinta liked her, whereas Jan had always been disapproving. Somehow Mary hadn't been quite the mother Jan wanted—although Mary wasn't sure anyone could have lived up to Jan's expectations. Jan resented the years they'd lived at the light station. She claimed the place had curtailed her childhood and that she'd missed out on *opportunities*—whatever that meant. Mary couldn't imagine what great things Jan envisaged would have come her way in suburban Hobart.

It was true their lives hadn't been easy at the light station. Challenges came with isolation. There'd been no other children on the cape. Dim lighting for schoolwork in the kitchen. Limited fresh food. No visitors in winter. Poor weather. But what they lacked in convenience, they had gained in simplicity and proximity to nature. Skies and sea stretching forever. Fishing. Exploring. Picnics on the beach. Space to roam. Mary's heart still settled to think of it. Even so, Jan was convinced she'd been denied the important things, society and friendships and culture. Ever since, she'd run herself ragged trying to create this life she believed she'd been deprived of. It had driven her husband away; of that Mary was sure.

And yet, Mary could still remember how Jan loved to ride the pony along Lighthouse Beach. How she and Gary had run across the hills with bed sheets over their heads pretending to be ghosts. The bonfires, and the glorious Christmases, making decorations and presents. Then, it was just the four of them—Mary, Jack and the two children—wandering on moonlit nights with the flash of the light slicing the dark. Mary remembered those jewels of Jan's childhood, even if Jan chose to forget them.

She remembered less of Gary, her second child. He was more often with his father working in the shed, or kicking a ball among the tussocks, chasing chickens, sprinting to the beach. Not long after the youngest child, Tom, came along, Jan and Gary went to boarding school in Hobart. Tom grew up on the cape alone, roaming wild. He was the only one who spoke of the light station with affection. By the time they went to school, Gary and Jan couldn't wait to escape it.

Parents weren't supposed to have favourites, but Mary had always felt protective of Tom. He was her sensitive child, the one susceptible to deep passion and grinding hurt. She loved them all, of course she did. But Tom was special. He needed her more than the others. Or was it that she needed him?

Now she thought of the letter and shuddered. It could ruin everything. Her family life. Her children's beliefs. She must make sure it wasn't discovered. Ridiculous that she hadn't destroyed it already. What was holding her back?

She sighed and struggled to suppress tears. Soon she would be on Bruny. With Jack. And everything would be clearer.

At Kettering, they waited in line with a small number of cars and an empty cattle truck. Jacinta disappeared into the ferry terminal while Mary stayed in the car watching ruffles of wind skip over the water. The skies had lifted a little but still reflected the steely grey of the sea. Across the D'Entrecasteaux Channel,

Mary could see the gentle hills of North Bruny. Not far out, the ferry had rounded the headland and was coming towards them.

It had been many years since she first crossed to Bruny Island, taking the ferry from further south at Middleton to the southern part of the island. She had made that unhappy passage alone, leaving her parents behind in Hobart and coming to live on her uncle's farm. Remaking her life—and not by choice—at the grand age of sixteen. Not for the first time, she wondered what shape her life might have taken if she had never been sent to Bruny.

Jacinta returned with hot drinks, and Mary accepted the cup of tea with relief. Thinking of the past made her feel cold, and yet what else was there to think of? She'd come on this journey to remember the best of it, but recollection could not be without pain. She sipped her tea too quickly and burned her tongue.

'How's Alex?' she asked, shifting her thoughts away from the past. Alex was Jacinta's boyfriend, the son of a lawyer. He was a quiet lad, positive and affable; Mary liked him.

'He's okay.' Jacinta paused. 'He's under pressure at the moment. From his family. Especially his mum.'

'Isn't that always so?'

Jacinta's lips compressed. 'They want him to take up a partnership in the firm. But it's too soon. He's only been out of uni a couple of years.'

'And what does Alex want?'

'That's a good question. I wish his mother would ask him. But she's hell-focused on getting what she wants.'

'Alex in the family business and you sidelined.'

'How did you know?' Jacinta glanced at her.

'Just a hunch. You're developing too much influence. Taking her son away.'

'Are all mothers like that?'

Mary laughed. 'Not me. I was relieved when Judy snapped up Gary. I thought he'd never find a wife.'

'What about Tom?'

Mary hesitated. Yes, Tom. It had been nine years now since he'd returned from Antarctica, and still no sign of healing. 'He'll sort things out eventually,' she said. 'But how about you and Alex?'

'I think he needs to experience a bit more of the world before the business takes over his life.'

Mary's smile was wry. 'Isn't that always the way with lawyers? Making money while the sun shines?'

Jacinta's forehead puckered. 'I don't want to be his sacrifice. We need to move in and commit to each other before he sinks into his career.'

'And is Alex ready for that?'

'I think so.'

'Good. A plan.' Mary liked plans. It meant you were more than halfway to working things out. Alex ought to be ready. Jacinta was a special girl. A bit of nest-making might accelerate things.

As they talked, the ferry had approached the landing, engines grinding, and bumped into position. Deck hands tossed heavy ropes over bollards, then the ramps lowered and the Bruny traffic clunked off and away. Jacinta followed the line of cars onto the ferry. There were few vehicles going across so only the lower deck was loaded. When they were all parked, the ramps were cranked up, and the throb of the engines shuddered through the decks as the ferry pushed away.

They churned out past the headland, swinging slowly south-east. Mary climbed out of the car, donned her coat and hat and walked slowly to the front of the ferry. This was her favourite place, watching the water froth up at the bow and the gulls cruising by on the chill air. She had crossed the channel many times before. Sometimes with the children, attempting to curb their enthusiasm to climb up for a better view. Other times, she'd been alone, with space to dissect her life.

On the surface, happiness seemed little enough to ask for. Mostly, she and Jack had been lucky. They'd managed to sew themselves back together in troubled times. She ought to be proud of what they'd achieved.

Shivering, she gazed towards North Bruny. The water was liquid glass and the cold cut through her like ice. It was a typical late-autumn day. The sort of day that gave the southlands their moodiness. The long, grey, misty light. It made her feel nostalgic.

Jacinta came to stand beside her and they hooked elbows. Warm against cold. Strength against weariness. Eventually, Jacinta led her back to the car. They sat with the engine running and the heaters on, watching the low wooded hills of North Bruny loom closer, widening into pastures with trees and wire fences.

Mary was surprised to find tears again welling in her eyes.

As they drove east over the island, Mary watched the paddocks blur by. Hunched in her seat, she was trying to retain every detail of the scenery. It was different, this trip—knowing she wouldn't pass this way again. The land was drying out, even here, where it used to be so lush. She remembered a time when rain pounded the whole island and cloaked it in green. These days, the storms that lashed South Bruny wore themselves out by the time they reached the north part of the island, and now it looked as cracked and weathered as her skin.

Her eyes scraped the landscape, seeking the old Bruny, the things she and Jack had loved. She had forgotten the way the road curved over the hills. Black swans were resting on a farm dam. And here were two white geese in a paddock. She was surprised to see piles of weathered grey logs waiting to be burned. With so much of the forest already gone, were people still clearing?

They turned south on the main Bruny road and drove past mudflats where pied oystercatchers waded in the shallows, plucking crabs. In the scrub, yellow wattlebirds clacked. There was a short section of tarred road through Great Bay then they were back on gravel, passing coastal farmland where dirty sheep competed with thickets of bracken.

They came to the Neck; a few cars in the roadside carpark. This was where a wooden walkway crossed the dunes and ascended the hill. Mary knew that path well. Beneath the walkway were the burrows of a thousand mutton birds and little penguins. If you knew where to look, you could see small webbed footprints crisscrossing among the waving grasses.

The road along the isthmus had only been open a few years when she first visited this place with Jack—before that people used to drive on the channel-side sand at low tide. She and Jack sat holding hands on the vast wild ocean beach, watching slick black penguins waddling ashore, moonlight glinting white on their plump bellies. The colony would be empty now. The last fat mutton-bird chicks would have left in late April, labouring on their migration to Siberia.

As the car whizzed low along the narrow passage of the Neck, Mary leaned back and closed her eyes, remembering the climb up the hill. Long ago, the walkway was just a rough track along the ridge. She used to puff her way up there with Jack and the children to marvel at the view—that wide expanse of sky and coast spreading south-east along the isthmus to Adventure Bay and Fluted Cape. There was the hummocky mass of South Bruny, the long lines of breaking surf clawing the beach. To the west, the silhouettes of black swans drifting on the channel. She could remember the heat of the climb. The delicious bite of the wind. The rain sheeting across South Bruny.

Now, the walkway claimed the ridge for tourists. The island had become a *destination*. And the word *isolation* no longer applied here. Bruny was still the place Mary loved, but it wasn't the same. She had to accept that. Change was the future. She smiled to herself. They called it *progress*. But she knew better. The island was her past. Her life with Jack. Her everything.

2

When the car mounted the rise over the dunes and the silver waters of Cloudy Bay spread out before her, Mary felt a sigh rise from deep within. The great flat stretch of yellow sand was just as it had always been. Quiet. Moody. The epitome of solitude. This place marked her beginnings with Jack. The two of them young and unscathed. They had grown wild in the wild air. Jack still lingered here with the sea mist; she could feel him. He was waiting for her.

As they drove down past the landlocked lagoon onto the sand, a white-faced heron startled from the shore, trailing gangly legs as it lifted into lilting flight. Pacific gulls rose chortling into the air. On the beach, Jacinta stopped the car, and Mary soaked up the ambience.

She opened the door and Jacinta helped her out. Then she patted her granddaughter's arm and Jacinta stepped away, leaving her to shuffle down the beach on her own. At the high edge of the tide, she bent stiffly to take a handful of sand. It was fine and grey, slightly muddy. Kneading the soggy graininess of it in her palm, she gazed into the distance where the beach arced east to the far headland: Cloudy Corner and East Cloudy Head.

Down by the water, the Pacific gulls had gathered again in loose flocks, facing seawards. Mary knew that if she could run and scare them, they'd lift as a unit into the air and then congregate once more further along the beach. They needed each other's company to stare so steadfastly south in this lonely light. Everything here was dense with latitude. If you headed south from this beach, there was nothing until Antarctica.

'Nana, let's get out of the wind. I don't want you to get cold.' Jacinta came up behind her, taking her hand.

Mary pulled gently away. 'I'll be all right. I'd like to walk a little more.'

She wandered slowly east, focusing on the distant dark shadow of East Cloudy Head where it humped against the sky. She used to go up there with Jack, pressing through the untracked scrub, scratching herself on bushes. They used to forge a route up towards the southern aspect of the head so they could climb nearer to the sky. They'd stand there, close and exhilarated, with the sea pounding over the rocks below, and the Southern Ocean all around, stretching east, south, west.

She paused to draw breath, taking in the cold stiff air. The hint of seaweed. The thick scent of salt. This place renewed her. It was life itself. She smiled and closed her eyes against the chill. She was right to come here.

'Nana. Please hop in. It's cold.'

The car pulled up beside her, and Mary realised she'd forgotten her granddaughter. There was so much within and around her that was not of this time. She glanced into the car, her features flushed, high on memory.

'Please, Nana. The wind is freezing.'

Jacinta helped her back in and they drove slowly along the sand, windows down so Mary could feel the air. The beach slid smoothly beneath the wheels of the four-wheel drive.

'Can you take me right down to the end?' Mary asked. 'I want to show you Cloudy Corner. There's a campground just short of the headland. You and Alex might like to camp there sometime.'

When she'd first come to this part of the island—on a camping trip with Jack's family—there was nobody else around. It was wilderness. They'd camped in the bush. At night they sat on the beach in the dark feeling the waves come in, soothed by the rhythm. And that view south; the arc of the bay, the dramatic cliffs etched with shadows.

'Does Alex like to camp?' she asked Jacinta, dragging herself back to the present.

Jacinta sighed. 'He does. But we don't seem to fit it in very often. Life's so busy.'

'You should bring him here. It might help you slow down. Give you some time for making decisions.'

'Yes. We need to get out of Hobart more. It hems you in, doesn't it? City life. Even in a small city. It's been months since we got away.'

Mary wanted to tell her that it was important to remember how to live. The young thought life was forever. And then, there you were, on the brink of decline, regretting time not used well. Yet if you lived with that knowledge of time passing—driven by intensity—perhaps meaning would evade you in your very quest to find it. Perhaps it was all right to live as Mary had done, letting life's tide drop experiences in her lap. She'd made the best she could of everything that had washed up over the decades.

'Thank you for coming here with me,' Mary said.

Jacinta smiled at her. 'I wouldn't have missed it.'

At the far end of the beach, Jacinta faced the car to the water and they sat quietly absorbing the atmosphere; the gush of the waves riding in, the buffeting of the wind at the windows, the scrub shifting and sighing behind them.

'I was five when you first brought me here,' Jacinta said, staring out over the rocks of Cloudy Reef where cormorants sat in a cluster, drying their wings. 'I thought this must be the end of the earth. You told me that if I sailed directly south for seven days I'd come to the ice. The edge of the land of penguins. That was magic for me.'

'Just like Tom.' Mary knew about the draw of Antarctica. She'd almost lost her younger son to its mysterious magnetism.

'Do you think he'll go back?' Jacinta asked.

Mary shook her head. 'I think he dreams of it. But he lost so much last time. I don't think he could go through that again.'

'Perhaps it'd be different if he went now.'

'And maybe not.'

'Poor Tom.'

Yes. Poor Tom. He still bore the wounds of his time south.

'Mum doesn't come here anymore, does she?' Jacinta said, looking out to the constant rush of waves. 'I've never understood it.'

'Maybe you can spend too much time in a place like this.'

'You don't feel that way, do you?'

'No. I miss it every day. But I'm not your mother. Not everyone feels at home in the wind.'

'It suited you and Grandpa,' Jacinta said. Then she laughed. 'Mum says you two were a good match.'

Mary hesitated. 'Your grandfather and I . . . complemented each other.' She thought of Jack's silences, and of her own fortitude. No-one else could have survived those years at the lighthouse with him.

'I didn't know Grandpa very well,' Jacinta said.

'He was a hard man to know.'

'Why was that?'

'He was probably born that way. His childhood wasn't easy. He worked hard on the farm from a young age. I suppose the lighthouse didn't help.'

'I thought he loved it.'

'Yes, but you can lose yourself in all that space and time.'

Mary often wondered what would have happened if she'd realised this earlier. Maybe she could have done more to help him. Perhaps she could have pulled him back. Stopped the drift. Softened his moods. But that would have required her to be a different person; someone without housewifely duties and children and their lessons. She had done all she could at the time: cooked his favourite meals, kept him warm, deflected the children from his impatience, massaged those poor arthritic fingers, so gnarled and wooden. But the wind was insidious. It had worn him down the same way it erodes rocks, and turns mountains into sand, and makes headlands into beaches.

Jacinta was gazing out to where the wind was picking up the crests of waves and flicking them skywards in fizzing white spume. 'It's beautiful here,' she said. 'But it's cold. We should close the windows and turn up the heater.'

'What? And blow away the smell of the sea?'

Jacinta reached over and squeezed Mary's hand. 'Your skin's like ice, Nana. Remember, you're my responsibility today. Is there a thermos in the picnic basket?'

'I forgot the thermos.' Mary's face folded into quietness. Now was the time. 'There's a cabin back along the beach a way,' she said, restraining the tension in her voice. 'Did you notice it as we passed? It's just over the dunes. Let's go and see if we can make a cup of tea there.'

Jacinta looked doubtful. 'Do you think we can do that?'

'I know the owners. They won't mind. It'll be unlocked.' Mary's skin tingled and she held her breath as she waited for Jacinta to acquiesce.

'I suppose we can have a look . . .'

Jacinta turned the car and drove back along the beach while Mary sat tight and still, struggling to subdue her mounting excitement. She waved a casual hand to show Jacinta where the track turned off, but as they swung up over the dunes, lurching over the rise, Mary's heart was dipping and curving too.

'Thank goodness for four-wheel drive,' Jacinta said, a smile lighting her face. She was struggling to hold the car straight while the sand grabbed at the wheels. They parked on the grass beside the small building.

It was a log cabin, painted brown, with three big windows facing seawards and a grand view over the low coastal scrub to the flat expanse of the beach. Mary could see the tide running in and the hulk of the headland stretching south across the bay. On the front verandah there was a wooden picnic table and an old barbeque collecting rust.

Jacinta turned off the engine. 'Are you sure it's okay for us to do this? Someone might be staying here.'

Mary was already opening her car door. 'I rang ahead to check. They're expecting us to pop in.' She slid out hurriedly, awkwardly, knowing she must usher her granddaughter inside before she could ask too many questions. Soon Jacinta would discover that not all had been revealed. She shuffled to the steps, noticing the sound of the sea rising over the dunes and the twitter of fairy wrens in the hushed lull between waves. 'Could you bring the suitcase, please?' she flung over her shoulder.

Jacinta was standing by the car, frowning. 'Why do we need the case?'

'Bring it inside and I'll show you.'

Mary opened the door wide. Then she picked up a box of matches and a handwritten note from the kitchen bench.

'What's that?' Jacinta asked from the doorway.

'A note from the owners.'

'Oh, good.' Jacinta sounded relieved. 'They really were expecting us.' She set down the suitcase.

'You didn't believe me?'

'I was beginning to have my doubts.'

'Now you can stop doubting. Let's turn the heater on. It's cold in here.'

Jacinta took the matches. 'Will the gas be on? Or should I go outside and check the bottle?'

'It should be on.'

Jacinta opened the curtains and then squatted to light the heater. 'Why don't you sit on the couch?' she said. 'There's a rug you can put over your knees.'

While Mary arranged the blanket around her legs, Jacinta filled the kettle and set it on the gas stove. She lit the ring and shook the match to extinguish the flame. 'So this is why you didn't bring a thermos.'

'I forgot the thermos.'

'But you knew we could get a cup of tea here.'

'Yes.'

Jacinta stared at her for a long moment and Mary could feel her suspicion rising. 'What's going on, Nana?'

Ignoring the question, Mary gazed out the window, unsure how to give her granddaughter the truth without making her angry. Conflict was rare between them. It was unfamiliar and uncomfortable. Stalling, she studied the weather. Rain was coming in off the sea and the grey curtains of a squall were closing in. 'How's that kettle going?' she asked.

'It'll take ages. The water's freezing. What about your tablets? Is it time?'

'They're in the suitcase.' They both turned to look at the case standing upright near the door. 'Would you mind taking it into the bedroom?' Mary asked, trying to control the quiver in her voice. 'The furthest one. With the two single beds. Not the bunkroom.'

Jacinta frowned and went to look in the room, leaving the case where it stood. When she came out she sat down on an old armchair by the window and stared at Mary. 'One of the beds is made up in there.'

'Is it?' Mary feigned surprise.

'What's going on?'

Over Jacinta's shoulder, Mary could see the sea rolling in. A Pacific gull flapped slowly up the beach, hanging on the breeze. This was the moment she'd been dreading. 'I've organised to stay here,' she said. 'It's all arranged. I've rented this place for a month, and I've paid for a Parks ranger to stop in and check on me each day to make sure I'm all right.'

Jacinta looked at her without moving.

'Everything will be fine,' Mary went on, trotting out the reassuring spiel she had rehearsed so many times in the past few days. 'The ranger can get me anything I need. If there are any problems, he can help me . . . if I run out of milk or whatever. And I've told them about my health. Everything I need is in the suitcase.'

'What about your medication? And what if you're ill? There's no electricity and no telephone. If you run out of gas, you'll freeze.'

'There's a spare gas bottle outside.'

'What about food? You won't feed yourself properly.'

'I've paid to have the place stocked. And I can cook, you know.'

'But you won't. You'll have a tin of baked beans or something ridiculous like that for dinner. Not real food.'

'I can look after myself.'

'Not if you get ill. They don't even have a hospital on the island.'

A taut silence spread between them. In truth, Mary's failing health was part of the reason for escaping. Part of the reason for being here, away from Jan's grip.

Jacinta's eyes brimmed with tears. 'You could die out here, Nana.'

'This is where I want to be.'

Tears slid down Jacinta's cheeks, challenging Mary's resolve. But she held herself strong. She had known she'd encounter opposition.

'Mum will be furious,' Jacinta said.

'This is my decision.'

'But it affects other people.'

'Like who? Your mother?' Mary's anger flared. If Jan had her way Mary would have been booked into a home months ago.

'You know she only wants what's best for you.'

'Is that so? Surely I'm the best judge of that.'

Jacinta scrubbed her face with her wrist, wiping away tears. 'Mum will say you're not rational.'

'Of course she'll say that.'

'You know she'll persuade Gary. And she'll work on Tom too.'

Mary shook her head. Of Tom's loyalty she was certain. She and Tom knew each other without words. 'Your mother might influence Gary,' she said, 'but Tom won't listen to her.'

They lapsed to silence again and rain started to patter on the roof. Outside, soft mist wrapped around the cabin. The sea was steely grey and chopped with whitecaps. Mary felt her nerves settling. She would hold strong. There was no argument that would take her back to rot in Hobart. She was here for her own purpose; for Jack. And she would not allow Jan to slot her into a home. That was the nub of it: she was taking action before Jan could make her a captive.

Jacinta tried again. 'I can't let you do this, Nana. It isn't safe.'

'Life isn't safe.'

Jacinta pleaded, 'Can't I just bring you down here on day trips? I can take time off work and go for walks so you'll be alone.'

'It wouldn't be the same. I need time by myself down here.'

Jacinta stared out the window. 'Mum's going to be so angry.' She sighed and stood up to check the kettle in the kitchen.

Mary regretted having to bring Jacinta into this. And her granddaughter was right. Jan would be furious. Down here, Mary was beyond her sphere of control. In recent times, as Mary deteriorated, it seemed Jan had relished the notion of taking charge. She was always asking about her health, almost swooning with delight each time Mary had an attack of angina. Mary wondered how such animosity had entered their relationship. Over the years she'd tried to appease Jan; taking her to lunch, meeting her for coffee after school, cooking roasts. When Jan's husband left, Mary had supported her through the anger and grief. She'd even gone to the movies with Jan a few times, despite the pain of her arthritis in those cramped cinema seats. But the rift was too great. Mary had accepted an uneasy truce.

'Why *here?*' Jacinta was saying. 'Why not at the lighthouse? At least there'd be someone around. And a telephone.'

Mary shook her head. 'It wouldn't have felt right, staying in my old house. It wouldn't be the same. And the keepers' cottages are too cold.'

It was more than that. Too much had happened at the lighthouse. If she stayed there, she couldn't dodge all that. She had needed to come *here*, where she could remember Jack at his best, before the distance and solitude of the cape seeped into his soul.

'I'm sure the cottages have better heating these days,' Jacinta said.

'No. It's more peaceful here. And I can see the sea.' The cottages on the cape hadn't been built for the view; the kitchen windows faced the light tower on the hill. The lighthouse authorities wanted people to have their minds on the job.

The kettle boiled at last and Jacinta made tea. She grunted when she opened the gas fridge and found it well provisioned—further evidence of Mary's deception. She placed some biscuits and a cup of tea on the coffee table and sat down again.

'I don't like this, Nana,' she said, taking Mary's wrinkled hand. 'But I suppose this hasn't been easy for you either. And it's not for me to tell you what to do.'

Now it was Mary's turn to blink away tears.

Jacinta's sigh was heavy. 'Why did you choose *me* to bring you here?'

'Because I knew you'd understand.'

'Not Tom?'

'He's less able to cope with Jan than you are.'

'You've thought of everything.'

'I tried to. I don't want to cause any trouble.'

'*This* is trouble.' Jacinta stood up, hands on hips. She laughed a little brokenly and Mary's heart twisted. 'You tricked me into bringing you here.'

'I didn't want to trick you.'

Jacinta gazed out the window and Mary felt distance swimming between them. 'I'm sorry, Jacinta.'

Jacinta smiled shakily down at her. 'It's okay. I'll get used to it. But I think I'll go for a walk, if you don't mind. The rain's stopped and I need some fresh air. I'll get my coat from the car.'

She gave Mary a hug and then went out into the wind. Mary heard the car door bang and saw her stride over the dunes onto the beach. It was good for Jacinta to get out into the weather. Her spirit would be soothed and the wind would settle her; when she came back she'd be calm. It always worked that way. There was space out there for a heart to grow large. Mary had lived her life knowing this secret.

And for life, you needed a large heart.

3

Something's happening, some sort of storm brewing. I've never been intuitive, but today there's a strange sense of tension and foreboding in the air. I feel it in the wind and the damp cold of the clouds pressing down on the forest. I'm lost in it, suspended in an eerie uncertainty.

From the front verandah of my house in Coningham, thirty minutes south of Hobart, I can see through the trees to the channel where the late afternoon light is pearl-grey. On the calm waters towards Bruny Island, the boats of the Sunday yacht fleet are finishing their picnics and returning home. I sit in my deckchair and watch the green rosellas crunching seeds on the feeder. All flutter and twitter, busy beaks and ruffled feathers, they know nothing of what I feel. They side-step around the edges of the feeder on ridiculously short legs, and bob to scoop up seeds with crooked bills. Then they husk them, twisting the seeds with grey bobble tongues. Their routine doesn't change. Today, I find this reassuring.

The birds may be oblivious, but the dog at my feet knows something's happening. Jess is a brown kelpie with triangular prick ears, a bushy tail and bright yellow eyes. She reads my moods exactly. I like it that she knows things without asking. I like it that she doesn't speak. People have too many words. They've fenced themselves in with walls and roofs and entertainment. Too much indoors, too little sky.

My house is close to nature and clouds and birds. I chose it because it's peaceful. In this street there are only a few scattered houses, mostly holiday homes. Some days I wave at the old couple next door and they wave back, but that's as far as it goes. I've never been particularly social. Probably it's because of the lighthouse, growing up surrounded by the wilderness of Cape Bruny. But I've been worse in recent years. More reclusive. These days my definition of contentedness is Jess and me, sitting here by ourselves, away from people's eyes.

Behind us the forest slides down the slope, hugging close to the back fence, and shade comes early in the afternoon. From the lounge room, the view to North Bruny, hunching against the horizon, reminds me where I have come from. It takes me back to the light station. If I close my eyes I can almost feel the wind lashing the cape. I could stand above the cliffs inhaling air with the bite of ice on its breath. I'd stay out as long as I could, waiting to see an albatross skimming over the waves far below or a sea eagle rocketing across the cape with its wings bent in the blast.

As early evening slips over the water, Jess and I remain on the deck watching the last boats trickle home. The light fades and the birds disappear. I hear a possum scraping its way down a tree adjacent to the house. It thuds onto the roof and gallops across like an elephant in army boots. Then it climbs onto the railing, brush tail waving and pink nose sniffing. I can feel Jess holding her breath. One of her front legs is raised as if her foot is listening. She sits and watches, her whole being straining against obedience. She wants to give chase and snap at that furry tail. But obedience wins and she sits tight by my knee.

The phone rings and Jess leaps to her feet, scrabbling on the deck. The scratch of her toenails startles the possum as it extends its nose to sniff the slivers of apple I've placed on the railing. As the phone continues to ring, Jess races to the front door and barks. She keeps barking after I go inside to pick up the phone. Even after I shout at her, she follows me into the lounge room, barking at the night, at the possum, at me for the tension I've been carrying all day.

'Hold on,' I yell into the phone. I shoo Jess outside and she dashes down the stairs and runs quickly around the house. 'Sorry,' I say into the phone. 'Who is it?'

'Jacinta.'

I can tell by the angst in her voice that this phone call relates to the sense of expectation I've felt all day.

'Tom,' she says. 'I took Nana down to Bruny Island today. She made me leave her there. She's staying in a cabin at Cloudy Bay.'

I know the cabin at the far end of Cloudy Bay, tucked behind the dunes, hiding from the wind. Jess and I have often walked ourselves into emptiness on that beach, and I've peeped through the window of the cabin. It looks homely and snug. I think of Mum sitting on the couch, remembering the past.

'Did I do the right thing leaving her there?' Jacinta asks. 'I'm concerned about her health.'

I hear the ticking of a motorboat out on the channel.

'She says it's what she wants,' Jacinta continues. 'To be down there by herself.'

I find my voice. 'Jan and Gary won't agree.'

'What should we do?'

'I'm not sure.'

'Alex says I should call a family meeting.'

Dread creeps beneath my skin.

'What if I arrange for everyone to come here to Nana's house tonight?' Jacinta says. 'Can you make it?'

'You're at Battery Point?'

'Yes, I came straight here. Tom, she's left it perfect . . . I don't think she's planning on coming back.'

So, Mum's expecting to die out at Bruny. I knew she didn't want to fade away in a nursing home, and I know she hasn't been well lately, but this Bruny escapade seems a bit extreme. And I'm surprised she didn't discuss it with me. I'm not like Jan and Gary, both loud and uncompromising in their opinions; I would have listened to her. Now I can't think what to say. Mum's death isn't something I'm prepared for. I can't imagine her not being around.

'I'll organise the meeting for seven thirty,' Jacinta says. She pauses and I stare blankly into silence. 'Are you okay, Tom?'

'I think so.'

'Drive carefully, won't you? And be on time. I don't want to be worrying about you if you're late.'

'No. I don't want to worry you.'

When I turn off the house lights and step out into darkness, Jess is there beneath my hand, pushing up at me with her wet nose. She snuffles under my palm and I run my hand over the velvet of her ears and the dome of her head. She's warm and soft and solid in a night that has somehow dissolved into air. I can hear her panting beside me as we walk down the steps and then down the steep concrete path to the car. The possum scrambles up a tree trunk as we pass.

I open the front door of the Subaru and Jess bounds in and dives to the floor on the passenger side. She knows where she belongs and she always obeys the rules. Tonight, she's as uptight as I am. She's panting so hard, I'm not sure which is louder—Jess or the old car engine.

'Hey, girl.' I slide my hand past the gear stick and ruffle her head. By the glow of the streetlight I see her yellow eyes staring at me. 'We're off to a party.'

The car rolls quickly down the driveway and I brake and put it into gear before we reach the bottom of the hill. We turn left onto the road towards the highway, passing shadowy houses brooding in the bush. The road descends to the water's edge, curving narrow and close to the shore. As I take one of the corners too fast, Jess sits up, whines and rests her chin on the front seat. Then she turns a tight circle and curls up on the floor again.

What was it Jacinta said about driving carefully?

But I can't concentrate. If Mum dies, I don't know what I'll do.

As usual, the street outside Mum's house in Battery Point is choked with cars. When they built the houses here, they didn't know this area was destined to become expensive real estate. It takes time to find a parking space. Then Jess and I walk back along the footpath, dodging vehicles with their wheels on the pavement. Jess decides to relieve herself on a small square of grass and I wait while she hunches in embarrassment and then tries not to notice me swiping up her droppings in a plastic bag. I tuck the bag in Mum's rubbish bin before approaching the front door.

I'm late and they're all in the kitchen waiting for me. I hear the drone of their voices when I open the door and step into the hall. Jess's toenails click on the wooden floor. We're almost through the sliding doors before I realise I haven't taken a breath.

'Here he is.' Jacinta rises to take my arm and guide me to a seat.

Jan and Gary are already at the table frowning into cups of tea. Gary has left his wife, Judy, at home, and perhaps that's a good thing tonight. Alex is at the sink setting out extra mugs. No doubt he's here to provide moral support for Jacinta. And she's going to need it, judging by the way Jan glares at me as I drag out my chair. She glances down at Jess with distaste.

'Couldn't you leave the dog at home?'

Jan doesn't understand dogs. She doesn't understand people either, even though she thinks she's an expert. I sit down and Jess curls under my feet.

'The dog's all right,' Gary grunts. He's spread on his chair like a Buddha. Over the past years his body has ballooned—too much time spent pressing buttons on his computer and remote controls instead of exercise. He nods his chins at me. 'How's things?'

I shrug. 'Not sure.'

'Bit of a shock, isn't it?' His laugh is short and strained. 'Trust the old lady to hit us with something like this.'

'She really didn't want to upset everyone,' Jacinta says quietly.

We all sit awkwardly, trying not to meet each other's eyes. Jan's shoulders are rigid: she's fit to burst. The rest of us breathe carefully into the silence, preparing for what's to come. Nobody seems to know what to say, but Gary's the first to find his tongue.

'You've had one heck of a day then, Jacinta, haven't you?' Ever the pacifist.

Jacinta nods. 'It hasn't been the easiest day.'

'Jacinta had no idea . . .' Jan leaps in quickly and then turns on Jacinta, 'although it amazes me you didn't ask her about the suitcase before you left Hobart.' I'm sure Jan has been berating Jacinta since she first heard the news, and now she's going to rehash it for my benefit.

Gary sets down his cup and leans back in his chair, hands folded behind his thick neck. 'How did she get you to take her to the cabin?'

'She was cold and she said she'd arranged with the owners to have a cup of tea there. It was out of the wind . . .'

'I suppose you carried the case in for her?' Jan rolls her eyes.

'She couldn't carry it herself,' Jacinta explains patiently. 'It was too heavy.'

'Surely you were suspicious by then. You should have left it in the car.'

Jacinta doesn't try to defend herself. She looks at her mother and waits.

'Did you try to talk her out of it?' Jan asks.

'Yes, of course. I was quite direct.'

'Did you tell her to just stop the rubbish and get back in the car? I bet you didn't put it like that.'

'Not quite like that. But I did press her.'

Jan clenches her fists on the table. 'Pity Mum didn't ask *me* to take her down there.'

At that moment, the kettle boils and the whistle shrieks. Alex jumps up to turn it off and waves a mug at me. 'What'll you have, Tom?'

'Tea, thanks. Black.'

There's an uneasy lull while Alex pours tea and passes it to me. Jan continues to sit tall and straight in her chair. She's like a river about to breach its banks. Once she starts, nothing will stop the flood.

'Are you set now, Tom?' she asks.

I nod into my cup.

'All right, then,' she says. 'What are we going to do about this?' She stares at each of us in turn, as if we are somehow to blame. Nobody responds. 'Come on,' she says. 'We need to work it out. I'm not going to have Mum dying down there on her own.'

'We could each go and visit her,' Jacinta suggests. 'I know she'd like that. Alex and I can go down on weekends.'

Jan shakes her head firmly. 'She can't stay there. We have to bring her back and make some arrangements.'

'What sort of arrangements?' Gary asks.

'We need to find her a room in a nursing home. So she can't pull this sort of stunt again.'

Jacinta interjects, 'She doesn't want to be in a home.'

'She's seventy-seven and obviously not in her right mind, Jacinta.' Jan sweeps her argument along quickly, like she's clearing the floor of crumbs. 'A home is the safest place for her.'

'Perhaps she doesn't want to be safe.' My voice echoes across the room and everyone looks at me, shocked that I've spoken. Nobody expects me to have an opinion, or if I have one, to voice it.

Jan's lips curl in a derisive smile. 'So you're happy to let our mother die down there alone, are you, Tom?'

'That's not what he's saying,' Gary says.

'No? Then what *is* he saying?'

'He's saying that Mum has a right to choose not to go to a home.'

Jacinta places a hand gently on her mother's arm. 'Nana was very clear about what she wanted.'

'But it's not acceptable,' Jan says. 'If she dies, it could be days before anyone finds her.'

'The ranger will check on her daily.'

Jan won't be appeased. 'It's not enough. She's going to need full-time care.'

'She's been living on her own back here,' Gary points out. 'Why the sudden need for constant care?'

'It's different down there,' Jan says, affronted. 'You know how it is, Gary. It's cold and windy, and the chill will eat into her. You saw Dad die. Heart failure's a terrible way to go.'

We sit numbly for a moment. Apart from Alex, the others witnessed Dad's decline first-hand. But while they clustered around Dad's bed here in Hobart, saying their farewells, I was stranded on a ship, lurching slowly back from Antarctica across the Southern Ocean. I was three days too late. Three awful days. My goodbyes were said into grey skies and icy winds, leaning off the helideck with the ocean stretching around me. It's a lonely feeling, losing a parent from afar.

Jan watches us all carefully, assessing the moment. She holds us captive in her pause. 'For God's sake,' she says. 'Someone has to go down there and bring her back.'

'You're not volunteering.' Gary's voice is edged with anger. 'Surely you can find some spare time to go and pick her up.'

'It's better that someone else does it,' Jan says. 'Then she can't blame me.'

'So you want one of us to drop her off to whatever home you decide to check her into?'

'I'll make sure it's somewhere reputable. Somewhere close, so it's easy to pop in and visit her.'

'Shame you didn't visit her more often when she was living right here in this house.' Gary's warming up now, feeding off Jan's self-righteousness.

'We all have busy lives,' Jan retorts. 'How often did *you* drop by for a chat?'

Gary smoulders into his cup and silence swells again in the kitchen.

'I'm not sure we have to do anything,' I say quietly.

Jan stares at me stonily. 'That's not a solution,' she snaps. 'She needs appropriate care. If worse comes to worst she needs to be in a hospital.'

I dredge up strength from somewhere in my boots. 'It's Mum's solution,' I say. 'She doesn't want to come back.'

Jan is incensed. 'She's an old woman who's lost her mind. It's up to us to make decisions for her.'

For a few tense moments nobody says anything. Then Jacinta speaks. 'Nana's in her right mind. She knows what she wants.'

Jan glares at her. 'I'm sorry, Jacinta, but if you'd handled this properly in the first place it wouldn't be an issue. She chose you to take her to Bruny because she knew you'd do as she asked.'

'Well, Mum wouldn't choose *you*.' Gary folds his arms across his bulging belly. 'You haven't been civil to her in years.'

'That's not true.'

'You haven't exactly had a close relationship with her.'

Jan stiffens. 'I think I've done quite well, given where we've come from. What have you done for her in the past six months?'

Things are descending into territory none of us have entered before.

'At least I haven't loaded her with grief and guilt trips.'

Jan and Gary face off like bristling dogs about to fight. This is not going well. Somebody has to stop the slide.

'How about I go down and visit her sometime this week,' I offer. 'I can take a day off, maybe Wednesday, and make sure things are set up for her down there.'

'What are you going to do?' Jan says. 'Build a hospital at Lunawanna?'

I shrug, baulking inwardly at the confrontation. 'I'll check she has everything she needs.'

'Like a ventilator? And cylinders of oxygen?'

'You can go down if you like, Jan,' Gary says.

'No. I won't be going. If Mum chooses to isolate herself like this and you all support her, then I refuse to go and visit.'

'But she might not come back . . .' Jacinta's voice trails off.

Jan stands up. 'Then that's her choice. I'm too angry to drop in for a casual visit. And what would I say anyway? *How's it going, Mum?* What rubbish! If you've all made your decision, I'm going home.'

Jess slinks out from under the table and paces nervously around the room.

'Can't you make that dog sit down?' Jan demands. Then her face crumples. 'Oh God, this is so awful,' she says, tears welling.

And she's done it again; the gathering has become a focus for Jan's despair. Jacinta hugs her and pats her shoulder while Alex rolls his eyes at me and pours Jan another cup of tea. My continued presence at the table is taken as solidarity. Gary mutters something into his chins and shuffles out to the toilet. When he returns, Jan sits down and wraps her hands around her cup of tea.

'I still think we should be bringing her home,' she says.

'She'll be all right,' Gary says.

'That's rubbish, Gary. She isn't capable. We all know she won't remember her medication. She doesn't even know what day of the week it is half the time.'

'It's her right to decide,' I say, and the same silence returns that follows everything I say. Jess wriggles against my legs as I pause. 'It's her right to decide how she wants to die.'

Jan is outraged. She thumps the table in frustration. 'This is ridiculous. You're all trying to put her in the grave. Am I the only one who cares about her?'

I dig deep for boldness. 'This isn't about you, Jan. This is about Mum.' There, I've said it, and Jan is turning purple. 'We're leaving her there,' I continue, legs shaking. 'You can visit if you want. But nobody's bringing her home. It's Mum's choice.' I stand up and Jess leaps up too. 'The meeting's over.'

And, amazingly, it is. Teary, Jan sips her cup of tea. Gary starts talking about his work and the possibility of visiting Mum next week. And Alex clears away the empty cups and squirts dishwashing detergent into the sink.

Over their heads, Jacinta smiles at me wearily. Her quiet nod is affirmation. We've won the first battle. For Mum.

4

When Jacinta left that afternoon, the cabin swelled with a beautiful quiet and Mary's soul hummed. Slowly she succumbed to the soft ripple of remembered happiness. There was work to be done, yes—places she must visit, plans she must make—but for now she could eddy with the flow of time and sit in memory, striving for nothing.

Gazing through the rain-streaked windows, she heard the whisper of the sea. Persistent, threaded through everything, it was the rhythm of life here. She remembered how she and Jack had delighted in it when they first moved back to the island from the grey dreariness of Hobart. Those first nights, as they lay together in the lightkeeper's cottage, taking stock of their new lives, the sound had murmured through their dreams. It was there each time they woke, reminding them of this chance to start over.

Jan and Gary were still small, and Mary and Jack enjoyed watching them expand into the freedom. Grim, confined poverty in Hobart versus the isolated, wind-scraped cape: Mary knew they had chosen well. The melancholy that had settled on her and Jack in Hobart shifted like mist. In Jack's few free hours, the family traipsed the cape together, making discoveries. At the same time Mary and Jack were finding each other again, uncovering the precious small gems that had first drawn them to one another. They had been good times, those early months on the cape. Jack had revelled in the return to physical work. The children had grown brown and strong and wild. And Mary had sung in the wind and thrived. Now, in this place at Cloudy Bay, she would find strands of peace like those that had cradled her life so snugly back then.

In the bedroom, she unpacked her case, laying neat piles of clothing on the spare bed. The photo album she placed on the coffee table in the living area. Down here, she would have space to meander through the past, exploring the peaks and valleys of her life with Jack. All this was regular and systematic—she knew the dimensions of these things. But whenever she thought of the letter, tucked in the side pocket of the case, something in her jolted. Frowning, she pulled it out and set it on the couch. She must not be afraid of it. She was in command.

As she lit the stove and set the kettle on to boil again, she contemplated this strategy of the letter. It was clever, she decided, grudgingly conceding the letter bearer's ingenuity. Naively, she had considered him safely submerged in history. But now he had resurfaced with a triumphal stroke.

Her immediate thought had been to destroy the letter. That would be the simplest and most sensible option. There was little to gain from distressing people. But the letter bearer could re-emerge. He could materialise again with another letter. And what then?

She didn't understand his thinking. Why had he given the letter to *her*? Why hadn't he delivered it to the addressee? Was it because he wanted to inflict pain on Mary? To make his intentions known to her? Or was it because he wanted the decision to rest with her? And yet, at that terrible meeting, which she did not want to recall, he had expressed an expectation that she would deliver it. He was cruel, forcing her to have a hand in her own demise. That was intolerable. And she could not yield to it.

Did he really think she had a conscience? Or did he consider that he still had a hold on her? How ridiculous, and how arrogant! The time to give him shape had passed. She'd smudged him out long ago. And she would not bend to him. She must burn the letter and be done with it.

Reassured by this decision, she poured tea and fetched a can of tomatoes to have with toast for dinner. It was an inadequate meal. But she wasn't hungry, and at least she was eating. Tomorrow, she would organise something more substantial. By then, she'd have settled in a little more. And if she had the energy for a short walk, she might even rouse an appetite.

Her first night at Cloudy Bay was a restless tussle with the strangeness of a new bed. She shifted and tossed, rediscovering her hip joints and knees. Solid sleep was rare these days, but this was worse than usual. Sometime during the night a soft cough started, rattling her upright. It was heart-related: she knew the signs.

The letter was drifting in the back of her consciousness too, denying her the luxury of rest. Exasperated, she lurched out of bed and scuffed barefoot into the kitchen with the envelope clutched in her hand. Holding it over the sink, she lit a match. When the letter was ash, she would find release.

But the lighted match hovered away from the corner of the envelope and she could not bring it closer. Was this the right choice? What would happen if this letter were delivered after she died? Would it really matter? But then again, could she die peacefully while it still existed?

Too weary to answer her own questions, and too uncertain to act without careful reflection, she blew out the match and took the letter back to bed. Tonight was too soon. She had days to resolve the matter. Blurry with exhaustion, she propped herself up with pillows so she could breathe more easily. At home,

everything was as she needed. Here, she'd have to improvise to
find comfort.

While she wafted somewhere between sleep and wakeful-
ness, the wind whined around the house and racketed at the
windows. It was noisier than she'd expected. She'd forgotten the
way it moaned in the eaves. How unrelenting it could be. How
it could seed doubt in the most determined mind.

Nights like this on the cape, she used to creep closer to
Jack, the large solid slab of him, soaking up his warmth. Now
she was alone. Jack gone nine years ago. She missed his secure
presence, the acceptance and lack of expectation. It had taken a
lifetime to achieve, a rough ride on a hard road. But surely that
was love; not the flare of a bright light that glimmered briefly
and then disappeared.

She lay there seeking steadiness. Thinking of Jack. Thinking
of the wind roaring up from the south-west. In time, she would
become accustomed to it again. The wind would once more
become part of her psyche. Instead of shrinking away you had
to embrace it. This place was not for the weak and suggestible.

In the morning, after a slow breakfast of porridge with partly
frozen milk, she adjusted the thermostat in the gas fridge then
sat wearily on the couch beneath the rug and stared out across
the bay. It was another world out there. The wind had whipped
the waves to white-capped fury and the scrub rustled and sighed,
branches waving in the blast. Clouds and sea spray swept over
the distant cliffs and the light was grey. Occasional rain spattered
against the window.

A thread of icy air from beneath the front door wound itself
around her legs, and she was cold despite the closely tucked rug.
She got up and lit the gas heater. At the lighthouse, she never sat
still long enough to get chilled. There were always jobs to do.

But here, the morning was long. She was waiting for the ranger to come. And he must come soon.

She was eager to meet this ranger. He was important to her plan, and she needed to befriend him quickly. Removed from her family, she had to rely on someone else to drive her around the island, taking her to places of importance to her and Jack. This ranger was it, whether he liked it or not. She disliked this deliberate intent to use another person, but it was necessary. And perhaps it mattered less if she manipulated a stranger. What else could she do?

Leaning back and closing her eyes, she listened to the dull thud of waves smacking onto the beach. Sometimes, it was clear and strong. Then it faded as her mind focused elsewhere—on a memory or the song of a bird down in the scrub. It was Tom who had taught her to notice birds. Even as a lad, he'd wanted to know all about nature: the birds' names, what they ate, where they nested, what their eggs looked like. When he was small, he chased robins around the cottages where they hopped and fluttered, common as chooks. He mimicked the bird calls—even the complex lyrical song of the tawny-crowned honeyeater that fluted across the cape in autumn. As he grew older, he would sit on the grass reading books amid the whirr of brown quails as they fled across the hillside. After lessons each day, he used to climb the hill past the light tower and follow the track down the other side where he had a special nook. There, he liked to sit watching sea eagles circling over Courts Island, or Tasmanian wedge-tails roosting on low branches in the scrub. When the mutton birds were nesting, he'd be gone for hours, coming back with stories of eagles plucking fat chicks from burrows and tearing them apart with their beaks.

Mary had realised long ago that a boy who grew up with eagles could never be ordinary. At age ten, he announced his theory on life. She had been in the kitchen, kneading dough, when he came in and flung himself into a chair. She saw his face, luminous. And his wind-tousled hair. His cheeks bitten pink by the cold. A person could be like an albatross or a sea eagle, he said, as she went back to pounding dough. If you were an albatross, you flew low over the waves where there was less wind and the flying was easier. You didn't risk landing too often, because there was a chance you might not get airborne again, and it took energy to get going after you'd stopped. If you were a sea eagle, however, you soared high and fancy on the winds where you could see everything, and pounce down on things that interested you. You perched on rocks and branches, because you were strong and could easily launch into the air again. But a sea eagle was visible and confident, and other birds didn't like you—they attacked, sweeping out of the sky and dive-bombing to scare you away. This, he said, was the cost of being magnificent.

He looked at her then, as she paused over the dough, hands dusted in flour. 'I'm an albatross, Mum,' he said. 'I like to be in the wind, but I want to be safe.'

She had taken him in her arms, aching with love for him, and snuggled him close, wrapping him up as safely as she could. Even then she had known that no-one could ever be safe. Within the cocoon of childhood she could protect him—that much was possible. But she couldn't keep him from the world. Instead of disillusioning him she had kissed the top of his head, burying her face in the wiry mop of his hair. How did you tell a ten-year-old boy that life and its dangers would find him? You could map out life as you hoped it might unfold, but there were always unexpected deviations. Nobody could plan for those.

Now she thought of her own younger self, before she met Jack and became a mother. Passionate. Impetuous. Quick to anger. Would she have listened if anyone had warned her about life? Likely not. She was too full of hopes and dreams, quite indifferent to her parents' acquired wisdom. When they sent her to Bruny Island to protect her from herself, had she believed she needed saving? Of course not. But in hindsight, perhaps there had been some wisdom in it.

Poor Uncle Max and Aunt Faye. There they were, quietly farming their patch of South Bruny close to Lunawanna, and she had arrived, furious and emotional, on their doorstep. Despite her moody reluctance, they had been kind and welcoming.

At first the island had seemed gloomy to her, with its small rough houses and few people. Ripped from life in Hobart and deposited in a strange, quiet backwater, she was determined to dislike it. Nothing was going to make her fit in. Her heart was elsewhere. Exile was meant to extract her from danger, but she clung to the mast of her dream. She would hold her attachment close and strong. Her parents would not break her.

But Uncle Max deflected her with gentle purpose, directing her sulkiness into lifting hay bales and milking cows, raking silage, picking apples. He kept her busy: digging and weeding the vegie plot, pruning fruit trees. She also helped her aunt with the multitude of domestic tasks: washing, making jam, mending clothes. Labour had gradually knocked the petulance out of her. Physical work bred satisfaction. It soothed her bruised soul and calmed her indignation.

Later, she could see what a special time it was. Her punishment was, in fact, a gift. Through exile, she had escaped grimy Hobart, the prospect of a job in an office, the oppression of her parents' house and rules. On the farm, she lived outdoors in clean cool air. And there was a pattern to the days, a weekly and seasonal structure. She came to love the rich smell of grass, the sour smell of cow manure, the sweet, musty scent of hay in the shed. She liked to hustle the cows up the muddy track for milking. Behind the cottage, tall white ribbon gums lined the stream, and when the wind was up, she liked to stand beneath them, watching the long loose straps of bark slapping against their trunks and the skirts of foliage in the high canopy swaying against the sky.

Back then, the farm was shrouded with eucalypts and constantly drenched by weather off the southern seas. Rain would sheet from heavy clouds, pounding the paddocks, creating small rivers that ran down the cow tracks to the stream. When the heavens were emptying, she often sheltered in the old barn with the rain hammering on the roof and her cheek pressed against the warm flank of a cow, shooting milk into a bucket with each squeeze of her hands. And that shed was where she had first met Jack.

It was a day of low grey skies, and she was inside clipping wool from a straggly old sheep. Darkness fell across her and she thought more weather was coming in, but when she looked up she saw a tall young man leaning silently in the doorway, watching her. She realised he must be one of the three Mason boys Aunt Faye had told her lived on the neighbouring farm. Her aunt felt sorry for them because their property wasn't big enough to divide. The oldest son would inherit. The rest would probably have to leave the island for work.

She went back to clipping the sheep, expecting him to go off in search of Uncle Max. But he stayed, and she felt her skin heating up beneath his gaze. Who did he think he was, observing her like a cow?

'Are you looking for my uncle?' she asked, shooting him a frown. 'He's down by the stream, working on the pump. You'll find him there.'

The young man flushed and mumbled thanks.

'I'm Mary,' she said, standing up. 'Who are you?'

She offered a hand for him to shake, but he was already turning away. 'Jack,' he said, over his shoulder. 'I'm Jack Mason. Didn't mean to disturb you.'

Initially she hadn't been interested in him; she was still consumed by anger and fixed on other dreams. But she was a maturing girl thrown into the company of three young men, so it was inevitable that something would happen.

The two farm cottages were quite close and the families exchanged tools and assistance. They also shared celebrations: Christmas, Easter, picnics, fruit-picking. An only child from a strict Protestant family, Mary's self-awareness was awakening and she was drawn to men, even though she knew little about them. And there she was, unleashed among approving male attention in the physical world of the farm. Strong bodies. Masculine work. She thrived on stolen glances and quick conversations. A joke here and there. Jack's brothers were bolshie and fun-loving; they became the siblings she'd never had. But Jack was different. He was quiet and solid and strong. Restrained. There was something attractive in his steady silent presence. Something reassuring. And in his eyes, she saw a sparkle of a guarded interest. Despite herself, she was drawn to him. She wanted to know more.

During hay season, the families helped each other out, lifting bales onto the back of the Masons' old truck to get them into the barn before the next rain. It was heavy work. Mary could still remember Jack, shirtsleeves rolled up, the tight muscles of his forearms knotting as he swung bales onto the truck. His face had glowed with a sheen of sweat, his lips red, eyes blue, dark short-cropped hair scruffy with dust and stalks of hay.

For part of the day she had worked with the men, bending and lugging bales for as long as her strength held. She could see they approved of her grittiness, the way she flung herself into the task, dragging and lifting and heaving with the rest of them. She had watched Jack secretly, peeking inside his shirt as he bent to hook his fingers into the next bale, his chest muscles twitching beneath a thin smattering of hair as he gripped the baling twine. She imagined the texture of his chest, the hair, the feel of those strong arms pulling her close. Later, when her body was aching with fatigue, she brought water and cakes from the house. As he swigged from a bottle, Jack caught her watching him. His eyes crinkled, a smile flickering on his lips. Tight with embarrassment, she held her face rigid, but his smile broadened.

'Good cakes,' he said, taking one from the tin she was carrying and wiping drops of water from his lips.

They saw each other often like this. Small exchanges in a day of work. Accidental encounters on errands. Picking fruit in autumn, they ended up on the same tree, reaching and bending to shepherd apples into buckets. Talk was minimal, but they were alert to each other. Sly glances through a shield of leaves. The flash of a brown arm stretching for the same piece of fruit. Helping to fill a tipped bucket. Watching each other bite into the crisp white flesh of a just-ripe apple.

He came often to the shed while she was milking, begging a jug of cream for his mother, dipping a cup into her bucket and drinking it warm, or simply standing at the shed door watching her, as he had done at their first meeting. She fumbled when his eyes were on her, making the cow tense up and interrupting the flow of milk. 'Go away,' she'd pout. 'You're bothering my cow.' He'd laugh, his eyes dancing, and then he'd wander off down the path to find Uncle Max so he could borrow some tool or other.

When she recognised her susceptibility to him, she saw a need to avoid him. If Max and Faye discovered her interest, she'd be parcelled off home. And by that stage, she didn't want to go. She'd fallen in love with the farm and the island: the trees, the space, the air. When they drove to Lunawanna to collect supplies from the store, she would see mainland Tasmania, shimmering bluish-purple across the channel. As she sat outside the shop with Uncle Max, eating fish and chips, she'd gaze across the water, reminded of where she had come from. The island wove a special magic, and its isolated beauty was emphasised by the proximity of the mainland. They were on Bruny, happy and free. Everybody else was over there, with their complex city lives, buried in urban Hobart.

In small windows of spare time, the two families went to Cloudy Bay for picnics, fishing afternoons, walking and scarpering through the waves. Sometimes, the older generation stayed home, and it was just Mary and the boys. They took the truck to the far end of the beach, built bonfires on the sand, climbed East Cloudy Head in the raw bite of the wind.

One afternoon she found herself alone up there with Jack. The others had forgotten to bring extra layers and they retreated back to the beach as the sharp wind sliced through to hot skin. Snug in a thick woollen jumper, Mary tucked her knees in tight and sat in silence, swirling with the cold air and revelling in the long misty view. Jack stood nearby, and when she glanced up at him, she saw in his expression a kindred exhilaration, a parallel delight.

He looked down at her and his eyes were warm blue beacons. She felt her stomach melting. He sat beside her, blocking the wind, and she could smell the male tang of his sweat and a grassiness like sweet freshly cut hay. Tingling and alert, it was as if Mary's skin was speaking to him, and her breathing was a butterfly trapped in her throat, tight and light and anticipatory.

She knew he was looking at her, but she was afraid to connect, frightened to look up again. Then his hand covered hers, gently, carefully, and she felt her cold fingers engulfed in the warm dry grasp of his work-roughened skin. He was staring away across the wild spread of land and sea, holding her hand in his like the fragile precious shell of an egg. They breathed together, each raggedly attuned to the presence of the other. He reached out and touched her hair, his hand softly gliding over the tangle of her curls.

She was waiting, her lips already warm for him. Soon he moved closer and kissed her forehead. He was so hesitant, so restrained. She wanted passion from him, released and fervent and strong. But he was cautious and unsure. He desired her, yes, but he was strapped by awkwardness. And yet there was beauty in it, and ardour too. The magnetism was powerful, and there was something in his constraint that only escalated her eagerness. She wanted to lean against that hard chest—her entire body was bent towards it. At last he wrapped her up in those capable firm arms and drew her close.

They descended from the cape like Pacific gulls skimming over sand. Not much had happened really: an embrace, a few tentative kisses. But they had traversed a social gulf; ahead was a long road of caution and concealment, but a seed had germinated and a tendril of promise was flickering. The farm became a landscape of opportunity: chance meetings, stolen kisses in the barn, hands clutched tightly. Eyes locking over tables, tools, behind backs.

Jack's younger brother, Frank, took a job at Clennett's Mill up the mountain beyond the farm. Sometimes she accompanied Jack up there to deliver special luxuries: cakes and biscuits, fresh bread, newly picked fruit. They rode on horses, winding up the track into tall wet forest till they came to the camp where aromatic curls of smoke wafted among the tree trunks, men shouted, metal clanked and saws rasped at dense wood. They would leave the horses near the huts and she would follow Jack's straight back over fallen logs and mounds of stripped bark. Frank would be either in the noisy clattery mill, hacking at chunks of wood to toss into the furnace, or he'd be off somewhere across the steep slope, on the end of a saw felling a massive tree. In quiet pockets of forest, she and Jack would linger, pressing tight to each other, breathing into urgency, kissing, discovering one another.

The island had defined them then. They were the cool green grace of the farm. They were the eclipsing grandeur of the tall forests. They were the rhythmic slump of waves on the beach at Cloudy Bay. Their love was entangled in the place. Looking back, she was unsure whether it was Jack she had fallen in love with, or Bruny Island and the exhilarating freedom it offered. Or perhaps, a typical young girl, she'd been in love with the idea of being in love. The heady romance of it.

The truth was she hadn't expected to meet her future husband on Bruny. And it wasn't the outcome her parents had planned. It was, however, a consequence of the exile they had arranged for her. The island had slung her together with Jack; their relationship was an inevitable conclusion born out of isolation and awakening sexuality.

For a year, they navigated a secret liaison, built on stolen touch. Then they grew bolder. By that time, Mary had been on Bruny Island almost four years, and at twenty, she felt she was old enough to make her own decisions. Her upbringing insisted on propriety, and Jack, too, wanted to do things the right way. She knew that integrity and commitment were important to him. They discussed the next step, and after dinner one night, Jack told her of his conversation with his parents.

'I'm very fond of Mary,' he had said. 'She likes me too, and I want to marry her.'

His father had initially gaped, but once he'd recovered from his surprise, he nodded his approval. But Jack's mother's face had immediately expanded with a warm smile. 'She's a lovely choice, Jack,' she had said. 'A lovely steady girl. She'll make a good wife.'

A good wife, Mary had thought. What a challenge!

Encouraged by his parents' support, Jack visited Max and Faye to gauge their opinion. They were privately pleased but also concerned; Mary had been entrusted to them for safekeeping and this development might not be so welcome back in Hobart. Predictably, her parents weren't pleased that she planned to marry a farmer. They had higher aspirations for her than that. But Mary was determined to have Jack. Her mother and father had intervened in her life once already, and they knew they had less hold over her on Bruny. After a series of discussions, they gave permission reluctantly. She was in charge of her own life now.

In the wake of the announcement, Jack and Mary felt released. Discretion was still necessary, but secrecy wasn't required. Now they could hold hands in public and no longer shield glances. Chaperoning was insisted upon, but they stole away for private moments to kiss, to touch, to explore. A path to increased intimacy opened before them, and they tried new things—kissing with tongues, caressing beneath clothes. Mary would have gone further, but Jack was restrained. Everything must wait, he said, until the ring was on her finger.

They were married in a Hobart church, but returned to Bruny to work on the Masons' farm. Jack's father was becoming increasingly crippled with arthritis, and with Frank still away in the hills cutting wood, Jack was needed to help Sam, his older brother. The farmhouse was crowded, but it functioned in harmony. It was the happiest of times.

Whenever there was a break in the work schedule, Jack and Mary visited Cloudy Bay, taking each other in privacy. It was the place where they first made love and they regarded it as their haven—the sea, the salt, their bodies. Alone, they ran naked on the sand, laughing and shouting at the gulls. They fished off the beach and the rocks, eating their catch after cooking it over the flames of Jack's efficient little fire.

At the farm, intimacy had been slower to evolve than Mary had anticipated. In Jack's narrow bed they spooned into each other's warmth. But the house was small and they were afraid of making noise, so their passion was restricted. They learned each other in careful, drawn-out ways. With so much expectation, dissatisfaction was possible, and yet Mary was strung so tight with desire that her pleasure flowered easily. Once she discovered how to manage him, she guided him with such subtlety he hardly knew she was in control. And Cloudy Bay was their utopia where they could cry out without inhibition.

Looking back, Mary saw that period as the highlight of their lives together. They were still enveloped in the tranquil world of the farm, they were growing in love and in understanding, pressures were few. Marriage gave them new freedom. They picnicked alone, making love in the forest, at Cloudy Corner, even up on East Cloudy Head on a calm summer's day. Life was busy and close, hard but rich.

Then things changed. An outbreak of blight in the orchard caused finances to tighten. Jack recognised the burden of their presence and started talking about moving to Hobart for work. And then Rose arrived, Frank's bride. Being the social member of the Mason family, Frank was always looking for fun. During time off from the mill, he met Rose at the annual dance in Alonnah. She lived on a farm between Alonnah and Lunawanna, taking care of her bedridden mother, a task from which she was obviously keen to escape. Her relationship with Frank progressed quickly, and soon she too moved into the Mason farmhouse.

At first, another woman was welcome in a house of men. But it wasn't long before Mary started to dislike Rose. There was something not quite honest about her, she was lazy and manipulative, evading tasks so Mary took on more than her share. The men, even Jack, were entranced by her. She wore her fingernails long and polished, and she slicked her lips red. Mary tolerated her, struggling to be polite. But Rose didn't function by other people's rules. When she had one of her 'bad patches' there wasn't enough room in the Mason house. Mary abhorred Rose's selfishness, the way she twisted things to her own advantage. Rose was a snake in disguise, and Mary wanted to be far away from her.

Eventually, Mary persuaded Jack to shift to her uncle's farm, back into her old bedroom. They stayed there only a short time, aware their presence was a financial imposition. It wrenched both of them, but the move to Hobart was inevitable. Rent was beyond them, so they lived with Mary's parents. Her father was an accountant who'd managed to retain his property through the Depression, and his old house in North Hobart had space enough for all of them. It was a beautiful house, with squares of coloured glass bordering the window, and cast-iron lace around the verandahs. But the reality of living in it was harsh. Little light penetrated the large rooms with their high ceilings and cold walls, and the house was dark and sullen. Mary felt stifled by her parents' laws and expectations. When she fell pregnant and developed morning sickness, her mother was grimly pleased. At last, Mary had become the meek and malleable daughter she had desired.

In the city, Jack changed too. He became quieter and more introverted, working long hours in a cannery. The days seemed endless and he hated it, stuck inside with no natural light. Evenings, he sat by the fire with Mary's father, reading the paper and smoking a pipe—a new habit picked up in the city. The atmosphere wasn't conducive for talking, and Mary was so nauseous and depleted, she had little to say. Melancholy sat on her soul. She knew she should be pleased about the baby; pregnant women were supposed to be radiant. But Hobart was heavy and Jack was distant and withdrawn, mired in fatigue. At an appropriate hour, they'd retreat to the bedroom and undress awkwardly in the hissing glow of the gas lamp. Then they'd crawl into bed.

Intimacy died quickly with Mary's morning sickness, and Jack was exhausted, so he slept while she watched the shadows on the roof and wondered what had happened to the passion she'd felt for him on Bruny Island. Mired in loneliness, she dreamed of Cloudy Bay and the farm and the sweet smell of the ribbon gums on a wet morning. It didn't occur to her that Jack might be homesick too.

Five years later, when the job at the lighthouse came up, they both leaped at it. By then, they had two children and were living in a rented house in Battery Point. Their relationship had become strained and empty, both of them depressed by poverty and the suburban grind. It was easy to leave Hobart behind. The lighthouse was their opportunity to return to Bruny Island. It was also their chance to rediscover happiness.

5

There's something reassuring about working on an engine. Perhaps it's the structure of it, or the predictability of how things go together. Or it could be the ingeniousness of a functioning machine, the cleverness of design that makes a motor produce energy to turn a drive shaft and put a vehicle into motion.

It's not just the concept of an engine that I like, but also the feel of heavy parts in my hands. The familiar smell of oil and grease. I like working out problems systematically. I like the geometry of engines. There's a logic to them. And there's also the solitude you can find beneath a truck.

Bill is my boss at the garage in Sandy Bay. He gives me the difficult jobs because he knows I'm good at them, and makes sure I have a clear couple of days to work them out. And if there's nothing but routine jobs, he books me up, one service on top of another. He knows I'll power through everything. I'm as efficient as a machine once I get going.

Fortunately, Jess is the kind of dog you can take to work, which is just as well, because she hates being left at home. In the back corner of the garage, she curls up on an old sack, only moving to get a drink from time to time. The other mechanics throw her biscuits and crusts from their sandwiches. If I didn't tell them to draw the line at chocolate they'd throw that to her too. Just as well she doesn't know what I'm making her miss out on.

Whenever I have a difficult problem or if I need access to a special tool or machine, I nip down to the headquarters of the Antarctic Division in Kingston—known as the antdiv—to have a yarn with an old diesel mechanic there called Bazza. Bill doesn't mind me going because he knows I'll be back soon with the problem solved.

Today's project is to rebuild the engine of an old truck. The owner is Bill's friend so the work will be done at mates rates. It'd be cheaper to install a new engine, but things are quiet at this time of year, and Bill's happy for me to spend time sorting things out for his friend. The antdiv has better equipment than the garage, and I have a few parts that need machining, so I decide a quick break with Bazza is the best plan.

When I hook my spanner on the wall of the garage and wipe my hands on an old cloth, Jess knows we're heading out. She slinks from her corner for a quick pat and is in the car as soon as I open the door, smiling up at me from the floor and tapping her tail on the mat to let me know she's pleased to have a break. It can be hard work for a dog sitting on a sack all day.

In some circles, the antdiv is referred to as the *Division of Broken Marriages and Shattered Lives*. When I first heard it called that, I was irritated. At the time, it seemed like sour grapes from people who'd missed the privilege of going to Antarctica. But then I discovered its truth. They've got manuals for everything that happens down there, except how to get on with life after you return.

The antdiv is a series of square grey buildings joined by covered walkways much like the tunnels that used to connect the old buildings at the Antarctic stations before the new big comfortable 'sheds' were built. Near the front entrance, a bronze leopard seal is stretched out on a concrete block beside a cluster of Adelie penguins with their crests raised. I like to think the sculptures are there to remind everyone what Antarctica's really about, but I don't reckon anyone who works here even notices them. I don't often see the sculptures myself because the workshop's round the back.

Bazza's in there working on a new Hägglunds—a twin-cab tracked vehicle that'll be delivered south with resupply to replace one that a scientist dropped through the sea ice. When they bring the other one back, Bazza's crew will give it a full analysis and decide if it's worth refitting for another season south. They swap them over every three years anyway, but if the Hägg's in reasonable condition it might be okay to send with the next trip. Häggs are costly machines, but they're invaluable on the ice.

Bazza has four other diesos working in the shed with him, so you'd expect them to be on top of things, but I know from experience that everything's on a ridiculously short time frame. The antdiv just lines up the jobs, expecting Bazza's crew will have everything ready to go south again with the October or December resupply. It's flawed optimism. You'd think by now they'd be familiar with Antarctic logistics.

After I machine my parts for the truck, Bazza and I have a cup of coffee. He looks at his watch—three o'clock—and says he'd prefer a beer, but I tell him I have to get back to work. He raises bushy eyebrows at me and asks his usual question: When am I going south again? He asks me this every time he sees me. They need good diesos like me on the stations, he says. I always fob him off with some pathetic excuse, like not being able to stand the cold. But we both know I'm kidding myself. Ever since I went down there I've been yearning for the space and the light, for those long horizons and the cold emptiness of the air—white that goes on forever, and the plateau like a low grey cloud.

Bazza catches me staring into distance. 'Go,' he says. 'Just go this season. You'll be right, this time.'

Everyone knows, you see. Everyone in the Antarctic Division knows what happens to you while you're down there. They know who's being unfaithful, whose marriage is collapsing. But nobody lets on. It's the code. So nobody says anything to the suffering person back home who suspects their partner is having an affair down south. Affairs can happen at the other end too. The tyranny of distance.

'Come on,' Bazza says. 'Take your pick. There are positions for diesos at every station. There's nothing to hold you back.'

But he's wrong. There's plenty holding me back. Doubt. Fear. Inertia. Mum. 'What would I do with Jess?' I say, digging for excuses.

Bazza shakes his head. 'Someone'll look after her. I dunno. What about that niece of yours?'

He's right; Jacinta would care for Jess if I asked her. But I just can't go. There are weights in my shoes holding me in Hobart. Something bad would happen and I wouldn't be here to deal with it. I learned that last time; when you go down south you're vulnerable to losing things. Unfortunately, it's a risk you don't understand until after you go.

'Not this season, Bazza. Can't do it. I've got too many commitments.'

'We've all got commitments, mate. I've got my name down for next year. Had it approved by the missus. The pay's better than it used to be, too.'

Bazza has his own reasons for going south: a break from his wife, not too much work to do, the money, jollies every weekend, drinking beer in a field hut with his mates, porn movies to combat other aspects of the isolation. Bazza's got an arrangement with his wife: she has some bloke she sees when Bazza's south and he seems to be okay with that. And his wife doesn't mind if something happens down there with a girl over winter—although he's getting a bit beyond the eligible age group. The girls who go south are mostly young and get snapped up by the enthusiastic young testosterone that moves quicker than old bulls like Bazza; the ship's hardly out of Hobart and it's happening. If the beer wasn't free down there, Bazza says he'd get sick watching it all. No, he says, you wouldn't want to let your wife or girlfriend go south without you. They're all into it, like a bunch of animals.

That's what we are really, I tell him. Animals. Even though we spend a lot of time trying to hide it. It's biology; people can't help themselves. And what do you expect when you put a group of men and women together in a ship for close to five weeks? That's how long it takes to reach Davis Station from Hobart: seven days to the ice and then another two or three weeks grinding west through the pack. The ship is laden with cargo for resupplying whichever station you're heading to, and the crew just wants to make it through the big seas as fast as they can. In the pack, the ice damps down the swell. One trip, the ship was only three days out of Hobart in heavy seas when one of the choppers broke loose in the heli hangar. All the helicopters were smashed to pieces and they had to turn the ship and back rustle up some other choppers. Just like that. The antdiv has money at its fingertips. Who else could summon up a couple more helicopters in a few days? They couldn't drop off staff or do resupply without them—especially on those voyages early in the season, when the sea ice is still thick and the ship can't get into station.

But things are starting to change down there now. They've built a runway at Casey Station so they can fly people in. The ship's still needed to deliver supplies and gear, but the isolation is reducing. At least that's what they say. But I wonder about it; they can't fly people down unless the weather's perfect. And how many perfect days do you get in Antarctica? Especially in spring when everybody wants to get there.

Bazza glances at his watch. 'Let's go down to the cafeteria and get some chips. And a pie or something,' he says.

I follow him out of the shed, towards the main building. 'Where's Jess?' he asks.

'In the car.'

'Got the windows down?'

'Of course, I always leave the windows down.'

'I don't like to see a dog suffer. And you're such a dopey bugger sometimes.'

'I always look after my dog.'

Bazza nods. 'Just checking, you dreamer.'

'You set me off, Bazza. Pushing me to go south again.'

'Yeah, I know it. Bloody southland.'

We're all just a breath away from memories.

We enter the building and walk down a long grey corridor to the cafeteria. It's afternoon tea time and there are plenty of people sitting down with a cuppa or a snack. I used to know most of them. Some of the old guard have been here forever. They've done their stints down south, and now they are office-bound, directing the field staff who go in their place. But many of the young ones are transient. They last a few trips to Antarctica and then they move on. If you don't escape, you're trapped by it. Ice in your veins.

Bazza buys a couple of pies and we sit down at a table. There's a dismembered newspaper on the table and some flyers for a seminar on Wednesday night: 'The ecology of Adelie penguins' by Emma Sutton.

Bazza sees me looking at the flyer. 'Why don't you go?' he says. 'You're into penguins.'

I do love penguins, especially Adelies. They're rugged little black and white nuggets, solid balls of muscle. You don't want to mess with one unless you know what you're doing. They can draw blood with their beaks or the leading edge of a well-placed flipper. It's amazing how they can swim from somewhere out in the endless Southern Ocean to the ice edge and then waddle over miles of ice to return to their breeding colony—the same island they bred on the previous year. I always wonder how they find their way back each time.

Bazza is watching me.

'I don't think I can go,' I say. 'I've got too much work on.'

'You should go. It'll only be for an hour or so. And they need support for these things. They're always asking the bios to give talks about their work and then nobody goes.'

'What about you? Are you going?'

Bazza winks at me. 'I go home early that day. It's card night. But if it was a Thursday . . .'

'You're full of it, Bazza.'

'Yeah, mate. But Emma's a nice girl. She'll give a good talk.'

I put the flyer down and pick up my pie. 'I'll see how I'm going at work. Now, about this truck . . .'

Bazza looks at me and shakes his head.

On my return to the car Jess greets me joyously. Bazza made me take one of the flyers for the seminar and I toss it on the dashboard. I rub Jess about the ears. 'How you going, girl?'

She tries to scramble onto my lap and I indulge her in a crowded hug for a moment before pushing her back down to the floor. She's all doggie smiles and wiggly body. I wish humans could show their pleasure as transparently as dogs. We're all so self-contained.

'We've got work to do,' I remind her. 'Then we can go for a walk after dinner.'

Walk and *dinner*, two words that she knows. She pants happily up at me from the floor on the passenger side.

On the drive back to the garage, the flyer slips from the dashboard onto Jess's head and then to the floor. I scoop it up and put it on the seat. I wonder what this Emma Sutton is like. The young female scientists are generally the most temporary of all the staff. They have a few seasons in them before their lives are screwed up by a series of ice-based relationships that usually fail to survive back in the real world. Then they leave for other pursuits and to sort out their lives.

But it's not always as simple as that. I only had one season south and I'm still not sorted out. Bazza thinks I should be over it. But I'm not. It'll haunt me all my life.

6

There's something about Antarctica that locks you in for life. Maybe it's the landscape; so wild and bare and sparse. Or maybe it's seeing so much white. Or the relationships, all so intense. Whatever it is, somehow, in all that vast space and luminous light, you become transformed. You discover a new self. An ability to melt into distance. An uplifting sensation of freedom. At the same time, eternal yearning is born. You want to return. To reunite with the self you uncovered down there, a self unchecked by normal boundaries. When you go back to your old world, along with the other injuries Antarctica has inflicted, raw longing rules you. Your soul is in bondage. The healing takes years.

As my wife pointed out later, Antarctica is not something you can share with people who haven't been there. You can't show them how light shimmers over ice or glints from the angled faces of icebergs. When you talk about Antarctica after you return, you see the reflection of your craziness in people's faces. It's like grieving a death; those whose lives haven't been touched can't understand. So your isolation thickens. You wonder how you can feel more alone in a city of sixty thousand than in a field hut twenty kilometres from base.

For just over a year, Antarctica was my reality. I went, and I came back. My old life tried to reimpose itself, but parts of the puzzle were missing. They were lost in light and space. Captured by wind. Trapped in a blizzard. That's the cost.

Antarctica keeps part of you forever. You can never bring your whole self back again.

My wife Debbie found the ad on the Antarctic Division website for a diesel mechanic to overwinter at Davis Station; which would mean two summers and a winter away from home. We'd been married a year and bought a house. It was nothing fancy, and the mortgage wasn't huge, but neither of us had impressive incomes, so the loan was a financial constraint. I wasn't much of a spender, but Debbie was into clothes and shoes and manicures.

The Antarctic salary was three times my wage. Debbie decided we needed this job to set us up. We'd pay a decent sum off the mortgage and that'd relieve the strain. It'd be easy. I could go south and work on engines and look at birds—my two great passions, she pointed out—while she'd stay home and organise a few renovations to the house. I'd be away fifteen months, and sure, that was a long time and she'd miss me, but she was confident it'd work out beautifully in the end.

Ten years ago, in October, I left for Antarctica on the great orange ship the *Aurora Australis*, her horn blaring as she inched away from the wharf. On the helideck, I clung to the end of a streamer while down on the wharf Debbie held the other end. The ship slid through the inky waters, engines thrumming, until the streamer stretched to breaking point and gave out with a flick. It was hard to look back with the ship pointed south. One hundred metres from the docks and distance was already asserting itself.

As the wharf shrank away, the other expeditioners disappeared inside the ship. I was left alone in the approaching dusk. I stayed there until Hobart was long gone and the *Aurora* hummed smoothly through the quiet waters of the Derwent then down the eastern side of Bruny Island. The sadness of departure was tempered by the anticipation of new experiences, and I was filled with guilty excitement.

Beyond the tip of Bruny, we churned through the peaks and troughs of the Southern Ocean. The motion plastered me to my bunk. Occasionally, I braved the deck, watching the heaving waters stretching south, and trying to catch a glimpse of an albatross riding the updrafts around the ship. The birdwatchers on the ship showed me lists of seabirds: cape petrels, prions, royal albatross, black-browed albatross, wanderers, light-mantled sooties. But I was too ill to spend long out of bed. I'd snatch a brief gasp of frigid air, then stumble below and collapse on my bunk.

On rough days, the sea sloshed at my porthole like a washing machine. My cabin mate told of cups rolling off dinner tables, of the swell riding up onto the trawl deck at the back of the ship, of someone vomiting on the bridge. Dinners were bowls of pasta with rich creamy sauces, lobster thermidor, lasagne, steaks. But my meals consisted of dry biscuits chewed gingerly in my bunk. Only horizontal did I feel vaguely normal. I lay there fighting seasickness, waiting to acclimatise so I could sit up for long enough to write home to Debbie.

It took four days to find my sea legs. I was like a bear emerging from hibernation—slow at first, then grasping life with increasing energy. The bridge became my home. During the day, I helped with seabird counts, watching petrels and albatross riding the icy winds as they followed the ship. When I wasn't on the bridge, I was down on the trawl deck where the albatross dipped low over the water, skimming the surface of the waves. Down there, I saw krill swarms kicked up in the ship's wake, and seabirds diving to feast on them.

While others worked out in the weights room in the bowels of the ship or raised a sweat pummelling a boxing bag, I jumped rope out on the trawl deck, finding some sort of lurching rhythm as the ship rose and fell with the waves, my breath rising in clouds of vapour. Some passengers did nothing beyond eating and sleeping and watching videos in the gloom of the lounge.

On Saturday nights, I braved the throng down in the bar, discovering another aspect of ship life. After the mess, the bar was the place for meeting people. The *Aurora* is a dry ship these days, but back then people survived for their beer rations. Our trip was a new adventure for many, but there were also lots of returnees, who talked endlessly of people I didn't know and previous Antarctic expeditions. It was hard to fit into the crowd. While everyone else socialised and drank too much beer, I sat and observed the behaviour evolving among the passengers. Liaisons were budding everywhere; you'd have thought everyone was unattached, but many had relationships at home.

While all this was happening, the ship steamed south, churning through the roaring forties and the furious fifties into the screaming sixties. At times, we pushed into fog with black and white Antarctic petrels fading in and out, still following the ship.

A week in there came a new sound, a swishing against the side of the ship. And now the ship rolled more slowly, almost lazily. Out the porthole, pancake ice stretched to the grey horizon in neat rounded plates with crusty upturned edges. From the deck, I squinted into brightness, watching the swell running slowly through the shuffling horde of frosted discs. In the space of a day the world had transformed. The pancakes became larger cakes and then ice floes, and we were into the pack ice.

Wherever possible, the ship followed dark open tracts of water called leads. But as the floes thickened we began to break ice. Down on the fo'c'sle I hung over the railing, watching the ship ride up, feeling the tremors in its metal hulk as bits of ice grazed, split and tumbled under the bow. Occasional deep judders jarred the decks as the propeller carved chunks of ice with a jerk and a shake. There was eerie booming followed by groaning and creaking as the ship cracked floes with her weight.

By email I tried to share my experiences with Debbie. But the words sounded distant even to me. A week and a half from Hobart and I didn't know myself anymore. I was in this strange luminescent place and home was a receding memory.

We clunked west through the field of ice for two weeks, lengthening the gap between us and reality. People wearied of the pack ice. The crunching, crushing force of icebreaking. The echoing, tinny sound of ice on metal, shrieking and grinding. And yet the days of sameness were laced with surprises. Emperor penguins appeared from nowhere and launched themselves onto floes, fleeing the bow of the ship. Crabeater seals lay like silver slugs on the ice, waking up as we approached and spinning spectacular three-hundred-and-sixty-degree turns, lashing their tails, hissing and lunging as the ship ground past. Spouts rose as we rode alongside minke whales in breaks of open water, their small curved dorsal fins peaking as they dived. Snow petrels of purest white fluttered over the mashed ice in our wake, hunting krill. Helicopters took off from the back of the ship, heading out over the vast icescape to survey seals or to search out open stretches of water to speed our progress.

I passed the days up on the bridge, watching for seabirds by day, staring into the spot-lit night looking for icebergs. The captain told me we could hit a berg at nine knots without sinking. I thought of the *Titanic* going twenty-two knots in a field of icebergs.

At least twice a day, I pulled on all my layers of clothing and braved the cold above the bridge, staring into the blinding light, or leaning out over the bow watching ice crumpling, splitting and fracturing. Sometimes we became icebound, locked by slabs rafted up against each other, all twisted and strewn. Then, after working back and forth for up to an hour, the ship would finally create a crack in the ice large enough to push through into easier territory.

At the end of the third week in the pack ice we approached Davis Station, gliding through Iceberg Alley at sunset. The light glittered on the carved faces of the bergs. On the ice below, Adelie penguins scattered from the path of the ship. Eventually, we could see the station; the blocky shapes of buildings nestled at the foot of the crumbling brown Vestfold Hills. The frozen sea was dotted with hundreds of icebergs, snow-dusted islands and lines of black penguins.

As soon as the *Aurora* shuddered to a halt in the ice, we were into the intense rush of resupply. Each day the ship was out from Hobart cost the Antarctic Division tens of thousands of dollars, so anyone with a free pair of hands was put to work. Hägglunds, tractors and bulldozers flocked around the ship, and cranes swung into unloading. On a rotating roster we whizzed into station over the bulldozed ice highway on the back of a ute. They fed us and slotted us quickly into rooms where we could stash our gear. People like me—the incoming winterers—had rooms in the lime-green Living Quarters known as the LQ. The rest—those who would leave at the end of summer—were bundled into faded red shipping containers lined up across the road like holiday units at a caravan park. The road was the separation zone. Winterers and summerers; us and them.

The ship was gone within three days. Apart from the nuggety shapes of grounded icebergs, Prydz Bay was empty—a frozen sea with a jagged scar where the ship had done a six-point turn and crunched back to sea.

Life on station started to take shape. The first beer allowance was distributed. Scientists organised themselves and their field requirements. Duties were delegated. Field training began. In the machinery shed we diesel mechanics were always in demand. A quad bike that wouldn't start. Fuelling up a Hägglunds. Repair and maintenance of motorboats, tools, skidoos. Chainsaws for cutting ice. Fixing and modifying equipment for scientists. Constant monitoring of the power house. Maintaining the firefighting Hägg—a vital task down there, where fire meant disaster.

Soon scientists commenced field work, disappearing over the ice. The days gained a regular sort of rhythm—breakfast, smoko, lunch, smoko, dinner. People whose weight had bloomed on the slow hours of the voyage south expanded further with the calorie-dense meals which were mostly covered with cheese. And all that food had to be prepared. Food for fifty, five times a day. The two chefs were the most important people on station: food was essential for morale. But they couldn't do all the work alone. Rosters, known as slushy duty, were set up to assist them in the kitchen: hands to peel buckets of potatoes, hands to pack and unpack dishwashers, hands to peel and chop carrots and onions, grate cheese, serve food.

Amid the routine, station dynamics evolved. On Saturday nights parties shaped themselves from nowhere. A birthday was an excuse for a binge. A few musicians formed a rough sort of a band and jammed in the lounge. Gossip was born and grew—some real, some fabricated. Clashes emerged, scuffles over girlfriends. Relationships developed. Others died. Marriages came under strain.

Among all this, I found my own way. I wasn't into the field-hut drinking trips or the binges on station. When I wasn't in the shed or in the computer room emailing Debbie I was away, hooking myself onto field trips to assist biologists: counting penguins, marking seals, taking samples from frozen lakes, grinding out ice cores with the glaciologists. One diesel mechanic always had to be on station, so the opportunities for escape from work were few. But scientists often looked for helpers, and they wanted someone quiet and useful.

I patched up my loneliness with the vast landscapes, bizarre animals and luminescent light. I skied out from station, passing Adelie penguins waddling urgently in single file to their colonies on the offshore islands. Among the powdery blues of the towering bergs was an iceberg of magical deep jade, its surfaces scoured by wind. Near the ice edge, a leopard seal was sleeping, its heavy head resting on the ice. The sinuous length of its powerful body stretched, and then it rolled and yawned, showing strings of sharp teeth.

As the season progressed, I assisted wherever I could. This included tagging and marking Adelie penguins on a nearby island. We laughed at their rock-stealing antics as they fought to build the largest nest of stones, the fury of flipper bashings as they squabbled. I sat for hours watching them courting: the ducking and weaving of heads, the slow rhythmic flapping. And always more penguins arriving, waddling towards the island or tobogganing on their bellies, propelled by strong-clawed pink feet. The deafening noise of the place—the chorus of squawking black bodies scattered over rocky hillsides reuniting with returning mates. As the summer unfolded, egg incubation began, and the busy clucking calls subsided to quiet restfulness. Penguins sat belly-flopped on their nests, eyes like slits, the wind ruffling their feathers.

Eventually, the sea ice melted and blew out. My breaks were reduced to snatched days walking the valleys and lakes of the Vestfold Hills, although I managed to score a few days helping with field work on remote islands. When data collection was done for the day, I watched fulmars soaring straight-winged in the stiff breeze. Snow petrels scuffling about the rock faces. Sometimes I sat listening to the water lapping beneath the melting ice that surrounded the island, watching Adelies porpoising in the shallows and the wind drawing patterns on the surface of the sea.

Through all of this, I missed Debbie. Once a week we spoke by telephone. In between, I wrote emails telling her of all that I had seen and done. I wrote of the bergs dotting Prydz Bay, their varied shapes and colours. I wrote of the late sunsets, the ever-lengthening light, the lone emperor penguin in Long Fjord that glided up on its belly and sat beside me for several minutes. I wrote of the ice gradually melting, the bizarreness of twenty-four-hour daylight, the ugliness of station once the snow had gone. I wrote of the long hours in the shed, of the emptiness without her. I wrote to Debbie of how I missed her, of how I thought of her in our little house, and of how we'd soon be back together.

It still amazes me that you can be destroyed without knowing it. Even as it gives, Antarctica takes away. So, after all that happened to me because of that place, why is it I still long to return?

The Lightkeeper's Wife

7

It was close to midday when Mary forced herself to make lunch. All morning, she had waited for the arrival of the ranger, and still he had not come. It made her anxious. What if he didn't show? What would she do? She hadn't much time to fulfil her debt to Jack, and if the ranger didn't turn up, all was lost. Her family would come and drag her back to Hobart; Jan's nursing home loomed terrifyingly large.

At the kitchen bench, she dutifully shook tablets from various vials and gulped them down with icy water. It was essential that she maintain her health as long as possible and not succumb to the absent-mindedness which hovered so close about her. A stream of recollections had stolen chunks of her morning, and she'd forgotten her ten o'clock medication.

She sat on the couch, a sandwich and a mug of tea before her on the coffee table, and stared vacantly out the window, fighting a surge of agitation. If only she could relax and absorb the view. She looked down at the sandwich with apathetic distaste.

Finally, she heard a dull bang outside that could have been a car door closing. Then there were rapid footsteps on the verandah and a shadow passing the window. It must be him, the ranger. A loud knock battered the door. He sounded in a hurry.

'Come in,' she called.

The door swung open and a young man stood there in the Parks uniform: khaki shirt and trousers with a green jumper. He was stocky with red hair parted in the middle and pale skin dotted with freckles. His hand was tight on the door handle and his face wore the bland lack of interest of a schoolboy. He frowned at her, saying nothing. Mary's turmoil increased. Obviously, he didn't want to be here: this was going to be challenging. She reached for her walking stick and heaved herself up, offering her hand. 'I'm Mary Mason. Come in and take a seat.'

He released the door handle reluctantly and stepped across the room to shake her hand. She returned his grip as vigorously as she could manage, wanting him to think she was sprightly and interesting, even though she was, in truth, a withered scrap of womanhood. In her enthusiasm, she clutched his hand too long. His eye was already set on the door, but she must not let him leave yet.

'I'm pleased to meet you,' she said. 'Perhaps you'd like a cup of tea.'

He recoiled, tugging his hand loose. 'Sorry. Not today, Mrs Mason. I'm just making a quick visit to check on you.'

'Yes. Well, I'm still alive.'

'You don't need anything?'

'Nothing beyond a bit of human company.'

'That's good to hear.' He was already backing towards the door. 'I'll look in on you tomorrow.'

'You won't stay?'

'I've got other jobs to do.' His hand was on the door handle again.

'And your name?' she asked.

'Leon.' His reply was a mumble, almost incoherent. 'Leon Walker.'

'How about tomorrow then, Leon?' she suggested. 'I'll have the kettle warm.'

Her persistence finally paid off. 'All right then,' he said grudgingly. 'Tomorrow.'

He left before she could say anything more, and she was piqued. Perhaps he was irritated by old people. Perhaps he was determined not to like her. What could she do? She needed to secure his assistance somehow. She decided to walk out over the dunes—likely he'd gone to check the campground, and he'd probably make a quick circuit of the campsites and return. There should just be enough time for her to get out on the beach, and when he came driving back along the sand, he'd think: *There goes that old lady, Mary Mason. She's a game one, out here in this weather.* It would elevate her in his estimation and he would no longer look at her like a bothersome fly around the barbeque.

She shuffled to the bedroom and dug for her coat amid the clothes draped over a chair. Tugging on the coat, she grasped her cane and hurried out the door. There was a fearsome wind outside, laden with salt and blasting through the scrub on the dunes. It was just as well she was wearing trousers. It wouldn't do to be out in a dress. Pulling up the collar of her coat, she leaned into the wind and stumbled down the hill. Her cough startled a scarlet robin from a fence post, and Mary paused to watch the bird dip away over the grass.

The track descended into sand. She followed Leon's tyre marks over the crest of the dunes where the wind seemed to accelerate, gushing up from the beach. With effort, she climbed down the dune, sliding in the loose sand. She was beginning to wonder if she was being sensible. But sensible or not, having come this far, she needed to go on. He had to see her out there. He had to engage with her.

On the beach, she turned her back to the wind and made her best show of striding along the sand. It took only ten metres to realise she was fooling herself. *Striding* was not something a seventy-seven year-old woman with heart failure was capable of. If Leon saw her now he'd think she was mad.

She stopped to watch the sea, feeling sogginess in her chest. She should get out of the wind, but being on the beach was so different from the view through the cabin window. East Cloudy Head was a great hummock rearing south. Across the bay, the grey dolerite cliffs rose and stretched in humps along West Cloudy Head, finishing in a series of jagged rocks. The waves were running in from the south-west and the horizon was a steely band, curving to the edge of the earth. A Pacific gull flapped over, craning down at her then lifting away on the wind. Sea spray tingled on her skin and she could feel the bite of brine. This was home—this air, the cold feel of salt on her cheeks. Life came back to her, became real again. She might be on the cusp of death, but she swore she'd go out living instead of mothballed in a hospice.

She turned away from the sea, pleased with herself, done with her display of independence for the day. And there, just as she'd hoped, was Leon's four-wheel drive coming down the beach, not fifty metres away. A white Toyota. She could see his frown behind the steering wheel—his eyebrows one angry line. He pulled up and leaped out.

'Are you sure you should be walking in this weather?' he asked, his voice shredded by a gust of billowing air.

'I wanted to feel the wind,' she called back defiantly.

'No need to come this far to feel it.' He jammed his hands in his pockets.

'And isn't it a fine day,' she hollered, choking down an impulse to cough. 'A fine Cloudy Bay day.'

His eyebrows rose, as if questioning her sanity. Perhaps it *was* lunacy to suggest it was a fine day. But this was Bruny Island, and all was just as it should be. He ought to know that.

'Do you live nearby?' she asked, leaning on her stick, trying to divert him with friendly conversation.

'No,' he said. He kicked at the desiccated carcase of a mutton bird, partly hidden among withered clumps of seaweed, half covered by sand. She heard the fragile skull crack beneath his heavy boot.

'So, you come over each day on the ferry from Kettering?'

'Of course not. I live over at Adventure Bay.'

He was being difficult. Adventure Bay was on the east side of South Bruny, perhaps thirty minutes drive away. A string of famous explorers had landed there: Cook, Bligh, Furneaux, D'Entrecasteaux, Baudin, Flinders. It had been a place of shelter—a suitable location for taking on water and wood, and for neutral meetings with the natives. The indigenous people of Bruny Island had amicably accepted the intruders—the explorers who came and then left; the whalers who stayed until all the southern right whales were gone; and then the settlers, who did not leave. But settlement was disastrous for the Aborigines. Some of their women were abused by whalers and sealers, and disease took most of the others, leaving a small group who were removed to Flinders Island. Adventure Bay was quiet these days, in spite of its sad history.

'Ah. Adventure Bay. A peaceful little place,' she said. 'Are you a peaceful soul, Leon?' His glare told her she'd overstepped the mark. He was standing astride, hands still firmly in his pockets. 'How was the campground?' She tried another tack. 'Anyone camping?'

'No-one,' he said. 'People don't like being out when it's windy like this.' He emphasised *people* to indicate her diversion from the ordinary.

'*I* like it,' she said, accepting the face-off.

He frowned again. 'But if you don't look after that cough . . .'

She couldn't be sure, but it almost sounded like a threat. And now the cough was bubbling up again, betraying her. She jerked her cane out of the sand and planted it, ready for her next step. 'I'd best be heading back,' she said. 'Do enjoy the wind.'

She'd struggled several paces across the sand when the hacking began. It'd be hard work getting back to the cabin, but she was too proud to ask for help. She turned away, trying to swallow the cough, almost gagging.

'Just wait, Mrs Mason,' Leon called, his voice condescending and impatient, as if he were speaking to a child. 'I'm not usually a taxi service, but I'll give you a lift today. You need it.'

She moved to wave him away, but he gave her no space to protest, grasping her elbow strongly and heaving her into the car. A stiff silence settled between them as he drove back to the cabin, bouncing mercilessly over the dunes. He was clearly impatient with her antics and wanted to be done with her for the day.

At the cabin, he swung open the passenger door and shepherded her out. Then he helped her into the cabin and sat her on the couch. 'Remember, I have a job to do. My brief is only to check on you.'

She felt humbled and reprimanded. He slammed the front door to punctuate his resentment, then threw himself back into the four-wheel drive and roared away.

8

Leon gripped the steering wheel hard as he hammered along the sand. He couldn't believe he'd been lumped with this chore. Who was this crazy old dame he had to check on every day?

'Mrs Mary Mason.' He said it aloud in a whining derogatory tone. She was not part of his job description; that's what he'd said to his boss when the idea had first been raised. But his boss had waved Leon's protests away, saying it'd be a simple task and worth every cent of the extra money. Yeah, right. He'd imagined it'd be a quick drop-in, a wave through the door and a distant cheerio. But he could tell already this old woman expected more from him than that. She wanted company. She wanted attention. Her very greeting today spelled *needy*, in capital letters. He had enough stuff going down at home without having to take this on too.

He slung the car up the ramp from the beach and made a circle around the empty carpark at Whalebone Point. Should he bother with the toilets today? Or could he just leave them till tomorrow, given that he'd have to pass this place every day from now on, for who knew how many weeks? What a waste of time. And where had this old duck come from, anyway? His boss said she'd paid plenty to enlist some support. It was just to put her family at ease, apparently. Nothing too demanding.

Leon snorted. What a pain in the arse. And she expected him to be polite and have cups of tea. To have conversations. That wasn't part of the deal as he'd understood it.

He slammed out of the car and marched into the restrooms. Some idiot had pulled on one of the toilet rolls and there was a trail of paper all over the floor. Once he'd cleaned it up, there wasn't much else to do. He ought to head back and confront the home scene. Not much to look forward to there either.

He'd been in this job a while now: three, maybe four years. It wasn't quite what he'd expected—stocking toilet rolls, clearing rubbish and counting money out of National Park permit envelopes . . . *if* the tight-arse buggers decided to pay. Most visitors slunk by the pay stations, pretending they hadn't seen them. Nobody would know, of course, because there were no manned booths; it was an honesty system.

When he'd done the ranger training in Hobart, he'd imagined himself in one of the big parks—Cradle Mountain and Lake St Clair, or doing track maintenance in the Eastern or Western Arthurs. That would have been his prize posting—being paid to go bush, and maybe even manning one of the huts on the overnight walks. But once things had deteriorated at home, he hadn't had a choice. With his sister gone up to Devonport years ago, he'd been the only one who could step in, like a United Nations peacekeeping force.

He hadn't been particularly keen to get back to Adventure Bay. It was too damned quiet. Tourists might think it was pretty; the beaches were nice and there was a spectacular boat tour you could take out along the south-east coast of Bruny. But the place was a backwater, just the musty old museum and a few monuments and a coffee shop. If he hadn't left Bruny for a spell to complete his course in Hobart, he'd have gone mad . . . although perhaps that was an exaggeration. He did love Bruny. And the coastline was in his blood.

But what was he going to do about this Mrs Mason? He cursed himself for agreeing to a cup of tea tomorrow. And what was he supposed to do, sit there and have a nice chat with her? What would he say, anyway? *How was it back in the time of the ark? When are you booked in for your next blue rinse?* But that was a bit harsh. He didn't really know anything about her.

He swung the car up the mountain road and fanged around the curves. This was the benefit of knowing the roads so well; he could drive this route almost in his sleep. Not that he'd boast about that to his mother. Christ! Still living at home at his age. What an embarrassment. If only there was a resolution in sight—then he could apply for a job somewhere else. He'd tried to hint to his mother that she should seriously consider moving out, but he already knew she wouldn't do it. The old man was a bastard. God knows why she stayed.

Up on the mountain, he pulled over for some fresh air, stomping up the Mount Mangana trail. The track was always wet underfoot and he found the smell of the damp bush soothing. It reminded him of compost, of the forest recycling itself. He liked that about nature, the cycle of things. It was a pity none of the big old trees were left. He'd have to get back over to mainland Tasmania for forests like that—where the trees had diameters larger than the distance around his four-wheel drive. Well, not *his* four-wheel drive. The Parks vehicle.

He often came here when things weren't good at home. It was only about a twenty-minute drive from Adventure Bay. Few people came through on weekdays, especially at this time of year, and he could yell satisfyingly at the trees and the sky without worrying about disturbing anyone. Yelling was good for releasing tension, he'd discovered. And it was best done alone.

He figured he'd be doing a bit of yelling about Mary Mason up here over the next few weeks. Then he snorted. Truly, the old dame didn't look too good. And that cough of hers was a shocker. It made him think of a death rattle. Maybe she wouldn't be around too long anyway. The thought made him feel guilty; he shouldn't wish her dead. And besides, guess who'd be the lucky sucker to find her if she did cark it? Living on Bruny, he'd sometimes imagined he might come across a body washed ashore—the coast was so remote around here. But this was different. Every time he went into that cabin at Cloudy Bay he'd be wondering if Mrs Mason was dead.

Well, the first hurdle was this cup of tea tomorrow. He'd hoped wearing his uniform today might discourage her, remind her of his numerous other responsibilities. But then again, he was being paid to check on her. And there was no such thing as a free lunch.

He climbed back into the car and drove down off the mountain to see what mess might be waiting for him at home.

9

Morning had always been Mary's favourite time of day. It was when she was freshest and most positive, and somehow everything seemed cleanest. In this corner of the world, it was also generally the part of the day before the wind came up and the rain closed in. This morning was surprisingly clear. The sea was calm—barely a ripple—and the odd wavelet collapsed noisily in the stillness. Across the bay, the features of the cliffs were emerging—brown and grey and deeply lined with shadows—and the sea reflected silver.

She was standing by the window watching fairy wrens bopping and twittering on the lawn. And she was thinking of her favourite son, Tom.

On peaceful days like this, he used to say the ocean was resting. That it was waiting for the weather to change, preparing to receive a battering when the wind returned. It couldn't always be quiet, he said, or the cape would become complacent and forget what it was there for; to be torn by wind and weather. He was right, of course. Periods of calm had a purpose. They were times for storing energy. And energy was essential to fuel a soul to deal with life's challenges.

Sometimes Tom seemed wise, but he did worry her. All that awkwardness and that sad inability to move on with life.

Forty-two and on his own. She hadn't envisaged it that way. She hoped there was someone out there for him, some nice girl who'd understand and nurture him. She'd been relieved when he married Debbie, despite the girl's imperfections. At least he'd been happy, his face beaming with a quiet steady warmth. For a while he'd lost the faraway look that had followed him from childhood: the legacy of the cape. But then, after Antarctica, the distant look had returned and it had never quite left him. Jess filled a few gaps, but a dog, however attentive, could never fill the void created by lack of human company. Tom needed another wife, and soon. While the chance of children was still within reach. He'd be good with children. She shuffled to the couch and eased herself down, tugging the blanket around her stiff legs.

Weather like this made her think of the cape. This time of the year, it was often overcast—all those grey days; heavy southern skies thick with low cloud weeping moisture. Then there had been miraculous days when the sky was polished clean and the clouds were like puffs of vapour on a mirror. The lighthouse reflected so much white it hurt your eyes, and the sea was a vast smooth sheet, achingly blue, with occasional whitecaps nipping its surface.

If you climbed the hill to gaze south to where the sky fell into the deep arch of the horizon, sometimes you'd see the southern sea stacks glimmering—Pedra Branca and Eddystone Rock, the last pillars of land before the sea stretched beyond imagination to the distant land of ice. On days like that, you could feel pleasure so acute it erased pain and transcended troubles. You could stand for suspended lengths of time when you were supposed to be hanging out washing, gazing instead around the yellow arc of Lighthouse Bay, or watching sea eagles lifting high over the cape on the breeze.

A cough rattled somewhere deep in her chest. She should take her medication. There was fluid in her lungs and the doctor would say she must increase her dose of diuretics. She twisted to peer at the clock. Nearly ten. The ranger might come soon. What was his name? She ought to remember. It was important.

Leon—yes, she was sure that was it. It was annoying the way names slipped from her these days. She had little patience for these memory blanks; they caused her to stumble mid-thought.

She limped to the bench and set out two cups, popped tea bags in them and tipped Arrowroot biscuits onto a plate. Everything must be ready when he came. Her offering looked pitiful, but it was the best she could do. She swallowed her tablets and sat down to wait. Finally she heard the car, then footsteps on the deck, and Leon's knock shook the door.

'Come in,' she called.

She stood up as the door opened, almost losing her balance, and grasped the edge of the couch. He frowned from the doorway as a coughing fit struck her, doubling her over. She'd meant to greet him enthusiastically, but now she was breathless. He moved forward and helped her back onto the lounge. From the skew of his mouth, she could see he was irritated.

'What are you doing, Mrs Mason? Next time, don't stand.'

'I didn't want you to run away again.'

He glanced at her with shuttered eyes, barely concealing his impatience. 'I have a job to do.'

'You resent looking in on me?'

He maintained a sullen silence.

'I have a cup of tea ready for you,' she said, struggling up once more. 'Yesterday you said you'd stay. The water's just boiled.'

He sank onto the couch with a resigned sigh, pushing the rug aside.

'Do you like your job, Leon?' she asked as she lit the stove.

He ran his hands through his hair, head bowed. 'What I like about it is not talking to people.'

This was not good. 'Well, I need some things today,' she said, cajoling. 'And it's hard for me to ask without talking, isn't it?' There was nothing she needed, but it was an excuse to keep him here. 'How's life at Adventure Bay?'

He grunted. 'Same as usual.'

'Anything changed?'

'Not much. New café owner, selling the same crap coffee.'

'You like coffee? I only have tea.'

'I like working,' he said. 'Not sitting around.' He scuffed his feet, stared at the floor and then out the window. Looked everywhere, except at her.

'Why do you live in Adventure Bay if you hate it?'

'I didn't say I hated it.'

'Well, it's not very common, is it? Young men like yourself living on the island?'

'I live with my folks.'

She raised both eyebrows at him. 'How old are you?'

'A quarter your age.' He was being insolent now, payback for having to talk to her, she could see.

'Nowhere else to go?' She should have bitten her tongue. Young people could be self-focused and oversensitive. He might stand up and walk out.

At first, he didn't respond. When he eventually spoke, he seemed quiet and subdued. 'You wouldn't understand. Sometimes it can be hard to leave. And I don't want to live across the channel anyway. I've been here most of my life.'

'But there aren't many opportunities here, are there?'

He glared at her. 'No. This is it. I check toilets. I check on old women. I get paid.'

She ignored the jab. 'Perhaps you could get a Parks job elsewhere.'

'You're not hearing me. I want to stay on Bruny.'

His face clouded with something she couldn't interpret. He was afraid of leaving the island, she was sure of it. But why, she was unable to fathom. Most young people were keen to leave home—unless it suited them to stay. She'd heard that children these days were like boomerangs, coming home to sponge whenever life became difficult. Parents were constantly bailing them out, providing financial assistance. It hadn't been like that when her children were young. She poured hot water into the cups and jiggled the bags. 'Do you have milk, Leon? Sugar?'

'Just black.'

Appropriate, she thought. His gingery eyebrows were still furrowed with dark thoughts. He seemed burdened with life. Trying not to spill the tea, she placed his cup and the plate of biscuits on the coffee table and then went to fetch her own cup. Leon didn't move to assist her. She sat down in the armchair and tried to resume conversation.

'Did you have a nice walk up on the Head the other day?'

He grunted and stuffed a biscuit into his mouth. 'I didn't go up there, remember? I had to scrape you off the beach.'

'Perhaps you should go there more often. It's a salve for the soul. When it's windy, you feel like you could fly.'

His eyes flicked away.

'I suppose it's still the same up there,' she continued, trying to draw him out. 'Those columns of black rock have been there longer than any of us. And they'll still be there when we're all gone. I find that reassuring, don't you?'

He looked bored, but there was the slightest tinge of curiosity in his voice as he said, 'When did you first come here?'

'More than fifty years ago. With my husband, Jack, and his family.'

She thought of Jack's long legs, pressing through the scrub, the square set of his shoulders, his profile gazing out to sea. He'd been an unfolding mystery to her then, as she learned his body and his mind. After they left the farm, he'd become a question she'd never quite found the answer to. Yet she'd made the best of it, as people of her era had been brought up to do.

'My husband's dead now,' she said. 'But the rocks are still there. The land still watches south . . . When you walk up there, it takes you away from everything, everything that's ordinary. And that can be comforting.'

Leon was watching her. 'What were you doing on Bruny?'

'Jack was a lighthouse-keeper at the cape. We lived there twenty-six years. Before that he grew up near here on the land, back towards Lunawanna.'

'I know about the lighthouse.' Leon's attention was ensnared. 'I've read about it in the history room at Alonnah. How it was built by convicts to prevent shipwrecks. The tower's thirteen metres high. And it was first lit in 1838. They used to run it on whale oil.'

Mary smiled. She had him captive at last. 'Not in my time,' she said. 'I'm not quite that old.'

'What was it like living there?' he asked.

'You can find out yourself. They rent out one of the keepers' cottages. You can stay there. See what it feels like.'

He shook his head. 'It wouldn't be the same. Not like when you were there.'

She knew now that she had found his weak spot. Her way in. 'You want me to tell you about it?' she asked. His nod was small but affirmative. She lifted her cup and sipped, wondering how far she could push him. 'Why don't you take me for a drive, then? I'll feel more like talking if I get out.'

He sat back, impatient. 'It wasn't part of the deal, you know. To drive you about.'

'A person can get housebound.'

He folded his arms. 'You chose to come here. You knew what it'd be like. I'm a ranger, not a tour guide.' He glared at her, brows knit low.

'Just to the end of the beach,' she suggested, tremulous with anticipation. Cloudy Corner was the first destination on her list.

He hesitated and then made a face. 'All right. But we'll have to make it quick.'

Outside, the breeze caught in Mary's chest and she covered her cough with a hand. Leon took her elbow and guided her to the car. He was stronger than he looked; with him holding her up, it was like walking on air. He pushed her into the vehicle. 'Do up your seatbelt,' he growled. 'I don't want to be picking you up off the floor.'

Not very tactful, but he was right. She was weak after two days of sitting. Back in Hobart she was always finding things to do, tasks to get her up out of her chair. But here all she did was sit at the window watching the waves run in.

Banging the door shut, he started the vehicle with a roar and they bounced over the dunes onto the beach. He drove in silence, even when they lurched over a dip where a small stream ran into the sea. She reached for the dashboard to steady herself, but he ignored her and remained focused ahead. Near Cloudy Corner he stopped and pointed. 'Have a look out there, across the bay.'

Bright sunlight was shining yellow on the cliffs. The sea was silvery blue.

'Magnificent,' she said.

He swung the car to face the sea just as Jacinta had done that first day, and switched off the engine. The sound of waves was muffled and small gusts of wind were butting against the windows. 'Go on then,' he said. 'I'm ready.'

She glanced at him, having already forgotten that this trip was linked to a commitment. Then she remembered. She was supposed to tell him about the light station. Perhaps this hadn't been such a grand idea after all.

'Did you like it?' he asked. 'Being a keeper's wife? You must have liked it—to stay so long.'

'It was wonderful at first,' she said. She was speaking to Leon, but it was like riding towards Jack on a wave of memory. 'When we came to the cape we'd been gone from the island too long. We both missed it. Both of us. Bruny was always a place of the heart for us.'

Leon watched her closely.

'Going to the cape was a reunion with freedom,' she continued. 'So much space and air. Birds. Seals. Sometimes dolphins. We slotted in there like cows into a dairy.'

'You weren't lonely?'

'Not to start with. There was so much to do. Jack was busy with work. And I was busy setting up the house. Cows to milk, briquettes to lug, baking and cooking, washing. We had visitors sometimes, but the roads were rough. We were very isolated.'

The lightkeepers' schedule was busy. Night work and then cleaning during the day. A sheep to butcher. Another coat of paint on the lighthouse. Weather observations. Time off was reserved for a day on the weekend. This had been their time to learn the cape, her and Jack and the children. She thought of the special nook they had discovered, a cove which was reached by scrambling down a steep slope. They'd perch and picnic there on black slabs of broken rock. It was calm and quiet, out of the wind, a sheltered place where they could gaze across the channel to the dimpled folds of Recherche Bay. Often a pod of dolphins would be playing offshore, curling and curving through the waves. Jan and Gary would paddle in the cold shallows, or stand tossing rocks into the water with showery splashes. Afterwards, she and Jack would piggyback the children up the narrow gully, scrabbling in the gravel. When they arrived home, they felt washed clean by tranquillity, smoothed like pebbles rolling in the sea.

She recalled how intimacy had returned for them in those first few months at the lighthouse. When Jack wasn't too ragged from lack of sleep or the cry of the wind, they clutched each other in the whispering dark, finding solace and release in each other's bodies. It had been a time for remembering how to love. Yes, it had been good, for a while.

'How did you get food?' Leon asked, prodding her back to the present.

'We had a delivery every month,' she said. 'It came by truck off the ferry from North Bruny. When we moved to the cape, the road from Lunawanna to the lighthouse had just been constructed, so the delivery of supplies was much simpler. Before that the lighthouse vessel, *Cape York*, used to take stores to Jetty Beach and then they had to be transferred to the keepers' cottages. We had it comparatively easy, although we still welcomed the appearance of the truck.' She remembered the old Ford grinding across the heath, horn blaring with the news of its arrival. 'Unpacking was a family affair,' she said. 'Jack hefted boxes and we sorted them onto shelves in the storeroom. My daughter Jan liked to do a bucket brigade—passing tins along to Gary and then to me. The sacks of flour were too heavy for the children, so that was my job. We ate simply, stews and dumplings, salted meat, canned vegetables.'

'What about fresh stuff?' Leon asked. 'Surely you had a vegie garden?'

'Not a successful one,' Mary admitted. She had dug herself to exhaustion in that sifting sandy soil, and any moisture she'd added had run away. 'There was plenty of rain, but too much salt. Everything withered.' Just like Jack, she thought. 'The island was good to us,' she said, picking up a more hopeful memory. 'People sent us anything in season: apples, apricots, cabbages, peas. But gifts like those were irregular and mostly we had to manage with the stores. Food wasn't the highlight of our existence. Having the cow meant we had plenty of butter, cream and milk. And when Gary caught something edible, we had fresh fish. Our luxury was a roast when one of the sheep was killed.'

'How many visitors did you have?'

'Very few.'

'Not even with the new road?'

'No. People were preoccupied with their own lives. It was busiest during mutton-bird season, but that all stopped when mutton-birding was banned.'

'And you definitely weren't lonely?' Leon seem fixed on this.

'It was harder when the children got older,' she said. 'They were looking for other company by then. Eventually, we sent them to boarding school.'

'What about you?'

Mary hadn't often thought about herself. 'I managed well enough most of the time,' she said. And yet there had been times when the solitude was difficult. She'd tried to befriend the other keeper's wife. However, there was a social hierarchy even out there. Help had been forthcoming in emergencies, but the head keeper's wife didn't seek her out. She and her husband didn't have children, and perhaps Jan and Gary were too wild and noisy.

'And the weather?' Leon asked.

Yes, the weather. It had shaped everything they did. 'On bad days, we were stuck indoors,' she said. 'Sometimes the wind was so strong, you couldn't stand up in it. Only the men ventured out. Anyone else would be blown off the cape. Even the birds were cautious. But on still days, it was heaven on earth. Perfect beyond perfection.' She remembered the sun kissing the land. The light licking the ocean. The mainland, visible and purplish to the west. Nothing could be better.

'Was it worth it?' Leon asked, fetching her back again. 'Was it a happy place?'

She looked at him and hesitated. Could she really say she'd been happy there over the years? It had been nirvana until things had begun to dissolve. But had that place given her lasting joy? Or had she just coped within a framework she'd come to know and understand, working with whatever fragments she and Jack had been able to give each other?

'I was content,' she said. And this was the best she could do. What was happiness, after all? And how many people could say they'd had it?

Drained, she stared seawards and saw herself in the foam as it shattered over the rocks. She hoped Leon would recognise her need for rest. And he did. He started the four-wheel drive and drove up the track to the campground, steering slowly around the loop, past shady campsites nestled beneath stunted coastal stringybarks.

He stopped at a campsite and helped her out. She was stiff and slow, a bit wobbly. He dragged a sawn-off stump into a triangle of light beneath the shifting branches of the trees and left her sitting beside the remains of an old campfire while he picked up his bag of toilet rolls and walked across to the long-drop toilets. The door banged as he went in and then banged again as he came out. He wandered around the campground, keeping his distance from her.

Mary didn't mind being left alone. It was such a long time since she had camped at Cloudy Corner. She used to come here with the Masons on family outings; they would drive the old truck to the end of the road and then trundle along the sand to the end of the beach. They'd light a campfire under the trees and make tea while she and Jack walked up onto the headland.

The first time she and Jack came here alone was their honeymoon. They'd arrived on an overcast day with brooding skies, having walked from the farm with makeshift packs and panted to the end of the road where the land fell away onto the long flat run of the beach. On the rise overlooking the arc of sand, they'd stopped together, feeling the slow breeze stirring as they inhaled the tang of salt. Mary had been wet with sweat beneath heavy clothes, and was ready to stop, but Jack wanted to walk to the end of the beach. She remembered the joy of this place—she and Jack alone beneath the skies, the glow of light on the water, the late flush of yellow on East Cloudy Head.

At Cloudy Corner, Jack had shouldered through the scrub and she'd followed him into the hushed dark beneath the trees. She'd been keen to sleep on the beach under the spray of stars, but Jack was worried the wind would come up; he thought they'd be more comfortable under the trees. They made camp among the scrub, their bed a piece of canvas on the ground covered by woollen blankets. Then they stripped off and dived and splashed through the freezing waves, chasing each other, stopping to kiss, their skin alive with goosebumps.

Afterwards, they scrubbed themselves dry with a rough towel, prickling with cold, and layered on clothes before wandering along the sand, fossicking for treasures. They picked their way around the base of the headland to a string of rocks where cormorants perched with wings spread wide, trying to dry off in the brisk wind. Further around, they scrunched through mats of pig-face pockmarked by mutton-bird burrows. They found a place to sit on a rock platform above the black sea. Mary sat between Jack's legs so he could wrap himself around her, and she leaned against him, high on freedom and love.

For dinner, they ate chunks of bread smothered with slabs of melted cheese, and preserved apricots for dessert. She remembered the light of the flames flickering on Jack's face as he fed sticks into the fire. And the shiver of breeze that flowed up from the beach, rustling the leaves. She could still see Jack squatting by the flames, his legs thin and wiry, his shoulders boxy and broad. His face narrow. His jaw angled, rough with stubble.

After dinner they had walked the beach under the white wash of the moon, stopping to grasp each other in passion, or to lean into each other's warmth while the air settled bitingly cold around them. That night, they lay together, listening to the sound of the waves breaking on the beach, their bodies enmeshed, warmth rising between them. Intimacy was something they'd dreamed of for years, and yet it was almost overwhelming when reality arrived. All that yearning. So much anticipation. So little experience.

After the farm, there had been the burden of their lives in Hobart; Jack's retreat into himself and her own misery. The lighthouse gave them a temporary reprieve, but then the wind wore Jack down. Truly, it was a wonder they made it through. If she hadn't been so patient, so committed, so determined, they could have easily blown away like the marriages of today. But a failed marriage was destitution back then. There were few options for women. A divorce was a public disgrace. And she loved Jack, despite his foibles.

Often she had wished she could teach her children how to prevent a relationship from going into decline. The art of marriage maintenance. But even if she had been able to verbalise all that was in her heart, she couldn't dictate how they should live their lives. It wasn't her place to steal from them the bittersweet pain of their own discoveries and mistakes. The resuscitation of a relationship was something you could only learn between the lines of your own history. And grief was not something you could save people from. It was the destiny of everyone. Yet, if she could do those years again, perhaps she would have done them differently.

From the grand plateau of age, she could see where she and Jack had allowed room for slippage. But it had taken her years to understand how words could become lost if they weren't spoken. And then it was too late to retrieve them. When she began to comprehend the barrier in her relationship with Jack, the thread of contact was already broken. The wind had carried it away, and all that remained was empty air.

Their lives at the cape were dominated by the lighthouse. It was there on the hill each time she looked out the kitchen window. Its rotating beam punctuated the night. And Jack's alarm woke them each morning at four so he could do the weather observations and then be ready to extinguish the light at dawn. The two keepers were busy: reporting the weather six times a day, servicing and fuelling the generators, washing the lighthouse windows, cleaning the lenses and prisms, painting the tower, maintaining fences and slashing the grass.

While Jack was occupied with keeping the light, Mary maintained the family. She kneaded dough, baked cakes, prepared the evening meal. As she worked, the children did their lessons, bent over books and pencils and little piles of shavings. Outside, she milked the cow twice a day, hung out the washing, cared for the chickens and the pony. In the evenings, she sewed clothes and knitted jumpers and socks. She made butter and cheese, and tended the miserable vegie patch, trying to coax the wilting plants to grow. Always, in the background, the kettle sizzled on the stove, ready for Jack when he came in looking for a cup of tea and some food.

As time wound around them at the lighthouse, the wind had started eating at Jack. It mottled him slowly, grinding him down. His hands, already stiff from working in rain and cold at the farm, began to warp. And there was no escaping the wind in that southern reach of land. At first, it made Jack restless. He came home each night with an edginess that could not be relieved by sleep. Then his mood progressed to grumpiness. Mary had to deflect the children from him, diverting them into their rooms, into books, into games, anything to give him quiet and rest.

On days off, the family retreated to their favourite cove where there was stillness beyond the lash of the wind. Jack sagged in the quiet; something invisible lifted from him, and if they stayed there long enough, there would be small flashes of warmth and engagement. But those moments were brief and increasingly feeble. Distance diffused into their relationship, its invasion so insidious that it spread wide and long before Mary realised what was happening. Somehow, they had evolved into different people, and a bridge had to be remade—a task Mary couldn't tackle alone.

At night, she lay in bed, listening to Jack's breathing. Sometimes she reached for him—darkness gave sufficient anonymity to ignore the rift—and they'd take each other raggedly, desperately, trying to clutch onto something they both needed but couldn't ask for. In the grip of each other's bodies, they held on in silence and pretended the chasm between them didn't exist. Then he lost his interest in sex, complaining about his arthritis. She worked to ease his load, busying herself with extra jobs to protect him from labour around the house. If she could just help him a little bit more, she thought, his impatience might soften. He might remember to embrace the children. He might lift his eyes for long enough to see her.

Love-making was the final thread that held them together. But when the wind blew even that away, they were left with nothing but a vast expanse of mist and air, both of them lost in fog.

They should have found a way back to each other in all that time and sky and wilderness. They ought to have found reconnections in a place they both loved. But the only element of Cape Bruny that penetrated their relationship was space—that great expanse of it stretching all around. Eventually, she stopped reaching across the bed for Jack, and he slept facing away. Instead of trying to pull him back, she turned to the children, and allowed Jack to retreat into his silences and his solitude.

It had been easy to lose herself in daily activities. She'd used them as a prop to carry her through. Built routine around her like a fortress. The tasks became the purpose, and everything else became obscured beneath the rigid pattern of life: a structured string of days adding up to a year, and then more years when the passing of seasons and the growth of the children marked the passage of time. Somehow, she and Jack had disengaged until they arrived at a grim place that was neither love nor hatred. They existed in an empty place which, over the years, she came to know as indifference. Left alone there, she was forced to depend on secrets and fantasy to feed her soul—a dangerous place for a woman to go.

Though she didn't like to remember those times (and she still wasn't ready to think about them now), she had always blamed the storm, her accident, and all that followed for the near-demise of her relationship with Jack. And, because of that, within the deepest recesses of her being, she had long blamed the lighthouse itself. It had been their making, their breaking, and their making again. The life–death–life cycle of everything. But it had been the fault of neither, really. She and Jack had been already crumbling. The other factors were simply catalysts. They had made choices which led them to a place where there were, perhaps, no choices. They'd created a situation where the actions that came after became the only possibility. And the events that unfolded were consequence, not causality.

The awful truth was that the aftermath to those events became the path which would eventually lead to that letter hidden in her suitcase in the cabin at Cloudy Bay.

10

It's the day of my visit to check on Mum. As I eat breakfast, Jess skulks around my feet under the table. Occasionally, she peeks out at me with tragic eyes which switch to hopeful when she sees the toast in my hand. She's disappointed I haven't taken her for a walk. Usually, we head out early to the beach and watch the sunrise creeping across the water. At this time of year, the mornings are often stunning and the sea is like liquid glass. When it's clear, smoke haze hangs over the mountains from the forestry burns and the sun is a blazing ball of orange. But this morning a walk is not an option, despite Jess's pleading eyes. She'll have plenty of time to run at Cloudy Bay, even though she doesn't know it yet.

As the car slips down the driveway, I notice a removal van outside one of the houses across the road. I see the dark shape of a man at the window of the house. I wonder who's moving in and what they'll be like, whether they will expect anything neighbourly of me. I'm not good at change and it's enough to start a churring in my stomach.

It's not far from Coningham to Kettering and I'm still brooding on the prospect of new neighbours when we arrive at the wharf. We don't have to wait long before boarding, and there's hardly anyone heading out to the island at this time of day, so loading is quick. When we push out from the terminal, I'm the only one standing at the bow.

As the ferry hums across the channel, I meditate on emptiness. The morning is quiet and sleepy, and a few cormorants beat across the water, flying low. I stand in the cold wind watching North Bruny inch closer, immersing myself in the grinding throb of the engines, feeling the rhythm of the lapping waves, doing anything to avoid thinking about Mum. But the restless workings of my mind won't be suppressed. I missed the opportunity to say goodbye when Dad died and I've been determined to be here when Mum's turn comes. Now the time is approaching, I can't think of anything to say.

Since Dad's death I've visited Mum every week. Usually I stop in after work for dinner and mostly we have something simple: sausages and mash, or chops and vegies. Sometimes I buy a nice steak for her. She can't afford much on her pension, so I often tuck something extra in her fridge: a small roast for the weekend, some chocolates, maybe a few rashers of bacon.

We sit and watch the news together and we don't talk much. There's simple comfort to be had in quiet company; she likes to know I'm okay, and I'm reassured each time to see her relatively well. At her age there are always health complications, but the medication has kept her stable for a while. Jacinta has me worried, though. If she's concerned about Mum then maybe her heart condition is worsening. Perhaps Jan is right and I should be bringing oxygen bottles with me. You can hire them from hospitals, I think. After I see Mum, I might look into that . . . or would she see it as unwanted intervention?

I wish Jan could work out a smoother way to interact with Mum. I know it bothers Mum that they can't get on. And it's a shame she and Gary don't visit more often. Since Mum's mobility has declined she doesn't get out much. It must be an empty life, sitting in that musty old house, listening to the radio or watching TV. Sometimes I leave Jess with her for the day. They're quite good friends and I know it can be uplifting for Mum just to have Jess around.

I try to think of sensitive ways to discuss Mum's heart disease. She's a shrewd old lady and she'll have her defence strategies worked out. I guess all I can do is express my concern and the rest is up to her. It's a pity, though; she might benefit from a proper medical assessment. And a doctor could have some suggestions to make her more comfortable.

I don't blame her for wanting to get away. With Jan lurking around talking nursing homes, I'd orchestrate an escape too. And her choice of Bruny Island shouldn't be a surprise to any of us. We all know how she loves the place. But it's typical of Jan to rant about it. She refuses to go there on principle, saying the island stole her youth. God knows why she has to be so dramatic. I'm not surprised her husband left her. And how did she produce someone as incredibly likeable as Jacinta? It's a mystery.

Off the ferry, I head east and then south over the island, driving through memories of my childhood. I'll be visiting Mum at Cloudy Bay today, but it's at Cape Bruny that I remember her best. Working at the kitchen sink with the smell of baking bread thick in the air. Gazing through the smeary window towards the light tower on the hill. Scattering pencils across the table for lessons. Serving dinner in the steamy kitchen. Digging in the vegetable garden.

She was always so affectionate with me when I was small. Always so generous with her hugs and reassurances. Perhaps she knew I needed it—I've never been a particularly confident person. I suppose she was my first friend; after all, there were no other kids around. That wasn't a bad thing; I learned to be self-reliant and independent. But I guess I was closer to her than most children are to their parents.

Dad was more of an enigma to me, though he did make an effort. We went fishing sometimes and he taught me how to play cards. But during the day he was rarely in the cottage, so then it was Mum and me. We did lessons, played board games, cooked, knitted, wandered around watching birds on the cape.

I remember what an upheaval it was when the school holidays came and Jan and Gary returned home. They were so big and noisy and they frightened me. It was never long before the arguments with Jan started, and then Gary would take to the shed with Dad to dodge the fray. My brother had an affable way about him and he could draw Dad out. I was less capable of this, and Dad was no artist at conversation, so when it was just him and me, the quiet always settled. I was never sure how to lift it. Hearing Gary and Dad joshing and bantering in the workshop always made me feel sad and inadequate.

We were an ordinary family, I suppose. Some good and some bad. Some happy and some sad. Isn't that the way it is for everyone? We did live in a strange place, and I guess it infused my soul. But even though I'm a little different, I have the same needs as other people. I need love and company and hope, work and leisure. Mum has always been there for me, the silent and invisible force behind my recovery. She never had to do much: just knowing she was there helped. But soon things will change and I'll be on my own. Then it will be all down to me.

At Cloudy Bay, I ease the Subaru down the track onto the sand. The tide is out and the sea stretches south into the distance. Jess scrambles onto my lap, panting in my face, so I swing the door open and she leaps out, running low and flat, kelpie-style, towards a group of gulls. I yell at her from the driver's seat and she dashes in a large arc and loops back to me, tongue flapping. When I tell her off, she yaps at the sky, head thrown back. The gulls rise, chortling, and fly out over the water following the wind up the beach. Jess yaps again. She's telling me the gulls have gone anyway and I ought to have let her chase them.

'It's a National Park,' I remind her. 'You know the rules. You shouldn't even be out of the car.' I bang the door shut. 'Go on! Run to the end of the beach.'

She tears up the sand, looking back periodically to make sure I'm following her in my vehicle.

Towards the end of the beach, I turn up over the softer sand onto the track I know leads to the cabin. As I step out, Jess lollops up to meet me. Everything is quiet. Even the roar of the sea is dull here behind the dunes. I pause, hoping Mum has heard the car and will come to the door. She doesn't appear, and I remind myself that she's growing deaf, that she's slow and I ought to save her the trouble. The truth is, I'm scared to go inside in case she's dead. The quiet is making me nervous and Jess is waiting for me to do something. I step onto the porch and rap the door with my knuckles. There's no answer. I open the door and call out. 'Mum. It's me. Tom.'

Inside it's warmer. I notice the gas heater along the wall with its red windows alight. Mum has it on low—forever frugal. It doesn't seem quite warm enough for her old bones. I know she gets cold just sitting. The smell of propane gas reminds me of Antarctica. We always had to open the vents as soon as we entered a hut to make sure the gas could escape so no-one would asphyxiate.

Mum's asleep on the couch with a rug tucked around her. Her breathing's moist and noisy. For a minute I watch, unsure what to do. Perhaps I should sit outside and wait till she wakes, or go for a walk on the beach. Perhaps I shouldn't be here at all. Watching her feels like an intrusion. She'd hate me seeing her like this, with her legs slung wide, her arms askew and her head lolling crookedly.

She stirs and coughs a little.

'Mum,' I say loudly, trying to fill the room. 'Mum. I've come to visit.'

She jolts and jiggles and her lips smack loosely, then she sucks in a drag of air and coughs it up again. Her eyes flutter open. 'Jack? . . . Oh, it's you Tom.' She startles and looks around wildly as if she's seeking something. Her hands scrabble around the couch and scrape beneath her blanket. What's she looking for?

'Can I help?' I ask.

'Did you see it?' she gasps. 'Was there a letter here? An envelope?'

'No, nothing. I've just walked in. Is there something you want me to post for you?'

'Thank you, but no. It's fine.' She waves me away, then slumps and wheezes and digs around for a handkerchief. 'Sorry. There's not much dignity in it.'

I stand by uselessly while she coughs some more. I don't know what to do for her.

'It'll pass,' she croaks. 'I'm having a bad day. It's always worse when I wake up.' Her face is horribly pale. She reaches out an arm. 'Here. Help me get up so I can hug you.'

'You can hug me sitting down.'

'It's not the same.'

'No. But it'll do.' I sit beside her so she can grasp me with her weak arms. It feels more like a clutch of desperation than a hug.

She sits back and looks deeply into me. 'You're a good man, Tom. You have a good heart.'

More like a *lonely* heart. I pat her hand then withdraw. It seems such a condescending thing to do.

'Could you put the kettle on?' she asks. 'It boiled a little while ago, so it won't take long to heat up. I could use a cup of tea.'

I go to the kitchen. The kettle is still warm, but it isn't hot. It's longer than she thinks since it last boiled. She watches me from the couch.

'You called for Dad when you woke,' I say.

'Did I? Perhaps I'm going mad.' She coughs again. 'Damn these lungs . . . I can't breathe to speak. Tom, bring me my tablets, would you? They're on the bench.'

I find her pills and give them to her, wondering if Jan might be right about Mum forgetting her medication.

'Glass of water,' she puffs.

I grab a glass on the sink and fill it for her.

'Thank you.'

She's so grateful for so little. I feel useless. When I bring her the cup of tea, she waves me into the armchair opposite her. After a few sips, small flushes of red appear on her cheeks. It's better than ghostly white.

'So, how's Jan taking it?' she asks.

'Badly.'

'Has she booked the funeral?'

'Not quite.'

'Then she must have a bed reserved in a nursing home with my name written in black ink on the card at the foot of the bed. How's Jacinta?'

'She's okay.'

'Taking a battering from Jan, I imagine.'

'The usual.'

'I really didn't want to saddle her with this, but there was no other way. Jan won't be very happy.'

'No.'

'Is Alex backing Jacinta?'

'Yes.'

'Good. What about Gary?'

'Surprisingly supportive.'

'Wonders never cease.' Mum rubs at her chest and clears her throat.

'Why didn't you ask *me* to bring you down?' I ask.

She glances at me. 'I considered it. But you've got enough to deal with. And Jacinta's young and resilient.'

'I'm not dealing with anything, Mum. All that Antarctic stuff was years ago.'

'Yes, but you're still carrying it. I keep wondering when you're going to meet a nice girl.'

'Not at the garage. They're few and far between in the workshop.'

Mum laughs. Perhaps she's thinking about the girlie posters some of the blokes have pinned up in the tearoom.

We sit in silence for a while. It's not quite a comfortable silence. I've never been good at conversation; Mum usually carries it along for me. But it's obvious that she hasn't the energy today. I dig around for something worthwhile or amusing to say, but I can't think of anything. Out the window, I notice the white tips of surf way out over the dunes. Mum follows my gaze.

'Not a bad spot, is it?' she says. 'It'd be a good day to climb the Head . . . The wind and the view.'

'You love it up there, don't you?'

'It's one of my favourite places. A special place with your father.'

'How long since you've climbed it?'

'I can't remember. Too many years. Once your father became arthritic, he couldn't handle the track.'

'You didn't go up alone?'

'There weren't many opportunities. When we moved back to Hobart again, we were too busy.'

She watches me keenly, but I can only occasionally meet her eye. I want to shift the conversation to other things, like her illness and what might happen next. But I'm not sure how to ask her about death. I'm not sure how to ask if she's ready.

'Why don't you go for a walk up there later and tell me what you see?' she says, her face soft. 'You can bring it home to me. Then I can remember everything through your eyes.'

'Yeah, I might.'

'You should. I want you to have a nice time here.'

'What about *you*, Mum?'

'What about me?'

'How are you going here?'

'I'm fine. Nothing to worry about.' For a moment she looks fragile, as if something in her might break. Then she musters a firmer look and leans back to inspect me as only a mother can. 'How's work?' she asks. It's safer territory.

'Busy.'

'You took a day off?'

'They'll survive.'

She looks around the room, searching for something. 'Where's Jess?'

'Outside.'

'Bring her in so I can give her a pat.'

I open the door and Jess trots straight to Mum, pushing her head up under Mum's withered hand. She'll sit there for as long as Mum will stroke her velvety ears. She stares up at Mum with eyes that are subservient and patient. Mum bends her head towards Jess and whispers meaningless nothings to her. Stuff women reserve for babies and dogs.

'So you like it here by yourself?' I ask, finding a strand of conversation at last.

'It's a little lonely,' she admits.

'What about the ranger?'

She shrugs. 'He's a bit sullen. Wouldn't even stop for a cup of tea the first day. But I'm working on him.' She pauses. 'Don't tell Jan I said he's sullen. She'll be on the phone to Parks in seconds, trying to organise a nurse.' She laughs, privately amused.

'Any jobs you want done?' I ask. 'Want some wood chopped or anything?'

'Not really. I've been using the gas heater.'

'Are you eating?' I go back to the kitchen and tip a few biscuits onto a plate, then carry it over to her. She chooses a biscuit and nibbles it.

'When I remember.'

'Jan would say that's not good enough.'

'Just as well Jan isn't here, then.'

'What about your medication? Are you taking it?'

'Same as the meals. When I remember.'

'Jan's worried.'

'Tell her not to be. I remember often enough. And it's only been a few days. Ask me again in a fortnight.'

She's being deliberately provocative, and I'm just about done with the questioning. At least I'll be able to report back, even if the answers aren't quite as Jan would desire. 'How long do you think you'll be here?' I ask.

Mum raises her eyebrows. 'As long as it takes.'

I nod and look away, gripped by a dull, dry-mouthed sensation. It's as I thought, she'll be here till the end. Now's my opportunity to pursue the issue. I should do it; I should ask her all the things I listed in my mind last night. All those questions that I've reserved till now—when it's appropriate to talk about life and death. But it's too difficult, and I start to come up with excuses: there will be a better moment when I can ask more easily; she's not really that ill. The coughing's abated; perhaps it was as she said, just bad on waking.

She bends and drops a biscuit onto the floor for Jess. I can tell she's not sure how to have this conversation either, and I allow myself to be diverted.

'You're spoiling her,' I grunt.

'That's my job,' she says. 'I wouldn't want to disappoint her.'

Jess taps her tail on the floor and smiles at Mum with delight.

'How did you find this place?' I ask. 'I didn't think you'd been to Cloudy Bay for years.'

'It was in a brochure someone gave me. And it was best to have everything organised before anyone found out. I couldn't leave any reasons for Jan to drag me back.'

'Other than the fact that you're old and sick with heart disease.'

'A minor point,' she says with a crooked smile.

'Tell me more about the ranger,' I say.

She leans back against the pile of cushions on the couch and breathes heavily. I feel a hard lump in my throat. I've been kidding myself. She's old and ill. And there's no denying the moist rumble in her chest; her body's tired. It seems as if death is creeping towards us across the ocean, riding slowly with the swell, biding its time until it washes ashore and finds her, whether she's ready for it or not.

She gazes out the window. The sky is chilly and grey. What does she see out there? I wonder. My father? The light station? Us, as kids, fooling around on the cape?

I stumble on. 'Jacinta and Alex are coming down on the weekend,' I say. 'They were talking about staying the night.'

'That's fine. There are plenty of beds.' Small soft coughs rumble in her chest.

'You don't have to be alone,' I say. 'I could stay here with you. I could take a few weeks off work.'

She bristles. 'No. I'm managing fine on my own.' Her eyes are penetrating as she stares into me. 'You think it'll be over in a few weeks, do you?'

I glance away, not knowing what to say.

'I am getting worse,' she admits. 'When your body's this worn out, you don't belong here anymore.'

'Don't say that, Mum.'

'Why not? Because you don't want to hear it? It's the truth.'

I shrug. 'Some of us feel like we've never belonged.'

She looks at me sharply. 'What's that supposed to mean?'

'I don't know. I must be like Dad. Not the best at putting it all together. Not a great communicator. I think I'm like him . . . with silence, and all that.'

She stares at me with a strange expression on her face. 'No,' she says. 'You're not much like him at all.' She continues to look at me, and then it seems she's looking through me. 'And it's the grip of Antarctica,' she says, as if she's talking to herself rather than to me. 'You've never quite got over it.'

'It was hard losing Dad while I was still on the boat,' I say.

And we've come back to death again, as much as I've been trying to avoid it.

'Yes,' she says. 'I know. I've often wondered . . .' She stops, flashes a look at me and then points out the window, changing the subject. 'Why don't you go for a walk? Make a sandwich to take with you. You can't come down here without getting outside.'

I make lunch as instructed. Sandwiches with jam for Mum, and small slices of apple, peeled, so the skin won't catch in her throat. While I chop up potatoes and pumpkin and carrots and put them in a container to soak, she sips tea on the couch with Jess curled up on the floor beside her. We'll have an early roast dinner and I'll carve up the leftover meat so she'll have some decent food for the next few days. After that, I'll head off and catch the late ferry back to Kettering. I should still get back in time for the seminar at the antdiv, unless the ferry's running late. Hopefully, Mum will manage to look after herself until Jacinta and Alex visit on the weekend—in the rubbish bin is nothing but empty tins of baked beans and tomatoes; there hasn't been much cooking going on in this kitchen since Mum arrived.

By the time I prepare the meat and gouge holes in it for small slivers of garlic, Mum is snoring. It's hard to believe our short conversation has worn her out. I slip the leg of lamb into the oven and scoop my sandwich from the bench. Jess barely looks up as I lace my boots and creep out the door.

Clouds are brewing over the mountains and mist scuds over East Cloudy Head. I walk fast along the sand, following the track up through the campground to the beginning of the trail to East Cloudy Head. The logbook is smudged with lead pencil and there are few recent entries. The number of bushwalkers drops off once the weather deteriorates.

Before I start uphill, I take off a layer of fleece and bury it in my backpack. Then I hit the track. It heads up through a recently burned landscape, hammered by a scrub fire about a year ago. Already, the fire-hardy species are rebounding—thick strappy *Lomandra*, tiny banksias and the needles of new casuarinas pushing up through the sandy soil. New leafy growth climbs the charred skeletons of stunted eucalypts. All this renewal around me while my mind hovers on thoughts of Mum's death. What will come after? I wonder. Is there potential for new things to sprout in my life? Or will I be like some of these dwarfed gum trees that have been burned by flames too hot, making regeneration impossible?

I puff up the slope, pausing to draw breath as the track steepens. The mountains to the north are now shrouded in cloud. It'll be a fog-drip afternoon up there. Out across the bay, whitecaps ride between the heads. I'm high enough to see the crags of a false headland below. Perspective clarifies as you climb. From down on the beach, not everything is as it seems.

I press on, ascending through fields of burned banksias and hakeas with their seed heads split wide. The track rises to a ridgeline and then climbs over a saddle and finally arrives at the hummock of East Cloudy Head. In a sweaty hour and a half, I'm on top, picking my way around the rocky summit, seeking sheltered vantage points where the stripping wind isn't so strong.

To the east are crumbling sea cliffs and caves; sculptured crags with the sea clawing at their feet. Offshore, the Friars are green islands with skirts of white. There's a seal colony on one of those islands, but it's not visible from here. The sea spreads south, marked by white ridges of travelling swell. The horizon merges with the mist.

Soon the wind begins to sharpen and I pull layers back on—fleece, a windproof coat, a beanie, gloves. I need time up here. Time to breathe and settle, time to locate somewhere within myself a steadiness that will help me through the coming weeks of my mother's decline.

I find a nook and sit down. To the west are the recesses of Cloudy Bay and Cloudy Lagoon. I follow the land along, riding the lines of the cliffs, and there it is, far distant—Cape Bruny, a grey smudge protruding from the sea. I linger there, testing the edges of memory.

At first, the lighthouse is invisible. Minutes roll past with the waves and the shifting sky. Then a shaft of light escapes the clouds and illuminates the tower—a solid white pillar jutting from the land. It's a beacon of safety rising from the ocean of life.

I stay hunched in the icy wind, staring towards the lighthouse until the cold squeezes me in its grip. Then I go down to tend the roast. I have the rest of the afternoon to sit with Mum.

PART II

Evolution

11

Seminars at the the Antarctic Division are held in the theatrette. You walk in the front door of the main building and go downstairs into a large open area decked out with memorabilia: photos, and glass cabinets containing ancient rusted crampons, dog sleds and outdated protective clothing. It's a good place to lose yourself if you're waiting to meet someone.

This evening, some of the staff members have set up a table down there with drinks and nibbles, and everyone stands around and talks among themselves, waiting for the show to begin. Of course, it helps to know somebody. I rang Bazza yesterday and tried to persuade him to come, but he wouldn't. He says the truth is that tradies like me—diesos, electricians and plumbers—don't much like going to boffin functions because it makes them feel inadequate. And that's pretty much how I'm feeling right now, even though I probably know more about penguins than most of them.

I wasn't sure if I'd come tonight. I don't go out much. But ever since Sunday's family meeting I've been fielding a barrage of phone calls from Jan, and this seminar was an excuse to escape the phone. After visiting Mum today, I called Jan to let her know that Mum would be staying on Bruny, and Jan almost leaped down the line, saying it'd be my fault if Mum died down there.

All she'd asked of me was to bring Mum back and apparently I've failed, yet again.

I wander around the foyer examining photos and trying to be inconspicuous. My favourite is a shot of the *Aurora Australis* at the ice edge near Davis Station at night, all lit up like a birthday cake. The sky's black and overhead there's the faintest green suggestion of her namesake—the southern lights, aurora australis.

I know a lot about that ship. Eighty-five metres sounds big, until the ship's engineer tells you they cut her short to make her come in closer to budget. She ended up not particularly good at anything. Average passenger ship. Average cargo carrier. Average ice-breaker. That's what happens when you try to make a cut-price ship.

Someone comes out of the theatrette. It's John Fredricksen, a lean man with a head too large for his body. I've never had much to do with him, but I know he's been into penguins for years. That's the way it is here at the antdiv. Someone hooks onto a topic and they're at it till they retire. It's a closed circuit for scientists. Hard to get in, hard to get out.

He claps his hands to get the crowd's attention. 'This way, everyone. Time to find a seat.'

I move into the auditorium with the general stream of people, but I'm peripheral to their chitchat. They swoop on seats as if their names are marked on them. I sit at the back on the edge of a row so I can make a rapid escape if I need to. Down the front is a shortish, dark-haired girl wearing jeans and a T-shirt. She's frowning over a computer linked up to a powerpoint projector. A few minutes pass as she fiddles with the connections and hunts around for a file, then she nods to Fredricksen to dim the lights and the talk begins.

Introducing herself, Emma Sutton explains that she's spent three summers at Mawson Station observing Adelies. The penguins come back to breed early in the season and they're all gone again by the end of summer. Working on an animal with a short breeding cycle is good for scientists, she says, because it means she can come home to work up her datasets and reorganise her gear ready for the next season.

Emma's work has focused on the feeding patterns of Adelie penguins on an island off Mawson Station called Béchervaise. For many years, every bird that has visited the island has been tagged and implanted with a microchip. Over the past few summers, Emma and her team have rigged up a penguin-sized fence to funnel all the incoming and outgoing birds over an automated weighbridge to record each penguin's weight.

Emma describes how her team glued satellite trackers onto the backs of some penguins so she could trace their foraging voyages after they left the island. When the penguins returned from a feeding trip, she retrieved the trackers. She grimaces as she explains the next stage, water offloading—whereby they pump water into the penguin's stomach to make it regurgitate the fish it was carrying to feed its offspring. She admits that her intervention means the chicks of that penguin won't survive and she's unhappy about that, but the data she collects will provide information on Adelies and the impact of fisheries in Antarctica.

Water offloading sounds horrible, and I see several people in the crowd shifting uncomfortably. I don't much like the concept either, but I understand the reason for doing it. Emma makes it sound well rationalised, and I'd like to ask her if her research has had any positive outcomes—whether any fisheries have been curbed. But I don't ask, because I know it's an awkward question, and it wouldn't be fair to ask her to justify her work in front of an audience. The bottom line is that it's unlikely anyone is going to modify their catch for a bunch of penguins.

Emma shows us a breakdown of the fish species she collected by water offloading. Then she shows maps of the foraging journeys of the penguins. It's amazing how far those birds will go to collect food for their young. And it's astounding how deep they can dive.

In the photos, Béchervaise Island looks rocky, wild and windswept. The field accommodation is a round red hut on stilts. Emma shows pictures of herself standing outside the hut cocooned in multiple layers of clothing. She shows shots of her assistant handling penguins. Then she steps us through the Adelie breeding cycle and clicks through a series of photos of the chicks, developing from little balls of fluff to full-sized penguins with white-spectacled eyes and flashy black and white plumage.

Among her photos are several of south polar skuas feeding on abandoned eggs and dead chicks. The skuas are the scavengers of the penguin colonies, bold brown birds that make their living on misfortune. Emma says she likes them and she'd like to study them. After all, she points out, skuas have to make a living down there too. And she's right. Most people are captivated by images of fuzzy penguin chicks and they can't see past the blood on the skua's beak.

But it's the look in the skua's eye that arrests me. I recognise that gaze. It's the same look you see in the eyes of expeditioners after a stint down south. They call it the thousand-yard stare. Emma has it too. That's how I can tell she has recently returned, and also by the way she glances at the audience when the lights are turned up again. Unaccustomed to walls, she's feeling hemmed in. She's used to skies and wind and a cold that can snap freeze your fingers. That look in her eye twigs something in me. It makes me want to go back.

I wait behind in the auditorium while the others file out. Emma is preoccupied with disconnecting wires and leads, and she doesn't notice me for several moments. I stay in my seat with my heart pounding and a crazy idea shaping itself in my head.

'Excuse me,' I say, approaching her down the aisle. My throat is dry and my voice is tight.

She looks up. Her eyes are hazel and her cheekbones angular.

'I enjoyed your talk,' I say. 'I'm a great fan of penguins.'

'Isn't everyone?' She smiles. 'They're cute critters. Not the easiest to work on. But I like their attitude. You have to have a bit of feistiness to survive in Antarctica.'

I hesitate and then clutch my hands into fists and press on. 'Are you looking for an assistant? I mean, do you need someone to go south with you next season?'

Her smile becomes faint and distant. 'I doubt it,' she says. 'We have people offering their services all the time. We're pretty right for helpers, thanks.'

She goes back to packing up. It's obvious she considers me dealt with, and I'm not usually a person to persist, but I hover and wait. I don't know what's making me so brave.

'I have skills that might be useful,' I suggest. 'I'm a diesel mechanic . . .'

She replies impatiently, 'But no experience with penguins.'

'I know a bit about penguins,' I say quietly. 'I've been south before.'

She stops again and looks up. 'How many times?'

'Just once.'

'And you haven't been back?'

'Family stuff.'

'Yes,' she says, a little wearily. 'There's always that.' She slips her computer into a case. 'So, why now? My seminar triggered something, did it?' She smiles to herself. 'Photos of Antarctica can do that.'

I shrug. Some things aren't easy to explain. How do I tell her it's the look in her eye that reminds me of being south? 'It's the wildlife,' I say. 'Especially the birds.'

She picks up her bags. 'Well, thanks. I'll let you know if we need someone.'

'Should I give you my name and number?'

She sighs and sets her bags down again. 'Yes. I suppose so. Just in case.' She finds some paper in her backpack and hands it to me with a pen. I write down my name, address and phone number. 'Thanks,' she says. 'I'll give you a call if we're interviewing.'

It's cold in the car and Jess is curled up in a tight circle on the floor. She sits up and smiles at me as I climb in. It's part of our routine greeting. Next, I'm expected to pat her and ask her how she's going.

'What would you think if I went south again?' I say, as I reverse out of the carpark and turn for the highway.

She pants, then drops her chin onto the passenger seat and gazes up at me. Her eyes glint yellow in the glow of the streetlights. She doesn't know what I'm suggesting and perhaps that's just as well. Then she'd know my loyalty is not as deep as hers.

'It'd help if you could talk,' I say. 'Then at least we could discuss this thing.'

A car toots behind me and Jess lifts her head abruptly. In the rear-view mirror I see a small white car, and Emma is behind the wheel. She probably thinks I'm a daydreamer sitting here at the highway intersection in the dark, going nowhere. Embarrassed, I bang on my indicator and swing left. Emma turns right towards the city.

As we head south through the roundabout, Jess whines and fidgets. She may not know what I'm thinking, but she knows I'm preoccupied. I forget to dip my headlights when another car approaches on an unlit stretch of highway and the driver hammers his high beams on just before he passes me. It's like a flash straight into my soul. I see my mind skittering like a kite let loose in the wind. On the floor, Jess starts panting with agitation. She leaps on the seat and I yell at her and she dives to the floor, cowering as if I might hit her. I shrivel with guilt.

'Jess, I'm sorry.' I reach to pat her head, almost veering off the road. 'I'll make it up to you. You can have extra food tonight. Just this once.'

Extra food! I'm breaking all my rules. How could a few slides of penguins do this to me?

At home, I pour dog kibble into Jess's bowl and toast a few slices of bread for myself. It's not much of a meal, but this evening it'll do. From the hall cupboard I pull out my old slide projector and set it up on a chair in the lounge room. I switch it on and place a couple of books under the legs so the light is at the right height on the wall. Then I insert a pre-loaded carousel and turn off the lights. Jess finishes her dinner by lapping up some water and drops onto her mat to watch the show. It's been years since we've done this together.

I have tons of slides from my fifteen months down south. Back then, everyone was taking pictures with slide film; we used to develop the film ourselves in the darkroom using special kits. It was fun dipping the film in the different solutions and seeing pictures appear like magic. I suppose if I went south again I'd have to update to something digital. Everybody seems to be into it these days. Although I think it'd feel strange to move away from my old manual SLR.

If someone looked through my slide collection without knowing about Antarctica, they'd think every day was fine during my stay. But when you're down there for months, you can choose when to take your photos. And nobody takes photos during a blizzard. I took great shots of many things: the brightly coloured station buildings, the folds of the undulating Vestfold Hills, Weddell seals like black slugs on the ice, Adelie penguins tobogganing in lines, icebergs lit pink by the sun, snow petrels fluttering against a steel grey sky. But among all my slides there are five that stop me. These are the ones I linger on now.

The first is a picture of a newborn crabeater seal pup lying on an ice floe beside his mother. He's all dark eyes, loose skin and soft brown fur. Within three weeks, sucking rich milk from his mother, he'll grow into that loose skin. And as he grows larger and stronger, his mother will become smaller and weaker. Nearby a male seal will be watching and waiting. When the mother is too weak to hold off his advances, he'll separate the mother and pup so he can mate with the mother. From then on the pup is alone. The bond between mother and pup was strong, but short. The pack ice is forever changing. Nothing is guaranteed. Relationships are intense but brief. The impermanence of things in Antarctica.

The second photo is of an Adelie penguin colony on Magnetic Island, just off Davis Station. It's taken from the top of the island, overlooking the colony. Beyond, the sea ice stretches into the distance, glinting with silver light and grounded bergs. The scene is luminescent. Somehow the photo reflects the intensity and transience of light in Antarctica. The light is a gift that comes magically; it illuminates your soul and then it is gone.

The third photo is of a Weddell seal hunched against the side of a breathing hole. She's using her bulk to create a platform so her pup can climb out of the water. Just before I took the photo, I was drawn across the ice by frantic splashing and braying. The pup was scrabbling at the sides of the hole while his mother tried to thrust him up out of the water. Every time she tried to nudge him up onto the ice, the pup would flail wildly and slip back in, gurgling underwater. Then he'd pop up, braying again, eyes wide. For several minutes, I watched the mother working to get her pup out, until she finally came up with the strategy of using herself as a bridge. Every time I look at this slide, I'm reminded how hard it is to survive in Antarctica, even if you've evolved to live there. You can die from misadventure even if you belong. Humans do not belong in Antarctica. It's important to remember this.

The fourth picture is of a dead Weddell seal pup lying in an ice hollow. The warmth of its dying body melted out its grave. The body was fresh—mostly intact—but the eyes were already gone, probably gouged out by the skuas and giant petrels that flapped reluctantly into the sky as I approached to take the photo. Death is always close in Antarctica, and once you die you become food for the scavengers. This slide reminds me that there is purpose in death as well as in life.

The fifth slide was taken among several immense icebergs just off Davis Station. I was exploring the area on skis and had paused to gaze up at the elegant curves of the bergs against the perfect sky. Within the cold blue shadows there was no wind, no movement. Intense quiet settled over the ice. Immersed within that stillness, I heard the sound of silence—a glorious deafening ache that reached to the bottom of my soul. This, for me, was Antarctica.

I turn off the slide projector and the room falls suddenly quiet. I feel very alone, despite Jess sleeping beside me on the rug. As always, I'm unsure whether Antarctic reminiscence is good or bad for me. It resurrects those tingling sensations of excitement and freedom. It makes my heart beat with the desire to go back there. Then those flooding feelings of guilt return. The pain of not being here when my father died. The fear of being absent should something similar happen to Mum. These are the burdens that have held me in Hobart for so long.

Looking back over these slides reminds me of the lessons Antarctica taught me. And yet I realise I still don't know how to use the intrinsic wisdom of that place. Perhaps I learned nothing there about the living of life. And what do I know about death, with the shadow of my mother's departure hanging over me? Since Antarctica, I've marked time. I haven't had the courage to try again for fear of injuries. It's difficult to trust when the deepest trust has been broken.

12

The phone call came about six months into my stay in Antarctica. The summer season was over, the last ship had departed, and the sea ice had refrozen and locked us in. I had just returned from a long ski around the icebergs near station, wandering out to Gardner Island, barren and quiet now with the Adelies gone and their nests a field of scattered stones.

Debbie sounded surprised when I answered the phone, as if she'd expected the answering machine. Her voice was distant, tinged with the sense of dislocation that had entered our conversations over the past months. 'Tom. I didn't expect to find you in your room.'

'I was just about to go down to dinner.' The smell of food was wafting up the stairs through the LQ.

'Is it dinner time down there? I keep forgetting the time difference.'

When Debbie and I talked on the phone, we usually chatted about the small things that made up our everyday lives. Debbie would give me a description of the curtains she'd ordered or the new items she'd bought for the kitchen, the colour she'd put in her hair. She'd tell me about the people that were annoying her at work, how her boss was giving her the creeps. And then I'd tell her what was happening on station. The silly things people were doing. The party that had spontaneously erupted on Saturday night while I was reading in my room. The tedium of work in the shed. The complexities of living in a small insular community. But this time, she was strangely quiet. People were passing my room, heading down to dinner. I got off my bed and closed the door.

'How are you?' I asked.

'I'm okay . . . Actually, I'm less than okay, Tom . . .'

Silence spun out, filling with my fear. This was the phone call all winterers dread. Something had happened at home. Maybe Mum or Dad; possibly an accident. I couldn't breathe.

'Tom?'

'I'm still here.' My soul was whirling with the wind outside, my eyes fixed on white distance. 'Are Mum and Dad all right?' I asked.

'They're fine. Everyone's fine except *me*.' She sounded mournful. 'You're such a long way away.'

Yes. So far away. A world away over ice. 'We knew it'd be like this,' I said.

'Like what, Tom?' Her voice welled with emotion. 'Did we know how lonely it would be for me? That I'd be sitting here looking at four walls with only the TV for company while you're down there with a crowd having a party?'

'I don't go to many parties.' I've kept myself separate for her. I've thought of her constantly, waiting at home in Hobart. The time passing slowly.

'. . . I've been so lonely, Tom.'

Silence again. I felt myself sinking. What could I do? Nothing could change the fact of my isolation. We sat. The quiet stretched awkwardly. Then I found something that barely resembled my voice. 'Tell me how it is for you.'

Another awful silence. Then Debbie, tight and hesitant. 'I just don't think I can do this anymore. It's too hard on my own.'

Warning bells in my head. 'You wanted this—so we could get ahead.'

'I couldn't have known it would be this bad,' she said.

'Isn't there anyone you can talk to?'

'Everyone's sick of me. *Antarctica, Antarctica, Antarctica*—it's all I ever talk about. How do *you* cope, Tom?'

'I work.' Hours in the workshop. Time measuring itself out in the systematic servicing of engines. 'And I read. And get off station whenever I can. Helping people. I write to you . . .' Silence. 'Perhaps you could try talking to the counsellors at the antdiv?'

Debbie's disgust hammered down the line. 'It's no wonder they have counsellors on tap. I bet this happens all the time. Counselling won't help. All they can tell me is that a bunch of other wives feel just like I do.'

Another silence.

'I'm sorry, Tom, but I've met somebody.'

The slow heavy sound of my breathing. The wind outside. The snow blowing. Everything drifting away.

'Tom. Are you there? I said I've met somebody. Someone who's here for me.'

A hollow sound. My voice, as if from very far away. *'I'm here for you.'*

Debbie, matter-of-fact: 'Tom, you're an impossible distance away. I can't do this anymore.'

'How long?' I asked.

Debbie's reply was less assured. 'It's been a while . . . I didn't know how to tell you . . .'

She'd met him months ago, apparently. Two, three, four months. She'd waited until the last ship had left for the season before telling me so I had no escape. No recourse. Why hadn't I felt her pulling away? Or perhaps I had. Maybe I'd ignored the signs.

'There was nothing I could say, really,' she continued. 'I mean, what would I have said? That the distance was getting to me and I could feel myself becoming vulnerable?'

'Something like that might have helped.'

She paused. 'It wouldn't have changed anything. These things happen, you know. Sometimes, you don't see them until it's too late. I'm sorry, Tom.'

The silence of a man drowning.

Then she hung up.

She had called me on the cusp of winter and her rejection destroyed me. It was too much to come to terms with. Too much to accept. My wife with another man—my *replacement*. And our relationship over.

The last ship was gone. The days getting shorter. There was no way back.

During those early weeks, I rang Debbie many times. If I found her at home, we talked and she cried.

'What can we do to fix this? I don't want it to be over.'

'There's nothing. It's too late. You're stuck down there.'

'If you'd just told me earlier . . .'

'But I didn't. Please don't blame me. I didn't want this to happen.'

'But I was doing this for you. For us.'

'I'm sorry it hasn't worked out.'

'Me too. I love you. I'm your husband. You're my wife.'

'I'm sorry, Tom. How many times can I say it? We couldn't have foreseen this.'

But perhaps we could have. At the pre-departure briefing they gave us the figures on marriage breakup. It was something ridiculous, like eighty per cent for overwintering staff. But you think you're immune from it. You think your own relationship is different, that you're stronger than everyone else, and that the figures are just numbers. And then, there you are, just another statistic. The Division of Broken Marriages and Shattered Lives.

She wouldn't tell me the new man's name or anything about him. 'It won't help, Tom. It'll just make things worse. You need to get on with things. Enjoy your stay down there. That's all that's left now.'

She was patient and she listened to my long silences. Often when I called she wasn't there and I'd sit dialling her number over and over, waiting for the phone to ring out and then dialling again. Her absence meant she must be with him. That man. She must be talking to him. Or making love. He was there, and I was in Antarctica. Trapped by winter. I couldn't even fight for her.

Then she asked me not to ring anymore. She said she'd cried all her tears, and there was nothing left. It was best to move on.

But move on where?

Nothing consoled me, not even the shimmering auroras that raged across the sky. Walking up to the workshed each day, I'd push myself as fast as I could, inhaling great breaths of freezing air, never quite managing to release the hysterical sensation of breaking apart. During blizzards, I'd force myself to work when others stayed inside. I'd drag myself up the rope that had been rigged from the LQ to the workshop, fighting with needling ice and blasting snow, almost wishing the roaring wind would blow me away. After battling the shed door shut, I'd hide beneath an engine, finding order in symmetry and pattern, the logic of pulling machines apart and putting them back together.

Alone in the upstairs lounge of the LQ, I passed long hours staring at the light slowly fading from Prydz Bay. Darkest winter came quickly and somehow I was at home in it. The long hours of night matched my internal wilderness. I wanted to suffer. It was as if I had been eaten by darkness and it had seeped into all the corners of my being until there was nothing hopeful left.

Around me, station life carried on. The two overwintering women fixed themselves in safe liaisons, causing resentment among some of the men. I was only vaguely aware of the friction.

Strange antics emerged with the shortening days; none of it made sense to me. One of the scientists started talking to his dinner plate. Names appeared on mugs and people became furious if someone sat in 'their' chair. With a party of only eighteen on station there were few choices for friends. Rifts developed.

Twenty-four-hour darkness brought my worst moments. People moved around me but I rarely engaged. I spent blocks of time in bed without eating or sleeping. By the time the sun appeared I was hollow and empty, eroded by grief.

It was my job that saved me. The winter cold meant that planning was required to complete any task. A machine that wasn't housed indoors needed three to four hours of heating before it could be started. If there'd been a recent blizzard, piled-up snow had to be moved first. This meant prewarming the loader or the Bobcat so I could shift the snow and ice. When a machine was finally moved into the workshop after being outside at minus thirty degrees Celsius, the dense steel sucked the warmth from the building. Two more days would pass before the shed and the machine were warm enough to begin work.

Nothing happened quickly. But it was this step-by-step routine that held the pieces of me together and enabled me to play out the actions of life as Tom Mason had known it. Each morning I showered and walked downstairs, one foot after the other, into the dining room. Food tasted like cardboard. There was a tightness in my throat from all the emotions knotted there.

When the light returned, I took to walking on the sea ice within station limits; as the sun grew in strength, I wandered the hills and watched the skies. There was solace to be found in landscapes and in distance and ice. The light was my saviour, and the colours of ice and sky: pinks, mauves and apricots, gradually intensifying to orange, silver and white. Light brought balance. In the shed, work increased. Spring was barely underway but preparations began for the summer season. I started talking to the others again.

And soon the Adelie penguins came tobogganing over the ice.

The first ship arrived in late October.

After seven months of isolation, we made a pretence at excitement about the new arrivals. But dread and anxiety soon took over. None of us was sure we could cope with the invasion. Who would be coming? How would they behave? What changes would they impose on the patterns of our lives? We were ready to prejudge the new expeditioners as insensitive, loud and pushy. And they were all three; how could they not be, after the months of quiet we had lived through, the months of space we had known, and our knowledge of the dark that we could not share? The summerers waltzed in like they owned the world. They violated our peace and privacy. They were boisterous, overly enthusiastic.

I avoided them by immersing myself in unloading the resupply ship. We worked around the clock, snatching meals when we could. The new biologists wafted around the LQ and skied out to the islands. Now that they'd escaped the ship it was as if nothing mattered beyond their leisure. In the dining room, the new crowd was amused by us, not understanding our strange little routines—the anchors that had carried us through the long days of darkness.

When the ship pulled away at the end of resupply, I sat along the wall of the LQ with a few other overwintering men and drank beer, speaking little. It was somehow shocking to watch the young women, some of them drinking too much and flirting outrageously. They danced provocatively and laughed too loudly. The old dieso sitting beside me grunted and stood up with his beer.

'They shouldn't be here,' he said. 'I can't stand it. I'm going to my room.'

Our world had transformed: giggling in the corridors, crowds in the computer room, always someone in the dining room, talking and making coffee.

I retreated to the workshop, trying to find normality among the machines. One of the new helicopter engineers came in to book a quad bike. 'Got your eye on any of the sheilas?' he asked jovially.

The question floored me. 'No,' I mumbled. 'I have a wife at home.' Still in denial.

He laughed. 'I didn't think any of that mattered down here.' He winked as I passed him the keys.

As usual, there was no privacy on station. Word quickly spread that I needed cheering up because of my marriage break-down. People invited me into the field. The new scientists soon learned I was useful. On a remote island, I helped the biologist studying snow petrels. With a different scientist, I captured and tagged Adelie penguins, helping to monitor populations on the icebound islands near station. I also assisted Sarah, who was working on Weddell seals for the summer. She hadn't worked with Weddells before and she appreciated the advice and experience I'd developed helping out the previous summer.

One night at a party on station, she came to me, drunk, and asked me to dance. But I declined and stayed in my post against the wall, swigging my beer.

'Come into the field with me again,' she said over her shoulder, as she swivelled back out to dance. 'You need to get off station more. And I need a hand. There's been a flush of pups up in Long Fjord.'

In the morning I packed my field bag, roped it to a quad bike and followed her out from station across the sea ice. We spun far out on the frozen waste, whizzing north past two islands locked like black hummocks in the ice. Far out, the sea ice was like a highway. We saw lines of black Adelies as they headed for their rookeries, their feathers ruffling in the wind.

Navigation in the Vestfold Hills wasn't easy and we had to look for specific landmarks that would direct us to the fjords. Until you knew the characteristics of the hills, they appeared featureless, rolling low and monotonous to the grey dome of the plateau. But once you knew what to look for, the hills became familiar friends, and the frozen fjords were the roads we raced along on our quad bikes.

The fjords were a place of relative protection from the wind and the blizzards; the wind could still barrel down from the plateau and along the valleys between the hills, but there were sheltered areas—often around islands in the fjords—and these were the sites where Weddell seals gave birth to their pups each year in spring. Bull males defended breathing holes where their harem of females hauled themselves out of the water onto the ice.

As Sarah and I drove through the frozen fjords, we passed several clusters of dozing seals. We stayed wide of them, not wanting to disturb them until we returned later with our tagging gear after offloading our luggage at the field hut.

Brookes Hut was a splash of red—a converted shipping container—at the end of a small bay overlooking the sea ice. Sarah and I bounced our quads over the rumpled tide cracks and drove up the track behind a mound of dirty snow to park just outside the hut. We lugged our gear inside where it was dull and quiet and the whine of the wind seemed distant. We stashed our food on the shelves among the existing cans of baked beans and powdered milk, sultanas and frozen cans of beer. Then we tossed sleeping bags on bunks, opened the vents and set up the toilet with a plastic bag that we would take back with us to station to be burned.

While Sarah boiled water for cups of tea, I went outside to watch tiny brown storm petrels flittering over the rocks near the hut. The morning light had shifted to grey and the ice was flat and featureless. Somewhere across the fjord the hollow bray of a Weddell seal echoed. Cold air froze in my nostrils and drew tears. The landscape was beautiful; it was rugged, harsh and wild. And it felt good to be off station, away from the gossip and pernickety human interactions. Sarah was easy to be with. She was undemanding and I knew we'd have a good few days. The mechanics' shed would survive without me.

After tea and chocolate, we gathered our equipment and set out across the ice, shattering the silence once more with the reverberating noise of our quads. Sarah led the way to the nearest colony—a gathering of dark grey spotted slugs lying stretched on the ice. We cut the engines and stood listening to occasional coughs and snorts. A pup barking at its mother. The hollow echoing bray of another seal, further along the fjord. Then the sound of our crampons, crunching and scratching on ice as we walked towards the group.

We circled the harem, counting pups and cows. Several seals raised sleek pointed heads to look at us, opening and closing their slit nostrils, prickling the air with pale whiskers. One spun to watch us, spreading its hind flippers to reveal a coloured tag in the webbing. The pups dozed, floppy bags of grey-brown fur lying prone on the ice. It'd be my job to dance in and drag a pup away while Sarah distracted the mother with a flag on a pole. While she kept the mother entertained, I would quickly tag the pup and let it go.

We had a successful day, tagging numerous pups and adults. That evening, Sarah cooked dinner with fresh vegies from the resupply ship, and served it with wine. It was a good start to the season. We sat rugged up on the deck watching the sky darken towards a midnight sunset, the air chilling our wine, our gloved hands fumbling with our forks.

After we'd washed the dishes we played cards. Then we pulled closed the blackout curtains and slipped into our sleeping bags on opposite bunks. The wind echoed in the vents and buffeted the walls of the hut. It was quiet inside. Quiet and safe.

I lay awake listening to Sarah breathe, feeling the night around me, thinking of Debbie at home in bed with a man I didn't know.

Like a shadow, Sarah came across the room. I had thought she was asleep, but she must have heard my ragged breathing and felt the weight of my grief. She unzipped my sleeping bag and lay down beside me beneath the cocoon of feathers. Her hands were gentle, running up and down my arms. Her body was a warm entanglement.

I didn't want to feel desire, yet I was unhinged by the soft touch of her fingers tracing my cheeks and lips. When she kissed me, I struggled to hold back, but she felt me rise even without touching me. I was too broken to refuse.

She was refuge.

My favourite field hut at Davis Station is the melon at Trajer Ridge. It's shaped like a watermelon—hence the name. To get there you walk out from station over the undulating brown hills. You climb over saddles and walk through rocky valleys, until suddenly you rise above a crumbling ridgeline and see light shimmering on a secret lake tucked below. Beneath the spacious sky you wander down to the lake's edge and squat by the still water. Early in the season the lake is locked by ice and laced with strings of ascending bubbles. By late spring it has melted to a mirror of light.

After you leave the lake, you bumble over endless rock fields and snowdrifts, descending gradually out of the hills until you step onto frozen Ellis Fjord. This is when you strap on the crampons that have been bumping and clinking against your pack, and begin crunching over the long flat drudgery of ice, working up blisters on your heels.

On a still day, the reflected light is hot. You sweat and have to stop to shed layers. Everything is quiet. When you start moving again, all you can hear is the sound of your breathing and the scratch of your spikes. The hills rise around you, and occasionally, along the edge of the fjord where ice meets rock, you find small pools, smooth as glass, melted by the sun.

At the end of the fjord the land climbs towards the plateau. You trudge up a long ridge with grand views across the desolate snow-patched Vestfolds. On a clear morning, the far hills are dark against the turgid blue of the sky. By afternoon, the light washes out and flattens the landscape, dissecting distance.

Cresting the ridge, you see the red dome of the hut, balanced on a slab of rock below. It's attached to the earth by wire, to anchor it in the fierce blast of blizzards and katabatic winds. Beyond, the plateau stretches white. It's a relief to step inside the hut and take off your pack. On the deck, you open a beer and sit in clean dry socks and thermals, watching the light wash over the hills until the cold drives you inside to cook dinner and read, listening to the voice of the wind escalating in the wires. At night, you slip into your sleeping bag and wait for sleep to find you. The wind buffets the walls and sings in the cables. You hear it whining in the vents, juddering at the door. Within the hut you are safe, curled up within your bag. You could be floating in a womb.

That is how Sarah made me feel in the aftermath of my marriage collapse. Through Christmas and over the summer, she continued to find excuses to invite me to assist her in the field. And, like a dog, I continued to follow her. Rumour quickly bound us together; this was good for Sarah, as she was safe on station, largely immune from flirtation and propositions. On the whole, there was no ill will towards me. We were discreet and people knew what I'd been through, they knew I had suffered. But questions accompanied me wherever I went. What was Sarah like in bed? How was it that I was the lucky guy? And how did I feel knowing Sarah had a boyfriend back home?

Sarah never mentioned her boyfriend to me. Other girls had photos of their boyfriends plastered over the pinboards in their rooms, but Sarah's photos were of her parents and her cat. I didn't ask about her home life and she didn't ask about mine. In the soothing comfort of rebound, I allowed myself to think our relationship could grow into something more. On station, I stayed quiet with my head bowed and my heart closed. In the field, Sarah was my cocoon.

But eventually the *Aurora Australis* appeared in Prydz Bay to deliver more supplies and to collect departing winterers, including me. When I told Sarah I'd like to meet her in Hobart when her ship returned, her eyes became cool and her face shuttered. She laughed a tight little laugh. 'But you *knew* I had a boyfriend. I thought you understood.'

The ground rocked beneath me.

'I'm sorry, Tom. It's been fun. But I'm engaged,' she said.

'Engaged?'

'You know how it is,' she said. 'It's not convenient to wear a ring down here.'

A ring was not convenient and yet *I* had been convenient. She kissed me blithely on the lips. 'Come to my cabin tonight. It's our last time.'

So why did I go to her that night? What was it that took me unhesitatingly to her door? Why did I lace my boots in the foyer of the living quarters, don my coat and walk down the dirty melted-out path to her donga where candles and soft music waited for me?

She let me in and undressed me, and in the space of that one night I was splintered again, smashed apart. There had been no healing from Debbie, only avoidance, replacement and self-delusion. But I let Sarah take me. I lay beside her that last night, clinging to the warmth of her body, feeling myself blowing away like dust in the wind.

The next morning, the helicopter took the husk of me to the ship and I returned to Tasmania.

13

Mary had imagined that returning to Cloudy Bay would restore the peace she had known here when she was young. But anxiety overcame the solace of solitude. And sleeplessness was dulling her short moments of pleasure. The insomnia derived from many sources: the wind, her cough, mulling on what to do with the wretched letter, fear that Jan might materialise and insist on taking her home. On top of that, she was aware of time passing, and her duty to Jack was far from complete. Of her list of promised destinations, she had only visited one, Cloudy Corner. There was still much work to do.

Her health was deteriorating, there was no denying it. At night she could hardly breathe and the tablets seemed to make little difference. True rest had become rare; much of her waking time was spent dithering over the letter. This was the irony of it all. She was here to disperse her guilt at last and the letter was a constant reminder of what she had done.

Jack was with her in this place, she knew it. She could feel him in the vast measure of silence. He was watching her, waiting. Sometimes he came riding on the wind, and other times he seemed to pass, invisible, through the cabin. Knowing he was present reassured her. The long ache of her loneliness was subsiding.

Whenever Leon came, she strived to enjoy his company—there was little enough of human companionship in her days. But his visits had become a drama of tension. Could she persuade him to take her out? How might she shift the conversation her way? Would she stir his pity or his anger?

He came every day as arranged, stopping for a quick cup of tea and a short discussion of the weather. She tried to ease him into longer conversations, looking for opportunities that might allow her to tag along with him on his duties. But he remained quiet and reserved. The only thing that interested him was the lighthouse, but his attention was fickle; often he was focused elsewhere, and he left again too quickly.

Today, though, he arrived like a thunderstorm, banging into the cabin without saying hello, and marching to the kitchen to put the kettle on. Mary offered a polite good morning, and he glared at her beneath knitted brows.

'What do you mean, *good morning*?' he said.

'It's not raining,' she pointed out. 'That's good for Cloudy Bay.'

He scowled at her. 'The weather's not the only way to judge a day.' He slapped the *Hobart Mercury* on the bench. 'Here's a newspaper. It's yesterday's, but I thought you might want to see what's going on in the world. And here's some milk.' He put the carton in the gas fridge. 'Is there anything else you need?'

'My granddaughter's coming this weekend, so you can have a couple of days off.'

He swung away to find some cups, and she heard him muttering, 'There's no such thing as a day off.'

'Perhaps you could have a day with your family,' she suggested. 'Go for a picnic.'

The look he gave her was ferocious. 'Who says I want to go for a picnic with my family?'

'It was just an idea.'

'Yeah, well, family picnics are not my idea of fun.' He set two cups on the bench.

'It sounds like you need a holiday,' she said, trying again.

'Not much chance of that at the moment, is there?' Even as he said it he glanced at her with a flicker of guilt in his eyes.

'This won't go on forever, if that's what you mean.'

'You're thinking of going back?'

'Not immediately . . . but I'll have to go back eventually.'

He slipped her a furtive look and she held back from saying she intended to be here till she died.

'Would you mind bringing my tablets?' she asked.

He poured the tea, delivered her tablets and sat down in a chair while she shook out the required medication and swallowed it. A long silence followed in which they sipped tea and stared out the window. The quiet seemed to soften him somehow, and eventually he turned to her, his face calmer.

'The weekend after next, there's going to be a scout camp out here,' he said. 'They'll be staying at Cloudy Corner.'

'That's fine. It won't matter if they're noisy. I won't hear them from here.'

'I had an idea you might talk to them,' he suggested.

'I'm sure I can be polite and say hello.'

He shook his head. 'That's not what I meant. I thought you might talk to them about being a keeper's wife. I think they'd be interested.'

The suggestion set her coughing. When she recovered, she stared at him, annoyed. 'As you can see, I can barely string two sentences together.'

'You won't have to speak for long,' he said, leaning forward.

She paused, considering. Perhaps this was an opportunity, an opening she could exploit. She must suppress her irritation and dive on her chance. 'All right,' she said slowly. 'I'll do it—in exchange for an outing.'

His expression soured. 'Where to?'

'Up to Mount Mangana.'

He snorted. 'Don't be ridiculous. You wouldn't make it more than twenty metres up the track.'

'I don't need to walk,' she said. 'I just want to drive through the forest.'

'When?' he asked.

'How about now?'

Surprisingly, he agreed. Still looking disgruntled, he deposited her inside the four-wheel drive and climbed into the driver's seat, slamming the door. Then he drove fast down the beach, flushing gulls from the sand.

Sitting quietly in the passenger seat, Mary wound down the window to let the fresh air rush in. Despite Leon's grumpiness, she was surfing on a surge of triumph and she couldn't keep the smile off her lips. Soon she'd have another place crossed off her list. And how good it was to leave the cabin again. Sea spray was rising above the beach and light shimmered over the sea with a pearly glow. The world was beautiful and here she was, whizzing through it, watching the sun cutting the clouds and glinting off the water.

At the end of the beach near the lagoon, Leon drove up onto the road and stopped in the Whalebone Point carpark. He grabbed a bag of toilet rolls from the back seat and swung out of the car. 'I won't be long.'

Mary watched him stride across the tarmac, head down, shoulders rounded. He was brooding today, stewing over something. She wished she could ask him what was wrong, but his body language didn't encourage questions.

When he climbed back in, he wound her window up. 'We'll be going faster along the road. You'll get blown away.'

Pulling out of the carpark they passed the Pines campground, where a man was bending over a camp stove and a woman was folding away a tent. Leon waved at them.

'That was nice of you,' she said.

He grunted. 'I get paid to be nice to people.'

They drove past paddocks dotted with sheep and bracken. Then the coastal scrub gave way to greener farms where plump Herefords grazed. Here, taller trees grew along the roadside verges, and occasionally there were quaint cold-looking cottages with smoke coiling from their chimneys. Up high in the mountains bald patches marked recent logging sites.

'Could you slow down?' Mary asked.

They were approaching the old Mason farm and the cottage where her uncle and aunt had lived. Years ago the two properties had been amalgamated into a larger farm; Jack's family home had been pulled down and her uncle's cottage had been renovated. These days it was let out to tourists looking for a 'taste' of Bruny Island. The old barn had gone too. Not surprising, given the years and the weather that had passed since then.

'Stop here,' she said. They were just near the gate.

'What is it?' Leon seemed interested now in spite of himself.

'This is where I used to live.' She pointed to the cottage. 'Jack's family lived next door. But the old house is gone.'

'Does it make you feel sad coming back?'

She shrugged. 'I'm not sure. I do feel very nostalgic. We had some good times here. The farm was a haven for us.'

Leon kept the vehicle idling on the verge and it seemed to be vibrating with the rhythm of life—accelerating backwards through seasons and years.

'We came here on our holiday breaks from the lighthouse,' she said.

'Why here?' Leon asked. 'Why didn't you get further away? Like up to Bicheno, or across to Victoria. Somewhere different.'

'Jack didn't earn much and our time off was short. Sometimes we stayed with my parents in Hobart. But mostly we came here.'

She looked once again at the cottage. Of course, for some years Rose had still been lurking around the Mason farm. Time had not altered Mary's opinion of Rose, so during their stays, Mary ensured her family did not often cross paths with Rose. Her sister-in-law was still studiously glamorous and annoyingly self-focused, and Mary had little time for her. However, visiting the farm was always good for Jack. On the property and out of the wind, he seemed able to relax. They had passed their limited leisure time in simple ways: fishing down at Cloudy Bay, picnics on the mountain, sharing fish and chips from the Lunawanna store. When they were here, Mary saw glimpses of the man Jack used to be. He smiled more often; sometimes he talked, played games with the children: chess, Monopoly. All the things he never did at the lighthouse. In bed, they snuggled close. No sex, but he tucked his arms around her and she felt his breath in her hair. Remembered how to love him again.

Tears welled in her eyes and she waved Leon on.

'Are you okay?' he asked.

'I'll be all right,' she said.

Just before Lunawanna they turned off on the Adventure Bay road, climbing into forest and slowing as the gravel deteriorated to potholes. This was the route Leon drove each day to and from Cloudy Bay. As it zigzagged up, the trees became taller and straighter with dense thickets of blanket leaf and mountain correa crowded round the trunks. The higher they went, the wetter the road became, and tree crowns rose in narrow spires with mist clinging to their tops.

'Could we stop near the old mill?' Mary said. 'I want to get out and smell the air.' Another item on her list.

Leon stopped at the pullout near the old Clennett's Mill site. 'Why here?' he asked. 'It's just a few old bits of metal buried in the bush.'

'This is where Jack's brother used to work when it was a functioning mill. We came up here sometimes. I want to remember.'

He offered to help her out, and she swung her legs around. But she was weak and he had to hold her arm to stop her from sliding to the ground. Shuffling away from him, she tried to wrap distance around herself, opaque as a cloud. She wanted to stand in this place and remember the past. Underfoot were straps of wet bark and the air was thick with the tangy aroma of mint and eucalypt leaves.

Forty, fifty years ago, when Frank cut timber up here, the trees were enormous old giants with huge trunks. Now they were spindles. These days the forest was turned over too quickly. Sawlogs had given way to woodchips and the forest was not the same, no matter what the foresters said about the trees growing back. But it was still beautiful and she breathed it all in, trying to ignore the cough brewing in her lungs.

In the treetops, wind shuffled the leaves. Fog-drip spattered her head and mist touched her cheeks with wet fingers. If she closed her eyes she could make the years dissolve. She could merge with the timeless grandeur of the forests and be here again with Jack. Beneath those watching crowns they had embraced urgently, mindful not to be caught. She recalled the song of the wind tossing high in the trees. The distant rasp of saws. Winches groaning. Yells along the tramway.

After she and Jack had moved to Hobart, Frank died here in a forestry accident. He was working a saw, felling an immense old tree; misjudging the moment to stand back he was crushed as the tree crashed to the ground. It was a dreadful accident, violent and devastating. Frank was the jovial son, the lively one who always carried a joke and a laugh.

Losing Frank had rocked the poor Mason family. Everyone missed him, especially Jack's older brother, Sam, who had been very close to Frank. And Frank's legacy had not been a welcome one. Instead of going back to her own family, Rose had asked to stay on the farm. Mary had known Rose was dodging her ill mother, wishing to leave the arduous task of nursing to her younger sister. It was an appalling abrogation of responsibility, but Mary couldn't say this to Jack's parents who felt duty bound to care for her.

Mary had often wondered how differently things might have unfolded if Frank hadn't died or if Rose had returned to her kin. But the past was set and could not be rewritten; and Rose was part of the story. Drawing in the mist and scents of the forest, Mary tried to fix on contentment. She could see the past shimmering in the leaves, but nothing could be changed and she must let it all go. Now was the time for acceptance.

She wasn't sure how long Leon allowed her to stand there in the damp of the forest with the breeze swirling around her ankles. Eventually, he took her arm and guided her into the vehicle, and they drove down the mountain with the heater blowing and the trees flicking by the window. It had been a tiring trip, and she dozed most of the way home.

As they spun along Cloudy Bay towards the cabin, she turned her head to smile at him, wanting him to know how she appreciated his patience and sensitivity. She couldn't tell him this, but he had helped her to achieve another goal in her pilgrimage for Jack. His nod acknowledged her thanks.

'Will I see you tomorrow?' she asked.

'Yes, of course. It's Friday and your family's not coming until the weekend.'

He pushed up his sleeve to check his watch and there, on the pale freckled flesh of his wrist, she saw dark bruises, purple and yellowish-green, in the shape of fingers.

'What's that?' Her breath caught in her throat. Had he been in a fight?

He glanced at what she'd seen and his face closed. 'Nothing.' Resolutely, he pulled his sleeve down and stared out the windscreen, refusing to meet her eyes. His lips were firm and his face was tight, demanding silence.

At the cabin, he helped her inside. She wanted to ask more, but his face was unapproachable. Had someone hurt him? Or had he hurt someone else? She hardly knew him. She thought of his dark moods. Was it possible he might strike her? Or could he be harming himself?

She tried to conceal her uneasiness as he settled her on the couch. Then he was gone, swinging sharply into the vehicle and accelerating recklessly over the dunes. She went to the window to watch him race down the beach. He might run away with his secrets for now, but she knew he'd be back. Within the story of that bruise was the reason for his self-imposed exile on Bruny, she was sure of it. Exile was something she understood.

Reclaiming the couch, she tucked herself into the blanket and leaned into memory once more, further back now. The story was strong and clear and it sprang from the corners of her mind with vivid intensity. It had all taken place in apple season. She was sixteen. Ten days that had shaped her life. It was the time of ripening fruit, when Hobart flooded with people and apples. From all around the state the crates came in. They came on trucks and trains to be loaded onto steamers bound for overseas. Pickers arrived in town. Stands appeared in the streets selling apples of all kinds: Cox's orange pippins, munroes, ribstons pippins, Rome beauties, New Yorks, sturmers and democrats.

She remembered the smell of stewing apples. Her parents' old house in North Hobart was thick with it, and the hallways were always congested with boxes. They ate apples in everything: apple pie, apple tea cake, apple crumble, apple sauce. She spent hours in the kitchen with her mother, peeling and cooking apples. With the stove burning and the pots boiling it was hot, and when the work was done each day, she would go for a walk to release the sweet scent of apples from her skin.

In the park one afternoon, she stopped to watch a young man chasing a dog across the grass. They were playful and energetic, almost silly—running and tumbling in the carpet of brown leaves, the man whooping, the dog barking. It looked like ridiculous fun and she turned away reluctantly, knowing duty awaited her at home.

A shout made her glance back. The young man was bounding towards her across the park. He approached her confidently and she waited; perhaps he was someone her parents knew from church. About ten feet away, he stopped and kicked a pile of leaves in the air. Then, laughing, he caught the dog as it leaped into his arms. 'I'm Adam,' he said.

He put the dog down and came up to her, offering his hand. She accepted it hesitantly. But his grip was warm and strong and his smile was captivating.

'I'm Mary,' she said shyly. 'Do you live around here?'

'No,' he said. His smile was still broad and he let her hand slip slowly from his grasp. 'I'm not often in Hobart. I'm a picker. But I'm tired of work today. I had to get away from ladders and go out for a run.' He glanced around the park and then focused back on her. 'Tell me, what do Hobart girls do on windy autumn days?'

'They cut and peel apples,' she said. They laughed.

'Well, my back's had it,' he said. 'I've been picking apples and shifting ladders and loading crates for weeks. If I didn't need the money, I'd be done with it.'

'Does it pay well?'

'Not particularly. And the huts are average. Grotty and old. But it's what I do. And I like to be on the road.' He stopped and swiped a hand through his messy blond hair. 'Anyway, Mary . . .' He paused to stroke her name with a fresh smile. 'It's so much nicer to have an afternoon exploring Hobart. And infinitely nicer to have met you. Shall we walk around the park?'

Turning slightly, he glanced at her hopefully and she laughed. 'Oh, all right. I suppose it won't hurt to walk awhile. The latest I can be back is dinner time.'

They wandered along the old stone fence, leaves swishing around their ankles. 'I've come down from the north,' he said. 'We move south as the fruit ripens, picking our way through the orchards. I started up near Devonport. Then Beaconsfield and George Town. After this I'm off to the Huon Valley for a few weeks. Then I might see if there are any pears left on the Tasman Peninsula.'

'You move around a lot,' she said. 'Don't you ever stop?'

He shrugged. 'I've been picking fruit since I was fifteen. It's what I know. Tassie's home, but I don't mind going across Bass Strait to pick in Victoria. It's grapes and pears and oranges up there. But apple season in Tassie is best. It keeps me in work for weeks. When it's over I go back north. Maybe take a job on a farm for a while. But mostly I like to keep moving. It's good seeing different places.'

They walked and talked for close to an hour, Mary bombarding him with questions. She had little of life to share, and he seemed to enjoy chatting, telling her of a world she'd never seen. When she went home, she was full of him, brimming with excitement. But she didn't say anything to her parents. She didn't think they'd approve of her conversing with a stranger.

The next day, she returned to the park, hoping to see Adam again. And there he was, waiting by the wall, his grin bright and welcoming. That was the beginning of her great deception. Each afternoon, she would tell her mother she was off for a walk, and then she'd meet up with Adam when his workday was done. They would sit against the stone wall and rekindle their conversation from the previous day. She'd never dared to think beyond the margins of her experience before, but Adam gave her new horizons. He fuelled her boldness. She talked to him as she had never talked to anyone.

Their attraction was mutual and magical. She was drawn by his assurance and worldliness. And he was fired by her naivety and the soft glow of her innocence. A young girl becoming a woman, she was vibrant with hope. She imagined his life to be bold and adventurous, so different from the strict confines of her family home. He told her he had witnessed things he hoped she'd never have to see; sordid events, like fights, domestic violence, gambling and theft. Human behaviour was rife in the pickers' huts—mostly alcohol driven. He'd chosen not to get involved in any of it, but there were things he'd been forced to do to defend himself. This was a topic he elected not to expand on.

He had left home at an early age to escape his strict and bitter father. Being on his own was better than weathering his father's criticisms and insults. His mother had been sad to see him go, poor oppressed woman that she was. He regularly sent her letters, but he hadn't been back home. A transient way of life suited him better; seeing new places, new people. He was happy when he was on the road.

Listening to him, Mary's world became larger. She believed they were destined for each other. Then, five days after they'd met, things shifted into new territory. They were sitting on the grass in the far corner of the park, conversing as usual, dreaming up plans for travels, when talk suddenly suspended. Adam was watching her, his eyes alight and his face luminous. She felt time lift and take flight. There was something different between them, something fresh but weightless.

He reached out and grasped her hand, the warmth of his fingers folding around hers, and her eyes locked with his. In his face was a liquid intensity, a hopeful question. A flush crept up her arm, spreading from the tips of his fingers. This was not right and she ought not to allow it, but the core of her was squeezed tight and she couldn't let go.

Perhaps he sensed her turmoil, because for a brief moment he relaxed his hold, giving her an opportunity to pull away. But she left her hand lying lightly in his. She knew it was wrong, but she wanted to trust him, to go on this flight with him away from the ordinary. Even now, all these decades later, she could remember the smile that curled his lips. With her permission given, the world of sensual touch unfolded.

Turning her hand over, he began to trace lines and soft circles in her palm while her stomach contracted and her toes clenched. Then, with a tingle that was almost unbearable, his fingers crept spider-like to her wrist. Overcome by wild recklessness, suddenly she wanted to feel his fingers on her face, her arms, beneath her clothes. It was a hot, hot feeling. A shocking feeling.

He looked at her knowingly, and ashamed, she pulled away. What sort of girl was she to enjoy this? What was she doing? But she allowed him to take her hand again. It was what she wanted. She couldn't pretend otherwise. Gently, he pushed up her sleeve and trickled his fingers along her arm to the tender crease at her elbow. The play of his fingertips made her shudder and tremble. She was a rose unfurling. Nothing else mattered. She was consumed. Lost in sensation.

By the end of the week they were kissing.

She was alarmed things had moved so quickly, but she'd never been gripped by such a sense of urgency. Artless and unsophisticated, she pulled him to her, seeking the taste of his lips. He was kind with her. Slow and in command. Gently steadying her with a smile. Between kisses they talked. Planning a future. Dreaming of a cottage and an orchard of their own. She was learning passion. And he'd met someone virtuous at last. A woman who was unharmed by hardship. Someone who adored him.

Then her parents found out. Her father was walking home from work and he saw them kissing. Icy with fury, he barked her name so loudly it rang across the park. Horrified, she wrenched herself from Adam's grasp and ran home. When her father came in, the slam of the front door rocked the house. From her bedroom, she heard the fast sound of angry voices in the kitchen. Her mother's cry of disbelief.

A knock on the front door brought sudden stillness and she rushed to the top of the stairs. But her father glared at her darkly from the bottom of the stairwell. He waved her back to her room and she went reluctantly, obediently, too frightened to argue. Through the bedroom window, she saw Adam on the doorstep, and then her father was out there, his back stiff and hostile. She watched their brief introductions. Her father was usually the correct gentleman, but this time he did not extend his hand. His body was tense, and beside him, Adam seemed forlorn and intimidated. She watched them walk into the street and then they were hidden by the hedge.

Her father was back too soon. There had been no time for discussion, no time for Adam to show her father who he was and how inspiring he could be. She was called to the kitchen, summonsed by her father's imperious voice. Her parents made her sit on a chair while they discussed her life.

'He's a *fruit* picker,' her father said, with demeaning emphasis. 'Entirely unsuitable. And she's not to be trusted. She's out of control. Ruled by impulse.'

Her mother's face was sharp with spite. 'What can we do about it?'

Her father had answers to everything. 'I've sent him away. He won't come back.'

Mary's heart contracted. Her breathing was tight.

'And what should we do with her?' her mother said.

'She'll have to go to your brother's farm on Bruny. It's the only place that's far enough away.'

Over dinner they worked out her future while she dripped tears into her food. She was not to ask questions. She must pack her clothes and be ready to leave in the morning. Her parents were not being unkind. They were doing this to help her. Later, she'd understand.

When they dismissed her, she organised her things as instructed. Then she stood at the bedroom window, straining into the dark, wondering if Adam was out there, waiting for her. She loved him and wanted to go to him. But how to get out? Her father had locked the doors. And how to find him?

She was humiliated and helpless. But what could she do? She was young and her parents had responsibility for her. She dared not disobey them.

The next morning, before first light, she was on the bus to Middleton to catch the ferry. And in the shadows, Jack was waiting. Her future. Quiet and serious, so different from Adam. He was the result of her exile.

14

Leon drove furiously down the beach away from the cabin. It seemed this was going to be his usual Cloudy Bay exit policy. The trip to the mountains had been painless enough, and the ride home had been quiet, with Mrs Mason pleasantly worn out by memory and the cold. And it had been peaceful, almost comfortable. Sure, they had a prickly sort of atmosphere between them, but at least it was largely honest. No pretence at niceness or anything. He hated the overly polite exchanges of most humans. His mother often said it wasn't sociable to be as blunt as he was, but he didn't care.

It was a pity, though, that he'd ruined it all. God knows why he'd lifted his sleeve to check the time. There was a digital clock on the vehicle dashboard. Why hadn't he looked at that? Habit, he supposed. Sometimes he could get quite obsessive about checking his watch. Especially at the end of the day, around the time his father would be getting home.

So Mrs Mason had seen the bruises. It wasn't any of her business. She might probe him with a few questions next time he saw her, but he didn't have to answer. He was good at evading tricky questions. And she had no right to hear anything he didn't wish to impart. Then again, if he wanted to hear more about the lighthouse . . .

He'd often wondered what it was like to live at the light station years ago, when the old tower was still operating. At least once each week his rounds took him down to Cape Bruny and the Labillardiere Peninsula. If he had time, he drove to the end of the road at Cape Bruny and parked the vehicle in the public carpark just past the cottages, then climbed the hill. The tower had such a sense of history and power about it. He would have loved to see it lit at night, the beams streaking out across the landscape and the sea.

The cape was so wild; it was like being at the end of the earth. Up by the light tower, he usually sat on the wooden bench chair—a memorial to a young guy who'd been swept off the rock pillars to the south while he was researching seabirds. On clear days, when Leon could see the rock stacks, he somehow felt close to that young man. He must have been really dedicated—even crazy—to put himself out there on a bunch of rocks like that. The sea could be demonic, Leon knew. The young guy had been well enough prepared, his camp anchored to the rocks. But when a ferocious wave came up, it simply swept him away. Leon often imagined that rogue wave flooding the rocks. He saw it surging, ripping out the young man's protection. And then he saw the rock, empty. A life gone. It must have been awful for the people who went to collect him after his stint out there finding the rock pillars teeming with their usual plethora of seabirds but nothing else. No smiling face or waving hand.

For Leon, there was a soothing rawness in sitting up by the tower, especially in bad weather. He liked to look out over the heaving sea where it merged into grey mist. If he walked along from the tower, he could look down over Courts Island and watch the waves dashing themselves to death against the cliffs and the rocks.

Sometimes when he was walking up from the carpark, he'd run into Tony, the caretaker, or his wife, Diane. Both of them were kind enough to him. They considered him part of the local infrastructure, like themselves. They'd been keepers at Cape Bruny before the old light was shut down. But they openly admitted they didn't much care for the tourists. The light station was now a historic site, preserved for the public, but somehow it seemed an invasion of privacy, with people wandering all over the hill.

Leon thought Tony and Diane blended with the landscape, in a way. Their faces were craggy and lined like the cliffs, and even though they always said hello to him, they kept their distance. He'd never been asked in for a cup of tea. But he didn't mind. This was something he understood. People had a right to their personal space.

It was his ranger training in Hobart that had kindled his interest in local history. Most of the other students considered history as something to learn for exams and then forget, but for Leon it had become a passion. History helped him understand his origins. It linked him with that sleepy place his parents called home. And the more he delved into Bruny Island and the history of the lighthouse, the more he wanted to know. Not just the facts, but also the feelings—what it had been like to exist there in another time.

Mrs Mason had suggested he should rent the keeper's cottage for a few days, but Leon reckoned he had a fair feel for the place in modern times from his regular visits—and he'd been there in all sorts of weather. No. What he was interested in was how it felt to live there when it was more isolated, like in Mrs Mason's time, and even before that. He'd read the archives in the history room at Alonnah, and he'd found out all sorts of stuff. They had folders full of newspaper clippings and writings going back years—about agriculture, the timber industry, and of course, the lighthouse.

Reading and learning about the history of the island had roused his interest further. And given Tony and Diane's preference for privacy, Leon figured Mrs Mason was his best bet to find out more about the light station. He thought maybe this scout talk might draw extra stories out of her. Perhaps it might open a few cracks and give him some openings to enter further into her life with well-placed questions. In retrospect, the trip up the mountain road had been worth it, even if she had spotted the bruises. But he'd be more careful next time. He'd button his sleeves so it was difficult to pull them up.

His thoughts turned to home and he checked the time once more—making a studious effort to use the clock on the dash rather than his watch. There should still be time to make the run through to Alonnah to check the mail at the post office and then go on to the campground at the Neck before he headed home. He'd heard from some locals that there were campers up at the Neck, and it wouldn't hurt to drop by and see how they were going, and whether they'd adhered to the honesty system. Perhaps it was a reflection on his character, but he liked to see them flush and squirm when he cleared the box and went to ask where their payment was. Some of them had pretty fancy set-ups, with intricate tarp riggings to protect them from the rain, and gas lamps and picnic tables. Everything but the kitchen sink. They had plenty of money for a snazzy rig but were too stingy to pay a camping fee.

Being bound to the clock was a big restriction in his job. From September to February, during peak penguin season, it would have been nice sometimes to stay with the tourists at the Neck and watch the birds coming in at dusk. But he always aimed to be home by six so he could be there when his father walked into the house. That way he could try to defuse the arguments that erupted when his father was drunk, and make sure his mother didn't receive the brunt of his father's rage. These days, Leon was physically stronger than his father, but in the midst of a fury, his father was unpredictable and could lash out suddenly. Leon would have liked to match his father's ferocity and teach him a lesson. But so far, he'd managed to restrain himself. Strength had to come from the inside, he kept telling himself, not from violence.

His father had been a steady man while Leon was growing up. He'd been a hard worker, toiling long hours at one of the timber mills on the island. They said he was a good cutter. Efficient on the saw. The island sawlog industry had dwindled over the years, but Leon's father had always managed to keep himself in a job. The accident happened a few years ago. His father's right hand got caught in a belt on the machinery that drove the saw. Surgery in Hobart hadn't been as successful as they'd hoped. And then he'd been pensioned off.

Reg Walker had never been good at sitting around. He liked being a breadwinner, and the job had given him power and status. To him, the disability pension was a public disgrace. After a lifetime of denigrating dole bludgers and those on sickness disability pensions, he couldn't accept his impotence. Leon had been studying in Hobart, and at first he felt sorry for his father, hearing second-hand from his mother how his morale had declined. Then the drinking binges started.

Leon hadn't known of his father's earlier trouble with the bottle. It was only after questioning his mother through her tears that he discovered his father had given up drinking before they were married. Apparently, he had never handled drink well—becoming boisterous and belligerent, and occasionally getting into brawls. But that was a long time ago. Since he'd given the drink away, everything had been fine. He'd almost been proud to be a teetotaller. And while he was steadily working, it hadn't been an issue. But after the accident, bored, depressed and restless, it had only taken one lapse at the pub for his anger and aggression to surface. Drink helped him forget. But it also brought out a deeply buried ugliness.

Before knowing about any of this, Leon had come home one weekend to visit his parents in their small white weatherboard cottage just across the road from the beach. He always liked the sense of quiet that settled over him when he turned off the car engine and climbed out into the fresh Bruny air. This time, he was surprised to find the house locked. The cars were in the garage, so someone should be home. Perhaps his mother was out walking.

He went for a stroll along the beach, waiting an hour or so before he returned. His mother rarely went out for long, and his father often visited friends during the day, so he wouldn't be home for a while. When he discovered everything still locked, he pounded on the door in case his mother was in the shower. All was quiet for a few moments and then he thought he heard movement inside. He knocked again and called out to her.

Finally she spoke to him from behind the front door, saying she was unwell and that he should come back next week. Her voice sounded strange and teary, and he knew then that something was wrong. Reluctantly, she let him in. When he saw the bruise around her eye, it was as if he'd been struck himself. He knew exactly what was happening.

It had been a terrible afternoon. Leon tried to talk things through with her; he wanted her to leave right away. After all, if it had happened once, it would happen again. But his mother said that she and Reg had worked this out before and they could resolve it again. Leon hadn't been so sure. His father was different now—so damaged and sullen. As a young man, leaving the drink behind had been possible, but now, with his life shattered, Leon couldn't see any chance of reform. His mother would not be convinced. Between binges, his father was conciliatory, even charming. He loved her and she was certain he was trying hard not to let it happen again.

Leon had grown frustrated. He couldn't understand why his mother refused to help herself; he was angry she hadn't told him sooner, and he told her so. But when she cowered away from him, he felt remorse. His mother had endured enough without him adding to her pain. He calmed and reassured her, a lump of sadness welling in his throat.

Back in Hobart, his anxiety had increased. He rang her as often as he could, and he suspected the situation was deteriorating. Eventually he'd contacted Parks and found there was a job for a ranger on Bruny Island. The Parks service had been keen: his knowledge of the island would be useful. So he took the job and moved home. Someone had to be there to protect his mother.

Being there for her was a commitment that imposed on every corner of Leon's life. It drained him, physically and emotionally. His father resented his presence in the house, which only added to the tension. And his father was erratic. One day he was charming and rational, and the next day he came home sinister and aggressive. His mother didn't realise how much she feared him, but Leon could see the change in her each time his father came in. He could feel the air prickling. Fortunately, if the old man became threatening, Leon was strong enough to fend off most of the blows. But he couldn't avoid them all, especially when he had to manhandle his father into the bedroom and hold him down while he roared and bellowed and filled the air with fists.

Leon always had a sense of guilt about his father's rages, as if he were in some way indirectly responsible. By not insisting that his mother leave, Leon wondered if he was perpetuating the pattern of violence. Surely there would come a day when he was delayed at work and his mother was beaten again. By allowing her to stay, he was leaving her exposed to attacks. Maybe his continued presence was preventing his mother's departure; if he hadn't been there, perhaps his mother would have found the strength to leave.

He figured there must be some way to help his mother escape from Bruny; he lay awake at night trying to devise plans, but they all came to nothing. And he'd reached a point where his mother avoided talking to him—she was afraid he'd pressure her and disturb that semblance of calm she managed to arrange so carefully around herself.

Living at home with his parents was therefore the only solution, and Leon truncated his workdays to fit his father's timetable. He had to be there when his father came home so he could take the blows that were destined for his mother. It was an untenable situation. It broke him apart. He didn't want to hate his father, but the aggression left room for nothing but anger, and he carried it with him constantly.

15

⚜

Evening at Cloudy Bay was not a good time for Mary. Just when she ought to be relaxing and finding her way gently into sleep, she was gripped by urgency, and anxiety blossomed in her chest. Another day over and what had she achieved? Yes, she had managed to tick off Cloudy Corner, the farm and Clennett's Mill today (getting all the way to Mount Mangana wasn't possible, and at least she'd paid homage to the forest close to the mountain, so she decided to let that one go). But her list was not yet complete—she still had to visit East Cloudy Head and the lighthouse, the most important places in her pilgrimage . . . and God knows how she was going to achieve this. If she couldn't organise it, though, she'd have failed Jack. And herself.

Worst of all, the letter was still in existence. She'd been deliberating and arguing with herself for days, but she still hadn't been able to destroy it. What was wrong with her? Did she really think she owed something to the letter bearer? And what would happen if she allowed the letter to be delivered? Unfortunately, she could foresee it all. Bonds would be severed. Faith and trust shattered. Could she bear the consequences? Not while she was alive. Giving credence to the letter would negate the purpose of her life's journey. Jack wouldn't be here to see it—that at least was reassuring. But did she have a right to rearrange the future by eliminating the letter? Should she display strength, deliver the letter and brave the outcome? No, it was too much at this stage. She couldn't endure it. Her health was too diminished. It would be distressing and vexatious. She would die without peace of mind and security. And what about all the things she had fought to restore and maintain in her family? The letter would undo everything. It would break the skin of calm that she'd struggled to stretch over them all.

She needed that thing out of her life. Disposed of. And now she couldn't find it.

Shoving the blanket aside, she levered herself off the couch and began another systematic search of the house—the third such foray in the past half hour. She had checked her suitcase and she was sure it wasn't there. She'd shifted all the cushions, shaken out her pillowcase, flipped through the magazines, rumpled all her clothes. Perhaps she'd slipped it in among the pile of newspapers stacked by the fireplace. (When was she ever going to get around to lighting a real fire?) But no, she would definitely remember grovelling down there on the floor. And her knees wouldn't handle it, of that she was certain.

Maybe she'd left it in the kitchen, or perhaps, dear God, she'd thrown it away. In a panic, she jerked the lid off the bin and peered inside. Just a few cans, sticky with baked beans. And a milk carton. Leon had cleared the rubbish this morning. Had he thrown out the letter accidentally? Must she go out in the cold to find it?

On the edge of tears, she scuffed into the bathroom for one last check, and there it was, sitting on the vanity beside the bathroom sink. She snatched it up. Why couldn't she remember putting it there? Perhaps she had set it down while she was washing her hands.

She carried the envelope into the bedroom and slipped it back into the side pocket of the suitcase. Then she struggled into her nightclothes. The cold here had weakened her, and her

joints were stiff. It had become a tremendous effort just to lift
her arms. In a nursing home she'd have help. But they'd stick
tubes in her at the end. They wouldn't let her go with dignity.
It might please Jan, but it'd be a horrible way to die. And where
was Jan anyway? She thought Jan would have visited by now,
hell-bent on dragging her out of here.

With the letter safely tucked away, she eased herself into
bed. She'd done nothing all afternoon, and yet she was weary.
Tonight, she'd get some decent rest.

Sleep came quickly, but she woke sometime after midnight with
a hacking cough that raked and barked and wouldn't stop. Only
upright could she control it, so she propped herself with pillows
and sat up.

It was a clear night. White light flooded the bedroom,
perhaps from a full moon. She prickled alert. Jack might be near.
She'd dreamed of him these past nights; whenever she tossed
uncomfortably on the edge of consciousness, he seemed to place
his brown fingers on her arm as if he was trying to stop her from
saying something she shouldn't.

Part of her knew he was a creation of memory, but his face
was so vivid—the prominent bridge of his nose, the speckled blue
of his eyes, that slightly jutting chin, the dimple beneath his lower
lip, the shadow of whiskers emerging. His lips were marbled with
sun cracks and the dry lick of salt. And his eyes asked questions
she couldn't hear, expecting answers she couldn't voice.

Perhaps if she could reach out and touch him she might
feel the texture of his skin, the roughness that came with weather
and too much wind.

Moonlight fell in streaks across the floor, and he seemed
close. She peered round the room, straining against shadows,
almost sure she could see him sitting on the chair in the corner.
He was so still. Maybe he didn't want her to know he was there.

For long moments she breathed heavily, waiting for him to move or speak. Such a stubborn wretch he was. He didn't utter a word.

She called to him. His shadow was long and tall. She knew it was him. But in the dark she couldn't make out his face.

'Why don't you stay?' she asked. 'I need to talk with you.'

She saw his shadow shift slightly. Then she wasn't sure whether he was there at all. Were those footsteps moving through the house? Or was it just the cabin creaking?

'Are you going outside?' She pushed back the covers and heaved her legs around. 'Don't go without me. I'm coming with you.'

Coughing arrested her, doubling her over on the side of the bed. She struggled up and shuffled into the lounge room.

'Jack. Please wait.'

There he was, his shadow by the door. She tugged her coat off the hook and pulled it on awkwardly, cursing the lack of strength in her arms. Then she stepped out into a white night, washed pale by the moon. The cold air caught in her lungs and coughing surged. While she huddled, waiting for the rattle to subside, Jack's shadow wafted down the hill and over the dunes towards the beach. No wonder he hadn't waited: she sounded like a dying dog.

'Jack. I want to walk with you.'

She stumbled downhill after him, over wet grass. Cold nipped her fingers. Behind the dunes the sand was firm but it softened quickly as she proceeded. Air swirled loosely around her. Grass prickled her feet. The track began to descend.

She stopped on the cold beach and saw light rippling on the water. The long white line of a wave collapsed. She could see Jack's shadow flitting along the base of the dunes. If she didn't know better, she'd have thought he was nothing more than a cloud passing over the moon. But he'd brought her here deliberately. It was a magic night. In this light on their beach, time was indefinable. Fifty years could be erased in a moment.

This could be any one of those bright nights when she and Jack had embraced here.

Pulling her coat close, she trudged along the sand, searching for him. When a tendril of cloud slipped across the moon, she saw him lurking not far away. She made her way towards him, the wind tugging at her legs.

'Jack. I'm here.'

He was gone again. So fickle. Had he really been so temperamental? Their love had been difficult to hold onto, and who could say love was forever? But they'd come through hardship and compromise to find the muted joys of a long marriage: the peace of secure companionship, dependability, quiet and unspoken understanding.

A larger, denser cloud shifted across the sky. She watched the fluid shape of its shadow spreading over the water. For five long minutes, she stood shivering in the wind waiting for the cloud to erase the moon. Sound travelled along the beach from east to west as waves folded on themselves. Then, finally, the cloud smudged out the light.

Jack came with the darkness. She felt his breath near her ear and his hand, warm in hers, drawing her on. In the close, cold dark, she shambled with him along the beach, feeling her way across the sand with icy toes.

The intimacy of being close to him set her trembling. It made her flush hot and tingly and then she was shaking with euphoria. Jack was here with her. He'd come to guide her. She felt love such as she had known when they were young. It pounded thickly in her chest. It made her pant, small feathery breaths. Her fingers tingling with it. Her head light.

Dark fingers snatched at her. Sucked away her breath. Everything curdled. Slumped.

Then there was silence.

•

Black night eased slowly to thumping nausea and weakness. She was sprawled on the sand like a swooning heroine, her feet and hands white in the moonlight. Her head was heavy as if she'd been struck, and her heart was knocking like an overwrought engine. She tried to work out what had happened. How long had she been lying here? Hadn't she been walking just a short time ago with Jack?

The cloud whose darkness brought Jack to her had evaporated. Dear God, she was cold. She pushed herself up, the blood whirling in her head. Her breathing was wet and gurgly. Had she had a heart attack or had she just fainted?

Slowly she turned herself onto hands and knees. With effort she forced herself up in the wind. But it was such a long way back to the cabin. And Jack was gone.

She hoped she could make it back alone.

Leon's voice woke her from a restless doze.

Daylight was washing through the window. She was in bed with her face pressed into the pillow. She'd slept in. The pillow was damp—she'd been drooling again. She tried to move but her body was stiff.

Leon called again.

She realised she was still wearing her coat, and her bed was full of sand. She could barely recall staggering in here last night and slotting herself under the covers. In the dark she had climbed the hill on hands and knees, dragging herself over the grass. It wouldn't do, she had told herself, for Leon to find her dead out there.

She had no idea how long it had taken, that painfully slow journey over the dunes and up the hill. She remembered seeing the cabin at last. The coughing had punctuated her every move, slowing her when she needed to be inside and out of the wind. She remembered the cold. She remembered Jack sitting in the corner of the bedroom watching her, shadowy and silent.

Now her body felt as if it had been hit by a truck. And Leon was calling again. 'Mrs Mason.'

She heard the cabin door opening. 'I'm here,' she croaked. 'In bed.'

He came in, face puckered with concern.

'Why are you here so early?' she asked querulously. A cough halted her, deep and racking, and her body bent in half with the force of it.

Watching her, his face darkened. 'I was on my way to the campground, but I had a feeling I should come here first. What happened?'

She struggled up, moisture gurgling in her throat, and spat quietly into the cup by her bed. 'I was cold last night and I put on my coat.'

'You've been out.' His face was expressionless.

'No. I was here in bed.' She didn't want him to know how desperate it had all been. How nearly she didn't return.

He glared at her. 'The door was ajar. And the floor is covered in sand.'

'Has someone been here?' she asked, feigning innocence. 'Don't tell me the scouts have arrived already?'

'It's not the weekend,' he said. 'And anyway, they're not coming till the weekend after.' He turned away.

She heard water running in the kitchen and the sound of the kettle being set on the stove. Then he was back at the door. He wasn't going to let her get away with it. 'There's no point having the heater on if you're going to leave the door open.'

'The wind must have blown it open.'

'There are footprints on the floor and they lead to your room. Get up and have some tea.'

She heaved herself out of bed and limped into the lounge room, leaning heavily on her stick. He pushed a cup of tea across the kitchen bench.

'What am I supposed to tell your family?'

She should have guessed this question was coming. 'You don't need to tell them.'

'I'm supposed to be watching out for you.'

She stifled a cough, unable to respond.

He watched her splutter into her hands. 'Look at you. If I tell them you've been wandering at night, they'll come and take you home.'

'Over my dead body.'

'Highly likely.' His voice was getting louder. 'You're supposed to be able to look after yourself. What about your tablets? You need a full-time carer.'

This prompted a rally. She would not go back into the hands of Jan and end up in one of those awful nursing homes. 'Don't tell me what I need,' she barked. 'I get enough of that from my family.'

He scoffed at her and started wiping the kitchen bench furiously. 'Your family? What do they care? Where are they? Someone should be here looking after you.'

She tried to hold back tears. 'They're coming tomorrow. They know I don't want them here all the time.'

He threw the cloth in the kitchen sink. 'Have you eaten?' he asked. 'Of course not. Look at you. You've lost weight since you came here. And it's been less than a week.'

'It's the coughing.'

'Perhaps you'd cough less if you remembered to take your tablets.' He dragged her pill bottles into a cluster on the bench. 'I can't stay here and ram these down your throat, so I'm going to set them out according to the instructions. I'll put each pill on a piece of paper with a time written beside it. Do you think you can manage to get yourself over here and swallow them four times a day?'

'You don't have to do this,' she snapped. 'I'm not a child.'

'I'm trying to help you.' He glanced at the clock and waved a bottle at her.

'Don't say anything,' she mumbled. 'Just bring them to me.'

He dumped the pills and a glass of water on the coffee table. 'Let's stop these little night-time walks, shall we? Before you get into more trouble. I can't always be here to rescue you.'

Her hands began to shake and tears spilled from her eyes. He turned his back on her and leaned against the kitchen bench, looking out.

'Are you all right?' he asked after a while, conciliatory.

'Yes. I think so.'

He walked around and flopped in an armchair, then rested his head against the back, staring up at the ceiling. 'You have to take better care of yourself,' he said. 'I don't want to be held responsible if something happens to you. One visit a day is the best I can do.'

'I'll make sure I take my tablets.'

'And you have to eat.'

'It's hard. I'm not hungry.'

'Promise you'll try.'

'I'll try.'

'And it's cold in here. I'm going to light a fire for you each morning when I come. I'll split the wood and haul it inside for you. Can you lift the handle and shove the wood in the heater? That's all you'll have to do.'

The fire. He was going to light the fire. And if it was lit, she could burn the letter. 'What if the handle gets hot?'

'There are oven mitts hanging on the wall. Hadn't you noticed?'

'No.' She felt sheepish and reprimanded, like a schoolgirl. 'I've been looking out the window.'

'And not in the mirror, obviously, or you'd know what I'm talking about.'

'Have you seen the mirror here?' Relief fuelled an attempt at humour. He wasn't going to send her home yet. 'At my age, you don't want to see your entire body when you step into the shower.'

Leon didn't laugh. 'Don't shower then.' He found newspaper and began stuffing balls of it into the wood heater. Then he shoved in kindling and wood and lit it. 'Okay,' he said. 'I'm going. Can you do the rest by yourself?'

The rest would be the burning of the letter. He could leave now, so she could get on with it.

He rolled up his sleeve to check the time, and her eyes were drawn to his arm. There it was. A new bruise just above his wrist. He covered it with his hand and looked away, his face studiously blank.

What was happening with Leon? Who was hurting him? 'I think you need to talk,' she said.

He shook his head slowly. 'Not today.' Then he pulled on his jacket and was gone over the dunes in seconds, the roar of his vehicle lost in the wind.

Mary sat by the window, watching clouds skating across the sky. Wasn't there something she meant to do? She couldn't quite remember.

16

Friday morning, I wake exhausted. I haven't slept well since Emma's talk. At night, every time I close my eyes, I see flashes of Antarctica, Adelie penguins, Sarah, the end of my marriage. The recollection comes with rushes of emotion. I thought I'd dealt with all that, but the seminar has released all the memories again.

I slip out for my early walk with Jess. Nature has always helped me through tough spots before and it's no different this morning. We wander along the sand; Jess sniffs around while I allow myself to unwind with the hiss of the wavelets as they skim up the beach. It's good to see that the world is normal, even if I am not.

After a shower and breakfast, I've just picked up my car keys when I hear footsteps on the verandah and a knock at the door. Jess scrabbles to take a look and her woof is a question, not an answer. I follow her to the door and open it.

A woman stands there, facing away from me, looking out towards the channel.

'Hello,' I say. 'What can I do for you?'

She turns and I notice that everything about her is pale: her face, her light brown hair, her cheeks, her eyes, and also the smile that stretches her lips. She's thin and small. Plain. Probably somewhere in her thirties.

'I'm Laura,' she says. 'I wanted to introduce myself. My brother and I have just moved in across the road.' She peers at the trees down the side of my house. 'Quiet place, isn't it? And the trees make it dark. A bit spooky, don't you think?'

'The trees are good,' I say. 'They bring the birds.'

She glances around uncertainly. 'I suppose so. I know nothing about birds.' She flashes a tight smile. 'Lots of possums, aren't there? They were all over my roof last night. Do they eat your roses?'

'I don't have any roses.' My new neighbour obviously isn't into trees or wildlife, which means we have less than nothing in common. This might be a good thing, because then there's little excuse for contact.

'You'll probably see me round a bit,' she continues. 'And you might see my brother too, although he won't be out much. He's not well. His name's Michael. I just call him Mouse.'

She's clearly keen to talk, but I pull my keys out of my pocket and jingle them. 'Sorry, I'm just heading off to work.'

'Oh.' She seems disappointed. 'You're leaving.' She looks down and notices Jess at last. 'What's your dog's name?'

'Jess.'

'Is she friendly?'

Jess's tail is beating slowly against the deck. This woman clearly does not know animals.

'Yes.'

Laura bends to pat Jess on the head. 'I didn't grow up with dogs,' she says. 'But I like them.' She strokes Jess cautiously. 'Mouse likes dogs too. Perhaps you could bring Jess down sometime to meet him.'

I shrug. 'Maybe.'

She smiles. 'I'd like that. It'd give Mouse a lift.'

I wait for her to leave, but she lingers on the deck, watching the light glinting on the water. I wonder what I can say to usher

her down the path. 'Sorry, but I do have to go. I need to be on time for work.'

'Yes, of course.' Her thin face is almost ghostly. 'Do you mind if I ask your name?'

'I'm Tom.'

'Well, it was nice meeting you.' She stretches out a hand and I'm forced to shake it. It's thin, soft and cool. Then, she turns and starts down the steps to the path. Her shape fades quickly among the bushes until she appears again crossing the road, moving like mist skimming over the ground. She's a strange one, shy and uncertain. Damaged in some way; needy. I hope she doesn't expect me to be neighbourly.

I scoop an apple from the fruit bowl and lock the door, unable to shake Laura from my thoughts. There's something uncomfortably familiar about her. As I climb into the car and watch Jess drop onto the floor, I realise Laura reminds me of myself.

At lunchtime I go down to Salamanca to see if the *Aurora* is in yet from her last voyage. I should keep away from things Antarctic, but Emma's photos are still haunting me and I feel the stirrings of craving. It's an addiction that's hard to break when you return from down south—the sensation of excitement and freedom you experience down there. I want to feel it again, even though it's no good for me.

Looking for a parking spot along the waterfront, I pass the wharf, and there she is, the *Aurora*, an orange giant, docked behind the smaller *L'Astrolabe*, another Antarctic research vessel. I park along the esplanade and wander into the shadows cast by the *Aurora*.

She always seems bigger than I remember: not in the league of bulk carriers, but loomingly large and loudly orange. In a chopper over ice you can spot her from miles away. Large ropes as thick as my arms hook her to bollards along the dock, and she shifts and rises against the tyres that buffer the wharf. Her hull is marked by gouges and scuffs where she has encountered ice, and even from here I can detect that familiar stench of diesel. I think of going south again and a worm of anticipation wriggles in my stomach. Up on the helideck, two crew members are sucking on cigarettes. They see me and wave. I nod and slip quietly away, feeling strange and dislocated. I should quit dreaming, buy some lunch at Salamanca and head back to work.

As I wait at an auto-teller to withdraw some cash, Emma walks past with another girl. She's the last person I expected to see and something in me backflips. I see her pause to look in a shop window, chatting to her friend. A man behind me waiting to access the ATM coughs impatiently, and I snatch my money and receipt and dive away.

Emma hasn't seen me and I shove my wallet in my pocket and follow them down the street. Then I stop. What am I doing following her? Have I lost my mind? I watch the girls wandering along the pavement. There's something about the way Emma moves—so easy and relaxed. Her shoulders ride low and the smile that curls her lips when I catch her profile is self-assured. She seems to smile easily and often. She's someone who's comfortable in company. She's everything that I'm not.

The girls stop and talk outside a café. They glance my way, but don't seem to notice me standing stupidly on the footpath. Emma probably doesn't even remember me. She's only met me once and it's unlikely I impressed her. They disappear into the café and I stand for a while, wondering what to do. Should I follow them inside? Is it wrong to want to see more of Emma? I slip my hands into my pockets and try to walk nonchalantly into the café.

Inside it's dimly lit. Most of the tables are full, but down the back there's a small round table with just one seat. Emma and her friend are at the counter looking at a menu. I grab a newspaper from the communal magazine rack and make my way to the empty table. My heart is pumping. What if they see me and Emma recognises me? What will I do then?

I hide behind the sheets of the *Mercury*, pretending to read. A waitress comes by and I order coffee. The girls have taken a table near the door and are deep in conversation. Sunlight casts a halo around Emma's head, but with her cropped short hair and sturdy build she doesn't look angelic. I feel a flush of pleasure and then succumb to confusion. Why do I care? I haven't looked at a woman in years. And now here I am, oscillating wildly between excitement and fear.

I'm still gazing at Emma over the top of the newspaper when the waitress asks where she should put my cappuccino. I reach for the cup and look at her for the first time. She's heavily made-up with bleached blonde hair but she's smiling at me, and I realise I don't mind the curve of her waist where her black apron is tied. The cup shakes in my hand as I take it from her, and froth spills into the saucer.

'Sorry,' she says.

'It's my fault.'

'No. I'll clean it up for you.'

'Don't worry.'

But she's already gone and I slide my attention from her hips to Emma's happy laugh, which mingles with the general hum from the other tables.

The waitress returns straightaway with a cloth and wipes out my saucer. Her eyes are rimmed with black kohl and her lashes are laden with mascara. It's impossible to tell what she really looks like underneath all that make-up. She raises her eyebrows at me and walks away, cloth in hand. Then she glances back at me with a half-smile that makes me nervous. She thinks I like her. How did that happen? I've never known how to act around women. I suppress an urge to escape. If I rush out, my exit will be obvious and Emma may notice. I should go back to reading, and hopefully the waitress will lose interest.

I bend my head over the paper and pretend to be absorbed, but in truth my senses are all focused on Emma. I'm listening with my whole body for the sound of her voice or the pleasant dry tone of her laugh. Even with my eyes fixed on the paper I can see her in my peripheral vision.

'What are you reading?' It's the waitress again, carrying a pile of dishes past my table. 'Must be a good article,' she says with a wink.

Fear cascades in my chest and my resolve falters. I have to leave or the waitress will be asking me out. I imagine myself blushing and stammering, trying to politely turn down her invitation. I envisage the amusement of the other café patrons, watching my discomfort. Emma or no Emma, I have to go. I drain my coffee, shake four dollars out of my pocket and leave it on the table, slinking past Emma and her friend as I escape through the door.

At work, I struggle with vertigo. Emma is with me beneath the car, her smile stoking my courage. I can't focus on the job. The strength of my imagination is frightening. It seems my Antarctic vault has reopened and I'm bogged in a thick sludge of memory.

On my journey south, one of the girls left her sunglasses in her cabin so she could fully experience Antarctica on her face—the wind and the searing light. She burned her retinas and lived in the shadow and pain of snow blindness for two days. When I think of Emma, a strange foolishness arrests me. I feel as reckless and as stupid as that girl on the ship, as though I could easily leave my protective layers behind and dive into something brighter than I can handle.

During the afternoon an idea starts brewing in my mind. Perhaps I should ring Emma and ask her out. But I haven't taken anyone out since Debbie and it feels risky. What if Emma says no? Jess is onto me, of course. She's been watching me from her rug against the garage wall, her yellow eyes steady and unblinking. She knows I'm feeling unsettled, and she's afraid to take her eyes off me in case I disappear without her. I stop tinkering with the undercarriage of the car and go to make coffee and gather more tools. Then I'm back under the hoist again, tightening a few parts and wondering what I should do. Finally, I go into the garage office and ring the antdiv number. I ask for Emma and the operator puts me through to her office. The phone rings several times and I'm just about to hang up when she answers.

'Hello. Emma here.'

'Hello. This is Tom Mason.'

She pauses. Of course she doesn't remember me.

'I came to your talk the other night, and I gave you my number . . . in case there was a job.'

'Oh yes,' she says, discouragingly.

I plunge on anyway. 'I wondered if you'd like to have a drink tonight. After work. We could just talk . . . about Antarctica.'

She pauses for a long time.

'It's not about getting a job,' I say. 'I just want to talk about going south. About what it's like being at Mawson Station. I haven't talked about Antarctica for so long.'

'Okay,' she says, a little hesitantly. 'Where would we go?'

'Somewhere down at Salamanca?'

'All right. Name a pub and a time.'

She's already at the bar when I arrive; I see her at the counter leaning on her elbows. Her face is blank and she looks slightly masculine. To survive down south she probably had to neutralise her femininity. I move up alongside, trying not to touch her. It's busy and she hasn't yet managed to attract the attention of a barman.

'Hello,' I say.

She looks at me. 'Hi.'

'I'll buy the drinks,' I offer. 'What'll you have?'

She steps back from the bar. 'A Cascade. They have it on tap here. And could you get me some water too? I just need to duck into the ladies'.'

I watch her thread her way among the tables; when she moves there's no denying she's a woman, something about her hips. I smile to myself, happy she came to meet me. Then I lapse to nervousness; when it comes to conversation, I'm sure to stuff it up.

She's gone quite a while. I fidget at the counter and finally the barman notices me and I order three beers and a glass of water. The first beer I drink quickly, leaving the empty glass on the counter. I don't drink often, but tonight I need steadying, and Emma won't know I'm on my second glass.

I find a table near the window and sit down. It's almost dark outside. Autumn is fading into winter even though it's only May. I think of Mum down at Cloudy Bay, the long grey light down there. I wonder if she's managing and I feel a pang of guilt. I should be down there cooking for her, and here I am at a pub.

Emma finds me and sits down opposite, thanking me for the beer. Sitting close to her like this, my heart thuds with excitement. She has a frank and friendly face.

'How did you like my talk?' she says. A good opener. I wish I had thought of something suitable to say.

'It was great. You've got some nice photos.' My response sounds so bland I almost wince.

She takes a long sip of beer and glances around the room. 'I'm still finding crowds difficult,' she says. 'Usually I'm just beginning to adjust and it's time to pack up and go south again. You know how it is.'

Yes. I know how it is. 'How long have you been back?' I ask.

'Just a few weeks. Haven't even unpacked my bags.' She laughs. 'Maybe I won't bother.'

I watch her fiddling with her glass.

'You look forward to coming back,' she says, 'and then you hit Hobart and all the confusion starts and you just want to run away again.'

She flutters a tentative smile my way and I nod in understanding. 'How long before you go back down south?'

'Four months. And counting.' She shifts restlessly in her seat, scanning the room. 'I can't wait to go.'

I understand her anxiety. After spending summer on base with just fifty people a bar like this must seem packed. 'How was it at Mawson Station?' I ask. 'I've never been there.'

'Well, you missed out. Where did you go?'

'Davis.'

'Summer?'

'Over winter.'

'Nowhere else?'

'We stopped overnight at Casey Station on the way home.'

'Kept you on the ship, did they? With the shrink?' She laughs. 'I bet a few of you needed it. The antdiv's worried about the number of maladjusted people they keep bringing back to so-called civilisation.' She glances at me, more serious now. 'How did you go? Coming back, I mean.'

I shrug. 'Messy, I suppose.'

She drains her beer. 'Isn't everyone?'

She goes to the bar to order more beers while I wait at the table. I try to assess how things are going, but I'm not sure whether we're having a good time or not. She comes back and sits down heavily, pushing a beer across the table to me.

'Well, south can be a pain when you're a woman,' she says. 'I should try to remember that when I'm desperate to go back. If I wasn't in the field most of the time, I don't think I could handle it.' She stares into her beer. 'You know how it is. You can't even fart without everybody knowing about it. And if you're a woman you only have to look sideways at someone and everyone thinks you're having an affair.'

'Some people turn into animals down there,' I say.

She shakes her head. 'No, it's worse than that. They *choose* animals to go down there. It's the army psych test. Designed to select lunatics.'

'I passed,' I say.

Emma grins. 'Me too. Remember the first question? *Which would you prefer: to live in a social suburb or to be alone in a deep dark wood?* For God's sake.'

I like the way her face opens up when she laughs. She loses her Antarctic guardedness.

She becomes serious again. 'So what was it really like? Overwintering?'

'Same as for everyone.' I try to dodge the question—there's too much weight behind it—but she's watching me intently, so I'll have to find a better answer. 'Winter's a strange time. Humans aren't meant to live without light.' I don't tell her how the dark penetrates everything. Or how it can sink you if you're carrying anything into it.

'At least you've overwintered,' she says. 'So that makes you a *real* expeditioner. Not like us summerers. It must be good when the light comes back.' She's letting me off lightly. Perhaps there's sadness in my face.

'Yes, it's magic,' I say. 'All those fragile pinks and mauves.'

She gazes pensively at her glass. 'I'm not sure I'd want to do it. Everyone I know who's overwintered is more than a little bit mad.' This could be a subtle insult or simply an observation. She glances up quickly and laughs. 'I wasn't meaning you,' she says. 'I don't even know you.'

With that comment she's underlined our lack of acquaintance, and I hesitate, unsure how to restart the conversation. Emma helps me.

'Let me tell you about Mawson base,' she says. 'That's what you wanted to hear about, isn't it?'

I nod.

'Well, it's every bit as amazing as they say. Even better than the photos. It blows you away.'

Her face lights up and she looks through and beyond me to another place. 'Station's ordinary,' she continues. 'Just a bunch of sheds up from Horseshoe Bay. But then there's the plateau and the mountains. And that's where the real Antarctica starts. I love it up there.' She smiles to herself. 'It's cold in the mountains, and tough for the fingers, but when you sit up on one of those peaks and look out, the plateau goes on forever. It's like something out of *The Lord of the Rings*. And then you turn and look out to sea, and there are islands and icebergs scattered through the sea ice as far as you can see.' She glances at me. 'I've been up Mount Henderson a few times. And once I went out to Fang Peak with Nick Thompson, the field training officer. Do you know him?'

'No.'

'He's been south a few times. Just thought you might have heard of him.'

The conversation briefly stalls again, but Emma picks up the threads and carries me along. Fortunately, she seems happy to chatter without much input from me. 'I've been to Scullin too,' she says.

Scullin Monolith is a massive wedge of dark rock that rises steeply out of the sea about one hundred and sixty kilometres east of Mawson station. It's a major breeding colony for Antarctic petrels—a protected wildlife sanctuary. Hardly anyone goes there.

'What's it like?' I ask.

'Incredible,' she says. 'Unbelievable. The air's thick with birds.'

'Don't you need a special permit?' I ask.

'Yes, and when someone scores one, every biologist finds a reason to help. You know how it is.'

Yes, I do know. When the ultimate jolly is on, everyone tries to use their contacts and wield whatever influence they have. Somehow, I was lucky enough to tag along on most of the good rides when I was south. It can pay to be quietly helpful and unaligned. In a melting pot of personalities, there's always a use for somebody neutral.

'What about Auster?' I ask. 'Have you been there?' Auster is the emperor penguin rookery on the sea ice out from Mawson Station. It sits among an amphitheatre of sculpted icebergs.

'Of course I've been,' Emma says. 'Several times. What penguin biologist wouldn't have? And it's every bit as fantastic as they say.' She nods at me and smiles. 'Close your eyes.'

'Why?'

'Just do it.'

I oblige reluctantly.

'All right,' she says. 'Imagine this: you're way out on the sea ice and there's a circle of icebergs—some are blocky, some are sloping, and there are melt caves beneath a few.' She pauses. 'Got that?'

'Yes,' I mumble. 'I'm there.'

There's a long pause and I wonder what she's doing, whether she's watching me, whether I should open my eyes. My heart starts to race and my hands begin to sweat. I keep my lids tightly shut. When she starts talking again, her voice is softer. It runs like a thrill up and down my spine.

'Okay. Now imagine the sky. It's sharp blue. Or it could be white-grey—one of those days when it's overcast, but everything's still reflecting white.'

'Yes,' I say.

'What is it for you?'

'Blue,' I say. 'The sky's blue.'

'Good.' Emma sounds pleased. 'I'm there on a blue day too. It's crystal clear and bitingly cold. My fingers are freezing even with three pairs of gloves on.'

I remember that kind of cold.

'Next, the penguins. They're scattered everywhere, with bergs all round. It's mid-season and the chicks are being creched, so they're all hanging out in clusters. Most of the adults are standing like soldiers—you know the way they stand, heads up, beaks pointed to the sky. Just passing time.' She laughs. 'Probably just enjoying the view. It's the best piece of real estate I've ever seen.'

'Noisy?'

'Of course. Lots of trumpeting. Smelly too. Just lean back and draw in a good whiff of all that penguin crap.' She sniffs loudly. 'Ah, the glorious smell of a penguin colony. There's nothing like it.'

Silence thickens for a moment. I wonder if Emma is still here with me or if her mind is wandering over the mountains near Mawson.

'You can open your eyes,' she says finally.

I lift my lids timidly to meet her eyes. She's watching me carefully, softly.

'Did you enjoy the trip?' she asks.

I nod, words catching in my throat.

'Another beer, perhaps,' she says, glancing towards the bar. 'I think I'll get a jug this time.'

It's late when Emma takes me home to her place. We walk. We're drunk and it's cold and there's nobody in the streets except us. Her house is several blocks away uphill in North Hobart. We wander along Elizabeth Street, past restaurants and pubs with groups of rowdy people clustering outside. We should have caught a taxi, but walking is good for sobriety . . . or maybe it's bad, because with sobriety I feel myself becoming tense again.

Eventually, we leave the shops behind and walk up another street past darkened houses. Beneath a street lamp, Emma stumbles and giggles. Conversation has dropped away, and our progress is punctuated only by the intermittent chorus of barking dogs and the occasional flare of headlights as cars pass by. In a dark stretch, she trips again over a crack in the footpath and lurches against me. A possum startles from the shadows of a tree and gallops across the path. Emma uses this as an excuse to grip my hand, and she holds it firmly as we walk up the hill, running her thumb back and forth across my fingers. My knees weaken. I'm too entranced to pull away.

Halfway along another quiet street, Emma pauses and fiddles with the catch on a low iron gate. It swings open with a musical creak and she leads me around the house to a bungalow in the backyard. She unlocks the front door and walks in, turning on the lights. Tossing her coat across a chair she swivels to look at me, hands on hips. My mouth dries and I lick my lips uncertainly. She smiles then—a slow confident smile that travels up into her eyes. My heart batters, and I stand there useless, hands hanging by my sides.

Time stretches and the moment subsides. I curse myself for my inaction. Emma couldn't have spelled out her interest more clearly. She shows me to a tiny bathroom and when she leaves, I stand in front of the mirror and examine myself. In the glare of the fluorescent light, I look gaunt and pale and there are dark hollows under my eyes. My cheekbones are too high and there's a shadow of regrowth on my cheeks. I shiver away from the emptiness in my eyes. It's like there's something missing. When I peer at myself again, I look afraid.

I splash water on my face and dry it on a towel, then wander through the lounge to the bedroom where Emma has lit a candle and is undressing. It's as if she knows I'm unable to do it for her. I glance around and watch the candlelight flickering warmly on the walls. There's not much furniture in this room. Emma is still living out of a suitcase; her shoes are in a pile in the corner and there are framed prints leaning up against one wall. She notices me looking around.

'I haven't had time to hang my pictures yet,' she comments, pulling off a sock. 'There was someone else using the room while I was away.'

I try not to look at her muscular thighs.

'Would you like to see them?' she says, and then laughs when she sees my face. 'I'm talking about the pictures.'

'There are hooks on the wall,' I say, dodging her gaze. 'We could hang them now.'

I pick up the first photo. It's a picture of Emma in Antarctica. She's standing outside a round red building a bit like a spaceship on stilts. Around her are rocks and ice and a line of Adelie penguins mid-waddle.

'Béchervaise Island,' she says, taking the print from me.

Now she's down to one sock, knickers and a singlet. My heart tumbles as I watch her reach up to hang the photo on a hook. She selects a picture of a grey-headed albatross perched over a moody view of Macquarie Island. The light is dim and the sea is a restless white, foaming over the rocks below.

'A friend of mine took this shot. It's good, isn't it?' She hangs it above the bed. 'I'd love to go there, wouldn't you?'

I'm staring at her toned body. 'Go where?' I ask vaguely.

'Macquarie Island.'

'Yes, yes,' I say.

I bend quickly to lift the next frame, but she grasps my arm gently. The candlelight is soft on her face as she looks up at me. A moment of breathlessness hovers between us, a fragment of time when we both wait. I know it's up to me to act, but I wallow in the luscious darkness of her eyes, quivering internally. The smallest smile flickers on her lips, and suddenly it isn't difficult to kiss her. Passion, long unfamiliar, floods through me. Her lips are full and eager. Her body curves into mine.

I didn't think I could do this. But now that I feel her, warm and strong and close, something releases, something that has held me in check for years. It eases out of me like a sigh. And slowly,

slowly I allow myself to go with sensation. The untapping of myself; an uncorking. Like a slow-motion replay.

Emma is soft, but firm in my arms. She draws me onto the bed and allows me to explore her with my hands: the tautness of her forearms, the tight curve of her back, the softer roll of her hips. This is like music, like summer, like the quiver of birds' wings. It's hot and searing like white light over ice. It's like finding myself again after a decade, and not knowing who I am.

17

The first time I saw an aurora I was awestruck. We were four or five days south of Hobart on the Southern Ocean and I had been asleep in my cabin when someone came clattering down the corridor, banging on doors. 'Hey, everybody. Get up. There's an aurora outside. The southern lights. Come on. It's incredible.'

My cabin mate flicked on the lights and we started donning layers: thermals, woollen shirts, fleece trousers, jackets, freezer suits, gloves, hats. Out in the corridor there was a buzz of activity and a flow of bodies heading for the bridge. I joined the trail of people clomping up the stairs and out onto the helideck. We then filed up again to a deck above the bridge where a group was milling quietly in the dark beside the warmth of the heating vent.

'There's a lull,' a girl said. 'But it'll come again.'

We waited in the shadows, tense with anticipation, willing the aurora to reappear across the black sky. Ahead, the spotlights from the ship glowed on the water, piercing the dark. I wondered if we'd really see anything as elusive and ethereal as an aurora with all this extraneous light.

And then, there it was, an awakening in a high corner of the sky. A flicker, then a soft rippling sheet of pale yellow light that rose and fell on itself like a veil of smoke. It shimmered, surged and swelled, reaching and twisting, before subsiding as suddenly as it had appeared.

Stunned, we waited.

Another part of the sky lit up, ghostly fingers of fluctuating light that flickered and swirled before dancing right across the heavens in a thin trail. Wavering in curtains, rising and falling, spreading, glimmering, folding, pulsing, flaring and receding. Quivering up and down. Dropping off again.

I realised I'd been holding my breath. How could there be such beauty as this?

'This is nothing,' an old-timer grunted. 'You haven't seen an aurora till you've seen them midwinter. They're stronger. More colourful. And they last for hours.'

Nobody listened to him. People who go south too often get jaded, and then even the extraordinary can become mundane. While he returned to his warm bed, the rest of us maintained our vigil on the bridge, creeping closer to the warmth of the heating vent as the cold pressed in. We were bonded in reverent silence, waiting for the heavens to light up again.

Lying awake beside Emma this morning reminds me of seeing that first aurora. Naked beneath her sheets, I'm achingly aware, alive with feelings of discovery and disbelief. Beside me, she is warm and incredibly relaxed, her arms and legs skewed and her head thrown back on the pillow. The fingers of one hand are tangled loosely in mine. Even in sleep, she seems confidently in possession of herself, so unalarmed by the enormity of the world.

It's pleasant to lie here watching her in the dim light. Her face is slack and her mouth partly open. My eyes trace the strong line of her nose, the high curve of her cheeks, the hint of white teeth. Her lips are full and soft and I recall the sensation of them moving eagerly beneath mine, biting at me last night in passion. Her eyelids are open a little too. I want to shut them to protect her eyes, yet I'm afraid to reach out across the short space between us in case I disturb her, for then my peaceful observation of her would end. You can't study someone as closely as this when they're awake. It'd be a violation of privacy.

I'm still unsure how we came to this last night—whether it was the beer, or the talk of Antarctica. Now that I'm sober, it's not regret that I feel, but an uncomfortable fragility, as if my skin is cracking open and I'm morphing into something else. As I bask in the warmth of Emma's body, I can feel something within me gaining a momentum that will soon be too big for me to stop.

I decide I must leave. Gently, I disentangle my hand from Emma's fingers, but her eyes open fully and engage me. She is momentarily languid and then her hand snaps onto my arm, pinning it.

'Don't,' she says. 'You're not going.' Her eyes are intense. 'Don't run. I'm not scary.'

'I have to go to work.'

'Will they sack you?'

Despite her grip on me, she looks sleepy again and the smile that creeps onto her lips makes my heart heave. It's either fear or desire, or both.

'You should stay,' she says. 'Ring in sick. Say your car's broken down.'

'I'm a mechanic.'

She closes her eyes. 'That excuse won't work then, will it?'

She's silent a moment and I'm blankly panicked. I don't know how to escape.

'Come up with something else,' she says without opening her eyes. 'Be creative.'

'I'm a mechanic,' I say again, as if that should explain everything.

'That doesn't mean you have to be a machine.' She looks at me and tugs my hand across, then lays it on the soft doughiness of her belly. She presses my hand beneath hers and slowly draws it over her silken skin. 'You can't go,' she says, rolling against me.

In that moment, with her body moving against mine, desire erupts in me. I want her body and her skin and the feel of her hands clasping my arms, exploring the contours of my calves, kneading my back.

Later, she makes me toast and coffee. I've showered and dressed, but Emma seems completely comfortable padding naked around the kitchen. With the curtains still drawn, it's as if we exist in our own secluded sanctuary.

Her breasts move every time she does. They're large but firm, and they suit her athletic frame. She sits on the wooden chair across from me to eat breakfast and it's impossible for me not to look at her, not to watch her nipples, like brown discs. She munches toast and looks at me flatly.

'Don't judge me,' she says. 'I am who I am. Far from perfect. You survive by being like a bloke down there. If you're feminine, they harass you. If you're sexless, you manage. I know my body's average, but I'm okay with that.'

I swallow and my voice is like gravel. 'I like it.'

She doesn't smile. 'It performs, and it's strong. That's all I require of it.'

I say nothing. I'm enchanted by her body. I'm glad she's strong and unpretentious. I force myself to stop looking at her and examine the room.

'These two buildings are like an Antarctic halfway house,' she says, following my gaze. 'People come and go all the time. I like being out here in the bungalow because I can have my own space without having to deal with share-house dynamics. Four people live in the house and this is the spillover accommodation. Two of them have office jobs at the antdiv and haven't been south for ages.' She laughs almost derisively. 'You'd think they'd be over it by now, wouldn't you? You'd think they'd be living in regular houses. But they like having expeditioners around. It reminds them of how it feels to be down there.'

She leans over a portable CD player sitting on the floor beside her chair and puts on some music—The Verve. The noise seems too large and loud for this small living space.

'I'm going to have a shower,' she says.

Alone at the table, I feel strange and out of place and the music chafes at me. I go outside and sit on the edge of the concrete porch looking across the overgrown backyard. The curtains in the main house are still drawn. One room has no curtains and I assume it must be the kitchen. I can't see anyone inside.

The day is cool and cloudy. I can still hear Emma's music, so I shut the door and sit down on the porch again. I should head off to work soon. The boss will be annoyed. Perhaps I should have rung and fabricated some excuse, but they'd know I was lying. And I'm not good at deceit. I like to keep life simple—work, Jess, birdwatching. Already this morning things have changed, and part of me wants to retreat. But a small voice is telling me I've already moved far beyond my usual solitude, and there's no going back.

Emma comes out freshly showered, her hair damp. She's wearing jeans, a shirt and Blundstone boots. There's no shape to her in these clothes; she's advertising nothing, but I'm still willing to buy. She sits down beside me.

'What are you going to do?' she asks.

My breath catches as I connect with her eyes. 'I have to go to work.'

She nods. 'How about tonight? Want to come over for a meal and some wine?'

I hesitate. Her proposition both excites and frightens me. Two nights in a row almost seems like commitment.

She tries to read my uncertainty. 'Do you have something on already?'

'No. I have a dog at home. Jess. She's not used to being left.'

'Bring her along, then. A dog is good. I like dogs.' Emma laughs. 'I thought you were going to say you had a girlfriend.'

'No girlfriend.'

The confession sounds lonely. A bit desperate. I wish I hadn't said anything. And Emma is looking at me strangely, as if she's wondering about something. Perhaps I should tell her upfront that I'm a social misfit, that I'm not sure where I belong.

She reaches out and a plucks a head of grass from the lawn, starts picking out the seeds one by one. 'You miss the smells when you're down south,' she says. 'Don't you think? Like the smell of grass. And the smell of moisture. All you smell is penguin shit and station food.' She waves the stem of grass and throws it away, and then she rubs her hand along my knee. 'Don't you remember that about coming back? The smell of land? The clouds? The smell of dogs and grass and trees?' She pushes me playfully. 'Go on. Don't tell me you've forgotten.'

'No. I remember. Smells. And confusion. Traffic. The craziness of everything. Everyone in such a hurry.'

She gazes off across the yard into grey distance. 'Down there you forget how to rush. It's a shame we relearn it so quickly when we come back. I think it's nice to take life slowly. To stop and appreciate things: landscapes, horizons. That's what's so addictive about going south. The joy you get from contemplation. Getting away from the hustle and bustle. The way we live life back here becomes so . . . irrelevant.' She leans back and stares up at the clouds. 'That's why it's so hard to settle down. Who wants to live the way everyone else does? They don't know what they're missing out on.'

'It *is* possible to live simply here if you want to,' I say.

She shakes her head. 'No, it's not. Look at you. You feel compelled to go to work this morning. Down there, you'd find a way to delay it.'

'Not if there were things to be done.'

'Maybe not. But you'd be doing real things. And you'd have time to stop and look at the sky, or to watch a snow petrel flying over. And you'd value that.'

She's right. Down south you can be fulfilled just by the way the light slants over the ice, or how it glows on an iceberg. You get hooked on distance.

Still, I want to tell her there are ways to find joy right here in Hobart. Simple things, like lingering over breakfast while watching the rosellas on my feeder. Or the sight of the morning light over the channel, the bright flash of orange that comes with the autumn smoke haze. I've learned how to find moments of happiness in normal life. It's a matter of rearranging your thoughts so you don't buy into the rush. It's not Antarctic euphoria, but a kind of peace is possible.

Now, though, Emma's face has folded into itself. She's focused on memories and she wouldn't hear me if I tried to explain. Even if she did, she wouldn't understand. She's still trapped in the southern whirl and the conviction that nothing can ever equal it. It takes years to adjust, not weeks or months. And yet, given the opportunity to go south with Emma, I'd do it to myself again. Just to share the place with her. To feel that wild sensation of freedom, of escape. The exhilaration of light. I suppose in a way she's right. I fill the void by finding pleasure in the winging of a cormorant over water, but it doesn't approach the thrill of watching snow petrels wheeling against a steely sky.

'I'd better head off,' I say, standing awkwardly. The ground feels unsteady beneath my feet.

Emma smiles up at me. 'Bring some wine,' she says. 'Bring two bottles. I'll be waiting for you.'

18

Jess is sitting by the side gate when I get home from work. She doesn't smile and she doesn't stand up. Her eyes are forlorn and my rising guilt is dense. I open the gate and she skulks out and cringes round my legs. She thinks she's done something wrong.

I sit on the path and she crawls onto my lap, curling up in a tight ball. When I pull on her ears, the sigh that shudders through her is almost human. She feels betrayed; this is the first time I've left her overnight without coming home. I'd like to tell her how happy I was with Emma, but now with my sad dog on my lap, all I can do is cry big wet tears that well out and drip onto her head. Where is this coming from? I haven't cried in years. One night with Emma and I'm breaking apart. How can I have a relationship with another person when I can't get it right with my dog?

Jess and I sit on the footpath for a long time in the mellow afternoon light. Soon we are sitting in shadows and even with my hot-water-bottle dog still coiled on my lap the cold is eating into me through the concrete path.

'Come on, Jess,' I say finally. 'We have to go inside.'

She leaps up and, follows me closely into the house like she's glued to my legs. I put on some music and shake food into her dish. Then I set down a bowl of milk as well. She looks up at me and beats her tail against the floor. I think she knows I'm saying sorry. For a dog, milk is like a bag of lollies.

I shower and change and then stuff some clean clothes into a bag. I suppose this means I'm expecting to stay the night at Emma's again. This may be a presumption, but if I buy two bottles of wine it'll be a necessity. I roll up Jess's rug and place it by the door. Still at her bowl, she lifts her head and wags her tail. She knows she won't be left behind this time.

As the light fades over the water, I sip tea in the kitchen and struggle to compose myself. Something is skipping and tumbling in my chest and my palms are sweaty with excitement. It's as if life is reawakening in me. The hope of a future very different from the past nine years.

A knock at the door checks me. It's Laura, with a hesitant smile on her face.

'Sorry to come banging on your door again . . . It's just that I need some matches for the stove, and I wondered if you had some. I'm a bit reluctant to drag Mouse down to the shops. He gets carsick.'

I wonder what sort of person gets carsick on a five-minute drive—or why she can't leave her brother at home—but I go to the pantry to see if I have a spare box. The phone rings and I take the call still ferreting around on the top shelf. It's Jan. Typical of her to ring at a difficult moment.

'What's happening with Mum?' she asks.

'I don't know. Isn't Jacinta down there now? With Alex?'

'Yes. But I thought you might have heard from them.'

'There's no phone coverage at Cloudy Bay.'

'That's another reason why I'm so cross,' Jan says. 'Mum has no way of calling if she needs help.'

'Do you want to come down with me next week?'

'Can't. I've got too much on. My whole week's booked out.'

Sure, her whole week is booked out. What does she expect me to do for her?

'Call me after you've spoken to Jacinta,' she says. 'Hopefully Alex will be able to talk some sense into her. And into Mum. I had a quiet word with him before they left and I think he understands my concerns. Not like the rest of you.'

She hangs up. Laura is still hovering by the door. At last, I find a matchbox at the back of the shelf and hand it to her, dropping it into her open palm. Transaction completed.

'Thank you,' she says. But she stays on the doorstep as if she expects an invitation inside. 'We're settling in all right,' she says.

'Good.' Monosyllabic answers work to discourage most people. I'm expecting her to get the message soon. She gives a slight awkward smile and I can't help comparing her with Emma. Laura: frail, timid and colourless, so thin she might snap. Emma: bold, robust and confident. I can't wait to finish this meeting so I can scoop up Jess and my things and take myself back to the warmth of Emma's presence.

'It's a bit of a run into town,' Laura continues. 'Mouse doesn't cope with corners very well.'

'Maybe he'll get used to it after a while,' I suggest.

She glances down at Jess, sitting by my feet. 'Do dogs get carsick?'

'Some. Not Jess.'

'I used to get carsick all the time when I was small. But I'm over it now.'

I shift restlessly and twiddle the doorknob. Surely she'll go soon.

'Where do you work?' she asks.

'In town.'

'Office work?'

'No, I'm a mechanic.'

'That could come in handy.'

'I work long hours.' I hope she doesn't ask me to fix her car.

'Saturdays too?'

'Yes, I've just got back.'

'You must be tired. Would you like some dinner?'

'Thanks, that's kind. But I'm going out. In fact, I'm supposed to be already on my way.'

'Oh, sorry. I'd better let you go then.'

'Maybe another time.'

She moves away at last, the matches in her hand. 'Thanks for these. I'll replace them next week.'

'Don't worry. I've got plenty.'

She shakes the box and steps down off the porch.

When she's gone I retreat into the house to collect my bag. And then Jess and I are on our way to Emma's, via the bottle shop.

The light outside the bungalow glows warmly and Jess and I stand there like shadows till I muster the courage to knock. Emma opens the door and looks down at Jess, steps back and swings the door wide.

Jess and I slink inside. Jess looks up at me with a worried expression and then at Emma. It's as if she's trying to work us out.

'You can put Jess's rug on the floor there,' Emma says, pointing to a corner where she has already placed a bowl of water.

I hand over the bottles of wine and roll out Jess's blanket. 'Here, Jess.' I point to the rug.

Jess sits obediently on the rug and smiles at me. She has an obliging lap of the water then glances at Emma, looking surprisingly relaxed. Emma has been clever giving Jess her own space. She hasn't forced herself on the dog. Perhaps she has a better understanding of animals than most biologists do.

'She's a good dog, isn't she?' Emma says. 'Most dogs aren't so well behaved.' She pours two glasses of red wine, hands one to me and leans over the bench to check a pot on the stove. 'Could you put on some music?'

I flick through the pile of CDs on the floor and pull out an Alex Lloyd album. While I'm figuring out the buttons on the CD unit, I hear the click of Jess's toenails crossing the floor. She taps into the kitchen and sits down near Emma, panting up at her.

'Would you like a bone?' Emma asks.

Jess follows Emma to the fridge and bats her tail wildly on the floor while Emma fishes out a plastic bag. Emma puts some newspaper down, gives Jess the bone and ruffles her head.

'Make sure you keep it on the paper,' she says. 'I don't want blood all over the floor.'

Jess looks positively joyous. She crouches down and gets to work on the bone. She seems to understand Emma's instructions about keeping it on the paper.

'I think she likes you,' I say. 'I wasn't expecting her to accept you so quickly.'

'She's a nice dog. You've done a good job with her. I'd love to have a dog, but I'm away too much.' She gazes down at Jess and then at me. 'What would you do with her if you went south?'

'I don't know. Find someone to look after her, I suppose.'

'You'd miss her.'

'Yes. It's a pity they don't have sled dogs at Mawson anymore.'

Emma laughs. 'She wouldn't pass for a husky anyway.'

She comes across the room and sits on the couch with me. She's still wearing the same clothes as this morning, but it's warm in here, so she's unbuttoned the shirt a hole or two. I can see her collarbone, the satin sheen of her skin, the rise and fall of her breasts as she breathes; it's very sexy.

'How was work?' she asks.

'Busy.'

'You don't get sick of it?'

'No, I like it.'

'Not too repetitive?'

'Every job's repetitive.'

'Yes, I suppose it is to some degree. Even mine . . . tagging penguins, water offloading, data entry.'

'I like engines—the way they work. It's clever.'

'It must feel good to fix things.'

'I enjoy finding solutions.'

Emma flicks at my knee with her fingers. 'What about in your personal life?'

I pause. 'That's a bit harder.'

She stands up to serve dinner and I move to help her. 'Just stay on the couch,' she says. 'It's a tiny kitchen. You're best out of the way.'

Jess is still on the kitchen floor working on her bone. She looks up as Emma steps over her, then glances over to me and wags her tail: four short beats against the floor. She wants my approval to like Emma, so I nod and Jess returns to her bone, pleased.

Emma serves beef stew with lentils and rice. We eat on the couch with our bowls resting on our knees. The food is good with the red wine and by the end of the first glass I can feel myself relaxing.

'Do you have family in Hobart?' Emma asks, sipping wine.

'Mother, sister, brother, niece.'

'Father?'

'He died a a few years ago.'

'Were you close?'

'Not particularly.'

I think of Dad at the lighthouse, his thin shoulders and long serious face. I can hardly remember a conversation with him; certainly no conversations on topics of importance. What I recall is his hurried, jerky gait as he headed up the hill to the lighthouse, his quiet presence at the kitchen table, my yearning for his approval. He wore so little of himself on his exterior; I used to think he must be full of secrets and that there had to be some trigger to release them which I couldn't find. When I was a teenager my relationship with him frustrated me. Later, I gave up and turned inwards to my own world. It was from him that I learned silence.

Emma is watching me.

'How about *your* family?' I ask.

'They all live on the north coast of New South Wales. I'm the only one with polar tendencies.' She takes another mouthful of stew and chews thoughtfully. 'I don't have a father either. He left when I was ten. Took up with the next-door neighbour, who was divorced. How convenient to have an affair with the woman next door! They bought a house in another suburb and Dad erased us from his life. His new wife didn't want to compete with us so she made him cut us out. Pathetic, isn't it? He didn't even come to my sister's wedding.'

Emma sloshes more wine into our glasses and raises hers high. 'To families,' she says with a twisted smile. 'To non-existent relationships with fathers.'

I clink my glass against hers and drink, watching her.

'What else can we drink to?' she asks.

'To going south?'

'You're obsessed with that, aren't you?'

'Only since I met you.'

She snorts. 'I don't believe you.'

I duck my head to avoid the knowing look in her eyes. 'Over the past few years I've only thought about it remotely,' I say. 'It hasn't been a possibility.'

'And now it is?'

'I don't know.'

She looks at me incredulously. 'Is that why you're here?'

'No. I'm here because I like you.'

She drinks her wine quickly. 'You *like* me. What does that mean?'

I wonder what she wants me to say. That I love her? That I lust after her madly? Sure, I'm swept up in all of this. But I don't really want to say *I love you*. What would it mean after only a couple of days?

'I don't mix relationships with going south.' She's issuing a warning.

I shrug. What am I supposed to say?

She presses harder. 'You said you wanted to go south.'

'Yes, I think I'd like to.'

'You *think* you'd like to?' She's making this very difficult.

'It's not always easy to just get up and go.'

'Why not?'

'People have commitments.'

'You mean things that tie them down.'

'Things that make it hard to go.' Like Mum. Like fear.

'Like what? Mortgages? I thought you said you wanted to go south.'

'I do, but it doesn't have to be this season.'

'And not necessarily with me.'

I grip my wineglass tight and try to halt the panic rising in my chest. Am I already ruining things between us? 'I'd like to go south with you,' I say. 'But not if it doesn't suit you.'

I reach out tentatively and take her hands in mine, but she tries to pull away. I wasn't expecting this. She seemed so secure in herself up till now. I hold onto her hands. I like her and she likes me. This much I can tell, even if she's confused right now. What does she expect? She's only been back a few weeks. She must have held herself so strongly down there, and now she's breaking open, like me.

All I can manage is a husky whisper. 'Emma, I *really* like you. Okay?'

She relaxes her hands, and I kiss her gently trying to communicate my understanding and empathy. I'm sure I fall short, but it's the best I can do.

She stands up, turns off the lights and sits down with me again. I touch her face in the dark, following her features with my fingertips, running my thumb along the soft line of her lips. Her compliance makes me bold; that, and her earlier momentary lapse in confidence. Her body moving eagerly now beneath my hands makes me feel masculine. She's so warm, so soft. Somehow she fits perfectly into me, straining against my thigh between her legs.

'Come to bed,' she murmurs in my ear. 'I think we'll feel more comfortable naked.'

Sometime in the night, Jess clicks into the room and pushes her head under my hand which is lying loosely on top of the covers. I stroke her head and rub my fingers slowly over the dense velvet of her ears.

If only women were as simple as dogs.

In the morning, Emma rolls over and rests her head on my shoulder. She smiles languidly, which is all it takes to set my heart tripping. I run my hand along her arm, observing the glow of her skin in the beige light cast through the curtains. She feels deliciously smooth.

'How old are you?' she asks.

'Old.'

'How old?'

'Forty-two.'

'That's okay. Nine years' difference. Age doesn't really matter.'

She closes her eyes a moment and I ache with the burden of caring. I think I more than like her and that makes me feel afraid. I'm used to owning my own heart.

'Have you been with many women?' she asks.

'Only three, including you.'

She grins, her eyes still closed. 'I thought so. You feel fresh.'

I wonder what she means. Inexperienced? Awkward?

'I'm sorry,' I say.

'What for? I like being with you. The others feel like they're working from a recipe.'

Others?

'Have you been married before?' she asks.

'Yes.' I wait for her to stiffen, try to sense a change, but I detect nothing. 'It was a while ago.' My voice is tight in my throat.

She rubs the sparse hair on my chest. 'Antarctica?' she asks.

'Yes.'

'What happened?'

'She met another man.'

'You couldn't come back?'

'It was after the last ship.'

'Of course. It always is.' She strokes my cheek. 'No wonder you had a tough winter.'

'Winter's tough for everyone.'

Her face is soft with compassion. 'Stop trying to be so strong. It's okay to be sad.' She kisses my forehead, my nose, my chin. 'That's why I don't do it,' she says. 'That's why I don't mix love with south. It ruins you.'

What's this, then? I want to ask. What are we doing? But she snuggles into me, and I like the warmth and the softness of her too much to ask any questions.

19

Jacinta and Alex had arrived on Saturday morning, filling the cabin with youthful energetic joy. Mary felt as though she'd been hit by a tornado; in they came, bearing rustling bags of food and radiant smiles. At first, their activity overwhelmed her, and there was a moment of panic when she realised the letter was still sitting on the coffee table. But she managed to conceal it in her blanket before Jacinta rushed over to embrace her.

'Nana. How are you? Look at you, you're so thin. We're here to feed you.'

They dumped more bags on the bench, stocked the fridge, boiled the kettle, stoked the fire. Mary was exhausted just watching them. While she sat sipping tea, they vacuumed the cabin, mopped the floors, cleaned out the bathroom and put on a roast for dinner. And now Alex was out chopping. Mary could hear the dull *thock thock* of axe hitting wood.

'How's your mother?' she asked dutifully. It was better to have the Jan conversation now or it might mar the evening.

'Oh, you know,' Jacinta said. 'The usual. She's worrying about you and cross that she can't change things.' The edge of her smile slipped. 'Have you given any thought to coming home? If you did, I'd make sure you could stay at Battery Point. I won't let Mum boss you around.'

Mary shook her head firmly. 'I want to be here.'

'You're not lonely?'

'No, the ranger comes every day. His name's Leon. Nice young fellow.'

'But he's not here for long, is he? I can't bear thinking of you sitting here all by yourself.'

'I'm fine,' Mary insisted. She wasn't completely alone. She had Jack.

'So Mum hasn't been down to visit?'

'Not yet. Neither has Gary.'

Jacinta's face tightened slightly, and Mary saw that she was upset about this. 'I suppose Gary's busy with work . . .'

'And your mother's just plain angry. She hates not getting her way.'

Jacinta tried to smile, but couldn't mask her sadness. 'She's stubborn,' Jacinta said. 'And sometimes a bit hysterical. At the moment, it's a full-time job calming her down. I wish she'd come here, though.'

Mary flattened her lips. 'She will when she's ready.'

She too wished that Jan would visit. It'd be nice to make peace with her daughter before she died—but perhaps she shouldn't hope for the unachievable. And if Jan did come, she'd arrive with a barrowload of plans and subterfuge. She'd concoct a way of shipping Mary back to Hobart and into a home. Better that she stayed away.

When Alex came in, Mary sat back to enjoy the company of her guests. Alex was full of admiration for Jacinta, and her grand-daughter basked in it happily. Theirs was a gentle relationship, and Alex was such an open and affable man. He was dedicated and unswerving; a good choice for a husband. Pity about his domineering mother. But then, you couldn't have everything in life. Mary was convinced Jacinta and Alex could do well together. They would have their ripples and waves, of course—no relationship could complete its journey without storms. But they had the tools to steer them through. Affection, patience and good communication were an excellent start. Perhaps more marriages might survive if they had such solid foundations.

Apart from the sheer pleasure of fellowship, there were other reasons Mary was glad to have visitors in the cabin. Over the past few days, in all the space and silence, she'd become aware of increasing patches of time when she suspected she might be losing her mind. It didn't seem unreasonable anymore that Jack might be lurking in the cabin. She knew he'd been there; she'd felt his presence. And she'd talked to him, encouraged him to show his face. Even invited him to take a seat so they could reminisce on their better times.

She knew she shouldn't indulge in these fantasies about Jack. But it was so reassuring to imagine him here with her. Despite the faults in their relationship, she missed him dreadfully after he died. Those last months of his life, she'd been consumed with caring for him. She wanted him to be safe from the torture of a nursing home and to have the dignity of dying in his own bed. When he passed away, a great emptiness had followed. His illness had given her purpose, and it was an immense wilderness to be without him.

Later, she had gradually found new activities to fill her time. She started helping out in the local opportunity shop. She signed up to deliver Meals on Wheels. It felt good to make her contribution to the community, and reminded her that she was fortunate to be in control of her own situation, for as long as it lasted.

Yes, it was good to have Jacinta and Alex visit for the weekend. And once they were gone she could resume her own agenda. There was information to be chiselled out of Leon—those bruises needed explanation. And next weekend was the scout camp at Cloudy Corner, close to East Cloudy Head. If there was some way she could get up the path to the head, even just a little way, then she could satisfy her commitment to Jack.

•

Jacinta and Alex left in an affectionate flurry on Sunday. Unexpectedly, two days later, Tom arrived.

Mary was at the window waiting for Leon when Tom's old car surged over the dunes and pulled up on the grass. She watched her son jump out. He was like a boy, slim and lithe. How had forty-two years passed so quickly? It didn't seem so long ago that she had folded him on her lap and snuggled him close. He had always been a serious child, and now he was a man, marked by hurt and fear.

But today was different. He swept into the cabin and gripped her in a hug, his face alight. Mary returned his embrace with as much vigour as she could muster. She hadn't seen him so elated in years, and the blue sky reflected his delight—it was clear and celebratory. Not even Debbie had lit him up this way. Indeed, she couldn't quite remember him ever looking so radiant and alive.

Jess seemed jubilant too. She bounded into the cabin and onto the couch with a shower of damp sand, panting unashamedly in Mary's face. Even a fit of coughing didn't shake her off. Tom was so distracted he failed to remark when Mary hacked up phlegm.

She waited a few minutes for him to divulge his news, but then gave in to her curiosity. 'What has happened to you?'

He hesitated. 'I don't want to get your hopes up,' he said.

'Tell me.'

'I've met someone.' The admission rendered him breathless.

'Wonderful. Your feet haven't touched the ground since you walked in.'

'Is it that obvious?'

'Yes.'

His joy was tempered by agitation. Happiness tinged with terror. It seemed to Mary that he was having trouble giving in

to the thrill of this new relationship, but at the same time he
was incapable of holding back.

'Where did you meet her?' she asked.

'At the antdiv. She gave a seminar. She's a penguin biologist—just returned.'

His face clouded slightly and Mary thought she detected
a shadow of doubt. When Tom had come off the ship from
Antarctica all those years ago, he'd been like a little boy lost.
His face was blank when he saw her waiting on the wharf. Mary
knew she wasn't the person he was hoping to see, but Debbie
had refused to come. And everything was made worse by Jack's
recent passing. Poor Jack had slipped away just days before the
ship docked, unable to hold on until Tom's return.

Mary remembered the phone call she made to the ship;
the anxious surprise in Tom's voice when he was summoned to
the bridge to receive her call.

Mum. What is it?

*I'm sorry, Tom, to call you like this. I'm sorry for what I
have to tell you . . . But your father died this morning . . . he was
so ill . . . he couldn't manage any longer . . .*

What a thing to have to tell your son over the telephone.
What unspeakable pain not to be able to put your arms around
him, not to be able to hold him when he needed you most. After
the phone call she had rung Debbie to see if she would meet
Tom at the wharf. But Debbie was convinced Tom would see
it the wrong way. She said he'd take it as a signal that she was
there for him.

As he came ashore, Mary watched him searching the crowd.
Just in case. Holding onto the possibility that Debbie might
surface from the sea of waiting faces. He had staggered off the
boat like a drunk. It wasn't just the ground that was unsteady
for him; his life was adrift.

Initially, Mary had thought it was the loss of his wife and
father that shut Tom down, but as time went on she realised it

was more than that. Tom's retreat into himself had also been due to the challenges of re-entering normal life after more than a year of Antarctic simplicity. The explosion of return superimposed on loss and grief had almost destroyed him. Somehow, he had continued to carry out the actions of life, but he had disengaged from it, as if it were all happening to someone else. For years now, he'd been moving around the periphery of things, always measuring the edges of life, rather than its volume. But now, in one blow, this new woman had flattened his fences.

'Tell me about her,' Mary said.

'Her name's Emma.' His mouth softened when he said the girl's name, and seeing him this way made her tingle with pleasure. 'And she's strong, Mum.'

Strength was good. 'What else?'

'She's confident. Not at all pretentious.'

'I like her already. She sounds lovely.'

He looked at her nervously. 'I wasn't sure whether to tell you, but I'm kind of hoping I might go south with her. To work with penguins.'

The thought of Tom going south again alarmed her. Did he think he'd be immune from hurt this time? But his eyes were bright and excited. What else could she do but encourage him?

As he told her more about Emma, Mary realised how her own death would release him. He wouldn't have to stay in Hobart waiting for her to call. That's what he'd been doing these past years, and it had taken her all this time to work it out. It was devastating to be suddenly aware of the limitations her existence had placed on her son.

She watched him in the kitchen, filling the kettle and lighting the stove. There were more questions she wanted to ask. But she held back for several minutes, observing him while he gazed out the window, the trace of a smile playing on his lips.

'When does Emma go south again?' she asked eventually.

'In four months.'

'Is that long enough?'

'Long enough for what?'

'To know if she's right for you.'

'I already know.'

'But does she?'

He shrugged, a frown darkening his face. 'She's whirling. She's only been back a few weeks.'

Mary smiled. 'You're whirling too.'

'Am I?'

'I'm happy for you.'

He sat down, hesitating, clearly fighting with himself over something he wanted to say. 'Do you think it's a good idea?' he managed finally. 'To go south?'

Their eyes connected across space, and Mary saw hope in his face. Freedom would come after her death. And perhaps, with this woman, he would have the courage to grasp that freedom. She nodded. 'I'm pleased for you. I want you to be happy.'

'I think I'm safe this time, Mum,' he said.

But she knew he was wrong. Nobody was ever safe.

The early years in Hobart with Jack just after she'd fallen pregnant with Jan had been difficult times. She and Jack were unhappy, both missing Bruny, both struggling to adjust to their new urban life. While Jack exhausted himself working long days in the factory, she was confined by morning sickness. When apple season came and the house filled with the aroma of stewing fruit again, the rich smells made her ill. Nauseous and miserable, her life seemed unbearably heavy.

Despite Mary's gloominess, her mother was delighted to have the young couple in the house. To celebrate their marriage and the pregnancy, her mother wanted to buy material to make new bed sheets for them. It seemed an indulgence to Mary, but her mother insisted, so they went to the haberdashery store to select the fabric. Mary was still in the early stages of pregnancy and had not begun to show, so an outing was socially acceptable.

They must have spent twenty minutes in the shop while her mother pondered over fabric, rubbing samples between her fingers to make sure the quality was right. In the musty store, Mary's morning sickness had surged, and she went outside into the wet Hobart morning to get some air.

Sheltered beneath the shop awning, she stared down the street at the grey bodies hurrying up the pavement with heads bowed to dodge the raindrops. Some were shielded by umbrellas, while others stooped beneath dark coats or held newspapers over their heads. Far down the street, she noticed a man coming towards her. He was tall and slim, walking fast. She watched his progress up the footpath until he lifted a hand to brush wet hair from his face and the gesture turned her heart to stone. It was Adam. She knew his walk, even though she hadn't seen him for years. And then he saw her too.

Just then her mother swept out of the shop, hooked elbows with her and swung her up the street in the other direction. Her mother moved with such speed that Mary wondered if she had seen Adam walking up the hill. After all those years of careful planning, her parents wouldn't want to risk her seeing him again, despite the fact she was now safely married.

When they arrived back at the house, she was feeling weak. The rapid march uphill in the cold air had taxed her. Her mother sat her in a chair by the fire, gave her a cup of tea and insisted she take a nap. Mary complied so she wouldn't arouse her mother's suspicion, but she lay on the bed in a flutter, wondering how she could escape to find Adam.

After what she deemed to be an acceptable amount of time for a rest, Mary emerged from her room. She forced herself to remain calm, ironing clothes, drinking tea and chatting with her mother for more than an hour. By then, the rain had stopped and the day had subsided to a dull grey. Mary finally persuaded her mother that she was well enough to go for a walk. Moving slowly and striving to suppress the panic in her chest, she collected her coat, hat and scarf and stepped out into the chill afternoon.

Just as she'd known he'd be, Adam was in the park, sitting on a bench, wet and bedraggled. He looked up as she walked to meet him, his eyes haunted and sad, and her throat clenched. After all these years, she still connected with him. She remembered the shape of his jaw and the line of his cheek, but his face was harder and somehow less hopeful than the boy she'd first met. Tiny broken veins tracked across his reddened cheeks, and his posture sagged with a heaviness that had not been there before.

Automatically, they headed to the top corner of the park, erasing the years in twenty seconds. They walked side by side, and between them there yawned an ocean of unshared life. Mary longed to reach for his hand, but she restrained herself. She had a ring on her finger now and a baby growing inside her. Time had altered her circumstances and there was no going back.

At the top of the park they sat down together. Mary was tense and straight-backed. She couldn't speak. And Adam was bent forward, defeated. Silence stretched over the short distance and the long years between them. When he spoke at last, his voice was dense with emotion.

'It's been a long time, Mary,' he said. 'What is it? Five years?'

'Yes. Something like that.' Nervous butterflies quivered in her throat.

'I've been here looking for you every year. Every apple season, I kept hoping I'd find you.'

'You're still picking fruit?'

'Yes, of course. It's my life. I'm still on the road.'

She looked at him, unsure, waiting to see what he would say next.

'We were going to settle down together, remember? We were going to have a cottage. Our own orchard. Our own apple farm. What happened to that?'

She didn't know what to say.

'They're lost dreams, Mary. I've had trouble coming to terms with that. Where have you been?'

'My parents sent me to Bruny Island. To my uncle's farm. They wanted me away from here. They knew I loved you.'

His shoulders slumped further. 'I wasn't good enough. I know that. Your father laughed at me when I told him I was a fruit picker. I said I'd look after you, but he wouldn't hear me out. It was over in five minutes. We could have made it work, you and I. We still can.'

'I'm sorry about my father. He's a hard man with strong opinions. I'm sorry he hurt you.' Without thinking, Mary reached for his knee, feeling the warmth of him through his damp trousers, surprised at the way her body ignited when she touched him.

His face softened, his eyes deepening as he looked at her. 'Do you remember the times we shared in this park?' he said. 'Our hopes? Our plans for the future?'

Unexpected tears tripped in her eyes. He took her hands in his and desire rushed through her. She was still the girl who loved him, the girl who had taken her first kiss from his lips.

He was bent over her hands, rubbing her fingers. Then he became very still. He'd seen the ring. Her wedding ring. His breathing became ragged and he held her hands tight so she couldn't pull away.

'How late am I?' he asked, his voice tight and hoarse.

'I've been married for a year.'

He couldn't look at her then and she knew he was ashamed of his own tears. 'I wrote letters to you,' he said. 'Here they are. I went back to my lodgings to fetch them for you.' From inside his jacket he pulled a small bundle wrapped in brown paper and tied with string. 'Take them. They're yours. Maybe you'll read them sometime.'

He handed her the parcel and she slipped it into her coat pocket. Then he stood up to go, his face wretched. Tortured, she reached for his hand, and he sat down again, folding her hands into his. Even after all these years he still owned her, still knew her, and his touch still made her flush with excitement.

Eager now, reading something in her eyes, he moved close, bending to kiss her. She drew back, trying to protest, thinking of Jack. But he pulled her to him, all the heat of his body pressed against her. And he kissed her till she was ragged and lost. Beneath his lips, she came alive. Jack had never stirred her in this way. He hadn't learned her body the way Adam had learned it in the few days they had known each other.

For a moment, she almost forgot. But as Adam paused to look at her, his face alive with want, she wrenched away. She straightened her coat and stood up, digging for strength. 'Adam, I'm having a baby.'

He paled and his face twisted, and then he extended his hand to her, desperation etched in his features. 'Come with me,' he said urgently. 'We can make this happen.'

But she backed away. 'I still care for you,' she said. 'I can't deny it. But I'm no longer the girl you knew. I love you, but we can't have what we want. I'm married to another man. To Jack.' She had to give him a name. 'I wish I could roll back the clock. But I can't. I'm married and I'm having a baby. That's the way it is. I can't be your wife.'

She walked away and left him there. She was agonised. Was she in love with him? Or was she in love with past dreams and a fanciful notion of what might have been? And what did she really know of him from those ten days in the park? Would he have stood by her when she bore the child of another man? Or would she have been left with nothing? No, she couldn't go with him. It was all too uncertain.

In the kitchen, she threw the bundle of letters into the fire. What was there to be gained from reading them? She was already shredded by remorse; she didn't need more anguish. All that was left was to focus on Jack. She must work with dutiful humility to improve their marriage. Since they'd been in Hobart, she'd let things stagnate. Immersed in morning sickness and despondence, she'd allowed their love to subside. Now she must revitalise it. Her fervour was guilt-driven. She had kissed another man. For a wild moment, she had even considered leaving. But she had chosen Jack and she had to make it work.

First, they must find a rental home—there was no chance of happiness in her parents' house. And then she had to learn to live with her guilt and deceit. She could tell no-one of her encounter with Adam.

She and Jack laboured on in Hobart until the lighthouse job came up at Cape Bruny. It was a beacon of hope. The island represented her bond with Jack. They needed to go back there to find each other again. And paradoxically, it was in that place of hope that she discovered the unreliability of hope.

At the light station, she'd made the mistake of allowing fantasies to pervade her marriage. When Jack had withdrawn, she sustained herself with daydreams of Adam. She indulged in idealised visions of a picker's life—the excitement of being on the road, going places, meeting people. She imagined the peaceful orchard cottage they would share. In her loneliness, she let Adam slip between her and Jack, causing damage, deep and wide. She clung to him long after she ought to have let him go. And there had been a cost. In the end, it had rendered her vulnerable.

And now here she sat, listening to her son Tom, and he was telling her that this time he was safe in love. What could she say to warn him? It had taken her years to understand that love was not safety. To comprehend the impact of her secret passion for Adam. Yes, she might have had a different life with Adam, possibly a relationship with more intensity and less distance. But then again, perhaps not. Love was more than desire. And Adam had not navigated life's storms with her as Jack had. He hadn't been with her in the wretched fog of parental tiredness.

He hadn't weathered the tedium of ordinary days, financial pressures, the anxiety of decisions, the concerns about their children's future. That was the sum of a marriage—tenacity, the strength to bear the mundane, and the accumulation of shared history.

20

I'm at home stirring up a bolognese sauce when the phone rings. When I hear Emma's voice my pulse lurches and I fumble the spoon.

'Two things,' she says. 'First, can you take Friday off? I want to take you rock climbing at Freycinet.'

I've already taken today off to visit Mum, but perhaps if I put in a couple of big days at work, I'll be able to catch up.

'Second thing,' Emma continues. 'I spoke to my boss about taking you south, and he wants to know if you can come for an interview at three o'clock tomorrow.'

More time off. Just as well Bill appreciates me. 'Where should I meet you?' I ask.

'Just go to the front desk and have them call me.'

She's about to hang up.

'Emma.' I try to hold her on the phone. I want to hang onto the sound of her voice.

'What?'

'I'm looking forward to seeing you.'

Her laugh is like music. 'You'll just have to wait.'

My dieso mate, Bazza, says Emma's boss Fredricksen is a typical boffin—aloof, a bit elitist and always dreaming up crazy, impractical ideas. He never lets his hair down or mixes it with the tradies.

We're having a cup of coffee in the workshop before the interview. I point out that not all boffins are like that, but Bazza won't back down. Emma's boss is one of the old school, he says; hasn't been south for years and does all his research from behind a desk. Bazza reckons he's never seen such a disorganised office. From the mess of the place it's a wonder he can get anything done. It's a regular fire trap. There must be data from twenty years hidden away somewhere in there. Years of field observations piling up. And for what? Bazza says he's heard that hardly any of it gets written up. The science is just about us having a presence in Antarctica. *Us* meaning *Australia*. That's why we tradies are so important, according to Bazza. Without us, the scientists couldn't survive down there. They depend on us.

I interrupt Bazza's rant to tell him I'm having an interview with Fredricksen at three o'clock; I try to gauge the look on his face. He says he wouldn't work for Fredricksen in a hundred years. If Fredricksen's office caught fire, he wouldn't piss on it to put it out.

'I'd be working with Emma,' I say, and watch Bazza's eyebrows rise.

'She's an interesting one,' he says, shaking his head. 'Roughs it like the blokes when she's south, I've heard. And you'll have to hit it off with Fredricksen if you want to go south. It doesn't matter how good you are at your job, if Fredricksen doesn't like you, he won't employ you.'

'Got any tips?' I ask.

But Bazza shakes his head. 'The man's a mystery to me. All I can suggest is to be non-threatening.'

I remind him that I'm the least threatening person I know, and he agrees. 'Whatever you do, don't ogle Emma while Fredricksen's in the room,' Bazza says. 'She's a tomboy, but I reckon half the antdiv fancies her. She's got a body like a rocket.

Built for a purpose. And there's no place for prissy girls down there anyway. They only get into trouble.'

I say I hadn't noticed Emma's body, at the same time feeling my knees and stomach melt. I hope I can hold it together and not reveal anything to Fredricksen.

Bazza shakes my hand and wishes me luck. 'When I told you to get yourself back down south, I didn't reckon you'd be up to it this season,' he says. 'But you're looking stronger. Shame you won't be going down as a dieso. We need good staff like you.'

'I'll let you know how I go,' I say. 'Keep a job free for me just in case.'

Bazza lets me into the main building with his swipe card and I walk down the long corridor, tucking all the loose pieces of myself back inside. I need to be pleasant, a bit dull, non-threatening, as Bazza said, but capable. This is something I should do well.

The receptionists examine me surreptitiously while they call Emma to advise her I've arrived. Soon after, Emma appears from a corridor. Her face is happy and enthusiastic, but the ladies are still watching us closely, so I keep my expression blank.

'Tom,' Emma says. 'Good to see you.' Her eyes are bright in her brown face and the warmth of her smile almost buckles my knees. She shakes my hand professionally and winks. 'Come this way. I'll show you the lab.'

I nod at the curious faces of the front-desk ladies and follow her up a gangway to the next building.

The antdiv is like a rabbit warren. I used to know my way around here, but I've cancelled it out of my mental directory. In the past nine years I've only visited Bazza out in the workshop or followed him down to the cafeteria, apart from going to Emma's seminar, of course.

Emma leads me up a set of stairs and then along a corridor past a string of offices. She turns to smile at me but says nothing and I wonder if I'm imagining the flash of daring in her eyes.

'This is the lab,' she says, opening a door. 'You'll have to excuse the mess. I'm still unpacking.'

She's right. The lab is in disarray. Boxes, equipment and papers are scattered across tables and benches. I don't know how she can work in here.

'Actually, do you mind if I just quickly finish an email?' She laughs airily. 'I ought to be cleaning up, but I can't stop emailing south. A friend of mine is wintering at Mawson and I keep wondering what she's up to.' She glances almost wistfully at the computer on the desk.

I perch on a stool and try not to watch the flurry of her fingers across the keyboard. There's a desperate urgency to her typing and it reflects the strength of her desire to be somewhere else. I've forgotten how it is when you return—feeling cut off from Antarctic happenings and dreaming of station life as if events taking place down south are somehow more real than anything going on at home.

Emma speaks to me while she's typing. 'My friend has hooked up with one of the physicists down south . . . *against* my advice. I told her she should try to retain some emotional independence, but she says it all just happened after a few too many drinks at the Saturday night party. She says she needs someone . . . I don't think her boyfriend back here is going to be very happy . . . not that anyone will tell him . . . poor bugger.'

Finally she swivels on her seat and looks at me. 'Are you ready?' she says. 'Fredricksen will be waiting.'

My mouth goes dry at the mention of Fredricksen's name and my palms begin to sweat. 'I don't know. It's a long time since I've had an interview.'

Emma smiles. 'You'll be fine.' She grabs my hand and places it against her cheek. It's a gentle gesture, but I'm shaken by it. I'm so unaccustomed to this rush of emotions. Small things seem capable of breaking me apart.

Emma stands and kisses me, rattling me further, and then she takes me through the maze of corridors to Fredricksen's office. He's sitting behind his desk with a mountain of paper around him, just like Bazza said, and his fingers resting on a keyboard. When Emma brings me in, he pushes back from his desk and stands up to shake my hand. He's bearded, like most of the older Antarctic fraternity and his eyes are assessing. He waves me to a seat and motions to Emma to leave us. I watch her go, suppressing a shaky desire to call her back. But I can't ask her to sit here and hold my hand through this. I have to do it alone.

Fredricksen leans back in his seat and asks about my previous stint south. He asks who was on my expedition, who I worked with in the field, what sort of tasks I was doing on station. I answer as best I can. He asks what sort of a winter we had, whether anyone lost the plot, whether I'd consider wintering again. I tell him that overwintering was hard and that I'd only consider a summer job in future. He nods knowingly. Fortunately, he has sufficient tact not to ask me why I haven't been back since my first trip.

He asks me what I know about Adelie penguins, whether I'm competent at sexing them and tagging them, how I feel about the ethics of water offloading, and what skills I have in electronics. These questions are easy for me to deal with and I'm honest with him. I tell him what I do and don't know, and that I'm willing to learn. I tell him birds are one of my passions, and that I can work all day among them without feeling tired. I explain that I'm not keen on water offloading, but if it's part of the job then I'll find a way to cope. He asks me how I'd deal with the isolation this time, given that I found overwintering tough, and I tell him that I grew up at a lighthouse and that isolation is not a problem. Home relationships, I explain, were the problem last time. He nods, understanding. I'm sure he has also had his woes.

Finally, he asks about Emma, and whether I think I can get along with her. I admit I don't know her well, but that I'm willing to work with all types of people. I tell him that I've helped many biologists in the field and that my tactic is to work around issues to make sure the job gets done.

Fredricksen regards me for some time before speaking again. 'Emma needs someone who's sensitive to her need for control,' he says, pulling on his beard. 'If you can work out a way around that, the two of you will achieve a lot. She's a nice girl, but strong. A head-on approach will not work with her.'

I tell him there are ways to suggest things without seeming to take control.

He stands up and shakes my hand. 'I'll let you know in a few weeks,' he says. 'Protocol demands I interview more than one applicant. I think you'll do, but I can't give you the nod yet. Understand?'

I thank him and make sure he has my phone number. Then I wander along the corridors again, trying to find Emma's lab. She said she wanted to know how my interview went, so the least I can do is report in before I go back to work.

Somehow I find the lab again. The door is open and I'm about to walk in when I notice Emma at the back of the lab with a short, burly-looking man. She's sitting on a stool with her head bent down and he has his hand on her shoulder and is standing close. There's something about their interaction that makes me pause. This might not be the right time for me to barge in.

Before they see me, I back out and walk away down the corridor, breathing hard. What was happening in there? Who was that man? Was I imagining the air of intimacy between them? I try to compose myself again. It may be nothing. I shouldn't get ahead of myself. I should trust Emma. She has invited me to go away with her for the weekend, so she must want to be with me. But I know what this place is like—liaisons around every corner, people falling into each other, almost by accident. And the returnees are the worst, immersed as they are in the chaos of their re-entry.

I hover in the corridor pretending to look at maps while I decide what to do. I could go back to the garage and get some work done, but I want to wait and say goodbye to Emma. Looking back towards her lab, I see the man now leaning against the doorframe. Whoever it is, he's still talking to her. I dive into the men's restroom and wait inside a cubicle. Surely he'll leave soon. Doesn't he have work to do?

Eventually I decide that hiding in the toilets is ridiculous. I can't work with Emma if it's going to be like this. I slip out into the corridor, somehow find my way back through the maze and then sweep quickly past the reception area and out the front door.

To my surprise, Emma is waiting beside the Subaru. She's patting Jess's nose through the partly opened window. 'Why didn't you come back to the lab?' she asks.

'I had trouble finding it.'

'How did it go?'

'Okay, I think.'

'Good.' Emma's smile is sunshine. 'What are you going to do now?' she asks.

'I think I'll go home.'

'Can I come?'

'I don't know. Is that a good idea?'

'I think it's an excellent idea. Just wait while I grab my bag. You can drop me back here tomorrow on your way to work.'

When Emma steps into my house, I feel the air move. It stirs like a faint breath through the room, and I wonder if I have sighed aloud. It seems so normal to be bringing her home.

'This is great,' she says, taking in the comfortable spread of couches and cushions and the dappled light falling through the windows.

I must admit this is a wonderful house. Being located on an east-facing hill, it loses the light early, but makes up for this with its long view across the channel. Over the years I've made it very homely inside. Given that I haven't had to share it with anyone except Jess, I've developed it to my taste. I suppose most men don't get that opportunity.

I fill the kettle and light the stove. Emma wanders through the lounge room and dumps her bag in my bedroom. I wait in the kitchen while Jess trots along behind her, having faithlessly discarded me for the attentions of her new friend.

'How long have you lived here?' Emma asks. She rolls up her sleeves as she enters the kitchen.

'About eight years.'

'I like it. Have you done much to the house?'

'A few renovations here and there. A new bathroom. Polished the floors. Put in the wood heater.'

'I wish I was practical,' she says.

'You have other skills.'

'Like catching penguins? And water offloading?' She walks to the front windows and gazes out over the channel. 'I'd love to have my own place,' she says. 'So I could fill it up with my own things.' She shrugs. 'But it isn't worth it. I'm never anywhere for long enough. I don't even have my own car anymore—I have to borrow from friends.'

'I could help you find a cheap one,' I suggest.

'I don't really need one,' she says. 'What would I do with it when I'm away?'

I pour two cups of tea and set them on the table in the lounge. Emma turns from the window and looks at me. I feel stupid, standing there looking at her so expectantly, my hands plunged in my pockets. I'm so desperate for things to go well with her, and now I can't think of anything to say.

Some of the spark seems to have gone from her as she comes across the room to join me. She throws herself down on one of the couches, legs carelessly apart, head tipped back. It's not an invitation, but seeing the taut skin of her throat makes me swallow. I have no idea how to shift the mood of the afternoon where I want it to go.

She sits up and looks at me directly, a hint of aggression in her eyes. 'What do you think about women in Antarctica?' she asks.

This is not quite the conversation I had in mind. Perhaps this is my interview with Emma, now that I've passed the test with Fredricksen. To delay answering, I pick up my tea and take a sip.

'Come on,' she says. 'Which camp are you in? Do you think women balance the Antarctic community? Or do you think they cause trouble?'

I set my cup down carefully.

'You're against it, aren't you?' Emma says.

'No, I'm not against it.' I choose my words cautiously. Emma's face tells me it'd be easy to offend. 'But I do think people should be careful about how they behave down there.'

'You're referring to some of the flirting that goes on,' Emma says.

'Flirting, yes,' I say. But I'm really thinking of women dancing provocatively at parties. Women drinking too much and leaning up against men without thinking how it affects them. Such a lack of awareness. Women playing more than one man at a time. Not all women, but enough to destabilise things. Enough to breed resentment. Feelings like that are magnified in a small community.

'Women should be allowed to have a good time down there without being crucified for it,' Emma is saying. 'What's wrong with a bit of flirting? Men flirt too. There's nothing abnormal about it—just go to a bar or a club in Hobart sometime.'

'Antarctica isn't Hobart,' I point out.

Emma runs a hand through her hair, considering. 'It's tricky, isn't it? Women want to go to Antarctica. They want to share the so-called last frontier, and it *is* more normal to have them down there. But there's all this resistance in the male ranks. If you flirt or get involved with someone, then you're causing trouble, and if you try to fit in by acting like one of the boys, that's wrong too and some of the guys look down on you. It's this us and them thing. And there's the tradies versus the boffins too. I'm not sure how to resolve it.' She looks at me thoughtfully. 'I suppose it's partly to do with this melding of two separate worlds. I mean, how many women do you have to deal with in your workplace?'

'None. They drop cars off for me to service and then pick them up again. The front desk deals with it.'

'That's just it. Tradies aren't used to working with women, whereas most of the women that go south are scientists who come from a mixed workplace. At university they're used to being respected for what they know. But down in Antarctica it's all reversed. The tradies rule because they run the station. No wonder it's difficult.'

In my mind, I hear Bazza carping on about how high and mighty some of the young female scientists are, and how they expect you to drop everything to cater to their work demands. But Bazza's not as old-fashioned as you might think. He says it's not about whether women should be there or not, but how they behave while they're down there. And how the men behave too. He says it's about people working out how to get on together, and about leaving some of their entrenched attitudes at home, or at least being able to keep a lid on it when things rile them.

'I try to avoid it all by staying out in the field,' Emma says.

I think of the man in her lab today and I wonder if she's as innocent and detached as she makes out. I want to believe her, but I know how it is down there.

Emma picks up her tea. 'I think all the problems boil down to a few bitter old men who don't want to share Antarctica with women,' she says. 'They want to keep it as a boys' club like it was in the past. They don't want to accept change. I'm sure they're the ones who insist on hanging porn all over the place.'

'All over the place?' I only remember a few pinups in the workshop, and they were pretty tame. It's the same in the garage where I work in Sandy Bay. Some of the men like having a few posters up. It's almost cultural for them. After a while you don't even notice.

'Normal women don't look like that,' Emma says with disdain.

'Nobody looks at those posters,' I say.

'I do,' she says. 'And I don't want to.'

I'd like to ask her how often she goes into the workshop when she's south. When I was down there we rarely had visitors. Especially not women. 'I think it helps some of the guys cope,' I say.

'With what?'

'Abstinence.'

'You shouldn't defend them. Can't they just work it off in the gym?'

'They do.' I remember the guys laughing about how strong they were from all the hours in the weights room. 'But it can still be difficult for some of them.'

Emma's laugh is hard. 'Because they're missing out? How pathetic. Women don't have that problem.'

How can I explain to her how it is to be in the body of a man? We're biologically different. Women don't seem to understand that.

'How about you,' Emma asks. 'How did you cope?'

I flush and mumble something inane. I don't want to tell Emma about Sarah helping me to survive the end of my marriage. 'It's a long time for people to be away from their partners,' I say.

'Then people with partners shouldn't go south.' Emma grins suddenly. 'That'd limit the application field, wouldn't it? . . . You know, the Brits only send down people who aren't married.' She laughs again. 'I wonder how many of them come back and get married to someone they've met down there? But sending married couples doesn't work either. They've tried that. Too much friction if they blow apart and the girl takes up with someone else. I've seen it happen.'

'It isn't safe for relationships,' I say, thinking of Debbie.

'No. And nobody should expect it to be safe. The problem is that people don't understand the risks.'

She's right, of course. You don't understand until it's too late. And then that which is broken can't be mended.

I stare out the window, wondering how things would be now if I'd been wiser, if I had stood up to Debbie and refused to go south. We'd have paid off most of the mortgage in a few years anyway, if we'd worked hard. We might even have two or three kids by now. A swing set in the backyard.

'I'm sorry.' Emma's voice draws me back into the room. 'That wasn't very sensitive of me.'

'It's okay,' I say, managing a smile. 'It's been a long time. I ought to be over it.'

She goes to the bathroom while I step outside. The porch is already in shadow and the air is cool. I sit on an old wooden chair and watch a rosella feeding on the bird tray. I watch it pick up a seed and crack it deftly with its beak, tucking the kernel into its mouth with its knobby grey tongue and then discarding the husk. Jess comes out and sits beside me. The birds are so accustomed to us they don't fly away. I watch the light over the water on the channel. When Emma comes out, I'm settled and calm. She touches my face with her hands and runs her fingertips over my lips. I am so easily undone by her.

'Come on,' she says, taking my hand.

Inside, she kisses me and releases my passion all over again. When her strong brown hands are on me and when I can feel the boldness of her curves, she is mine and I am hers.

21

In the pale light before dawn on Friday morning, I guiltily desert Jess, leaving her at home with a large bowl of dog food and an enormous placatory bone. Then I collect Emma and we hump piles of gear into my car: tent, sleeping bag, sleeping mats, an esky full of food, and milk-crates containing gas bottles, plates and pots. Emma tosses in an old rucksack weighed down with climbing equipment, as well as a rope and two harnesses. With her things added to mine we could be going for six weeks, not just overnight.

We drive north out of Hobart. At the wheel I am fizzing with excitement. Emma sits beside me, my hand warm on her knee. The sunlight is spreading across a watery blue sky. Nothing could be better.

The campground at Freycinet National Park nestles beneath the jutting rocky peaks of the Hazards. It's dotted with contorted old banksias, their bark as thick and wrinkled as an old man's skin, and it's rimmed by an arc of golden sand and softly lapping waves that hiss gently on the shore. As Emma and I step out of the car blue skies and cool air wrap around us. Honeyeaters dart between banksia flowers, twittering.

We're alone in the campground, so we can pitch our tent wherever we like. It all looks fine to me, but Emma fusses over flat ground and aspect until she settles finally on a spot beneath an ancient, gnarly banksia. We make a game of putting up the tent, flicking each other with tent poles and having mock fencing duels with the pegs. It's been a long time since I played like this with another person.

After organising our camp, we make tea over a small gas stove and have something to eat. Then Emma hauls out her climbing pack and lays her gear on a tarp. She tosses me a pair of funny little rubber shoes and tells me to try them on. They're as tiny as women's ballet slippers, but somehow I manage to cram my feet into them and stand up. Emma laughs, telling me to stand straight and to stop looking so awkward. She says I'll see how useful these shoes are when we're climbing; for now, it's a relief to change back into my runners. Next she pulls out a harness she has borrowed from a housemate, and I adjust the leg loops—my thighs are clearly not as bulky as those of the owner.

Once she has sorted out her gear, she packs everything away again and we drive through the coastal bush, winding onto a gravel road that takes us to a carpark above a small cove with golden sand. We're some distance above the beach, and I can see two people strolling along the water's edge. At each end of the beach are mounds of rocks painted red with lichen. The air is still and the steady rushing sound of the waves rises up to mingle with the smell of dew on the damp bushes.

Emma leads me along a tiny path that branches off the main beach trail, winding through prickly scrub and over rock slabs until we arrive at the base of a smooth granite dome. The view from here is stunning. Above and below us and stretching around the headland are sheets and domes of granite. The sea laps energetically at the lower rocks, and to the north I can see the couple still walking on the beach.

We unpack and wriggle into our harnesses. Emma clips an armoury of metal equipment around her waist and then tugs on her climbing shoes. As she moves, the belt makes a pleasant clinking sound. She has a furrowed look of concentration on her face as she goes over everything again, making sure she has all she needs. She seems capable and confident, calm and in control. It's both reassuring and sexy.

'Okay,' she says. 'Let's check you out.'

She tests the fastenings on my harness. Then she starts teaching me how to tie a figure-eight knot, but I stop her, showing her I already know this, at least. When I went south, we had to learn some basic climbing knots, how to rope up for glacier travel and how to rig a pulley. I use knots for work too, tying loads, securing tarps. Still, Emma seems surprised. 'I thought you'd have forgotten all this,' she says.

'I'm good with knots, and I've worn a harness before, but I'm not comfortable with heights. I've never been climbing.'

She grins. 'You'll be all right.'

Concentrating, she watches me tie in to my harness, and then she hooks me up to a big camming device she has placed in a crack near our feet. It expands to wedge itself tightly in the crack.

'I'm not particularly heavy,' she says. 'And even without this you should be able to hold my weight if I fall. But I prefer to be safe and make sure we have backup.'

I like backup too, especially when I'm off the ground. Emma ties herself into the free end of the rope then shows me how to thread the rope through the belay device attached to my harness, and how to feed out length as she climbs. If she falls, the belay device will lock the rope so I can halt her descent. There's a trade-off between having the rope too tight or too loose. She wants enough slack so that I'm not pulling on her as she ascends, but not so much that she'll fall a long way if she comes off the rock face.

I have to be ready, she says, and I have to watch her all the time. She's not planning to fall off, but it's important that I'm prepared if she does. Then she runs through climbing communication, all of which sounds funny to me, but she says that after a couple of times it will become automatic; climbing is a dangerous sport and it requires a thorough and pedantic approach. Watching Emma's serious face I have to resist the urge to kiss her.

Now we are ready to begin and I have so many things to think about I barely notice the view. I start to get nervous. The rope is in my left hand, running through the belay device to my right hand, which is ready to tighten the rope at any time. Emma gives me a final check over. My palms are sweating.

'Okay,' she says. 'Climbing.'

I feed out some rope and watch her inspecting the rock for finger- and toeholds. She reaches up to a tiny ridge, sticks her toe in a little crack, makes a few swift moves and is already a couple of metres above my head. How did that happen so easily? Emma pokes a camming device into a crack above her and tugs on it firmly once it's in place. She snaps a clipdraw into it and pulls on the rope. 'Rope,' she puffs. In my anxiety, I am holding on too tightly. Quickly I feed out some slack and she clips the rope through the hanging carabiner.

'Good,' she says, wedging her hand in the crack next to the camming device. She pauses to inspect the rock above and plan her next moves. 'What you have to remember on granite,' she says, 'is that the footholds may not be obvious. It'll seem scary at first, but if you put your weight on your foot, you can use friction to help you step up. This climb is not too steep, so take your time and you'll work it out.'

Right now, this seems overwhelming to me, so I focus on watching her instead. Shifting a little on her foothold, she reaches up, brings up her feet, and in no time she is ten metres above me, stopping to look for the next suitable crack or crevice to insert another piece of equipment for protection. It looks amazingly easy, and my heart swells with the excitement of watching her. She's good at this—carefully placing her feet on the rock and cleverly using her body to gain elevation. She moves smoothly and expertly. Even so, my hands are slick with sweat and my feet are damp in my runners.

Eventually, she climbs out of sight. Somehow it's easier not watching; instead, I listen for her directions and pay out rope as she needs it. The clinking sound from above tells me when she is moving again.

Glancing below, I see the sea swelling and frothing over the red rocks. Small puffy clouds have appeared on the eastern horizon and out to sea a bulk carrier is moving slowly north. Standing on this dome of granite in the warm sun, I can smell the rock; it's a dry hard smell, quite distinct from that of dirt. It mingles with the sweat of my fear, reminding me that I am yet to climb.

Soon Emma calls that she's safe, and I take myself off belay then sit down to jam my feet into the tight little shoes. I lace them firmly and tie my runners to a loop on the back of my harness. Emma is pulling in the rope from above; soon it will be tight and then I will have to climb. I check my harness and knots for the tenth time. It's a long way down if I fall. The rope tugs on my harness.

'That's me,' I say.

'Is that you?' Emma yells. 'I can't hear you.'

'Yes.' I try to muster a bigger voice. 'That's me.'

There's a pause before Emma's voice floats down again. 'On belay.'

So this is it. My heart is in my mouth. 'Okay. Climbing.'

Emma tugs reassuringly on the rope, but the rock wall above me seems blank, with nothing significant to hold on to. A long time seems to pass and I haven't made a move. My feet are already killing me in the tight shoes.

'Are you all right?' Emma calls down.

'I'm not sure how to start,' I say, wiping my arm across my forehead to dislodge the sweat.

'Okay,' she says. 'Look up a bit and you'll see a little crack. Can you get your fingers into that?'

I grope around to find the crack and push my fingers in, scrabbling for something to grasp.

'Slide your fingers along. There's an edge in there you can hook onto.'

A couple of seconds later, I've found it.

'Now, look down and across to your right a bit. There's a ledge you can put your foot on sideways. Place your other hand flat against the rock, push up on your right foot and pull with your hand in the crack. That'll get you off the ground and you can look for something else.'

How can she remember all these nuances of the rock? I try to follow her instructions, psyching up with shaking legs, and then I take the first move off the ground. I feel air all around me. I grapple around for another handhold and find one, a reassuring lump near a crack.

'Did you find that jug?' Emma calls.

'What's a jug?'

'A big handhold. Did you find it?'

'I think I'm hanging on to it.'

'Good.'

As I move slowly up the rock face, I find several solid locations to place my feet and there are plenty of cracks and edges to cling onto. I'm breathing like a windstorm, huffing with each breath. I try not to look down.

'Make sure you unclip the rope from the clipdraws as you go and pull out all the gear,' Emma reminds me. 'I don't want to have to climb back down to retrieve anything.'

Unclipping and pulling out the equipment is harder than it sounds. On trembling legs, I have to maintain my balance, hold on to rock with my left hand and try to wangle the rope out of the carabiner with my finger and thumb. Then I have to work out how to remove the gear—a camming device or wire with a blocky sinker on the end of it—and hook it into a loop on my harness. After removing the first piece, I feel exhausted.

'How are you going?' Emma calls.

'I think I'm okay,' I say, hoping I sound more confident than I feel.

'I've got you.' Emma pulls up on the rope. 'Do you need a rest?'

'No,' I pant. 'I'll keep going.'

Still out of sight, Emma gives me instructions and makes helpful suggestions, and I make slow progress up the rock face. She seems to know when to call out and when to leave me alone to work it out myself. Always, I am conscious of the voluminous feel of air and space around me, of the awful drop below me, the headiness of height, my tenuous grip on the rock face.

Eventually, I drag myself over a ledge and there's Emma, sitting about three metres above me.

'You're nearly there.' Her smile is luminous. 'How is it?'

'Great,' I puff.

'How did your legs go? Did you get sewing-machine leg?'

I remember one point, when I was partway up the rock with my right leg shaking uncontrollably.

She smiles knowingly. 'It happens to us all.'

She points out some good footholds and finger cracks for the last moves, and I finally haul myself up onto the rock beside her.

'Sit down and have a rest,' she says. 'It's beautiful up here.'

I lean back weakly against the rock and look out across the flat expanse of the sea. The beach is a sheltered cove below. I didn't realise we had gained so much height.

'Look at the light on the rocks,' Emma says. 'I just love all those oranges and reds. Impossible really—such bright colours in nature.'

We sit together a long time, eating the snacks we brought and drinking water. I've sweated buckets.

'I generally prefer to keep my feet on the ground,' I say.

'But how do you feel now?' Emma asks.

I notice the unweighted feeling of my body, the spreading looseness of my mind, the pleasant sensation of cool air on hot sweat.

'Euphoric.'

'That's why it's fun,' Emma says. 'You feel more alive. The hardest part is learning to block out the distance below you. You have to delete it somehow, so that when you look down, you don't register how far you could fall.' She catches me shaking my head, and smiles. 'If you see the height, you'll get vertigo,' she says. 'It paralyses you. And then you can't climb. All you'll be able to think about is the risk, and you'll miss out on the buzz. But taking risks is part of climbing. The trick is to take only calculated risks. Then you can look up and out without worrying about falling. It's all about enjoying the ride.'

She reaches out and squeezes my hand. And it seems to me she's not just talking about climbing. She's talking about life.

That night, sated, mellow, every muscle aching, we drink red wine with dinner. The shared experience, the dark around us, the campfire with its glowing embers and gently flickering flames, the wine—it all breeds an atmosphere of intimacy.

Emma admits she's finding it difficult to apply herself to grinding through all the data she collected last season. All she can think of is the news that comes dribbling back from Mawson Station. It's like an addiction, the way she has to dash into the lab each morning and check her emails to find out what happened overnight. After a few seasons she thought she'd be over it, but the yearning is as strong as ever.

'It's the freedom,' I say. 'The distance from normal routine and responsibility.'

Emma shakes her head. 'I have routine down there. Every day is routine. Rugging up for the cold. Checking the weighbridge. Catching birds. Water offloading. Data entry . . .'

'But you're not hemmed in to ordinary life.'

'What do you mean?'

'You don't have to go shopping. Or buy petrol. Or clean the house.'

'I suppose that's part of it,' she says. 'Life isn't very ordinary down there, is it? It does have its own routine, but each day is special and there's something different to look at. Like a leopard seal hauling out on the sea ice and scaring the hell out of the penguins. Or a skua hanging around the hut trying to steal the soap. Or a visitor you didn't expect making a trip out across the sea ice for dinner and a glass of wine.'

I watch Emma's face glowing in reminiscence. Her cheeks have a red sheen from the fire. She stares into the flames and there's a soft smile on her lips. I feel the warmth of the wine in my veins.

'I'm leading you astray,' she says. 'You were normal and stable before you met me, weren't you?'

'What's normal?'

'Were you thinking of Antarctica every day? Every waking moment? Like you are now?'

It's not Antarctica I'm thinking of every waking moment. 'I'm thinking of you,' I say.

Emma laughs. 'You've got things mixed up in your head. Me and Antarctica. You can't separate us. You can't think of one without thinking of the other.' She's gazing into the fire again, her eyes glistening in the liquid light.

'You don't have to go,' I say.

She looks at me blankly.

I say it again. 'You don't have to go south.'

'Everyone wants to go south.'

'If you want to settle back into life here, you could find something else to do . . . You could get a job at a university. Research, or something.'

'Who said I want to settle?'

'You'll have to eventually. You can't keep going south forever.'

'Why not?'

'Eventually you'll want a normal life.'

'I don't want a normal life. And neither do you. That's why you're here with me. Because you want to go south again.'

She doesn't understand. Being with her is about much more than wanting to go south. I like being with her. I like the feeling of her body wrapped around me. Her smell. Doing things with her, even climbing. The possibility of Antarctica is an added bonus.

'I like you even without Antarctica,' I say.

She shakes her head. 'No, you don't. You're wrong. It's Antarctic magic that has drawn you to me. If it wasn't for that, I'd just be another person in the street. And do you really think you could work with me down there?'

'Yes.'

'How do you know?'

I hesitate. 'I'm not very imposing.'

She laughs and winks at me. 'I don't mind a bit of imposition.'

I pretend to ignore the hint. 'I'm talking about the work-place. I'm not a bulldozer. There are ways to work things out.'

Emma stares off over the fire into the dark. 'Yes,' she says. 'There are always ways to work things out.' She seems suddenly abstracted and I wonder what she's thinking. 'We had a successful season,' she says eventually. 'Lots of data.' She pokes the fire with a stick and a log crumbles and flickers into energised flame. 'My assistant was good most of the time—when she wasn't trying to run back to station to see her beau. But this year I've decided I need a man. To help with the heavy work.'

I swallow the tightness in my throat, waiting for her to tell me whether she thinks I'll get the job, but she remains silent, and I force myself to speak. 'I'd really like to go south with you,' I say. 'But only if you think it can work.'

'If what can work?'

'Us . . . and being together in the field.'

Emma lifts her head and laughs. The light of the flames flickers on her throat. 'You want to try it?' she asks. 'Even after your marriage breakup?'

I nod, unable to speak.

'And it'll be all right this time?'

'Yes.'

She studies me carefully. 'How can you know?' she asks.

I shrug and her face softens in the firelight.

'You loved her, didn't you?' she says.

'Yes.'

'So why did you go?'

'To pay off the mortgage.'

Emma stabs at the coals with a stick and stands up. 'We all think we're safe,' she says quietly. 'But all of us are vulnerable.' She tosses the stick into the fire. 'Let's go to bed.'

PART III

Disintegration

22

'The scouts are here!' Leon burst through the door with a blast of fresh air, enthusiasm written all over his face.

Mary was on the couch, folded up in her rug. She was slow and bleary-eyed after a bad night; Jacinta and Alex had stayed over again and she'd relinquished two of her pillows. Unable to prop herself up she'd had no rest, struggling to breathe through fluid-filled lungs. They left early to catch the ferry back to Kettering and it was a relief to collapse on the couch, drifting in and out of weary slumber.

She peered blurrily up at Leon, trying to look responsive. 'Are you ready?' he asked.

She shook her head. 'I don't know what I'm going to say.'

He brushed away her reluctance. 'You'll think of something. And they're looking forward to it. I've told them all about you.'

'I can't do it. I'm too tired.'

He continued as if he hadn't heard her. 'Just think! You could be sitting in a hospital bed accepting cups of tea from grumpy nurses. But instead, here you are, still giving public speeches.'

His attempt at humour failed to move her. 'When you put it that way, a hospital bed sounds blissful.'

'You'll be fine. Now, where's your coat?'

237

While Leon gathered her things, Mary hunched beneath her blanket and gazed miserably out the window. Curtains of rain blotted the cliffs, and the bay was flat and featureless, obscured by drizzle. Wind gusted under the eaves and there were whitecaps riding angrily in to shore. It was silly to think she could go out there. But Leon would not be persuaded. She supposed she should capitalise on this opportunity to convince him to take her part way up East Cloudy Head.

He came back with her scarf. 'I see you've written a letter.'

She jolted. 'What letter?'

'The one on your bedside table. Do you want me to put a stamp on it and post it for you? I'll be going by the post office later today.'

'You'll do no such thing,' she snapped.

His face fell. 'I was only trying to help.'

'It's not help. It's interference,' she said. She knew she was over-reacting but his intrusion was dangerous. If he saw who that letter was addressed to, he might deliver it. And what then? Her whole life could come tumbling down.

Huffily, she scrambled to her feet and shuffled into the bedroom. How could she have left the letter somewhere so obvious? She'd had it out this morning, ready to tear it up and burn it, but she'd put it down while she made her bed and had forgotten it. Now she swung back to see if Leon was watching. No, he was out of sight. She grasped the envelope, her hands shaking. Where to put it? Nobody must find it. Dear God, how many times had she hidden this thing, only to lose it for a day? This time she must remember where she concealed it.

She folded it into her nightgown and tucked it beneath her pillow. It would fall out when she readied herself for bed tonight. She couldn't possibly miss it.

Back in the living room, she sat down again. 'Please, Leon, I'm in no state for public lectures. Can we just drive down and say hello?'

He looked at her, and she knew he wouldn't relent. 'We have a deal,' he said. 'And it won't take long.' He found her coat on a hook behind the door. 'Here, let's put this on. We can't have you freezing out there.'

He helped her up and lifted the coat over her shoulders. Then he bundled her out into the four-wheel drive. From the driver's seat, he paused and examined her, his face puckered with something that hovered between confusion and concern. She drew breath raggedly, fear hammering in her chest. He might be thinking about that letter. He might be wondering at her extreme response. She tried to look grey and strained and exhausted. She wanted him to feel guilty for forcing her into this. And she didn't want him to ask about the letter.

He looked out through the windscreen and she thought he was about to say something. Then he started the vehicle and she knew she was safe. A tacit truce had been declared.

The scouts had set up camp all over Cloudy Corner. It wasn't just an influx, it was an inundation: there were tents everywhere, and wood had been dragged into stacks, ready for the cold night ahead. Adults strutted about like commanders, marshalling hordes of children. Packs were lumped in piles and two big campfires blazed, billies sizzling over the coals. Mary had never seen so many people here, and the noise was startling.

Leon jabbed stubby fingers in his mouth and emitted a piercing whistle. The scouts stood quickly to attention. 'Gather round,' he yelled. 'Mrs Mason's here. She's going to talk to you about the lighthouse.'

The scouts flocked around them, the youngest flinging themselves to the ground and the older ones approaching more slowly and casually, feigning disinterest. Mary thought of Jan and Gary when they were teenagers—trying to appear grown up when they were far from it, struggling to subdue that flagrant enthusiasm of youth. Even so, she was overwhelmed by the proximity of so many energetic young bodies, all those unlined faces staring up at her expectantly.

'I need to sit down,' she said.

A campchair appeared from nowhere and Leon helped her into it. As soon as the weight was off her legs, the shakes took hold. It wasn't nervousness, but excitement—adrenalin competing with all the medication in her body.

Leon waited till the restless movement subsided, and Mary observed his patient demeanour. He wasn't uncomfortable with this group. In fact, he seemed quite confident. He was under-utilised here. He ought to be involved in greater duties than checking toilets and clearing rubbish bins. She wondered why he stayed, deliberately limiting his future.

'This is Mrs Mason,' he said, deferring to her with a polite nod. 'She's a walking encyclopaedia on Bruny Island and the lighthouse.'

Mary smiled. These days she felt more like an encyclopaedia of ailments.

'Mrs Mason lived at the lighthouse on Cape Bruny for twenty-six years,' Leon continued. 'Her husband was the light-house keeper. They had three kids and there were no schools nearby, so her children had to do lessons at home until high school. Imagine that.'

He nodded to her to begin. The scouts were regarding her like a museum specimen, and some of them were already staring up at the trees or pinching their nearest neighbour. The older scouts wore an air of faint boredom. She decided to make her speech quick so they weren't standing around for too long.

Struggling off her chair, she was surprised at how stiff she had become. Her bones were protesting at the cold. She clutched the arm of the chair, aware of her heart pounding. The wretched coughing started and she sat down again, accepting that it was too hard to stand. Then she began to tell the boys about the light.

'Cape Bruny is a place of vast distance and secret magic,' she said. 'When you drive out there, it's like a camel hump on the horizon, and the lighthouse is a pillar on the highest point of land. The tower's blinding white, so you can't miss it. If you climb this headland here, up onto East Cloudy Head,' she pointed to the start of the track, 'and if the weather is clear, you can see the lighthouse, even from this far away. That's why lighthouses are so important. And they were especially useful in the olden days, well before my time, when ships didn't have radar and GPS like they do today. Back then, the lighthouses were the eyes of the coast. The lights told sailors where there were rocks and reefs to avoid. Each lighthouse has its own special signal. In my day, the Cape Bruny light had a group flash. That meant two flashes every thirteen seconds with two dark periods in between, one short, one long. That's how sailors could tell their position, by the character of the flashes from each lighthouse.

'We lived in a red-roofed brick cottage below the lighthouse. To get up to the tower, you had to climb the concrete path. The weather was often terrible—so much wind. You could feel it through your clothes and aching in your ears. As you climbed the hill, you could see crumbling cliffs around the edges of the cape. And way out was the shifting face of the ocean, always heaving up and down. Below our cottage was a lovely stretch of sand called Lighthouse Beach. And to the west, you'd see all the jagged shadows of Recherche Bay.'

Mary noticed most of them were only half listening and she wondered how she could draw them in. 'Close your eyes,' she said, and they obeyed. 'Imagine you're standing on the cliffs near the light tower, looking south. You have to *think* south. And you have to take your mind out over the water and ride the waves as far as they go until you reach the ice. That's where the wind is born, and by the time it reaches Cape Bruny, it's still carrying Antarctica on its breath.

'Now turn around and walk to the door at the bottom of the tower. It's black and heavy, hard to open. You have to undo the lock and swing the door inwards. Then you step inside out of the wind. You can feel the stillness of the tower. And then you can hear the clank of your boots on the iron steps as you climb. When you speak your voice bounces around the walls.

'Now you're in the lantern room. There's a huge lens almost filling the room. It's domed like a beehive out of *Winnie the Pooh*. Prisms and faces of glass, all yellow with age. Imagine you're looking out through the windows. Way down below, the sea is foaming over the rocks around Courts Island. But the sound of the waves is dull because of the stone walls of the tower. And the wind is echoing. You're gloriously high. The view is wide. The ocean is rippling far to the south.'

She paused. 'You can open your eyes now.'

The boys' eyes flashed open. There was some squirming and giggling.

'Now we'll go back down to the keeper's cottage,' she said, trying to regain their attention. 'It wasn't very fancy back then—just bare walls and high ceilings. No posters or paintings or anything like that. There's a black kettle always hissing and simmering on the stove. And on the table there are pencils and paper. That's where my children did their lessons. They're all grown up now. But when they were younger they had maths and grammar to learn just like you. I had to be their teacher. They didn't always like that.'

Some of the boys laughed.

'And what do you think we did on bad days?' she asked them.

'Watch TV?' one of them said.

Mary shook her head. 'No. TV was only just coming in back then, and reception was poor out at the light station.'

'So what did you do?' Leon prompted her.

'Well, sometimes the wind was so strong you couldn't go out or you'd get blown over. So we used to do inside things. Like make pom-poms. Or draw pirate maps. Write letters and poke them into bottles to send out to sea. If the weather was good, we were outside flying kites, making bonfires, jumping over waves.

'Our beach was good for fossicking and we collected all sorts of things: shells and stones, feathers, lots of beach junk, like broken buoys and penguin skulls and old rusty knives. My children used to make things from sticks too: spears, bows and arrows, skis and poles. Sometimes, on a really good day, we'd go up past the tower and down the path on the other side. If the tide was low, we could go across the stony walkway to Courts Island. In among the grass, there were mutton-bird burrows, and at the right time of year, we'd pull out fluffy chicks with black shiny eyes.'

She stopped, drained of energy, and the children stared up at her, their imaginations fired, and shot out questions. Had she ever seen pirates? Could the wind really blow you off your feet? Did she see any wrecks? What happened when there was lightning? Was there treasure on Courts Island? Could kids go up the tower?

She answered as best she could. Unfortunately, no pirates. Yes, the wind really could bowl you over. They had seen a few sailing boats wrecked, and they'd assisted stranded sailors. No treasure had yet been found on Courts Island, but perhaps it might be there. And finally, yes, children could go up the tower these days—on guided tours with their parents. Back then, they were only allowed on special occasions.

'Is the tower still functional?' a scout leader asked.

Mary explained that yes, the tower could still be used, but it wasn't. The old light had been decommissioned in 1996, replaced by an automated beacon on the adjacent headland. She smiled sadly; Jack had detested automation. The beacon was a stunted thing, locked into the ground by concrete. It was cheaper to run and more efficient than the original light. Now the lighthouse keepers had become caretakers: they maintained the light station as a historic site and recorded weather observations for the Bureau of Meteorology so aeroplanes could land confidently at Hobart airport.

The caretakers were custodians of the stories of the lighthouse keepers. This was as precious as the lighthouse that stood as a monument to them. To those that lived there long before Mary's time.

The boys were getting restless and Mary could see their legs jiggling from inactivity. Of course they were done with it. They had listened well, but history was for old people, not for young things zinging with energy. She should stand up to finish and thank them . . . but as she struggled out of her chair, her legs wobbled and the breath seeped out of her. She felt herself sway, and there was an unusual lightness, as if all her blood was draining to her feet.

Suddenly, Jack was there in the branches above her, swimming in light. She felt a flush of heat. The trees spun. She heard panting. Then, all was quiet and black.

When she woke, Leon was leaning over her. She recognised his shape, hazy and undefined. The blur of his frown. Above him, the tops of trees swayed.

She was cold. So very cold. And heavy. Leaden. She closed her eyes, hearing the wind sighing in the leaves . . . or was it the pumping rush of blood, the sound of her own heart magnified in her ears? When she opened her eyes again, Leon was lifting her head to place a blanket beneath.

'Are you all right?' he asked.

She tried to struggle up, but he pressed her down gently. 'Lie still a moment. You fainted.'

She relinquished herself to heaviness and felt blankets being drawn over her.

'Here's a cup of tea,' someone said.

And then someone else: 'Is she going to be okay?'

Leon was sitting beside her on the ground. 'Don't get up till you're ready.'

It seemed she'd never be ready. She lay beneath the weight of the blankets, breathing shallowly. There was a great lump somewhere on her chest that was pressing, pressing, and then she was coughing, curled in a foetal ball. She rolled to her side, looking for something to spit into. Leon pressed a bowl beneath her face and then, thank God, she could breathe again.

He helped her to sit up and someone placed a warm cup of tea in her hands. She was feeble. Cold. Stiff. And her body was slow. Her lips were stubborn and refused to form words.

'Don't try to talk,' Leon said. He paused. 'Should I find a doctor? I can send someone for the nurse at Lunawanna.'

'No,' she croaked. 'I'll recover in a while.'

As she slurped tea, she began to feel stronger. Leon sat by, his face furrowed with worry. The scouts and their leaders had dispersed to other activities in order to give her some privacy.

'I'm better,' she said, after a while. 'And I have a request.'

He raised surprised eyebrows.

'The track up East Cloudy Head. After I've rested a little longer, could you support me so we can walk up there a short way?'

'What?' Leon laughed. 'That's a joke, right? You're having me on.'

'No,' she said. 'I want to go up there.'

'You just fainted. I'm taking you back to the cabin.'

She saw the firm line of his lips and knew that the issue was closed. She felt a twinge of regret. She wouldn't be communing with Jack up on the head today. And there wasn't much time left. Her opportunities were shutting down.

Leon reassured the scout crowd that she was recovering. Then he lifted her into the car, the cup of tea still in her hands, and drove back down the beach. In the cabin, he propped her up in bed with pillows and a hot-water bottle, and then he sat down beside her, his face pale.

'What happened out there?' he asked.

She shrugged. 'I must have sat for too long . . .'

He shook his head. 'I doubt it. You're always sitting. So it can't have been that.' He smiled wryly. 'Just remind me not to put you on the speaking circuit again. You upset a few people, fainting like that. The kids thought you were dead.'

'Was it all right—the talk?'

'It was fantastic. Everyone loved it . . . until you collapsed.' He contemplated her solemnly. 'What are we going to do with you?'

She clutched at his hand, frightened now. This could mean the end of everything. He might send her back. 'Please don't let them put me in a home.'

'You need more help than I can give you. And what's your family going to think when I tell them?'

'Don't tell them.'

He stared at her, his expression strained. 'I think they should know. Your daughter called me the other week. What's her name? Jan.'

Mary became sullen. 'Yes. But she shouldn't have rung you. She has no right. It's my death we're talking about here, not hers.'

'That's what I'm afraid of,' Leon said.

Silence fell between them. Mary had entered forbidden territory—discussion of her death. She slid into another coughing fit and Leon's eyebrows rose in accusation. He stood up. 'I'll make you another cup of tea.'

She listened to him banging around in the kitchen and soon he returned with a mug. The cabin was warm now, with both heaters pumping. Leon had rolled up his sleeves. 'If I can't tell your family, then I'll have to move in,' he declared. As he placed the cup on her bedside table, she saw new bruises on his forearm. They were dark red, turning green.

'Perhaps that'd be best for both of us,' she said, nodding pointedly at his arm.

He glanced down at the bruises and covered them slowly with the palm of his hand. Then he took his hand away.

'They're not pretty, are they?' he said. He sat down and gazed blindly out the window. Mary waited.

'What do you do . . .' he said slowly, 'when you're desperate to escape, but someone needs you so badly you know you can't go?' His jaw locked square and a muscle twitched high in his cheek.

'Perhaps you can find a way to help them help themselves.'

'And if they're powerless?' His voice was dense with pain. 'Alcohol makes him violent and my mother can't leave him. She's like a beaten dog. Comes back again and again, hoping for a pat. I have to be there to protect her when he comes home.'

Mary watched him carefully, beginning to comprehend. He stayed to take the blows for his mother. And his mother probably stayed out of a misplaced sense of duty. Mary understood that. She felt tears rising. Leon was a brave young man. A lesser man would have left long ago. It was no wonder he resented her presence at the cabin: she was yet another burden. She reached to touch his hand and he allowed her to do it, even though his face was screwed tight with anger and his hands were bunched in fists.

'I can't leave,' he said.

'He's your father?'

He nodded bitterly. 'I wish he wasn't.'

'Yes. But you're not like him. You're strong. It takes strength to stay.'

He looked at her now, tears in his eyes. 'It should be him dying,' he said. 'Not someone good like you.'

Mary managed a feeble smile. 'I've fooled you then, haven't I? I'm not good at all.'

He turned away to wipe his eyes. 'It could be in me—his weakness. It could be genetic.'

'You're not weak, Leon.'

'You can't know that.'

'I *do* know that.'

'But you're biased,' he said, smiling faintly at last. 'You *like* me.'

'I didn't at first,' she admits.

'I didn't make it easy for you.'

She grasped his arm, squeezing to make sure she had his full attention. 'You'll leave one day, you know.'

He stared at her without hope. 'You think so?'

'Yes. Something will change and you'll be able to go.'

His face became stony. 'If he puts her in hospital, she might leave him. But if he hurts her, I'll kill him.'

'You don't need violence, Leon. That's his game.'

He paused for a while, struggling with something in himself. Then he patted her hand where it rested on his arm. 'It's all right. I won't kill him. If that was in me, I'd have done it months ago.'

They sat quietly together for a long time, watching the shadows slipping on the walls. Now that the unsayable had been said, there was a strangely uplifting peace between them.

23

We drive home from Freycinet on a Saturday afternoon full of sun and blue skies and with a warm glow that started at the campfire and extended into everything we've done since. This morning, before our departure, we walked to Wineglass Bay. It felt like a dream—Emma's hand in mine, a rare wedge-tailed eagle circling above, and pademelons waiting for us on the white sands of the bay.

Now, in the car, the kilometres melt by. I'm bathed in happiness and I want this to last forever, but we arrive in Hobart all too soon. Emma invites me to stay the night and I agree willingly, unable to tear myself away. We unload her things, then I race to collect Jess and drive quickly back to Emma's. I know it's ridiculous, but I'm terrified things might change in the short time I'm away, afraid that she'll stop wanting me. But when I walk through the bungalow door Emma is still smiling, and the choking sensation in my throat gradually subsides.

I lie beside her through the night, drunk with love.

In the morning, we're dressed and having breakfast when the door is shoved open and a figure fills the doorway. I recognise him immediately: the man from Emma's lab at the antdiv. He's wearing tight black fleece trousers and a maroon top, both emphasising his bulky muscles. He leans against the door, hands in his pockets, and stares at us for several long seconds. His face is flat and his eyes are small and set too far apart. I can tell he has recently returned from down south—he has that faraway look, the tightness of not belonging. The same look I saw in Emma when I first met her.

'Emma,' he says, eyes flashing with outrage. 'What's happening?'

Her face is arranged in an appeasing smile. 'Nothing, Nick. We're having breakfast. That's all.'

He looks me up and down then swings back to Emma. 'I was expecting you up at the house last night for dinner,' he says. 'I thought we had an arrangement.'

Emma stands up. 'I didn't say I was coming to dinner.'

He steps into the room and I clear the dishes into the kitchen, keeping an eye on the door.

'You *always* come to Saturday dinner,' he says. 'I was waiting for you.'

'We were at Freycinet till late.' Emma is flushed and defensive.

I wonder if the shoes and harness I used belong to this man. He certainly has the leg-size to match. I slip along the wall to roll up Jess's blanket. She's at my heels with a growl rumbling in her chest. The room feels small with three people and a dog in it.

'Who is this guy, anyway?' Nick asks condescendingly. 'He comes with a dog, does he? Like Barbie comes with a handbag.' He stares at me and I tuck Jess's blanket under my arm.

'Stop it, Nick.' Emma is looking at me uneasily. Perhaps she's afraid I'll retaliate.

'I didn't know you were making new friends, Emma.' Nick moves closer to her. 'Aren't you going to introduce us?' The atmosphere in the tiny room is uncomfortable. He places his hand on Emma's arm and glares at me. 'Isn't it time for you to go?'

I hesitate, glancing at Emma, wondering what to do.

'The dog wants to leave,' Nick says.

Jess has slunk across the room and is standing by the door with her lips curled. Her eyes and ears are flat. She doesn't like Nick, and she's not the only one. I follow her to the door.

'Tom,' Emma says.

There's not enough room in here for all of us but I'm not sure whether she wants me to stay or go. I seek her face for a signal. I know it's weak to run out, but I can't bear confrontation. And although Nick is belligerent, he doesn't seem aggressive. Emma will be safe if I remove myself.

'Perhaps I'd better leave,' I mumble. Jess is at my heels.

'Let him go,' Nick growls.

'Tom,' Emma calls again.

I look back. Emma's face is troubled. She wants me to stay, but she has business with Nick that needs to be resolved. I can't help her with that. Nick is still glaring at me, his face as dark as thunder. My legs continue to march along the path, taking me away.

'Tom,' Emma says. 'You don't have to go.'

'Don't worry,' I call over my shoulder. 'It's fine. I'll leave you to it.'

I remember a time during my stay in Antarctica when a small group of us explored an ice crevasse on the plateau, just for fun. I was a reluctant member of the party, not quite convinced I would enjoy dangling above an abyss, but the others persuaded me to come. We rattled out early from station in a Hägglunds, juddering north over the uneven frozen fjords then up a steep snowy slope onto the ice field. It was a clear day of raw blue skies and brilliant white ice, and when the battering engines of the Hägg were finally quiet, a silence spread around us as infinite as the view.

We slathered on sunscreen, drank hot soup and ate chocolate biscuits, gazing out over the glossy plateau and the long stretch of sea ice below. The Vestfolds creased away to the south, and north of us only a few black islands broke up the featureless white.

With crampons strapped to our feet and harnesses fastened around our freezer suits, we crunched in single file over the ice behind Andy, the field training officer. It was his job to oversee all dangerous field activities and to train people for situations that might arise during their stay in Antarctica. We trudged over the plateau until a suitable crevasse was found. Then we dumped our gear in piles and stripped off layers of clothing.

A few metres back from the edge of the crevasse, Andy drilled several screws into hard ice. Methodically, he rigged anchors, ropes and a caving ladder so we could lower ourselves into the slot one at a time. When the first person disappeared over the lip of the crevasse, his helmet slipping from sight as he sank within the ice, the sweat chilled on my skin. Around me, the others jiggled happily, seemingly heedless of the risk. Andy stood on belay, solid as a fortress, checking the rope tension. He was chatting and joking, but I could see by the tightness in his body that at least he knew this was a dangerous game.

I waited till last, hoping we'd run out of time and I'd miss out, but the others pushed me forward. Andy watched me tie in to the rope and then snapped an extra line to my harness for security. Then he nodded at me to lower away. I backed up to the crevasse one crunching step at a time.

When I reached the edge, Andy barked instructions. But I stood there, upright, holding my breath, unable to lean back into space. He talked me through it with calm authority. I forced myself to lean backwards, and my feet scratched at the edge of the crevasse as I let out the rope one jerky frightened inch at a time.

Snow dust scattered as I descended. I lowered until I was three or four metres down, spinning slowly on the rope. The caving ladder was dangling beside me and I reached to grasp it. Below, a dark crack yawned. There was quiet, a dense stifling quiet. Just the noisy huffs of my breathing. Showers of fine snow crystals danced down on me from where the ropes sawed at the crevasse edge above.

Around me was another world. A world of layered meringues and ice puffs, cascading over each other like tiered wedding cakes. Powder-blue ice castles with fluffy turrets were mounded on top of each other. As my breathing eased, I could feel my heart knocking in my ears. The quiet pressed in. The walls. That sliver of light above. The deep blue crack of sky. The shaft of light fragmenting and glinting off a universe of tiny ice crystals.

Time stopped. Welded to the magical beauty was the possibility of a suffocating death. It was at once exhilarating and terrifying.

As I flee Emma's bungalow now, I remember the crevasse and how I felt that day. I'm still wrapped in Emma's magic, but Nick is the unexpected slump of my snow bridge. He's an outcome I hadn't anticipated, and everything within me is tumbling into darkness—a place I've always feared, where rescue is uncertain.

I should have known Emma had a boyfriend.

I haul open the car door and watch Jess leap up. Then I'm in, dragging the seatbelt across. I have to leave before Emma comes out. In case he follows her: Nick. That hard face of his, flat with anger. I turn the car uphill, misjudge the clutch, grinding a gear change; something a mechanic never does. Maybe I shouldn't be driving. I barely notice Jess whimpering on the floor.

The car turns itself onto the Mount Wellington road and rides up damp curves past driveways that plunge down to houses tucked deep in wet forest. We climb through Jacksons Bend, then Fern Tree, and on through the tight turns that lead to the summit. The roadside rocks are patched with white lichens. I notice rocks etched with the names of vandals. In breaks between trees, I see the hazy light of autumn hanging over the valleys and the city

below. The silver skeletons of dead trees reach up from the green
blanket of forest.

As I drive, my hands are tight on the wheel. I think of
Nick touching Emma. I think of him running his hands over
her body. It makes me shake with disbelief.

The road rises from wet forest into moody grey skies strewn
with fast clouds. We're in the zone of small stunted trees and
rumbled boulder fields. The low alpine heath is razed by cold
winds. I pull up at the summit beneath the white spire of the
telecommunications tower. There's no-one else around.

For a long time, I sit. I notice my hands trembling on the
steering wheel. From the back of the car, I scrounge a coat. Up
here, it's several degrees colder and the air has the feel of snow.
I let Jess out, even though dogs aren't allowed. She clings to my
calves, tail between her legs, the cold flattening her ears.

The summit is an explosion of rock and I'm as disordered
and chaotic as the scenery around me. It's fitting for me to be
here. I feel the wind flushing straight through my head. The
air's so cold, it is without scent. It's possible to imagine that
Antarctica exists.

I follow the boardwalk around to the lookout and stand at
the edge, watching the clouds scudding across the sky. Far below,
the metal arch of the Tasman Bridge reaches across the Derwent
River as it meanders its way north. The blanket of suburbs is
studded with the green dots of trees. Wind buffets up the cliff
face. It's hard to believe that yesterday I walked to Wineglass
Bay with Emma. Hard to believe that we watched a wedge-tailed
eagle in the sky. Hard to believe that yesterday I felt as high and
triumphant as that eagle.

I stand in the updraft until the wind freezes me to numb-
ness. Back inside the car, I fondle Jess's ears with cold stiff hands.
Her yellow eyes gaze into me. She understands better than any
human could.

I turn the key and start driving. I have to do something. I have to go somewhere so that I stop thinking about Nick, so that I stop imagining him with Emma.

We drive down the mountain, swinging into the curves, and then over the Tasman Bridge and out of town, to Cambridge, and then north to Richmond.

24

Richmond is a tourist town famous for a stone bridge built by convicts. It has quaint historic sandstone buildings and a main street lined with antique shops, cafés, galleries and a pub smothered with cast-iron lace. Gary and his wife, Judy, have a bed and breakfast on the edge of town. It's a life that suits Judy: greeting guests with her superficially friendly smile, and preparing breakfast trays. Fancy bed coverings. Payments and insincere goodbyes. Gary just goes along for the ride.

He looks surprised when he opens the front door and sees me with Jess at my heels. 'What are you doing here? Mum isn't dead, is she?'

'No. Just thought I'd drop in.'

'Nobody drops in to Richmond.'

I shrug.

He looks back over his shoulder into the house. 'We can't go inside. Judy's vacuuming.'

'Let's sit over there.' I point to Gary's ridiculous rotunda.

'Okay.'

We wander over the lawn past the rose garden, still blooming even in May. The seats in the rotunda are wet with dew.

'I'll get a towel,' Gary says, and ambles back to the house.

Jess is trotting around the lawn sniffing at things. She hunches to relieve herself and I go to the car to get a plastic bag. There'll be no making friends with Judy if Jess leaves a deposit on the lawn.

Gary returns and wipes the seats with an old towel. 'I should have asked if you wanted a cuppa,' he says.

Gary and I have never really been comfortable in each other's company. Gary went to boarding school just after I was born and only came home for holidays. He and Jan were like strangers invading the house: Gary spent most of his time helping Dad or reading, while Jan clashed with Mum in the kitchen. Usually I took to the hills, keeping my distance till they left again and I could slot safely back into my usual routine. I remember the sad look on Mum's face whenever I grabbed my coat and slipped out the door. But I had no qualms leaving the warm kitchen for the cold winds of the cape. The kitchen was too crowded for me.

'I wouldn't mind a cup of tea,' I say.

'How do you have it?'

'Just black.'

'God!' Gary snorts. 'Fancy having to ask my own brother how he has his tea.' He glances at me almost guiltily. 'Means we don't have enough cuppas together, doesn't it?'

'I don't like to get in the way.'

He laughs. 'You're always in the way trying to get *out* of the way. Anyway, I wouldn't mind you coming over more often.' He looks towards the house. 'It's Judy that's the problem. She's difficult. All women are difficult. I reckon you've got the right idea not having one.'

I say nothing and Gary grunts. 'I'll just get that cuppa,' he says.

I watch him walking across the lawn. When he was younger he used to walk like Dad, loping with long, forward-leaning strides. Now he's put on so much weight he takes short steps with his body tipped back to balance his weight.

It's cold in the shade of the rotunda. In summer, Gary spends hours on the ride-on mower to keep the lawn looking like a bowling green. Judy would have it green now, if the weather wasn't against her. Having a showpiece home is Judy's number one goal in life. She and Gary decided long ago not to have kids.

Gary comes back carrying a tray with two cups of tea and some slices of cake on a plate. He looks ludicrous tiptoeing over the grass concentrating on not spilling the tea. I don't mind a bit of tea in my saucer.

'Here.' He passes me a cup. 'Judy said we could have some chocolate cake. It's delicious.'

'Thanks.'

He sits down beside me. 'How are things?' he asks.

'Same as usual. How about you?'

'Sick of work. It's boring being in front of a computer all the time. But it's good money.'

'And you're good at it,' I say.

Gary works in IT for the state government in Hobart. Judy keeps telling everyone what a good reputation he has. She says he's indispensable. She really means that his income is indispensable. All her renovations and redecorating would be impossible without it.

'Are you hooked up to Foxtel yet?' he asks. Gary hangs out for the weekends so he can watch the sport.

'No,' I say. 'I don't watch much sport.'

He looks bored. 'No. You're always off looking for birds or some goddamned thing.' He snorts. 'I've got a nutter for a brother.'

'Thanks.'

'Thank God you've got Jess. At least she's normal. You didn't let her crap on the lawn, did you?'

'No, I picked it up.'

'Dogs always want to take a dump on this lawn. Judy wants me to get one of those scare guns they use in vineyards. The

ones that fire off every few minutes.' Gary snorts again. 'Reckon
I'll get a shotgun instead.'

I try to smile.

'When are you going to see Mum again?' he asks.

'Wednesday.'

'Mind if I come?'

'Sure. Why not? She'll be pleased to see you.'

'I'll take a flex day. I've got plenty of time owing. What
time are you leaving?'

'We can take the eleven o'clock ferry. So you don't have
to rush.'

Gary picks up a second piece of chocolate cake. 'How's
Mum going?' he asks.

I shrug.

'What about Jan? Has she visited Mum yet?'

'Not as far as I know.'

'If she had, you'd know about it. She's on the phone all
the time. Bloody Jan. Too much pride.' He shakes his head. 'You
heard from her?'

'Once or twice.'

'Isn't she chewing your ear off? She won't leave me alone.'

'She's been ringing a bit.'

'If Mum dies before Jan sees her, we won't hear the end of
it. What about Jacinta? Have you spoken to her? Last I heard she
and Alex were planning some fool expedition to the lighthouse.
Jan was going off her brain.'

'I don't think they've taken her yet. Mum hasn't mentioned it.'

'Maybe they'll take her next weekend then. Stupid idea.'

'Why?' It seemed to me that taking Mum to visit the
lighthouse might be a good thing. Perhaps I should have thought
of it.

'Don't you know what went on down there?' Gary says.

'What do you mean?'

'Before your time. Before you were born.' He leans back and laughs. 'You were probably the result of it all. The cure for the disease.'

I don't know what he's talking about.

'You'd better ask Jan,' Gary says. 'She knows the story best.'

'What story?'

'Of how Mum and Dad nearly blew apart. Around the time Mum broke her leg. Auntie Rose had to come and take care of us while Mum was in hospital.'

This is all news to me. 'Why didn't anyone tell me?' I ask.

'Because you're younger. And because you're different.' Gary stuffs down the rest of his cake and stares out over the garden while he chews and swallows. 'Ask Jan,' he says. 'She'll tell you.'

After Gary's, I find a long lonely beach to walk on. I stay out till dark to be away from the house. I'm afraid Emma might ring and I don't feel up to her excuses.

Sure enough, the light is flashing on the answering machine when I get home. I press the playback button and sit down when I hear Emma's voice.

'Tom, I'm really sorry about this morning. Nick shouldn't have come barging in like that. Will you ring me when you get in? . . . Please?'

I look at the phone but can't bring myself to pick it up. Instead, I thaw lamb chops to cook for a late dinner. Then I cut up a few vegies to go alongside. Jess is satisfied with her usual bowl of kibble. I'm rummaging around in the fridge looking for broccoli when the phone rings. I let it ring a couple of times, but I have to answer it. It could be Jacinta with news about Mum. But it's Emma. Her words tumble out in a rush.

'Why did you run out?' she asks, then blusters in again before I can reply. 'Actually, I don't blame you. Nick can be very

intimidating. He likes to think he owns me. We've had a bit to
do with each other since I got back—you know what it's like.'

There it is. The admission.

'I'd just like you to know that he doesn't own me,' she says,
talking through my silence. 'I can do what I like.'

I don't know what to say.

'Pick me up tomorrow after work,' she says. 'I'll wait for
you out the front of the antdiv. Five o'clock.'

'All right,' I say. Stupidly.

'Good. I'll be waiting for you.'

Later, when I've retired to bed, I hear a noise on the porch. It's
probably a possum looking for a morsel of apple. But Jess tenses
and leaps up from her rug, so I slip into the lounge room to
check it out. A torchlight is flashing through the window and
when I open the door Laura is there, ghostly in the dim light.
Her face is a mask of white, a dark streak on one cheek.

'Sorry to wake you.' Her voice is a whisper, barely audible
above the wind in the trees.

'I was awake.'

'Mouse has cut himself and I need to get him to hospital.
But I can't drive while he's in such a state.' She rubs a hand across
her cheek and looks down at her fingers, wiping them absently
on her jumper. I realise the dark smudge is blood.

'What about an ambulance?'

'It'll take twenty minutes to get here. And I don't want
anyone manhandling him in the house. I want him to be able
to come back home without fear.'

For a moment I hesitate, wavering indecisively. But who
else can help her? 'All right. I'll get my keys.'

'Thank you.'

When I return she's already running down the hill and
across the road, legs flashing beneath the street light. I walk

quickly to the car and Jess slips through the door and onto the floor on the passenger side before I can stop her. There's no time to take her back. I roll the car down the driveway.

Shouting and banging noises are coming from inside Laura's house. I wait in the car for a few minutes, unsure. Then I go to the front door, which is open. Laura is in the hallway holding onto the wrists of a large dark-haired man. He's clearly resisting her and his movements are strong and wild. He's very upset.

'Mouse,' she says, not in the wispy fragile voice I've heard before, but loudly. 'Mouse. You stop that right now. Put your hands down and listen to me.'

The man sees me in the doorway and drops to the floor like a frightened animal. He cowers against the wall, his hands covering his face. There's blood running down his forearm.

'Please go back to the car.' Laura's face is tight. 'He's not used to strangers.'

I go back into the cold night and open the back door on one side of the car. Then I turn on the headlights and the interior light. If this man is afraid, he might not want to climb into a darkened car. It might be less intimidating if he can see where Laura wants him to go.

Five minutes pass and exhaustion threatens to swamp me. I couldn't sleep in my own bed, but here in the cramped discomfort of the car, sleep rises unbidden and tries to claim me. Finally, I see the shadows of Laura and Mouse outside the house. I can hear Laura coaxing him. She tells him he'll be all right if he gets in the car. That he'll be safe. She's taking him to get his arm fixed. To stop the blood.

Then they're both sitting in the back seat. Laura pulls the door shut and locks it. I drive as smoothly as possible along the road and around the bends and twists of the cove towards the highway. In the rear-view mirror, I can see Laura's brother crouched beside the door moaning while she strokes his head, humming to soothe him. Streetlights intermittently flash on her face, but her features are blank and featureless. I see no fear in her. No self-pity.

By the time we reach Hobart, she has her brother's head hugged to her chest and her eyes are closed. Small whimpers come from his lips. There's blood on both their faces. She keeps his eyes covered as we stop at traffic lights. When we pull up outside the emergency department, Laura speaks quietly from the back. 'Could you please go in and get some help? I don't think I can do this bit alone.'

Lights illuminate the hospital entrance into a blinding white. The duty nurse at reception listens to me unmoving and then lifts a telephone. Within minutes four large men have come out to talk to me, their faces serious and attentive. They follow me to the car. There are cries and a scuffle in the back seat. Laura yells out, her voice edged with pain, and there's an awful growling and howling. I stand back while the men wrestle Laura's brother out of the car and restrain him. They bundle him quickly through the no-public-access doors, Laura close behind. Then I'm alone outside, blinking in the bright lights.

I linger on the pavement, waves of shock pulsing through me. Jess crawls from the car like a liquid shadow and shivers at my feet. I had forgotten she was there, huddling on the floor. She must have been terrified—first Mouse and his animal-like cries, then the four men leaping into the car, the shouting, the struggle. I bend and stroke her quivering head, guilt now mingling with my horror. I should have left her at home. But how could I have known?

The hollow siren of an approaching ambulance startles me. I scoop Jess up and deposit her on the front seat, then start the car. We'll go home now, slowly, and sit quietly in the dark.

25

I always go for a walk early in the morning; it's fresh and cool and quiet. This morning I particularly want to do normal things for Jess after the horror of that trip to the hospital last night. Like me, Jess is a creature of routine, and she takes comfort from these rituals.

We never usually meet anyone on our dawn jaunts, so it's a surprise to both of us when we see Laura wandering along the bush track ahead. She floats through the scrub, her gaze focused somewhere out over the channel. I slow down, hoping to avoid her, but she hears Jess rustling in the grass and she turns.

'Oh, hello.' She doesn't smile and her face is drawn. 'Sorry. I wasn't expecting to see anyone.' She waits for me to join her. 'You walk often?' she asks.

'Most days.'

She nods and I follow her onto the beach.

'Is Mouse okay?' I ask.

'He'll be all right. It was pretty horrible, though.' She stops walking and sighs. 'I didn't sleep much.'

I hesitate, unsure whether to push on with my walk or whether I should wait for her. Jess trots along the beach and up into the grass along the shore, sniffing animal trails.

'I didn't stay at the hospital,' she says, staring across the water. 'There wasn't much point. Once they sedated him, he slept. And they said they wouldn't let him wake properly for a while. So I caught a taxi home.' She turned to look at me. 'I don't like seeing him like that.'

'No.' I thrust my hands in my pockets.

'He has paranoid schizophrenia,' she says. 'I thought he was taking his medication, but apparently not. After I got home last night I found a pile of pills stashed in one of my pot plants.'

'Will he be home soon?'

'Not for a couple of weeks. They have to wean him off sedation and then stabilise him on medication before he can come home.' She looks up at me and I notice dark patches under her eyes. 'Thank you for what you did for us,' she says.

'That's all right.'

She glances at Jess snuffling up on the bank and then she gazes along the beach. 'Do you mind if I walk with you?' she asks.

I'd rather be alone, but what can I say? I shrug. 'Okay.'

We wander along the sand, not exactly walking together, but not completely apart. Laura strolls along, distracted. At the end of the beach, she follows me up along the cliff trail. I feel a bit awkward, but I try to pretend she isn't there. Unperturbed by the addition to our party, Jess trots quietly ahead.

The bush along the cliff is drier and we see thornbills and scrub wrens. A butcherbird chimes from high in a straggly eucalypt. I keep hoping Laura will turn back, but she comes all the way to the next beach and we walk back together along the road. At my driveway, I bid her farewell, but she stops and looks at me.

'That was nice,' she says. 'Can we do it again? Maybe tomorrow?'

'I'm not sure what I'm doing tomorrow,' I say. What if Emma's here? Laura could go walking by herself. She doesn't need to come with me.

'I'll look out for you if I'm up,' she says. 'Walking's good for me. I feel a bit better already.' She stares down at her house where it snuggles behind a string of tree ferns. 'It's so quiet without Mouse,' she says. 'I suppose I should enjoy the break.' She smiles at me sadly and I feel the weight of her loneliness.

'I'd better go,' I say. 'I have to get ready for work.'

'Thanks again for last night,' she calls after me.

When I leave the garage that afternoon, the car is in a rush to get to the antdiv. I try to slow it down, but it takes corners recklessly and drives too fast along the highway towards Kingston, swinging into the carpark.

As arranged, Emma is waiting on the pavement in front of the building. But there's a complication: Nick is standing there too. He's standing too close to her, staking his claim. What did she say about him not owning her? I stop the car at the far end of the carpark, about fifty metres away, and sit, watching them converse. Neither of them has seen me yet and I'm unsure whether to stay or go.

Nick is leaning in towards Emma as they talk, and even from here, I can see him gazing at her intently. They look accustomed to being in each other's space. Their body language makes my suspicions harder to deny. I want to think of Emma as my girlfriend, but really, I have no idea what goes on during the day when she's at work. For all I know, she could go home with Nick at lunchtime. There are many hours in a day during which Emma could explore options other than me. I've been a fool to imagine that Emma could be mine. A few dinners and a night away together and I'm gone.

Finally, I move the car forward. I might be outshone by Nick's predatory masculinity, but I won't sit by watching like this. Emma asked me to pick her up. And if she asked *me*, then she didn't ask him.

Nick notices the Subaru before Emma does, and scowls when he sees me behind the wheel. He murmurs something in her ear. She turns and looks at me, her face flushing pink and her body tensing. The intimacy between them is erased as she pulls away, holding him off with her hands. 'I'm going with Tom,' I hear her say.

'What?'

'You heard me.'

Scooping up her backpack, she bounds towards the car, pulls the door open and flings herself inside, closing the door with a thud. Nick bangs the top of the car with the flat of his hand. He bends down to stare in the side window at Emma, his eyes possessive.

'See you for morning coffee,' he says. 'The usual. In the café. Nine o'clock.' He mouths something else, but Emma is already looking away from him. She's looking at me, it makes my skin tingle.

'Rescued,' she says with a laugh. 'He's persistent, isn't he?'

As we drive home, unspoken questions are thick between us. I want Emma to negate Nick. But she keeps her thoughts hugged close and prattles on instead about tidying her office and a trip she's planning up north to visit her family. She'd like to see them again before she goes back south, and now's the time to do it, before the frenetic pre-expedition rush begins. Her sister has two kids and she's only seen them once or twice. Perhaps she should take a gift for them, but she doesn't know what to buy. She doesn't know much about kids, she says. In fact, she knows more about penguins.

I tell her we have something in common—I know more about birds than about people too. The look she casts my way is tinged with annoyance. She was only joking, she says. Of course she knows more about people than penguins. She was just speaking figuratively.

I don't know what to say after that. All I can think of is
Nick, and yet I can't bring myself to say his name aloud. I can't
make myself ask her what's going on between them. I'm afraid
she'll admit everything and then ask me to turn around and
take her back to the antdiv. I couldn't bear it. Last night after
the hospital, I lay awake in bed thinking of her. Remembering
the feel of her skin against mine. Trying to recall the smell of
her hair and the curve of her smile. Trying to convince myself
that Nick doesn't exist for her.

At home, I light the fire and boil the kettle.

Emma doesn't give me a chance to pour tea. She descends
on me with a look of fierce determination. I wanted to allow
room for discussion, but with her hands and eyes on me, it's
impossible to resist, and I submit willingly. This is what I've been
wanting, after all—Emma's lips on mine, her body against me,
tight with need, her hands gripping me close.

It's desperate love-making. All my unasked questions slip
away, knocked aside like vases of flowers spilled in our wake. We
grasp each other in the kitchen, tumble into the lounge room
then make our way slowly to the bedroom, peeling off clothes,
sliding shivery beneath the doona, feeding off the combined
warmth of our bodies.

After a makeshift dinner, Emma pulls a bottle of whisky
from her backpack with feigned stealth and a provocative smile.
'Leftover duty-free,' she says. 'I brought it back from down south.'

I shake my head. 'I'm no good at whisky.'

She strokes the stem of the bottle with a finger. 'Let's see
if we can help you to become friends.' She finds ice in the back
of my freezer, cracks several cubes into a couple of tumblers
and pours a generous shot into each, then passes me a tumbler.
'Cheers. And hey, we're having a party on Saturday night. Eight
o'clock start. Will you come?'

'I'm not good at parties either.'

'You'll be fine. Bring your own grog.'

We sit down together in the lounge room. The fire burbles quietly, the flames licking at the glass, the muffled crackle of burning wood. Jess is curled up in the corner on her rug. It's dark outside, and here in our circle by the fire, all is cosy.

'Drink up,' Emma insists.

I take a reluctant sip and brace myself as the whisky burns down to my chest.

'Good, isn't it?' Emma smiles. 'Have some more.' She jiggles the ice around her glass and takes a gulp, sighing with pleasure.

Mincingly, I sip a little more, preparing myself for the shocking burn.

'Not like that,' Emma says. 'That's pathetic.' She crawls forward across the couch and takes the glass from me. 'Tip your head back. I'm going to teach you how to take a proper mouthful.'

She pours a slug of liquor into my mouth then covers my lips with hers and kisses me, forcing me to swallow. I gasp as the whisky scalds its way down. It doesn't take long to feel a creeping warmth oozing through my body. Emma pours more whisky into my mouth, kisses me again, teases me with her tongue and with her hands, then passes whisky from her own mouth into mine and forces me to swallow that too. She sits back laughing, and the room is warm, and my body is comfortable and growing looser by the minute.

'You need this.' She smiles at me persuasively. 'You're so tied up inside. Here.' She sloshes more whisky into my glass. 'I'll just get more ice.'

I sip obediently while she fetches the ice tray and drops a handful of cubes into my glass. She tops up her own glass and then switches off the light as she sits down. Now the room is dark except for the dim glow from the lamp, and the rosy shimmer of the fire.

'There, that's better.' Emma tugs off her fleece and stretches her legs out across the couch. 'How are you feeling now? Do you like it?'

'I'm not sure.'

'Have more, then.'

I take another good sip and the spreading warmth is wonderfully soothing. A smile plays on my lips as smooth as liquid.

'Hold your glass towards the fire and have a look,' Emma suggests.

I do as she says and find myself entranced by the fiery swirling bronze liquid. It really is a fine drink—complex, structured and colourful.

'It's like your skin,' I say.

'What?'

'It reminds me of your skin.'

Emma laughs. 'You want to feel my skin?'

'Always.'

She laughs again and comes across the couch to kiss me. Everything about her feels fluid and light. I run my hands over the curves of her face, tracing her cheekbones, her lips, her eyebrows, losing myself in the outline of her face, the texture of her skin, my whole being swelling to have her close, pressed against me like this, intimate. My hands move urgently over the contours of her body, discovering and rediscovering, memorising her.

She pulls back too soon and pours more whisky into my glass.

'So, are we going out?' I ask bluntly, my tongue blurring in my mouth.

She laughs. 'Of course we're not going out. We're staying in.'

She's deliberately misunderstanding me, teasing me. I drink more, trying to find a way to overcome my shyness. I want her to tell me what Nick is to her.

With each sip of whisky, the next mouthful becomes more appealing. The urge in my groin simmers and subsides, eases to a mellow warmth. Her hand on me is heaven. I'm a bottomless well. Feeling is flowing in me, rippling back and forth, swirling and tumbling. And then the room is gently tipping, the curtains swaying, the couch rocking.

'You need to talk.' Emma massages my head with her fingers. 'You need to let it all out. Let it come.'

Her voice seems thick around the edges, her words less distinct. I wonder if she's riding on the same wave as me. I toss back the contents of my glass and reach for hers, toss that back as well. Pleasure shivers through me as the whisky intensifies its hold. Emma is staring at me, her face still with concentration, her eyes great wells of studious empathy and understanding. She's hearing what I'm saying without words. She's feeling my grief, my emptiness, my loneliness.

I lean back on the couch and start to talk without looking at her. 'Emma, there's so much I need to tell you . . .'

The sentences are halting at first. It's easier without eye contact so I fix my gaze on the fire. 'I had such a hard time down south . . . The winter was terrible. So dark. And so isolating . . . It had just started when my wife left me . . . Her name's Debbie, my wife . . . My ex-wife, I mean . . . But the ship was gone, so I couldn't go back . . .'

I have a sensation of stumbling over rocks and logs, trying to find my feet. But I struggle on. Emma is right. I need this. It's good for me. Slowly I gain momentum. I allow the flickering flames to soothe me, and I talk and talk, the words rolling out like a hidden river.

'Antarctica was tough for me. I loved it but I hated it.' It's the first time I've acknowledged this. Nine years to permit myself an honest analysis. 'I blamed Antarctica for losing Debbie. And I blamed myself for going. Our relationship was good before I left. We were solid. Antarctica was our plan to get ahead. To make some money . . . I had this feeling I shouldn't go. But I didn't listen. Going was a choice. A conscious decision. I knew we were at risk, but I overrode it. The promise of the south was too good.'

Memories wash through me with the whisky, gaining strength in recollection. I am immersed in my own world and I continue, talking about Antarctica, the devastation of my marriage breakup, followed by Sarah's rejection of me, and then my father's death. Then all my baggage about Dad comes tumbling out, surprising me. 'I keep remembering all those times I watched him leave the house when I was a boy, and I wished he'd ask me to come. I should have just tagged along; I'm sure he'd have let me. But I was afraid of him. Mum was easy. So kind and full of love. I felt safe with her. But Dad and I weren't quite connected. I regret missing my chance with him. I can't forget that.

'And now my mum is dying.' The last of it is welling out now. 'But this time I'm here to watch over her. I'd be with her now, but she won't let me. She's in a cabin on Bruny Island. All I can do is make sure I'm there when the time comes. It's what I want to do. To see her through to the finish.'

As I talk, I feel the weight coming off me, rising like a heat haze. Emma listens in silence and I talk until I'm spent and there are almost no more words to say.

For a suspended moment, I watch the flames licking slowly in the wood heater, not looking at her. Finally, I know I can tell her what I feel. 'I didn't expect to meet you, Emma. And you've changed me. You've given me back part of myself I didn't think I'd find again . . . You're so bold. So alive and confident. And you've made me feel like living again. You've made me want to embrace life. To clutch it with both hands. The way you do. I love you.'

Then, I'm ready to ask her about Nick. Having emptied myself out for her, at last I'm able to mention his name. 'Emma . . . is something happening with Nick? Or are you with me?' I turn to look into her eyes, to see what they reveal. And what I see is a woman asleep on the couch. Her head is cushioned on her elbow and her mouth is slightly open, her body slack.

I have no idea how much of my confession she has heard, if anything, and for a moment it is almost amusing. I allow myself a wry smile at the bungled timing of all this—my life story poured out to deaf ears. Then it occurs to me she certainly hasn't registered the question about Nick. And with that realisation my soul folds.

I pour another whisky and drink it quickly, both despising and enjoying the renewed burn of it as I swallow.

And then, a glimmer in my mind. The birth of release. Despite the sludge of my drunkenness, I am aware enough to understand that whether Emma remembers any of it or not, she has triggered my purging, which was, perhaps, all that I needed of her.

I should thank her for that.

26

The morning was wet and miserable, and even though she'd been in bed since eight the previous evening, Mary was tired. Nights were no longer a time of rest. She propped herself up with every pillow in the cabin, but she still couldn't breathe. If she lay down it was easy to imagine what it'd be like to die from drowning.

She'd been awake since dawn, listening to the weather. Intermittent rain drummed on the roof and spattered the windows and the clouds were low and sombre. She would have stayed in bed, but she couldn't sleep for the coughing. And because of Jack, wandering through her room all night. He'd been watching her. Reminding her.

Since the scout camp, time had somehow folded in on itself. Leon came each day, and now he sat with her for longer. Or at least it seemed he was there for longer. He was kinder too, and wore a look of endless patience. Sometimes they sat together for hours. And perhaps sometimes Leon came more than once a day. But there were blank patches in her memory now, as one day collapsed into the next so she was no longer sure whether she'd been to bed, or whether she had slept or eaten. Days were as indistinct as the tufts of grass waving on the dunes in the endless wind.

Earlier in the week, her two sons had come, Gary and Tom. Was it Wednesday or Thursday? It didn't matter. At least she remembered that they visited. She had known things must be getting worse for the two of them to show up—in her lucid moments she was aware of her deterioration. But Jan hadn't arrived, so the end was not yet nigh.

It saddened her that Gary was so large these days—he was so big he seemed to fill the cabin, everything soft where it should have been firm. She now had to look hard within her son's heavy features to see the slip of a boy he once was—all arms and legs, with Jack's smile. Of course, Gary had never had Jack's aloof shyness. Tom was comfortable saying only what needed to be said, but Gary seemed compelled to fill all the spaces with words. While Tom set the kettle on to boil in the kitchen, and found cups and biscuits, Gary reclined in the armchair and spun an endless monologue about work, Judy, the B&B, and Jan's opinions about Mary's health. Instead of listening, Mary found herself staring vacantly out the window, tuning in to the wind and the short blasts of rain that flushed in and out over Gary's one-way conversation.

Tom was in a strange mood, very different from his last visit. Mary vaguely remembered something he'd said about a girl and the possibility of going south, but she couldn't quite recollect the details. Perhaps the girl had already knocked the buoyancy out of him. Tom wasn't very resilient when it came to relationships. He wasn't very good at relationships at all. Poor lad.

She sensed he was brooding on something while he waited for the kettle to boil, but she concluded that he was blunted by the overwhelming presence of Gary in the room. She used to wish her two sons could be closer; however, there were too many years between them. They had spent too little time together as boys, and their personalities were too different.

If she'd anticipated what Tom was building up to, she might have been more prepared. But she had no idea what was brewing in his mind, no idea that he could rattle her so suddenly and so unexpectedly. Numbed by Gary's constant blather, when Tom's question came, she felt as though she'd been hit with a brick.

'Mum, what happened in that storm on the cape before I was born?'

Gary spluttered tea and coughed biscuit. And Mary was breathless, unable to speak.

'Something about a broken leg,' Tom said. 'Gary mentioned it the other day. Something to do with Auntie Rose.'

Gary tried to stop him with a voice like iron. 'I told you to ask *Jan*. Not Mum.'

But Tom was looking at her, hopeful, unaware that her breathing had stalled and that she was drowning in shock and in lungs full of fluid. Drowning in a past that wouldn't leave her alone.

Then the boys were hopping around her, white-faced and anxious, rubbing her back, holding her medication, pressing a glass of water to her lips. She was weak, and Tom was so horrified that he didn't push further. But Mary knew she must provide some sort of answer. When she could talk again, she gave the boys her edited version of the saga. Not the veins and muscles and flesh of it—that was the stuff she planned to die with. Instead, she gave them small pieces of the facts.

'There was a massive storm on the cape and the pony got out,' she said. 'I was trying to get him back inside when I had a fall from a cliff, breaking my leg. Prior to the storm, your father and I had been having a difficult time in our marriage. I suppose the accident saved us, in a way. We'd been on the cape so long we had forgotten how to appreciate it. Over the years we'd started taking things for granted. Like the beautiful place we lived in. And each other. It's not hard to do. Life gets busy and you forget to look after one another. Then the accident happened. Your Aunt Rose came to stay for a while to help out while I was in hospital. While we were apart, your father and I realised how far our relationship had slipped. When I came home, we worked hard to fix things between us. It took time, and not all couples could do what we did. But we had your father's courage and my perseverance. And hope arrived, in the form of you, Tom. I fell pregnant. You were unplanned—I'll admit it. But you were a wonderful and fitting motivation for our recovery.'

Mary continued with her story, watching the attentive looks on the faces of her sons. She described Rose's selfishness. Her laziness. The way she did little to help Jack around the house while Mary was in hospital. How Rose was more of an impediment to Jack than an assistant. She gave them a coloured truth.

Coloured truth, she believed, was far less sinful than a direct lie.

They had received an early storm warning from Maatsuyker Island to the south-west of Cape Bruny. Radio communication between the three south-eastern lights—Bruny, Maatsuyker and Tasman Islands—was a regular part of the daily routine. But even before the warning, they'd known the storm was coming. Purple clouds had been massing to the south all morning and the mountains of mainland Tasmania were obscured by a darkness that only came with heavy rains. By early afternoon, the skies were dark as dusk and the wind was shrieking.

From the moment they'd received the message from Maatsuyker, Jack and the head keeper had been skating over the cape, checking that everything was tied down. The grounds were always meticulously tidy, but they were worried about damage if the storm lived up to its potential. While the men were busy, Mary worked with Jan and Gary, bringing toys and bikes inside off the verandah. The cow was pleased to be led into the shed but they were unable to catch the pony. He was excited and skittish in the wind, galloping wildly across the slope, charging through each attempt to secure him. As the wind escalated, Mary and the children retreated to the cottage.

Jack dived in for a restless lunch, tossing back sandwiches and tea. His eyes were fastened on the window and the racing clouds. Little was said. Spattering rain was blowing in and out. He left quickly, hurrying to finish his tasks. Within the cottage, Mary knew they were safe; it had been built to withstand immense storms. And the light, too, had been constructed to stand for eternity. Jack would be safe up there.

For a while, she sat in the lounge room with the children, trying to knit. Gary was on the floor working on a piece of wood he'd been carving for days and Jan was curled up on a chair, reading a book. Outside, the wind gusted and shuddered under the eaves, whistling around the walls and pressing under the door. Eventually, Mary set her knitting aside and went to the kitchen where she could watch the tower. Jack was up there somewhere, observing the weather, like her.

She wished this thought might give her comfort, but the vibe between them had not been good lately. She couldn't remember how long it was since they'd turned to each other in intimacy—Jack had locked that part of himself away. And they hadn't talked about anything of consequence for months. At the dinner table, they kept up appearances for the benefit of the children, but beyond that it seemed there was little love left. And yet, there must be something in her that cared for his well-being. In threatening conditions like this, she still worried that he might be injured. He was her husband, and she felt loyalty towards him, even though their relationship was hollow.

She watched as the rain arrived in large fat drops, slung into long smudges on the windows. Her view of the hill became bleary, and the tower seemed bent and twisted. Time moved slowly as she watched the clouds sink and the raindrops thicken. Halfway down the paddock, the pony huddled against the wind, his tail pressed into the rain. She felt sorry for him, alone out there when he could have been in the protection of the shed. Perhaps he'd let her catch him now. She set the kettle on the warmer and pulled on her coat and hat, calling to Jan and Gary not to venture outside. On the porch, she paused to listen to the wind roaring across the cape and the sheds banging and clattering in the blast, the rain pounding on tin. Then she hurried to the paddock. It'd be best to get this job over quickly and retreat inside.

The pony hadn't moved. He was standing by the fence, and as she approached, her coat flapping, his eyes widened and nostrils flared. She managed to tie a rope to his head collar and turn him uphill, but he strained against her, trying to keep his rump into the wind.

At first she handled him gently, but as the cold and the rain beat into her face and he wouldn't budge, she grew rougher and more insistent, dragging at his head. Exasperated, she leaned against his shoulder and tried to push him backwards. He took a step back, then another and they slowly progressed up the hill and out through the gate. Then the real trouble began.

Beyond the security of the paddock, the pony became even more skittish and uncertain, prancing and jostling and stepping on Mary's feet. The wind was unbelievably strong and Mary clung to the rope, trying to use the pony as a shield as they laboured down the track towards the shed. The door had blown open and was slamming against the wall. At the sound, the pony propped, shied and snorted, wrenching the rope from her hands. Then he took off. Cursing, she followed him over the hill.

On the western side of the cape, the land fell away quickly, diving through grasses and scrub then arriving suddenly at the cliffs. Mary was worried the pony might not see the edge until too late. He could go over, scrabbling at the lip with his hooves. She ran down the slope after him, exposed to the full force of the gale. The rain was dense and sharp, driven by the wind. Further west, she saw the pony bounding across the slope. She tried to hurry towards him, but he disappeared into cloud. She paused, unsure whether he'd fallen or was just out of view.

Then she saw him again, trotting jerkily across the slope to the north, zigzagging among the scrub, head low. She followed him, clutching bushes to steady herself. He stopped at a high point where the vegetation grew dense. Quickly, she scrambled across, feet skating in the gravel. Suddenly her foot slid on loose rocks, caught for a moment then slid again. She grasped at a tussock but it whipped out of her fingers, and then she was sliding, slipping down a steep gully, too close to the edge.

She dug her fingers into the mud, and scraped at anything solid. Her fingers raked on stone. There was a scream in her throat. Then air, all around. And space. She thudded against dirt. Rock.

It ended in a thump and a crack as her leg folded. Air huffed out of her like closed gallows. Slipping in and out of awareness, she wondered whether she was warm or cold.

Eventually, she felt rainwater running inside her coat and realised she'd have to move and find a way up the cliff. It took forever to edge up the rock wall and then roll over and arrange herself in an awkward sitting position with her leg stretched in front of her. After heaving the leg into place, she slumped against the cliff with her coat tucked around her. Rain sluiced over her. She melded with the darkness all around.

Hours passed before Jack and the other keeper found her. They scrambled down ledges to reach her, and then carried her up to the cottage while she reeled in a fog of pain. Jack was needed on the cape; he couldn't leave. So his brother, Sam, came from the farm and drove her to hospital in Hobart. It was a wretched journey: her leg throbbed, and despite blankets and hot water bottles, she couldn't get warm.

At the hospital, they confined her to bed in traction until the leg straightened. Then they set it in plaster and sent her to her parents' place to recover. She was furious and bereft. The pony was safely back in his usual paddock, but she was here, stranded away from her family. Her mother patted her arm, smiling maternally. *You'll be all right, dear. They'll manage without you.* But Mary knew they wouldn't manage. Jack was useless in the kitchen and Jan was too young to shoulder the load. The head keeper's wife wasn't well, so it was too much to ask her to care for the children.

It was no surprise when Jack's letter arrived.

> Dear Mary,
>
> I hope you are recovering well. It has been very difficult to manage both the light-station duties and the family on my own. I have decided that I must call on Rose to come and help us while you are away. She can cook and look after the children while I attend to the many jobs that must be done after the storm.
>
> Get well quickly. The children are missing you.
> Jack

Mary was irritated. Rose was an ineffective solution. She was simply too lazy, and she'd be no use around the house. But of course, Jack, would be blind to that—all he'd see was an extra pair of hands.

Sitting by the fire in her parents' home, Mary had much time to contemplate. She thought about Jack's letter and everything it represented. She read it over and over, looking for something that wasn't there. The fall and the broken leg had shaken her and she needed something from Jack, some reassurance that she mattered and that she was important to him. She wanted to know how he'd felt when he discovered she was missing. She wanted him to tell her about the search and rescue. She wanted to hear of his concern, the revival of his love and affection when he knew she was hurt. But the letter gave her none of this.

She wondered what would have happened if she'd died. The children might have grieved for a time, but what of Jack? How long would her death have affected him? Over the years they had become like ghosts to each other, shadows passing along the walls, beings without substance or reality. At best, she figured Jack would have noticed her absence more than he noticed her presence. The space in his bed. His dinner plate unfilled. The empty kitchen. Nobody to nurture the children. The cow waiting by the gate to be milked.

Their conversations, he would not miss—they were devoid of anything that mattered, littered with necessary facts, but bearing nothing of warmth, no connection or intimacy. In recent years, their eyes had flattened during speech. They had closed each other out like a door pulled shut. And their jobs had become the reason for existing. Jack, the lighthouse keeper. Mary, the mother.

If she had died in the accident, Mary was aware that Jack could have written a new future for himself, one without the burden of a wife. He could have sent Jan and Gary to boarding school. He could have become one with the wind and melted into the solitude he wrapped so closely around himself. She often wondered if he would have been happier that way.

After ten weeks, the leg mended and she went home, aware there was much work to be done to knit her marriage back together. But it seemed she was too late. The *Jack* she arrived home to was a stranger, aloof and unwelcoming, disinterested in her return. Aware of her own fragility, and shocked by Jack's detachment, she took the children and went back to her parents' house. She needed space to find her way out of the debilitating grip of despair before she could attempt to revive her relationship. Two months later, she returned once more to the cape; this time she was ready to fix things with Jack.

At first, she and Jack edged around each other like skittish crabs, not knowing how to reconnect. There were times when she considered leaving for good, but commitment was something her parents had taught her, and divorce never seemed a real option. It might have been possible if she'd been a different person in a different era. But society frowned on separation, and she was in her mid-thirties with two children. Jan and Gary had to be considered too. Jack was their father, and they needed him.

There was also the burden of her guilt. Over the years at the lighthouse as Jack had become more distant, instead of retreating and dreaming of a life with Adam, she could have put more effort into her marriage. Jack might not be passionate like Adam, but he was solid and dependable, with an inner strength that matched the place they lived in . . . Bruny Island. Yes, the island was part of what held them together. How lucky they were in their mutual love of this place. It gave them a base on which to reconstruct themselves.

In the end, it was Mary's task to remake the family. She strived to avoid conflict, steering cautiously around prickly issues. She organised weekly picnics down in their quiet cove where sometimes they saw seals or dolphins. She re-ignited their sex life. Despite his initial resistance, she could see this was important to Jack. Sex reunited him with his physical self and it brought touch back into their relationship. Touch and intimacy. She also ensured they holidayed away at the farm, where Jack fished and walked and laughed with Max and Faye.

Jack started to put in more effort too. Instead of hiding in a book or escaping early to bed each evening, he stayed in the living area with the family. He talked books with Jan and spent more time with Gary: fishing, walking, teaching him carpentry in the shed. Then, when the children were in bed, Mary and Jack played canasta, five hundred, Scrabble. They reminisced on good times, unearthing their favourite memories. It was all so laborious and forced at first, but the new habits gained momentum.

Then Tom came along. The gift and the inspiration. The precious one who made them whole again. Mary didn't tell Jack she was pregnant until they'd begun to heal, and when she gave him the news, he wept. Jack liked babies. If he hadn't been so crushed by Hobart life, he'd have been more involved when Jan and Gary were small. Even so, he'd done as much as he could, cradling them to sleep, walking them in the pram, bringing them in to be fed. When Tom arrived, he took extra care with him. If Tom cried at night, Jack was there, taking the baby in his arms and walking up and down the corridor. Or he would sit on the couch stroking Tom's feathery little head with a hand already twisted with arthritis.

Jack could not be remade. Yet he did mellow, and she loved him for what he had been and also for what he was—a man of commitment. He was never particularly close to the children as they grew up, being too awkward and inscrutable for that. And he never completely recovered from the air and distance of the cape. But he and Mary were at ease together. And there was satisfaction in the achievement of a long marriage. By staying together, they had accomplished something valuable and intangible—an unspoken trust and solidarity that came from the knowledge they'd survived hardship and had not been destroyed.

There was cause for celebration in that.

27

Saturday night is Emma's party, and I don't think my acceptance was a particularly good idea. I haven't been to a party in years. I'm useless at small talk. And I don't want to see Nick again. If Emma gets a chance to line us up side by side in a social setting, I know which man will be found wanting. I'll be the gangly awkward one who can't even paste a friendly smile on his face.

I don't know why I'm going to this party anyway. I should be down at Bruny with Mum. She looked dreadful when I visited with Gary on Wednesday, weak and vague. That cough is killing her. Gary said Dad was the same.

I pull on jeans, a green shirt and a grey fleece top. It's not even worth looking in the mirror—all I will see is my inadequacy. I grab my keys from the bench before I can convince myself not to go.

Jess is waiting at the front door. I'm not sure if I should take her: I don't want to leave her in the car for three or four hours, but then again, if I have to check on my dog perhaps it'll give me an excuse to leave. I open the door and follow Jess to the car. She's joyous to be going out and I wish I could share a fraction of her excitement. All I feel is dread.

Outside Emma's house, I sit in the car with the radio on, waiting for eight o'clock. When the ABC news fanfare starts, I stay in the car a few minutes longer to hear out the news and get the weather forecast. Then I get out and shut the car door. I stand awhile in the street. The house is lit like a birthday with fairy lights strung up specially for the party. I jingle the keys in my pocket, open the gate and plod up the steps to the front door to ring the doorbell. There are footsteps and a shadow moving inside and the door finally swings open. It's Nick.

'Oh, it's you,' he says, his face expressionless. 'Emma must have asked everyone she knows.'

Now Emma appears behind him and grabs his arm to pull him out of the way. 'Isn't that the idea?' She smiles up at Nick and then at me. 'Parties are best when there's a good crowd. Come through to the kitchen.'

Nick stomps off down the hall and I follow Emma through the house. She's wearing jeans and a purple top glittering with silver sequins.

'I like your top,' I say as we come into the kitchen.

'Borrowed it from a friend,' she says. 'I don't own anything like this. It's a bit glitzy for me.'

'I think it suits you.' I feel like I'm trying too hard.

Emma glances down at my hands and then opens the fridge. 'Want a drink?' she asks.

A drink? Oh God, I feel like a complete idiot. She did say it was BYO. 'I'm sorry,' I mumble. 'I forgot to stop at the pub.'

'No matter,' she says vaguely. 'There's plenty here.'

'No. No.' I'm hoarse with embarrassment. 'I'll just pop down the street. It won't take a minute.'

I retreat quickly down the hall to the door. No wonder she was looking at me like that. I've committed a major social *faux pas*. *And* I'm here too early. Nobody else has arrived. Only a fool is on time to a party. I've forgotten how to be a normal human being.

'Tom,' Emma calls. 'Don't worry about it.'

She appears from the kitchen, while I stand with my hand on the doorknob. Her face is flushed and smiling. She's not judging, I realise; it's me who is doing all the flagellation here.

'There's plenty of grog.' She slips her hand over mine on the doorknob. 'Just stay.'

'I won't feel right.' My heart is beating hard at her proximity. Perhaps she doesn't mind me being early after all.

'Let him go.' Nick comes down the corridor doing up the cuffs of a white shirt. He looks brown-faced, healthy and masculine. 'It's going to be a big night. Won't hurt to have a few reserves.'

'I'll come with you.' Emma is right beside me at the door.

'We have to light the candles and put out the food,' Nick says.

'Emma,' another voice calls from the kitchen, 'where's the hummus?'

'It's okay. I'll be back soon.' I back out the door, feeling Emma's hand slip off mine, and then Nick has his arm around her waist and is shepherding her towards the kitchen. She might have said that he doesn't own her, but he's acting like he does.

In the street, I can breathe again. The best thing I could do right now is to get in the car and drive home. But Emma is expecting me to return, and, pathetic though I am, I can't let her down. I shove my hands in my pockets and start walking down the hill. My car is the only one parked in the street. Why didn't I notice this before? I'm so out of practice, it's a tragedy. If a party's happening, there should be cars everywhere.

I manage to take more than an hour buying half a dozen beers and a bottle of wine. When I come back up the hill, cars are parked up and down the street. I'm now fashionably late. I stop by the Subaru and let Jess out to stretch her legs. She squats with some embarrassment on the nature strip then bounds back into the car and snuggles down on my seat. She's happy that I'm back and that I haven't deserted her. I guess she's keeping her eye on me, just in case.

I drum my fingers on the roof of the car and watch people climbing out of another vehicle further up the street. They're laughing, talking animatedly. How nice it would be to enter a party with the added confidence of being with a friend. But I can't delay much longer. It's time to go and face the mob. I sweep my plastic bag of clinking bottles off the top of the car and walk through the gate and up the steps to the front door for the second time tonight.

Through the window I can see the lights have been dimmed and music is now throbbing. I bang on the door. Wait. Knock again. Then I let myself in. Music swells out. Music and smoke. I hear laughter from the kitchen, so I shut the door behind me and walk tentatively towards the sound. Somebody sweeps past me in the semi-dark, and then I have to push past bodies in the doorway to get into the kitchen. Everything is candlelit. Faces glow in the flickering light and the smoke haze softens outlines. The hubbub of conversation is loud as I move towards the fridge, weaving around the overheated bodies of people I've never seen before.

'No room in the fridge,' someone yells. 'Go to the laundry. There's ice in the sink.'

I wave and squeeze through another door and someone points me to the laundry where a candle is shivering on the windowsill. While I'm pulling the beers out of their packaging so I can bury them to keep them cool, a guy leans over me and fishes out a couple of drinks. He's sweaty and his dark hair hangs around his face. I can smell the smoke on his breath. The party's only been going an hour and this guy is smashed.

'Get one into you,' he says. 'Bloody good party.' He stumbles out.

I linger in the gloom of the laundry with an open beer in my hand before I muster the courage to search for Emma. I can't face going back into the crowded kitchen, so I follow someone through to the lounge room where party lights are strung around the curtains and light fittings as well as the mantelpiece above the gas fire. I see the glow of Nick's white shirt in one corner; he's with a group of people. I can't see if Emma is among them. In another corner, a cluster of guys is laughing loudly and clinking beers.

I slide further into the room and stand against the wall, sipping my beer. On the couch, a couple is deep in conversation. The guy is obviously chatting up the girl—he's playing with her hair and her hand is on his leg. Even *I* can interpret the signals.

Nick breaks away from his group and comes towards the door. Of course he notices me standing there like a wallflower.

'You're back,' he says, eyes and voice flat. 'You haven't seen Emma, have you?'

I shake my head.

'She's got the shits with me tonight. For sending you off.'

'I took myself off.'

'Tell her that, will you?' He puts his empty bottle on the mantelpiece. 'How are you off for a beer?'

'Just started one.'

'Drink up, then. I'll get you another.'

He shifts by me, through the door. I hope he won't come back, but he returns quickly with two bottles. The one he passes to me is dripping. It's straight out of the ice.

'Where'd you meet Emma?' he asks. He twists the top off his beer and takes a swig without moving his eyes from my face.

'She gave a talk at the antdiv.' I don't want to get into a conversation with this guy.

'How'd you hear about it?'

'Friend.'

'You got friends at the antdiv?' Nick looks disbelieving.

'A few.'

'Who?'

'Mostly diesos.'

'You're a grease monkey, then?'

'Mechanic.'

'Same thing.'

This guy has a knack of making me feel small. I wish I could tell him it isn't necessary, that I already feel small.

'Emma seems to have taken a liking to you,' Nick grunts. 'She's always picking up new people.'

'She's a nice girl.'

'You know she's going south again,' he says. 'She won't be round for long. I'd advise you not to get too involved.'

Just at that moment Emma breezes in through the door, smiling broadly and clearly tipsy. 'Guys,' she says. 'Good to see you getting on.'

Nick looks straight at me and then turns to Emma and rubs his hand up and down her back. 'Having fun, baby?'

She gives him a kiss on the lips. Obviously she's forgiven him for any disagreement they may have had earlier this evening. 'Great party, isn't it?' she says to him.

'The best.' He's looking her up and down approvingly. It's sickening to watch.

'Your turn for a kiss now,' she says, smiling at me.

Nick's smile disappears and then he's blocked out altogether as Emma leans towards me and touches her lips against mine.

'You taste nice,' she giggles. 'Hey, Nick, have you introduced Tom to anyone?'

'No,' he says. 'We were just having a cosy chat together.'

'Cosy?' She narrows her eyes at him. 'How about you go and get cosy with someone else.'

Nick scowls and reluctantly crosses the room to join a couple of guys near the window. Emma hooks her arm through mine.

'You were gone a long time,' she says. 'I was waiting for you.'

'It took me a while to find a pub. Plus, I didn't want to come back too early while you were still getting things ready.'

She giggles again and presses her face against my shoulder. 'I don't think I've had enough to eat. Can you get me some food?'

I'd prefer to sit with her on the couch. It's empty now—the couple must have gone elsewhere to grope each other. On the couch she could curl up close to me like a cat. I'd be happy just to snuggle. She wouldn't have to say anything.

'Food's in the kitchen,' she reminds me. Nick glances up as we leave the room.

The kitchen is still congested. I tug Emma through the tangle of bodies and find a bowl of hummus and some crackers on the bench.

'Load me up with it, will you?' she says. 'You dip and I'll eat. I've lost count of the drinks.' She stuffs crackers into her mouth and crunches them up as quickly as she can. 'Water?' she asks.

I'll never make it to the sink through this crush. She must read hesitation in my face.

'Get out of the way,' she yells at the throng. 'I'm going to be sick.' The crowd parts like the Red Sea. 'Magic, that.' She finds a used glass on the sink, rinses it and sloshes some water in clumsily. 'Still not sober,' she observes. 'Take me back to the lounge.'

I take her hand and carry the hummus and crackers with the other. The crowd stands clear. I could be leading a celebrity on an opening night. 'They're scared of you,' I murmur.

She smiles.

On the couch, she shovels in more dip and crackers. It should soak up some alcohol, at least. Nick's back with the group in the corner and there's a long row of empties lined up along the mantelpiece. I had forgotten that's how it is down south. Everyone gets very good at drinking. Socially, that's all there is to look forward to—your quota of grog, supplemented by home brew.

I ask Emma if Nick is her boyfriend, but she's so busy munching on a cracker that she doesn't hear me and the moment is gone. My resolve to ask her shrivels like plastic in an open fire. And anyway, if she says yes, what would I do? Get up and leave? Or bat out the evening feeling ill? Maybe it's better to live in doubt. Emma seems happy to sit in silence. She pulls my arm around her shoulders like a rug and nestles in. It's a good feeling. If I could just remove everyone else from the picture, it'd be romantic.

Several quiet minutes pass while we watch the other people in the room. I look down at her to pass some comment about the party, but she has slipped into a drunken doze. I hadn't realised she was so out of it. I thought the hummus would be kicking in by now. Perhaps another glass of water would help.

I make sure she's comfortable and then head to the kitchen. Somebody has turned on the lights in there and I see Nick by the sink so I grab a plastic cup off the bench and take it to the bathroom to fill. On the way, I pass what must be Nick's bedroom. A pile of climbing gear lies tossed in the corner, and on top I see the harness I used at Freycinet just over a week ago. I try not to imagine Emma in this room with Nick. I try not to think of him fondling her, touching her, kissing her but I have little success blocking it out. The thought of his hands on her darkens my mind.

Why doesn't she see it? Even *I* can tell that Nick's a womaniser. There's a reason he knows exactly what to do and say: too much experience.

When I return to the lounge, Emma is up dancing with a group of girls. She skols the cup of water I hand her, strokes my cheek and resumes dancing. I lean against the door with a fresh beer, enjoying watching her. Someone is doing a good job of mixing the music—a tall guy with a mop of dishevelled brown hair remains for hours by the sound system, squinting at CDs between swigs of beer. I watch him deftly flicking discs into the tray and jabbing buttons to find the right songs. It'd be nice to know your music like that; to be able to keep people dancing and entertained, to seamlessly keep the music flowing.

Sometime after midnight, I slip out to check on Jess. It's cold outside and the sky is dotted with stars. Jess raises her head from the floor to greet me, and I sit in the car with her for a while. I'm tired and I've had enough beer. For a few indulgent moments, I contemplate going home. But Emma might need me.

People keep moving in and out of the house: couples mostly, finding a dark nook to kiss in. Every now and then small groups bundle into cars and weave off down the hill, probably on their way to another party. Occasionally a taxi appears and ferries a load of people away. By the time I go back in, the party is winding down. Emma is still dancing, and I stand beside the door again to watch. Nick is stretched across the couch, half passed out, completely drunk. Perhaps that's his idea of a good time. His shirt is hanging out and has red wine stains on it.

I find myself watching the candles sinking low on their wicks and the sleepy shadows flickering on the walls. Finally, Emma comes across the room and takes my hand. 'Come on.' Her eyes melt in the dim light. 'Let's go to bed.'

She leads me out the back door, stopping to kiss me at the bottom of the stairs. She's hot and sweaty from dancing, and the smell of her excites me.

'Can I get Jess?' I ask between kisses.

'You and your bloody dog.' She waves me off. 'Just shut the door behind you when you come in.'

I walk around to the car realising I've killed yet another moment of promise. By the time I've dug a blanket out of the back of the car and laid it out for Jess in a corner of the bungalow, Emma is asleep in her clothes, spread-eagled across the bed. I shift her limbs gently and tug the doona from beneath her slack weight.

Then I tuck it carefully over her sleeping shape. I sit on the edge of the bed watching her, smiling at the soft grating of her snore. Then I undress, switch off the lamp and crawl in beside her.

Emma barely moves during the night, even though I wake several times to the sound of bottles being tossed into the yard and voices from the main house. Once, I slip out from the warmth of Emma's body to lock the door. I don't want an early-morning confrontation with an angry and hungover Nick, although I don't think he'll be up to much till midday. I hope to be long gone by then.

When sunlight floods in through the windows, I draw the curtains and leave Emma sleeping while I make a cup of tea. Jess clicks around the kitchen, pressing her nose up beneath my hand to remind me she's there. She doesn't seem comfortable; perhaps she remembers Nick from last time. I sit at the table and read yesterday's newspaper, including the jobs and real estate. Then I'm out of reading material.

I notice a black notebook under the newspaper and open it without thinking. The pages are full of dark flowing handwriting. Probably Emma's. I study the loops and curls of it, wondering what it tells me about her, and then my curiosity surges and, I am reading.

> *Busy few days with the Adelies. The weighbridge is giving me the shits. It works for a few days and then some connection goes wrong and we're off the air again. I just can't work out what's going on. I need some electronics genius to sort it out for me, but they're few and far between on station.*

> *Sophie went into station last night to visit her beau. God, it makes me sick. Saturday night and she has to go into town for the party. It's the same every week—same old music, same old grog. Station leader doesn't like me being on my own out here, so they*

sent Nick out to keep me company. A pointed comment. We've tried to be discreet, but everybody knows anyway. I suppose it's hard to disguise body language. And who can blame me. It's so hard when chemistry takes over, and God, Nick sets me on fire.

I put the book down. It's none of my business to be reading Emma's journal. It's a disgusting intrusion and I'm ashamed. I'm also deflated. Everything I've feared has been confirmed.

For ten minutes, I sit looking at the notebook, then reluctantly flick it open again.

Nick's been staying out at the hut quite a lot lately, and Sophie isn't complaining. I think she's just about had it with water offloading, and I have to admit it's a shitty job. Especially when you can't even get a shower afterwards. To his credit, Nick doesn't seem to mind. We boil up a big pot of water at the end of each day and wash ourselves where it matters. Then the evening is ours. It has been quite romantic actually. I guess I didn't expect it of Nick, but he can be very nice. And he's bloody good in bed.

I shove the notebook back under the newspaper, furious with myself for spying. Emma would hate it if she knew. I sit for another thirty minutes, staring at the clock, hoping she'll wake before Nick appears. Eventually, I hear a groan from the bedroom. I stand and walk to the bedside.

'Oh, Tom,' she says groggily. 'You're still here. That's nice.'

I sit on the bed.

'Did you tuck me in?' She closes her eyes.

'Yes. You were asleep when I came in.'

'Oh, and I had hoped for passionate sex.'

Me too.

'I'm too wasted this morning,' she says. 'Can you get me a coffee?'

I go to the kitchen and make her coffee, still riddled with guilt for having read her diary. I place the cup on the bedside table, shifting aside her pill packet and a glass of water. 'I'm really sorry,' I say. 'I accidentally looked in your journal.'

'Oh that,' she mumbles, her face partly concealed by her pillow. 'It's full of bullshit about Nick. Amazing the rubbish you can write sometimes.'

'Aren't you cross with me?'

'Yes, of course I'm cross,' she says sleepily. 'But it doesn't matter.'

I'm surprised she isn't more upset. I want it to matter. Reading someone's private journal goes against all my values. Perhaps she's too bleary to fully realise what I've done.

'Do you think it'd make a good book?' Emma asks, rolling to look up at me.

'What?'

'My life in Antarctica? Perhaps I should call it that. God, I think I'm still drunk.'

'Do you want some breakfast?'

She turns away from me again. 'Just a slice of toast and butter. Then I'm getting dressed and coming over to your place. I can't face any of the others today. I think I need a holiday.'

I return to the kitchen to make the toast.

'You don't mind if I come over to yours, do you?' she calls.

'No, that's fine.'

Of course I don't mind. I don't mind at all. But when I go back in with the toast she has fallen asleep again.

I wait at the table just sitting and thinking for another hour, and then leave. This might be the best thing I can do.

28

Sunday morning, Mary was staring at the bathroom mirror when she heard banging in the kitchen, as if someone was going through the cupboards. She stiffened, listening for a voice she might recognise.

Then she remembered. Of course; Jacinta was here. And Alex. They'd arrived early this morning, enthusiastic about the trip. She sighed, wiping the corners of her mouth with a tissue. She'd forgotten they were going to the lighthouse. They'd discussed it last weekend. And perhaps she had mentioned it to Leon. But she'd lost the thread of things somehow.

She ought to be excited about this excursion. For days, she'd been manoeuvring to make it happen. It was the last tick on her list of tributes to Jack. When it was done, she would feel she had atoned for her mistakes in some way. Her duty would be finished. But she was tired, so tired.

She finished in the bathroom and shuffled to the bedroom where she gazed vacantly at her suitcase. She kept forgetting things, finding herself in the middle of a room wondering what she was meant to do. Wasn't there something she had to attend to? Yes. She needed warm clothes. She gazed into the jumble of underwear, unpaired socks, rumpled shirts and trousers. She couldn't even maintain a tidy drawer anymore. She fumbled through her clothes until she found what she needed. But wasn't there something else she ought to remember? Something else she must do?

Yes. A letter—hidden in the side pocket. She tugged the envelope out with clumsy fingers and turned it over three times before sliding it carefully back in. Hadn't she'd made the decision to dispose of it days ago? Or was it only yesterday? Time had warped recently and she couldn't find logic in its fragments anymore. Tonight, when Alex and Jacinta had gone, she would burn the letter and be done with it.

'Nana?' Jacinta was at the door. 'Are you ready?'

'Yes . . . yes.' She looked up unsteadily.

Alex smiled at her as she hobbled into the living area with a bundle of clothing. 'Are you off to Antarctica?' he asked.

'There's a sou'westerly today,' she said. 'It cuts right through you.'

This morning before they arrived, she'd sat by the window watching the wind straining up over the dunes and flailing the shrubs, flicking upward sprays of spume off the waves. Wind like that was the breath of ice.

Now she moved towards the door, but Jacinta grasped her arm gently. 'I'm not sure we should go, Nana. You're not looking well, and if you catch cold, you could die of pneumonia. I'd never forgive myself.'

Mary was alarmed. There was no option. They had to make this trip today. 'I'll be fine,' she said, summoning a persuasive smile. 'I haven't been sleeping well, that's all.'

'But it's so exposed at the lighthouse. I don't want to take you out in the cold.'

'This is what I want, Jacinta. It's important to me.' Mary could sense her granddaughter's indecision so she pressed her advantage. 'If my cough gets out of hand then I'll let you bring me home.'

'Do you promise you'll tell me if you're feeling unwell?'

'I promise.'

'All right then.'

Alex took her clothes and put them in the car. When everything was packed, he helped her into the front seat.

They scaled the dunes and whizzed along the flat beach as if it was a highway.

'How fast are we going?' Mary croaked. She hadn't left the cabin since the scout camp last weekend, and the speed triggered somersaults in her chest.

'Only forty k's an hour,' Alex said. 'Is it too fast for you?'

'No,' she lied. 'It's fine.'

She reminded herself that, despite her agitation, it was a grand day to be out. The sky was patchy with clouds and Pacific gulls lifted at the car's approach and wafted overhead.

Halfway down the beach they passed a man and woman walking. They were young and they stared at Mary without smiling. She knew the car was an intrusion in such a beautiful place. When she was young, she'd have been mortified to see a vehicle here. Jack would have called it an abomination. He had always been a traditionalist.

She glanced back along the beach and was startled to see herself walking there on the sand with Jack—his tall shape and her impatient strong legs. Yes, there they were, walking fast together to the end of the beach. To Cloudy Corner. In the campground, they'd drop their packs and climb the headland to search for sea eagles and smell the cold air. They would embrace up there. Kiss and hold each other close. Young bodies straining tight.

She heard Alex talking and she turned to gaze into his expectant face. He smiled at her as he swung the car up off the beach and onto the road. 'So what do you think?' he said.

'About what?' Mary was lost.

'About Tom meeting a girl.'

'. . . he's met a girl, has he?'

'Yes,' Jacinta said from the back. 'He said he told you about her.'

Mary struggled to catch the slipping edge of a memory. Had Tom said he'd met someone? 'How are they going?' she asked.

'Well, I think,' Jacinta said. 'He seems happy.'

Good. It was time for Tom to be happy. Mary looked away, trying to hide her uneasiness. Hadn't she noticed Tom was happier? She ought to have seen that.

'He said he might go south again,' Jacinta added. 'And that you were pleased. He said you encouraged him.'

Was it really a good idea for Tom to go south again?

'He's hoping to work with this girl,' Jacinta continued. 'Emma.'

Emma. She did remember something about that name. 'What about Jess?' Mary asked.

'If he goes, I'll look after her.'

The road was turning towards the old farm, and Mary could see the tall white trees down by the stream. She remembered how she used to love standing beneath them in a strong wind, listening to the long strips of bark slapping against the trunks. Smiling, she closed her eyes, imagining herself as a girl again, milking cows in a shed that was no longer there. She saw herself up a ladder picking apples; in the paddock raking silage; standing in the shed where she'd met Jack, straining to see his face in the shadows.

At Lunawanna, Jacinta suggested stopping for coffee, but Mary wanted to keep going, so they drove past the shop onto the lighthouse road. These days the road was well graded with only a few potholes and corrugations, and it curved past houses and shacks overlooking the still waters of the channel. Beyond lay rough farmland dotted with bracken and tussock grass. They drove through stringybark forest, passing fences and gates and *No Trespassing* signs. It was drier here than at Cloudy Bay. Soon the shining mirror of Cloudy Lagoon appeared close beside the road. It was vast, edged with mudflats, and a breeze rippled across its surface.

When they finally came to the National Park, Mary was already tired. They stopped to collect an envelope at the pay station and then drove on through forest and roadside bracken. As they rounded a corner, a break in the trees revealed the view over the heath to the lighthouse. Alex stopped the car and turned off the engine and they sat in silence watching cloud shadows sliding across the terrain. The lighthouse stood white on the cape, unchanged. Below, on the leeside of the hill, tucked away from the prevailing winds, were the two keepers' cottages and the sheds. Waves were washing steadily into Lighthouse Bay and frothy skirts of foam laced the rocks.

Looking across to the lighthouse from the depths of the forest, it seemed to Mary as if she was looking back over her life to a place she didn't know anymore. Today could be yesterday, or it could be twenty, thirty, forty years ago. It was even possible when they arrived at the keeper's cottage that her younger self might come out to greet them. Or that Jack might emerge from the shed with a tool in his hand. Or maybe it would be Rose with her sly smile and threatening eyes at the cottage door, offering her hand as if she was a friend. Tom might even be there—a scruffy windswept boy, running up the track from the beach.

They drove on through twisted banksias and short, spreading rough-barked eucalypts. In the lower carpark just outside the lighthouse reserve, Alex stopped the car again and they all sat for a moment, staring up the hill. The gate was open.

'I think it's all right to drive in,' he said. 'The sign says it's okay till four thirty.' He put the car in gear.

'Wait here a minute,' Jacinta said, opening her door. 'I'll run up and speak to the caretaker.'

She was gone for several minutes and Mary took the opportunity to lean back and close her eyes. Memory lurked beneath her eyelids. She could see herself in the keeper's cottage right now, listening to the wind fetching up under the eaves and scuffing the windows. If she concentrated she could almost hear Jack hammering away at something in the shed. Tom whistling somewhere up on the hill. The pony snorting in the paddock.

Jacinta returned with a smile almost as wide as her face. 'I've got the keys to the lighthouse,' she cried, jingling them above her head. 'Don't get out. They're going to let us drive right to the top.'

As they drove up the road, Mary saw a lady waiting for them near the cottages. She was middle-aged and dark-haired, weathered. Alex lowered the electric window and the lady reached in to shake Mary's hand.

'Hello, Mrs Mason. I'm Diane.' Her smile was warm. 'Would you like to come in for a cuppa? I've got the kettle on.'

Mary hesitated, shaken. This woman could have been her, forty years ago. 'Thank you. But not just now . . . Perhaps after.'

'I'd love to talk,' Diane said, still holding her hand. 'It's a shame you haven't come before. You've always been welcome.'

Mary released her hand to cover a rising cough, aware that everyone was watching her. 'Sometimes it's hard to come back,' she said, smiling wearily at Diane. 'It's not quite the same.'

'Well, maybe another time . . .'

Mary could see herself in the caretaker's gentle nod and her far-reaching eyes. 'Your family?' she asked.

'All gone now,' Diane said. 'We schooled them here by correspondence until high school. Same as you.'

'Yes.' Mary said, remembering. The children and the books. The gloomy daytime light in the cottage. Then the children gone. The quiet in the house. The wind eating at the walls.

'You'll see the light hasn't changed,' Diane was saying. 'My husband Tony does the upkeep. But it's years now since she was lit. There's still a lot of work to do, of course. Tony maintains the site and I look after the cottage. It's different now, with all the visitors, but we still love living here.'

Mary felt tears welling. Ridiculous. A few kind words, a sliver of memory, and here she was on the verge of crying. She squeezed Diane's hand to thank her. Then she nodded to Alex and they drove on up the road, past the large new sheds and around the sweeping curve to the top of the hill.

At the foot of the lighthouse, Jacinta helped her out into the chill wind and they walked around the tower to the lookout. The engine room was gone now from the base of the lighthouse—only a slab of cracked concrete remained. But the view was marvellously constant. Exactly as it had been the last time she stood here. Courts Island wasn't visible—you had to descend the rough four-wheel-drive track to see it, a feat she wasn't capable of today. And she couldn't see the sea stacks to the south as they were visible only on the clearest of days. But the heaving sea was miraculously eternal. Its colour might change, and its texture and the direction of its seething whitecaps. Reassuringly though, it would go on forever, rolling and rising and driving towards shore. It soothed her to think of the ocean through time: the predictability of the tides, the endless renewal of waves. When she was gone, the sea would not change, and the land would continue to lean into its thrust. It steadied her to think of this.

When she started to shiver in the wind, Jacinta took her elbow and guided her back around the tower. Alex had already unlocked the lighthouse door and was holding it open for them. They passed through into the hush of the tower, their footsteps echoing. Alex closed the door and all was quiet.

Above, the shadowy spiral staircase wound upwards. In the light chamber, the curtains would be drawn. It used to be Jack's job each night to open the curtains and start the light; at dawn, he'd be up there to turn it off and close the curtains again. Every day, weather permitting, he'd go out on the high balcony and up onto the rim to clean the windows, rubbing off the salt smears.

She'd love to contemplate the cape from that elevated platform where the light used to wink out over the sea, but she didn't need to go up there. The tower was already dense with memories for her. And she didn't require the view to remember all that had taken place here; she could still see Jack's shadow in the lantern room and hear his voice echoing and rolling around the stone walls. She drew breath to explain all this to Jacinta and Alex, but as she gazed upwards a wave of emotion collapsed over her. Then dizziness. She was whirling in slow motion, on the brink of unconsciousness.

Strong arms grasped her. Then everything darkened.

She was lying on the concrete floor. Cold and winded. Breathless. Her body was light and then heavy. Her heart was flipping. The floor was freezing against her cheek. She was struggling against blackness.

She felt hands stroking her face. Soft warm hands, Jacinta's fingers flying like butterflies over her skin. Her granddaughter's face slipped from light to shade, light to shade.

It was cold in the tower. So cold. She could see the bottom of the lighthouse stairs, blurry, not far from her face. She blinked upwards. The stairs spiralled above her like a lazy snail shell. And the light was blinking again. Light and shade. Light and shade. Darkness. Humming. A cough racked.

'What happened?' The voice was faint.

'I don't know. We'll have to carry her back to the car.'

Someone was crying. The voices were far away. Tinged with humming and flashes of light. Like the tower at night. Sooner or later it would stop.

There was Jack's voice, furry around the edges. He was looking after her. She could feel him close. His arms lifted her and crushed her face against his chest. She could smell the warm male scent of him. She could feel the protection of his arms. She felt air rustling somewhere. Fluid gurgled.

'Her lungs are rattling.'

The voice boomed. Her head was held close. Flashes of coloured light, green, red, purest white. Jack was warm and near. She could die like this.

Then she was moving and there was bright light in her face, a rush of cold air. Jack was bending over her, folding his long straight back in two to reach her, a smile on his face to show he forgave her for everything. Those blue eyes. But now the shadows were eating him. They were mottling his face, erasing his eyes. He was nothing but mist again. Foggy.

She was aware of a roof closing over her, a seat to lean against. She was in the back of the car and Alex was frowning down at her.

'Is there an ambulance here?' he was saying. 'A doctor? A hospital? Is there anything on this island?'

And then, Jacinta's voice: 'I don't know. We can ask the caretaker's wife.'

'She should be in hospital where they can look after her.'

Mary struggled to form words. 'No hospitals. Take me to the cabin.'

Jacinta climbed in beside her, face pale and lined with tears. 'What was that, Nana? Can you hear me?'

'Yes, I can hear you.' Her vision was stabilising. The flashing had stopped. The humming dissipated.

'What happened? Are you all right?'

'I had a turn.' Her voice was quavering. 'But I'll be fine. Take me back to Cloudy Bay.'

'We should go to hospital,' Jacinta suggested. 'It's for the best.'

'I don't want to die in hospital.'

Jacinta was torn. She looked to Alex.

He shrugged. 'I think we should go to Hobart.'

'No. Not Hobart.' Mary clutched Jacinta anxiously. 'I know what I want.'

Alex looked at her. 'Well then.' His voice was heavy. 'I suppose we go to Cloudy Bay . . .'

He started the car and they eased slowly down the hill, stopping by the cottages while Jacinta returned the keys. Then she was back in the car, leaning forward to talk to Alex.

'There's no doctor on the island,' she said quietly. 'We'd have to drive to Hobart, or have her airlifted out. They can land a helicopter here.'

'No hospitals,' Mary asserted again. She was still shaking with after-reaction.

Jacinta took her hand and stroked her with gentle fingers. 'It's all right, Nana. We'll take you to Cloudy Bay. I promise we'll do what you say. Now, you rest while we drive home. Alex and I will take care of you.'

Mary sagged against her granddaughter, weak and exhausted. They drove through the gate and up the road. The thrum of the wheels on the gravel lulled her; the soothing shift and sway as they took the corners. She fought to keep her eyes open as the car crossed the heath. Then they were climbing the hill. Soon they'd be at the viewpoint—her last glimpse of the cape, her last view of the lighthouse. But fatigue washed over her and her eyelids slid down. She was riding on a tide that was carrying her elsewhere, back into memory, returning to Jack . . .

It was dark now and she couldn't see. She was on the cape and everything was black, even the tower. Why wasn't the light flashing? Jack had never forgotten it. The sea was roaring too. She could hear it. The cliffs must be nearer than she'd thought. Or was it rain on the roof? Another storm coming in? Storms came so quickly here, rushing across the sea from the south. If the light wasn't stone buried in stone, it'd be blown across the cape, shattered into pieces. Such winds they had on the cape. The children would be frightened in such a storm. There was thunder, and flashes of light. Mary hoped she could get the pony in the shed before the storm came. She didn't want to live through another storm like the last one.

And finally Rose was there. Yes. Mary had known she would come.

She was waiting in the doorway of the keeper's cottage, claiming Mary's territory, her face smug. Mary felt a twinge of anger. Now she was home from hospital, Rose would have to pack and be gone. She'd have to go back to the farm, back to her selfish, sedentary life.

But Rose's face was sliding inwards, rippling like smoke. Oh, how Mary wanted to wipe that smile away—that sly, self-aware smile, slightly mocking. Rose had seen the limp, despite Mary's struggle to hide it. Ten weeks of recovery and rehabilitation and now Mary's homecoming was flattened. Rose's smile was triumphant—she thought she could prolong her stay.

'Jack's up at the lighthouse.' Rose's voice warped and flexed. 'We didn't know when to expect you.'

We, as if she was the mistress of the house.

Mary felt an ache at the site of the fracture. Her leg was heavy with the memory of plaster. She'd been so hopeful when they cut the cast away, but what they gave her back was not her leg. It was a shrivelled pale thing, useless without a crutch. She thought she'd be going home immediately, but it was another four weeks before they'd let her go.

'Where are my children?' Her voice echoed down the empty hallway. The worn lino of the keeper's cottage. Her house.

'Doing their lessons.' Rose's face contorted with derision. 'Their schoolwork is important.' Rose was sneering at the leg as if she could see through Mary's trousers to the sallow skin, the itchy flaking redness, the wasted muscles. 'You're limping.'

Rose's eyes were dark holes. 'I hope you haven't returned too soon. We haven't time to nurse you.'

That *we* again. Mary tried to push her aside, but her hands dissolved through Rose as if she was made of air. Wind gushed. When Mary turned, Rose was gone.

She limped down the hallway. There was the sound of chairs scraping in the kitchen. Footsteps running. The children. But they were mirage-like, ghostly, running by her, through the wooden door.

And now she was in the kitchen. Condensation was wet on the windows. The kettle steaming on the stove. Mist billowing over the cape. Wind whistling under the window.

She heard the bang of the cottage door opening. Jack's footsteps, strong and heavy down the hall. He swung into the kitchen, his arranged smile turning crooked on his face. He seemed taller than she remembered. Thinner.

He went to the window and gazed up the hill. Mary followed his eyes. There was Rose, standing beside the light tower, her coat flapping in the wind.

'She's welcome to have tea with us,' Mary said.

'She didn't want to interrupt your homecoming.' Jack spoke without looking at her. His voice was strangled and strange.

'And what about you?'

He glanced at her, frosty. 'I'm glad you're back, Mary.'

She poured tea—thick black stuff that oozed from the kettle like treacle. His large hands encircled the cup. Hands that had touched her skin in intimacy, the long brown fingers toughened by wind and work.

She placed her hand on his arm. It was hard as wood. She had to draw him from the window, away from Rose's magnetic silhouette by the tower.

In the lounge room, flames danced in the heater, green and orange, licking at the briquettes. He leaned against the mantelpiece, staring at nothing, eyes wild. 'Rose stays till you can

climb the stairs.' His voice was gravelly, harsh. Then he walked
out through the wall, his body melting through stone.

Up the hill, Rose was still standing by the tower, her outline
flickering like the flames.

Mary raced to the kitchen, clattering her cup into the sink.
She grabbed two tea towels from the drying rack, and tucked
them in her pocket. At the front door, she tugged on her coat.
Her heart was thudding.

Outside, boiling cloud dissolved to a rare day of blue.
She could feel the chill freshness of the air. The silvery ripple
of the wind. Smell the close-clipped grass. To the west, across
the channel, the mountains dimpled up and down in a cloak of
purplish-blue. And now she could see the cliffs of Cape Bruny,
hunched in shadow. Her heart racketed as she turned the handle
of the lighthouse door and pushed it open.

Inside, the air was still and cold. Above, the staircase rose
in a spiral of seventy-eight steps. She could hear murmuring
voices. They were up there together, Jack and Rose. Talking.
What were they doing? Access was restricted; only keepers on
duty. Jack knew the rules. So did Rose. Mary only came up here
when Jack was ill.

She tied the tea towels over her shoes in rough knots. Her
coat was on the floor like a great black bear sleeping. Then she
started up the staircase, measuring each step with her breaths.
Breathing in. Breathing out. The air rasping in her lungs. Such
slow breaths. Each inhalation an effort.

The stairwell darkened. Clouds were scudding outside again.
The dim light shivered. Was it dusk now? Or the darkness of a
storm? The wind was scraping, rustling, gurgling. The effort of
climbing was too hard. There was no air.

Rose's face melted across her vision, swimming in and out
of focus. She struggled to concentrate on the climb. To breathe.
She was making progress up the stairs. The platform must be
coming.

One slow revolution of the snail shell. Two.

The stairs spiralled up and away. She tried to steady her breathing so as not to warn them. They had underestimated her. She would confront them. And Rose would have to go home.

The spiral narrowed at last.

Above, a dome of stars—the pinprick silver lights of the Milky Way. There was darkness outside the tower. Night black. Then suddenly the light ignited, a bright flare of whiteness slashing the night.

Up on the platform, two figures. Tall. Enmeshed.

The light revolved and flashed. There they were, Jack and Rose, gripped in an embrace.

Then there was darkness. The light extinguished. Everything collapsing. Her scaffolding was gone. A cry, the whoosh of air escaping.

She had fallen from the cliffs again. Only this time there was no ledge to stop her fall.

29

At midday, Emma is on my doorstep. As I open the door I hear the rough sound of a poorly tuned engine and see an old crimson Commodore rumbling down the hill.

Emma looks messy, red-eyed and pale. Probably not feeling particularly good after last night. 'You left,' she says.

'Yes. I waited, but you needed to rest.'

'You didn't look after me properly last night then, did you?'

I shrug.

'Can I come in?'

I stand back and she scuffs inside and collapses on the couch. Jess jumps up and lays her head in Emma's lap. They lie there together, limp and lifeless, while I fill the kettle. There is a long silence as I wait for it to boil.

'You said you'd been reading my journal,' Emma says eventually.

'I'm sorry.' I place the teapot and two mugs on the coffee table. 'I didn't mean to.'

'So why did you do it?' She's prickly and hungover.

'I don't know. It was lying there and I just picked it up. I wasn't thinking.'

'That was an invasion of privacy.'

'Yes. I'm sorry. As soon as I realised I put it down.'

'What did you read?'

'Just a few references to Nick.'

'A *few* references? I thought you put it down straightaway.'

'I did.'

'Anyway,' she says flippantly, 'don't believe everything you read.'

I wonder what that's supposed to mean.

'Everyone has a few lapses down south.' She flicks at Jess's ears. 'Did you enjoy the party?' she asks.

'I'm not much of a party person.'

She laughs, disbelieving. 'I don't know how you survived on station then.'

I pour the tea.

'Nick wasn't very happy about bringing me down here,' she says. 'But you know I don't have a car.'

So the Commodore was Nick's. I hedge carefully. 'I told you I'm happy to help find a car for you.'

She ignores this. 'He was pretty cranky about it, actually. I don't think he likes you very much. I think he's jealous of you.'

I pass her a mug, but she sets it aside and pulls me down to her and kisses me. We make love on the couch, our bodies pressed together, her mouth still tasting faintly of beer. It leaves me breathless and confused.

'I'm sorry I wasn't up to that last night.' She wipes her mouth absently.

I roll onto my back among the cushions and stare at the ceiling. What does this woman want from me? Without speaking, she gets up and puts on her clothes. Her mood has changed in the blink of an eye. 'Can you take me home now?' she asks.

I reach forward to stroke her knee, but she pushes my hand away.

'I want to go *right now*.' She walks out onto the front verandah while I dress.

'Can you tell me what's wrong?' I ask, coming outside, keys in my hand.

'You ought to know,' she snaps.

I follow her down to the car and open the door for her. She's hostile, not looking at me. 'It'd help if you'd tell me,' I say. 'I'm not good at these things.'

She gets inside and slams the door and we drive back to Hobart in silence. She stares out the side window, her face tight and closed.

When we pull up outside her house, I try again. 'Are you all right?' I attempt to place my hand on her leg, but she pushes me away. Then I realise she's crying. Her whole body is shaking with it, tears running down her face like water. 'I'm sorry,' I say, not knowing why I'm sorry or what I've done.

She bursts out of the car then comes around to my door and yells, 'You just don't get it, do you?'

I wind down the window.

'You can't set boundaries for me, can you? You can't tell me to keep away from Nick. I need a man who will fight for me.' She begins crying again and turns away, covering her eyes with her arm, and staggers up the path alongside the house.

I sit in the car with my head against the steering wheel, mind spinning with emotions.

I wonder what to do. Should I go in after her? Try to find her? Talk to her? I've been sitting here for some time already, and Nick's car is parked just in front of mine. What if she has already gone to him?

I start the car and sit with it idling for a while. Then I turn it off again, and sit some more. Eventually I get out and walk along the side of the house, knock on the door of the bungalow. There's no answer. Maybe she's gone up to the main house.

I knock again. This time, I hear a noise. Tentatively, I let myself in, and walk through to the bedroom. Emma is curled up on the bed, turned away from me, quivering with sobs. For a long moment, I stand awkwardly at the door, then sit beside her and stroke her hair. She doesn't turn around.

'I'm sorry,' I say. 'I'm sorry.' And I wish I could stop saying it. Not all of this is my fault. She's hungover and miserable and irrational. There's nothing I can do to console her.

She rolls over, finally, her face tear-streaked, and looks up at me. 'I'm ruining everything,' she sniffs. 'I'm messing up everything between us.'

At least she's acknowledging she has a role in this warped sequence of events. I help her sit up and she leans against me heavily, burying her face against my chest. Her cheeks are wet on my shirt.

'Are you all right?' I ask.

She shakes her head against my shirt. 'No. I'm a mess. It's so damned hard coming back. I forget each time how awful it is.'

'You'll get there.'

'Oh God, I hope so. I can't cope with being like this for long.' She lifts her head and snorts into a handkerchief stashed under her pillow. 'Can we try again?'

I nod helplessly, but my heart is churning with doubt.

She kisses me on the lips and pads into the bathroom, leaving me sitting on the bed. I glance at the picture of her at Béchervaise Island, standing outside the field hut. She looks so incredibly alive in that photo—so wild and released and open. She's wrapped in layers of thick windproof gear and her face is alight and vibrant. That's the Emma I want. The girl that grasps life. Not the one who shies from it and creates complications where there don't need to be any; a bit like me.

When she comes back, I offer to make tea, but she smiles tiredly and says she needs sleep. She'll be more rational tomorrow, she promises.

I watch as she undresses and tugs on pyjamas. Then she turns to me forlornly, like a child. I wrap her in my arms and she snuggles against my shoulder briefly before wriggling under the doona. I tuck it around her, and after I kiss her on the forehead, she rolls away, cosily drifting towards sleep.

I feel more like her father than a lover.

When I get home the answering machine light is blinking. I play the message; it's Jacinta, and she sounds distressed. My mouth goes dry with fear as I listen.

'Tom, I've been trying to call you, but you're not answering . . . It's bad news. We took Nana to the lighthouse today and she had a turn. We wanted to get her to hospital, but she won't have it, so we've brought her back to the cabin and now she's recovered a bit. Unfortunately, we can't stay here tonight because we have a commitment back in Hobart. Nana keeps insisting she's all right, but I don't want to leave her on her own. Given that I can't get onto you, I'm going to ring Leon now and see if he can keep an eye on her till you get here. Hopefully, you'll get this message and make it across before the last ferry. I'm ringing from the carpark at the end of the beach because this is the only place you can get reception without climbing a mountain or driving for miles. Ring me as soon as you get this message, will you? We'll probably be on our way back to Hobart by then.'

I look at the time. Four o'clock. I ring Jacinta's number.

'Tom, thank God it's you.'

'What's happening?'

'We're on the ferry.'

'What about Mum?'

'Leon's down there with her, and he says he doesn't mind staying the night, which might be just as well, because the wind has really come up and they're talking about shutting down the ferry.'

'I need to get down there.'

'Tom, I think she'll be okay. It was pretty scary when she had the turn, but she brightened up at the cabin, and we left her tucked in bed with a hot cup of tea. She should be better after a rest.'

'I feel like I need to do something.'

'Maybe you could make some phone calls.'

'Gary and Judy are away at some hospitality conference in Melbourne. Should I leave a message on their mobile? Or will that just panic them?'

'Gary will be fine. Leave a message. We should let him know.'

'Do you want me to ring Jan?'

'Could you? I don't feel up to it.'

She gives me Leon's mobile number in case I need it. Then I hang up and call Gary. He doesn't answer, so I leave a tactful message explaining what has happened to Mum. Next, I ring Jan. She answers the phone quickly. She must have been sitting on top of it.

'Hello.'

'Jan. It's Tom.'

'Have you heard anything? I've been waiting all day for Jacinta to call. She and Alex were going down to see Mum today.'

'Jan, I've just spoken to Jacinta. Apparently Mum had a turn at the lighthouse, but she's okay.'

'What do you mean *okay*? I told them not to take her there, but of course they wouldn't listen to me.'

'They say she's perked up now.'

'They're still down there?'

'No, they've had to come home.'

'Who's with her then?'

'Leon. The ranger.'

'Why aren't *you* down there?'

'I'm just about to leave, but I'm not sure if I'll be able to get over the channel. Jacinta said the ferry might not be running because of the wind.'

'Well, if you can't get across you should come here.' Jan doesn't want to be alone. She's worried about Mum and she wants me to distract her. She wants to use me to salve her guilty conscience. I try to think of an excuse, but I'm not quick enough. 'I'll cook for you,' she says.

At Kettering, the wind is sweeping the water into breakers and the ferry has been cancelled till further notice. I stand at the landing with Jess sheltering behind my legs, and stare out across the white-capped waste, wishing there was some other way to go to Mum. This is my time to be with her, and I'm powerless, grounded by the weather. There's no chance the ferry will resume tonight when waves like these are churning on the channel.

I linger in the blast until the cold chills me then I go back home to ring Jan. It's a shame I can't concoct some adequate reason to dodge having to visit her in her lonely house. But she grasps me like a life-buoy and works on my sympathy till I agree to have dinner with her. When finally I've extracted myself from her gushes of remorse, I ring Leon's mobile and leave a message to let him know the situation. Before I hang up, I provide Jan's number so he can find me. Then I swing into the car with Jess.

When I arrive at Jan's place, she collapses in tears on my shoulder, and I find myself stroking her as if she's a child. I tell her she's welcome to come to Cloudy Bay tomorrow morning, but she's inconsolable and her dramatics tire me. We sit in the kitchen drinking tea while she unburdens her conscience. I'd like to feel sorry for her, but Jan has created her own hell. Over the past weeks, I've offered several times to take her down to visit Mum, but she's always been too busy. She makes teary phone calls to Jacinta and Gary, raking over everything and blaming everybody until my mind starts to spin.

We're halfway through a bowl of pumpkin soup when her phone rings. She answers it quickly then passes it on to me.

Even though Leon's voice is buffeted by wind, I can detect his tension. I take the phone from the room, seeking privacy from Jan.

'I'm down at the carpark,' Leon says. 'I had to leave her for a few minutes, but I thought I should ring you. She's not too good, Tom. She was holding it together while Jacinta and Alex were here, but she's deteriorated since they left. I'm not sure what to do.'

'I can't get over there,' I tell him. 'They've shut the ferry down.'

'I'm happy to stay with her, but I'm worried. She's not talking any more.'

Not talking? This is unexpected. A fist of panic clutches my throat. 'Does she know you're there?' I ask.

'I think so.' He sounds hesitant. How could Mum have declined so quickly? Jacinta said she'd be okay.

'Was she all right when you first arrived?' I ask.

'She was resting. But her breathing's turned bad now, Tom. I don't like it. She seems to be struggling.'

'Look. I'll be there first thing in the morning, even if I have to swim the channel.'

I hang up and turn back to the kitchen, but Jan is behind me, her cheeks wet with tears.

'She's going to die, isn't she?'

'I don't know,' I say, staring past her.

'I can't cope,' she sobs.

I look down at her, unmoved. She wants my support but I can't help her. I have my own fears to deal with. 'I'm going home,' I say.

She follows me to the front door. 'I'm coming with you tomorrow.'

'Be at my place early then. I'm going on the first ferry. Either that, or you'll have to go with Jacinta and Alex.' A moment of guilt grips, and I hesitate by the car. My sister is watching me, her face sagging with the burden of regret.

'Wait till the second ferry,' she says. 'It can't possibly make any difference. I want to shower before I come.'

I shake my head in disbelief and climb into the car. Our mother is dying and all Jan can think of is taking a shower.

The night is dark as I head south on the highway, and it's heavy with the weight of my concern. At Kingston, I turn the car east to the beach and walk along the sand. There's no point going home to sit in silence when my thoughts are so heavy and sad. A cloak of clouds drapes the sky and the only light is from the buildings along the foreshore. My eyes adjust to the gloom and I shed my shoes, feeling the way with my toes. Jess pads behind me—I hear her panting in the breaks between waves. Sometimes she snuffles at invisible treasures on the sand. We walk and walk, seeking an emptiness that just won't come.

Some time after ten o'clock, I drive home, wishing I could fly over the channel to Bruny to be with Mum. When I see the shadow of Nick's Commodore parked beneath the streetlight at the bottom of my driveway, I want to turn and drive away. I'm worn out and I want to go to sleep. Has Emma driven herself here, or has she brought Nick along? Perhaps she's asleep in his back seat. I swing my car up the driveway past the Commodore and step out into the feeble light.

It's quiet. Jess and I slip along the path to the front door. If we're lucky we'll make it inside before anyone realises we're home. But there's a dark shape humped on the doormat. The body is too small to be Nick, so it must be Emma. Jess trots forward to sniff and lick her.

Emma's face is pressed against the doormat; leaning forward, I smell beer on her breath. She must be pretty drunk to sleep with her cheek on the bristles of the mat. I unlock the front door and open it. She doesn't move. It'd be easy for me to step over her and go inside to bed. But it's cold out here, and if she's drunk, she won't be thermoregulating properly. I'll have to get her inside and find somewhere to put her. I care for this girl, but tonight I don't want her in my bed.

I switch on a lamp in the lounge room, then grab a blanket from the hall cupboard and find a bucket in the laundry, just in case she throws up. I pour a large glass of water and set it on the floor beside the couch. Returning to Emma's limp body I shake her gently, trying to rouse her. She moans and rolls over, her lips red and swollen, her eyes pressed shut. I kneel beside her on the mat and loop my arm around her back. Then I lift her to her feet with effort, and she staggers into the house beside me, weak and uncoordinated.

'Do you need the bathroom?' I ask.

'Tom,' she slurs, 'is that you?'

'Yes, and you're not well.'

She slumps against me. 'Where were you? I made Nick bring me down here so I could see you, but you weren't here.'

'I've been at my sister's place.'

'Why weren't you here? Nick wouldn't leave, so we went down to the pub to wait for you.'

'And you drank too much.'

'Yes. Can you take me to bed with you?'

'You can have the couch. But first we'll visit the bathroom.'

I half carry her down the hall, and she closes her eyes against the light. In the bathroom I lean her against the wall. 'Can you manage?'

'I don't know,' she says, then, 'I need to lie down.'

I take her back down the hall again and roll her onto the couch, her head lolling onto the cushions.

'Tom,' she mumbles, as I turn off the lamp. 'What about Nick?'

'What about him?'

'He's in the car. Can you bring him in? He'll freeze out there.'

'Does it matter?' Tonight of all nights, I don't care about Nick. My mother is dying.

'We had an argument. I wanted him to go, but he wouldn't. And you weren't here.' She says it again as if it's all my fault.

'I'll bring him in,' I say. 'Then I'm going to sleep.'

Fortunately, Nick is capable of walking up the driveway unassisted, and when they're both ensconced on couches, I switch off the lights and retreat to my bedroom. I move woodenly through the shadows and lie on my bed fully clothed, staring at the ceiling. On the phone this evening, Leon said Mum was having trouble breathing. I envisage her face, pale and strained, her lips tinged with blue. I imagine the wheezing sound of her respiration, the labour of each inhalation.

A frightening void has opened up in me. I picture Mum lying in that lonely Cloudy Bay bed. Perhaps she really is dying. And now I'm truly afraid. Not scared for Mum—she knows what death holds for her. I'm afraid for myself. My feelings for Emma have been my life raft these past weeks: I thought Mum's death would be my release and Emma would be my future. But Emma's not the solution I first imagined her to be. Nick is the unexpected factor and I can't seem to delete him. Now he's here, in my house.

Jess jumps onto the bed and curls up beside me. I lay my hand on her head; her soft ears are reassuring beneath my fingers. Sleep floats just beyond reach: I yearn for it, but each time I'm tilting on its downhill edge, consciousness leaps at me, making me jolt, shifting my restless legs. This will be a night of fitful dozing.

I wake early and take Jess for a walk. Normally, I'd have breakfast and enter the day through the curling steam rising from my first cup of tea. But this morning there are uninvited guests in my house, and I don't want to listen to them snoring in the lounge room.

Outside, it's crisp and cold, and in the east, light is just beginning to glimmer on the horizon. Jess and I head down the hill past Laura's house. The curtains are drawn and the house is dark, so she must be still asleep. On the beach, I squat on the grey sand and stare across the channel while quiet wavelets lap at the shore. Dawn spreads slowly across the sky and soon a couple of gulls come strutting along the sand, jabbing at crab holes exposed by the tide. Jess is subdued too, picking up on my mood.

Last night at Jan's, I agreed to wait for the nine o'clock ferry. But I want to be down at Cloudy Bay *now*, spinning along the sand in the awakening light, running across the deck, sitting down beside Mum's bed, holding onto her hand. I pace the beach, hoping I'll hear Nick's Commodore start up and that they will both leave before I get back. But there's no sound from the road and soon Laura comes wandering out of the bush. I'm standing down near the water, and I hope she'll leave me be. But she meanders up with a hesitant smile.

'Are you okay?' she asks.

'Yes,' I say, keeping it short.

'You've been walking up and down for quite a while. I saw you from the road. Are you sure everything's all right?'

'Yes, it's fine,' I say dismissively. I wish she'd leave me alone, but I'm not sure how to send her away tactfully.

'It's not fine, is it? There's something wrong. I can feel it.'

Her concern makes something break inside me and words gush out. 'My mother's ill. She's dying of heart disease. She's down on Bruny Island in a cabin and I'm stuck here waiting for my sister. But I don't want to wait. I want to be there. I want to sit beside my mum even if she doesn't know I'm there.'

Laura listens silently, her eyes full of compassion. I'm surprised by her empathy, but then perhaps I shouldn't be—she's been through a lot with her brother. Suddenly, her company doesn't feel like an imposition, and I find her quiet attention almost comforting.

'You should go straightaway,' she says. 'Don't hang around. Just get on the road.'

'What about my sister?'

She shakes her head. 'She can make her own way down. Don't wait. You need to be there now.'

She's right. I do need to go. A little voice has been telling me that all night. I'm about to hurry off when I remember her trouble. 'How's Mouse?'

She shakes her head. 'Not now. I'll fill you in later. Just go.'

I hurry up the beach. She's given me a gift—the permission to put myself first for once. Before I dive through the bush, I turn and wave to her. I'll thank her later. I have a feeling she'll understand.

Up at the house, Nick and Emma are in the kitchen. Nick has found himself a bowl of cereal and is pouring coffee. He knows exactly how to make himself at home. Emma is slumped at the kitchen bench with a mug and a piece of toast in front of her. She's holding her head in her hands, and I'm not surprised she feels awful. The smell of beer is still oozing out of their pores.

She turns slowly when I come in. 'Tom. Where have you been?'

I look around for my car keys, I can't see them. 'I went for a walk.'

'There was a phone call for you. A man. Something to do with your mother.'

'Was it Leon?'

'I don't know. I didn't catch his name.'

A surge of impatience washes over me.

'I'm sorry,' she mumbles. 'I'm not the best this morning.'

I pick up the phone. Then I stop and look at them. What are they doing here, sitting in my house, watching me at this time? I want them gone. I take the phone to my bedroom and shut the door to block out their voices. My hands are shaking as I dial Leon's number.

There's no answer and the phone clicks to messagebank: *'You've called Leon Walker from the Tasmanian Parks and Wildlife Service. Please leave your details and I'll ring when I can.'*

His phone must be out of range. I leave a message. Perhaps he didn't call. Maybe it was Gary trying to contact me. Maybe everything is still all right with Mum. I ring Gary's number and he answers with a grunt.

'Gary. It's Tom.'

'What is it?' His voice is slow, like a cat stretching.

'Did you call me?'

'No. I'm having breakfast. You know how it is—don't ask me questions before I've had my first cup of coffee . . .'

'You didn't call?'

'No. I'm still in Melbourne. We're trying to rearrange our flights.'

Who could have called me then? Maybe it was Alex. I hang up and call Alex's mobile, but it wasn't him who rang either. He and Jacinta are getting ready to leave. I ask him to pick up Jan so I don't have to wait for her.

I go back to the kitchen to find the car keys, avoiding Emma's eyes.

'Is everything all right?' she asks.

'I have to go,' I say. 'Lock the door when you leave.'

Emma traps my hand. 'What is it, Tom?'

I stare right through her; it's as if I'm talking to air. 'My mother's dying.'

I tug my hand free. Jess is at my heels and we are outside the house, walking down the path. I open the car door. Then Emma is there, tears on her face. 'Tom.'

I look at her and feel nothing.

'I'm so sorry,' she says. 'I didn't know. You didn't tell me.'

I told her the night we drank whisky, but she doesn't know that. It doesn't matter now anyway. 'I have to go,' I say. 'I haven't much time.'

She grips the open car door and looks down at me. My hand is on the keys in the ignition and I'm ready to go. Her face is stricken. 'I'm so sorry. If I'd known about your mother things would have been different, I can promise you that. And I'm sorry I brought Nick here. It was the wrong thing to do. Will you call me when you get back?'

'I need to go,' I say.

She releases the door. 'Say you'll call me. I feel so bad.'

I can't reassure her. All I can think of is the road ahead of me, to Kettering and on to Cloudy Bay. Beyond that, nothing else has meaning.

Then Nick is on the deck waving the phone. 'Tom,' he shouts. 'It's for you. A guy called Leon.'

I swing the car door open again and run back up the path, breathing hard.

30

Afternoon. Soft mellow light melting through closed curtains. Mary was in her parents' house, coiled in a chair. Jack was at the lighthouse alone. Rose was gone now, he said, she was leaving the island. Mary had been grimly pleased about this. After all that had happened, the Masons didn't want Rose back at the farm. They had tolerated her presence all these years, but even *they* had their limits.

On the low table in front of Mary was Jack's letter, begging for her return. She had read it, but felt nothing. It was all too much.

Slowly she drifted, fragile and damaged. The fire crackled intermittently. Hurt and rejection had swallowed themselves and she was numb. She didn't know what she should do.

A rap on the door startled her. She knocked her cup of tea from the broad arm of the chair and watched the sepia stain spread across the carpet. The sound came again, but she didn't have the strength to get up. She was buried by an immense inertia, eyes fixed on the fire, watching the flame trickle lazily along the glowing log. Back and forth. Back and forth. The clock ticked on the mantelpiece. The fire popped and flickered. The house was so quiet with the children and her parents having gone to the circus.

She heard the click of a handle being turned. Wind gushed through the door and then subsided. She heard footsteps in the hall. Then there was nothing. It was just a trick of the wind. Her eyelids drooped shut.

She dreamed of a soft hand touching her hair, fingers sliding through her loose brown curls. Soothing fingers massaged her head, warm and real. It had been a long time since she had known such tenderness. She was cold, but these fingers were bringing her back. They belonged to someone alive and warm.

Gently the fingers crept over her scalp. They circled at her temples and made tracks across her forehead. She felt the soft whisper of exhaled air on her head, heard the steady sound of breathing. The fingers slid down the bridge of her nose, below her eyes, across the arches of her cheeks, around her chin. They lingered on her lips, tracing them. Her heart fluttered and her breathing deepened. She was afraid to open her eyes.

There was a rustle of movement. A shifting shadow. A body, blocking the light and heat of the fire. She sensed someone kneeling. Her hands were enclosed by strong fingers, warm palms. Hands that belonged to a man. He guided her fingers to his face and drifted them over his cheeks, his eyes, eyebrows, across a corrugated brow. She felt hair—wavy, longish—and hooked her fingers in it, feeling the texture, her breathing light.

Her hand was drawn to warm lips and then her fingertips were kissed, one at a time, slowly, deliciously.

She woke, eager; her eyes flew open and he was smiling at her. A mouth that she remembered. Eyes she still fell into. 'How did you find me?' she asked.

'Apple season,' he said. 'I come looking for you every year. I waited near the house and watched the others leave.' He smiled, something hidden in his eyes. 'The girl is you all over again, but darker, less hopeful. I see you in the boy as well.'

He lifted her left hand. Studied it. Then he turned it over and traced circles in her palm. Goosebumps spread up her arm.

His smile was thick with intent. He kissed her palm and the touch of his lips was almost unbearable. She grasped his hair again, this time to push him away, but her hand softened amid its coarseness and her fingers tumbled to his ear, then his cheek.

'What have you done?' she whispered.

'By coming here? By touching you?'

She pulled her hand away, trying to withdraw, to hold down the surge in her chest. He sat back, smiling.

'How long has it been?' His voice was a purr. 'How old is the girl?'

'Her name is Jan.'

'I don't need names.'

No. He didn't need names. But it reminded her. It recalled her to the fact that she had a life beyond this moment, beyond the liquid depths of his eyes, beyond the heat of his hand resting on her knee. 'Jan is thirteen. Gary's eleven.'

'They should have been mine.'

His eyes flashed and she felt a chill. There was much more to this man than the little she knew. She suspected he had violence within him. But he quickly smoothed his lips to that gentle smile.

'Fourteen years since I saw you last. In the park.' He lowered his head and touched a finger to her ring. 'It was torture to see this on your finger. You cheated me. You gave him what was mine.' His eyes brimmed with tears; he gripped her hand again and the warmth of his touch shot through her.

'I'm still married.'

Still married. What sort of feeble defence was that? Thank God, he didn't know the half of it. Married, in what sense of the word? Her husband at the light station dreaming of another woman. And here she was, broken and unable to rise from her chair.

'So where is he now?' His face was triumphant. He *knew.* He bent over her hand again, kneaded his thumbs into her palm, kissed her fingertips. She moved to protest, but he slipped her sleeve up and ran his fingers along the underside of her arm, and she sat transfixed, watching him.

He led her to the couch and her body followed him, her mind receding. She was cold and his fingers had warmed her. She wanted to know more.

Softly, he made circles on her thigh with his thumb. She was all at once liquid and light and hot. The touch of his lips on her neck was the promise that had faded from her dreams over the years.

As he kissed her, the pain flowed away, draining like sand through straw. She wanted his hands on her. Wanted him to reach beneath her clothes. Wanted him to take what had always been Jack's. Surely, it was hers for the giving. Jack hadn't wanted it for years. She'd been invisible to him. And now, here was a man who made her feel alive again. All need. How could it be wrong?

It happened in her bedroom. A small death that made her a woman renewed. Afterwards, he lay replete beside her, his sweaty skin sticking softly to hers. She knew she ought to feel guilt, but all she felt was euphoria. What she had done felt right. It felt good. And if she had this past hour over, she'd do it again, and without regret.

His hands explored her lazily, languorously, a fat smile on his lips. Then he became insistent, teasing her, seeing what was left of her. And she was his all over again, drowning in the delight of it, years of desire unleashed.

When it was over, he lay looking at her, his cheek on the pillow beside her. 'You should have seen yourself when you were sixteen,' he said.

'That was a long time ago.'

'You were so beautiful. So untouched . . . That's the way I always think of you. Young and undamaged. The only woman I've ever desired.'

'Everything changes,' she said. 'Nobody stays sixteen forever.'

His eyes were soft with the image of a girl that no longer existed. 'You don't have to go back,' he said.

She hesitated for a moment before slowly shaking her head. It wasn't a future she could seriously consider. Maybe in her dreams, but in reality, she had only ever seen herself with Jack. 'He's the father of my children.'

Adam's face flickered with sadness. 'So that's your last word?'

She nodded silently.

His smile was resigned. 'Well, I suppose that's it then.' He sat up, swiped moisture from the corner of his eyes. 'You see, I promised myself this was the last time. All these years my life has been on hold: picking fruit and shifting to the next town. It's amazing how fast the days slip by. And then your youth is gone and you wonder what you've got to show for it. I've been hoping you'd come back to me. But I've been fooling myself, haven't I? Using you as an excuse to avoid commitment. You've never come seeking me. So I have to stop doing this to myself. There might still be time to find a wife and have a family of my own.'

Her cheeks were wet with tears for him. She reached out and drew him back down to her. And he took her once more and then dressed and slipped quietly out the door.

31

She was lying sprawled, her legs heavy, when the light came on and she thought she heard a murmuring of voices, a conversation far away. The light went off again. And then it came on. Blindingly.

She dreamed of a voice, vaguely familiar. 'It's the sun, Mary. See, it's come out from behind a cloud.'

The sun?

Then it was dark again. And cold. She thought perhaps she wanted to speak. But everything in her was so slow. So weighty. She wanted to open her eyes, but it was too difficult.

Light, dark, sound, breathing. All of it, a burden.

Someone was speaking again, a breathy whisper of sound. 'We're outside, Mary . . . Let me sit you up a bit. I'm going to cup my hand over your eyes to shield out the sun . . . There it is, blazing from behind a cloud again.'

She was vaguely aware of movement; somebody shuffling her arms and legs and propping up her torso. She struggled to open her eyes, and tried to focus on the blur before her. Blue and grey, shadow, fog.

'You're on the beach, Mary,' the voice said. 'I've brought you out so you can see the sky. I wanted you to feel the wind.'

The light disappeared once more to bleary grey. She thought she heard a rattling sound. Or maybe she just felt it. Gurgling. Hollow rumbling.

Everything about her was rigid. Her body, unyielding. She was dissolving into the ground. Cold creeping through her. Such coldness. Her body not her own anymore.

She forced her eyes open, fluttering, and thought she saw the outline of a face, misty, framed with ginger hair. Her eyelids slid down again thankfully, into darkness.

'Mary. It's me. I'm here to look after you.'

Jack was with her. He was holding her. His arms strong around her. He forgave her for everything. Even that which he didn't know. He had to forgive her. She needed his forgiveness.

'Do you feel the wind on your face, Mary?'

The wind. Yes, the wind. They had been at home in it together. But she couldn't feel it now. She couldn't feel anything. Just heaviness. A great weight. A sense of sliding. Of light fading. Flashes of light returning again.

'I promised I'd bring you out here, didn't I?'

She felt Jack's breath on her face. His head beside hers on the pillow. She had always liked to feel him close to her. Such comfort.

There were shadows slipping across her face. Then the voice again, like an echo. 'The clouds are skating across the sky, Mary. There's a strong wind high up. Cirrus clouds. A front coming in.'

She struggled to open her eyes again. She was beneath the skies at Cape Bruny. This was a grey she knew and loved. It was the colour of her southern home: the long, shimmering silver light.

She waited for the shadows to come again, flitting, her head feeling light.

'It's a big cloud this time. We'll have to wait awhile before the sun comes through . . . Are you warm enough?'

What was warmth if it was not these arms around her?

The flashes of light and dark. The cold of the wind. Lightness. Her body detaching.

'Mary. The sun has come out again. Can you see it?'

She felt a strange warmth. Jack reaching for her. Adam's touch.

Then the warmth was giving way to cold again. But she was not afraid. She would be safe. All was glowing around her.

She heard humming. It must be Jack. But no, not Jack. It was something more. The rhythm of all things. The hum of life. She felt it deep within. The glow of living. The joy of knowing that Jack was waiting. And Adam. The great release of letting go. Of knowing all things would be happy in their own way. As she had been.

The humming.

The light.

Yes. She could see it. The light of the sun. So great. So beautiful.

Yes, Jack, I am coming . . .

PART IV

Resurrection

32

'It's a guy called Leon. Says he's calling from Cloudy Bay.' Nick passes the phone to me as I dash up onto the deck. 'Thanks, mate,' he says. 'We'll be off now. Hope everything's all right.'

I curl my fingers around the receiver and Nick ceases to exist. I barely see him as he slips down the driveway and tucks Emma into his car.

'Hello?' I'm hardly breathing as I wait to hear Leon's voice.

'Tom.'

'Yes?'

'I'm really sorry, mate . . . but she's gone.' He sounds exhausted, bereft.

'Gone?'

'Yes. It was just a little while ago. On the beach.'

'On the beach?' I feel like an echo, distant, hollow. 'How did you get her out there?'

'I carried her. I promised I'd take her out. She wanted that. Said she didn't want to be trapped under a roof. That she wanted to be beneath the sky.'

'She told you that?'

'Yes. She mentioned it a week ago. When we were talking.'

I sit down on the hard wood of the deck. Jess presses against me, her body warm against my arm. 'Where is she now?'

'In bed. I tucked her in . . . to keep her warm. I know it's strange but I didn't want her to get cold . . .' His voice drifts off, and the silence stretches. I can't comprehend that my mother is dead. I was going to see her this morning. I was going to sit with her and hold her hand. But I'm too late. 'What do we do now?' Leon asks. 'Who do we call?'

'I don't know. I'll find out. Then I'll come down. I'll be there as soon as I can.'

'I'll stay with her till you get here.'

He hangs up and I begin dialling. First Jan, then Gary. Jan is distraught, weeping, hysterical. She's too late, she says. And I say yes, it's too late for everything. Gary is more rational. He says he was expecting something like this; Mum looked so terrible the other day. I ask him to find out what to do about Mum's body. I trip over the words. *The body*. It's such a term of separation. The body disconnected from life, separated from contact, from affection. I feel nauseous.

I call Jacinta. She and Alex are on their way to pick up Jan when I tell her about Mum, Jacinta is silent on the end of the phone. It's as if she has been frozen. I stammer out broken condolences and hang up.

Around me, the day resumes its shape, thick with ludicrous sunshine and wavering shadows. I glance down at the road—the Commodore is long gone. It's hard to believe Emma and Nick were ever here. It's all so incongruous: my mother's death, Emma drunk on my doorstep last night, Nick sleeping in my house. I rest my chin on my knees, hugging my legs tight. Everything looks so normal. The trees, the quivering leaves, the sky, the puffy clouds. How can it be this way? How can everything go on like this when my mother has died?

I stand and walk slowly down the hill with Jess at my heels. We slot ourselves into the car and drive.

•

On the ferry, I leave Jess in the car and wander to the bow, leaning against the cold metal railing. Beneath my feet, the deck throbs. The light is shimmering on the water. I breathe with the rhythm of the engines, trying to empty myself, to be one with everything, to be non-existent. Wind pours over the bow as the ferry swings around the headland south of Kettering and angles across the channel.

Closer to Bruny, the wind increases and chops the water to small waves, spray hitting my face. In weather like this I should be cold, but instead I am numb. I grip the railing with hard fists, trying to feel some sort of emotion, to feel pain, or grief, or sadness. Anything.

When finally I release the railing and return to the car, my body is rigid, and then I'm gripped by a deep chill that leaves me shaking as if I'll never stop. I can hardly steady my hands to fit the key in the ignition.

Jess stares at me sadly. Usually she'd jump on the front seat for a pat, but today she sits miserably on the floor. She sniffs the hand I extend towards her and cautiously licks my fingers. Her tongue is soft and warm and my hands are icy. I tuck them beneath my armpits and gaze through the windscreen. Vapour fog creeps quickly around its edges as I breathe.

North Bruny passes in a blur and I can hardly recall disembarking from the ferry. The sky above the Neck is brooding; no patches of blue or breakthrough shafts of light. It seems appropriate.

I swing around the bends and curves of South Bruny, skipping from gravel to brief breaks of tar and back to gravel, through Alonnah—the school, the playground, the post office—and on to Lunawanna, past the mudflats, thick with mustering gulls. I turn east towards Cloudy Bay, past the store, and then the road sweeps out of town, passing cottages with thin streamers of smoke coiling from their chimneys and washing hung beneath their eaves. When at last I arrive at Cloudy Bay, I pull over in the Whalebone Point carpark and clamber out, unable as yet to tackle that final stretch down the beach to the door of the cabin where my mother's body lies.

I walk to the edge of the carpark and gaze south where the grey sea travels in between the heads. Those long arms of headland reach to embrace the bay, but fail to curb the magnetism of the ocean. Closer in, the waves are tinged with red. I've only ever seen this phenomenon here: the colour of blood in the waves. It flies up in the spume as the swell rears and collapses on itself. Today, it seems as if I'm watching the essence of my mother slipping away. I stumble west on the trail from the point, stopping eventually to lower myself onto a damp bench seat. I sit with my head in my hands, the heels of my palms pressing into my eyes creating spirals of colour.

Time withers. The sea roars, my heart beats—two separate rhythms. Eventually tears come, another rhythm rising from somewhere deep in my chest, the choke of contorted sobs, a welling emptiness. I lose myself in the sludge of it, thought dissolving.

Then a wet nose presses against my hands. A lick. A quick swipe across my fingers. I release my fists.

Jess is watching me with steady eyes. She doesn't shy from my grief. My hands sag to her head and knead the softness of her ears, feeling her warmth beneath my fingers.

Slowly, we walk back to the car together.

The cabin at the end of the beach.

Leon's four-wheel drive is parked on the grass, and I pull up alongside. Jess gallops around the lawn, her belly damp and heavy with sand after her run up the beach beside the car. I dig an old towel from the back seat and rub her down.

She bounds onto the deck where Leon is leaning against the wooden railing, his face ashen. I reach to shake his hand and he grips mine hard. He nods at me sympathetically, taking in my red eyes. 'You made it,' he says, releasing my hand.

'Yes. Tough trip.'

'Pretty tough night too.' His voice is rough with feeling.

'I should have been here. I should have stopped work a week ago to look after her.'

Leon shrugs a little uncertainly, as if afraid he might offend me. 'She talked about that a few times,' he says. 'But she really didn't want anyone. She was quite clear about that.'

'You don't think she was lonely?'

'No,' he says.

'Perhaps we should have called a doctor . . .' I'm riding on a moment of guilt.

He shakes his head. 'She didn't want to prolong things.'

I know what Mum wanted, but I need reassurance. I considered discussing death with her, but it was too hard. Now I feel inadequate; it seems Leon managed to achieve what I couldn't. He sighs deeply and I see tears brimming in his eyes.

'She was my friend,' he says.

I pat him on the shoulder. It's the best I can do.

Jess whines up at me and I glance uneasily at the front door. 'I suppose I should go in,' I say. Hesitantly, I step inside. Leon follows.

It's hot in the lounge room, unbearably so. The wood fire is glowing and the gas heater is on too, pumping out heat. I peel off a couple of layers. 'It's hot in here.'

Leon's face is haggard. 'She was cold.'

'Yes, but she'll turn to soup.'

His lips quiver. 'I didn't think of that.'

He slams the flue shut on the wood heater and extinguishes the gas while I open windows. Jess is sitting by the door to Mum's room, whimpering.

'She knows,' Leon says. 'Dogs know everything.'

I glance into the room and swallow hard. Jess looks up at me. We step slowly inside.

The bedroom is dim. Mum is in the bed by the window, and a flickering candle on the bedside table makes her look not of this world. Her face is waxy and grey, and her eyes stare into nothing. There's a strange smell permeating the room, slightly rancid. Leon has pulled the blankets high under her chin. I reach forward and touch her cheek with the back of my hand. Jess whines. Mum's skin is cold and firm, like plastic. Something in my chest tightens. I sit on the bed and run my hand over the covers. Mum is so flat under there. So depleted. So absent. The silence that lingers over her is oppressive; the lack of movement, of breathing. I bend my head and weep while Jess circles restlessly. Mum wasn't supposed to die without me. I wanted to be here with her. That's what I promised myself. I let her down.

Then suddenly I need to speak. I meant to do this while she was alive. To thank her for everything—for my childhood, for her love, for being patient with me.

'Mum,' I say gently. 'I'm here . . . It's me, Tom.'

I shift the covers slightly and touch her arm. It's cold and wooden and heavy. I fold my hand around hers and lift it. I want to cradle her fingers in mine and warm them. I want to inject back into her all the vibrancy of life that has carried her these past seventy-seven years. Emotion curdles in my throat and for a moment I can't talk. Then I collect myself.

'Mum, you came down here to prepare yourself for this, didn't you? You've been sending messages to Dad. Maybe you found him here. I guess I'll never know. If he's anywhere, I'm sure he's with you.

'You've been a tremendous mum, you know. Nobody could have been better. When I came back from Antarctica you had enough of your own strife, with Dad just gone, but you propped me up. I couldn't have come ashore without you . . . And the way you never expected me to talk about things. That's a gift. You've always accepted me the way I am . . .'

I try to press heat into her freezing fingers. 'It was wonderful growing up at the lighthouse, Mum. You know how I loved it. Just like you did. I appreciate you giving us that opportunity. You were the rock of our family . . . I don't know what I'll do without you . . .

'But you don't have to worry, Mum. I'm going to be okay. I've been doing better lately. Things haven't worked out with Emma, but I'm looking forward to things now. Not hiding away. I'm going to be all right. And Jan will be fine too. She's got Jacinta. And you know Gary's always good. He's the solid one among us—in more ways than one . . .' A sniffy gasp of a laugh escapes me.

'I only wish I'd asked you more about Dad. That's the only thing I regret.' I bow my head and drip tears onto her hand. All those years I could have talked about this, and now it has to come surging out when Mum is gone. 'I wish I knew more about him,' I murmur. 'I think he loved me, I'm sure he did. But he was a tough father, Mum. Not easy to love, not like you. I guess it's hard being a kid. You don't have the confidence to make things happen. If I'd been more relaxed, I could have spent more time with Dad like Gary did.'

I falter again and look down at Mum's fingers. The best memory I have of Dad is when I was eight and he showed me how engines work. Over several afternoons he demonstrated how to pull generators apart and put them back together again. We didn't talk much, but it was comfortable, just doing things with him. I suppose that was his way of teaching me about life. How to fix things.

He was a strange man, my father. So serious about weird things. I remember when we used to play Monopoly on windy cold days. He was so triumphant whenever he won, hotels on all his properties. That was one of the only times I recall him being truly happy, and also when we went fishing down at the cove. When I was small, he'd be pulling in lots of fish, and all I could catch was beach junk. Once we went fishing off the rocks and I kept snagging my line. He had to set up my tackle over and over, and we didn't catch a thing. He came home so grumpy he didn't talk all evening and went straight to bed after dinner.

My tears fall onto the sheets. Here I am with my dead mother, and I can't stop thinking about my father. 'Mum, there are so many good times I remember with you. Like wandering across to the heath to go birdwatching—all those tawny-crowned honeyeaters, they were my favourites. And sitting on the cliffs watching dolphins out herding fish. You had the wind in your hair, and you looked so smooth and peaceful, as if your heart was singing.

'You've had a grand life, Mum. Not all happy, I don't suppose. But nobody gets it all good. And it's the hard stuff that makes you. I've been dodging all that for too long, haven't I?—how to get on with life. But I won't anymore. I'm going out there, Mum—in my own way. I'm getting into living. The way you'd want me to . . . I love you . . .'

My voice breaks and I give up talking. I linger, holding Mum's hand, watching the still mask of her face, open-mouthed and expressionless.

The curtains shift as air leaks around the window and light washes across the room. The candle flame bobs and flitters in the draft.

Mum's gone and there's nothing I can do.

After a long while I leave the room. The front door is open and Leon is slumped at the picnic table on the porch. I grip the railing and stare out.

'You okay?' Leon asks.

I shrug.

'It's a bugger saying goodbye to people you love.' He brushes his hand through his hair. 'She helped me a lot, your mum. She listened to me. Most people are too busy for that. Too self-absorbed to hear you talk.' He nods at me. 'Your mum was a special lady.'

'Yes,' I say. 'She was a good woman.'

'It was a brave thing to do, coming here alone in her condition.'

'She knew what she was doing.'

'Yes, but it must have been difficult to allow it. Knowing something like this could happen.'

I recall Jan nagging at me on the phone. 'It caused a bit of friction . . . I suppose she talked about my father too . . .'

'Yes. And life at the lighthouse. She loved this place. It feels lonely here now . . . without her.'

'You were a great support to her.'

His eyes fill with moisture. 'I tried to spend more time here as things got worse. I only knew her a few weeks. But she knew me better than my own mother.'

My own tears threaten and I look away. Silence swallows us then. Eventually, I encourage him to go for a walk on the beach. He has sat out a difficult vigil overnight and I want him to take a break. As he steps off the deck and glances back at me, all the pain of the past eighteen hours is reflected in his face. I nod at him in mute thanks, and he wanders down the hill. Turning, I see a four-wheel drive spinning towards us along the sand. It will be Jacinta and Alex, bringing Jan with her bucketloads of guilt and grief. The timing is excellent: Leon has borne enough. He doesn't need to be here for this.

33

The week after Mum's death passes in a blur of preparations for the funeral. You'd think the death of a parent would have the potential to bring siblings closer, but not so with my family. Mum was the glue holding us together, and without her, we have nothing to bind us. Despite our common sadness, we drift from each other like feathers on the wind. Jan descends into a dark world of self-blame and remorse. Gary closes down around his hard little core. And I do what I always do in a crisis—retreat into silence and find solace in nature: the flight of a bird, the nuances of light over water, the sound of wind shuffling leaves.

We grind through a series of difficult meetings to decide on everything from a funeral MC and songs to flower arrangements and burial clothes. Mostly, I spend time alone.

Laura comes timidly to the door with lilies from a florist, and she leaves soon after. I'm not capable of being in company yet, and I'm relieved she respects my space. In the mornings, I see her watching through her kitchen window as Jess and I trudge down the path to the beach. Each time, she waves and I nod. It's nice to know someone is looking out for me. It makes me feel less alone. Often, when I'm home, staring out the window over the channel, I see her leave in her car, driving away somewhere—maybe to see Mouse.

Before the funeral, I visit Mum's coffin in the dim hall of the crematorium. It's quiet—only the muffled sound of my footsteps on the slate floor and the dull rustle of my breathing within the dense silence. The lid of the coffin is open and there's nothing to fear, but my heart tumbles and my palms sweat.

They've dressed her in fresh clothes—a dress Jan selected from her wardrobe. Her cheeks have been padded with cotton wool and her lips have been tweaked into an almost smile. She's been carefully made up with powder and lipstick, and her eyes have been somehow fixed shut. It's not the face I know. She's a study of absence, nothing of life left in her.

Seeing Mum resurrects the pain of my return from down south. It reminds me of all the losses I bore back then. My father. Leaving Antarctica. My marriage.

Debbie wouldn't meet with me till three months after I disembarked in Hobart. Every time I rang she fobbed me off with excuses. I was still reeling from the implosion of my life. Debbie could no doubt hear it in my voice, but I was preoccupied with finding my feet on non-Antarctic ground. I didn't realise how broken I was. How maladjusted.

Debbie finally agreed to meet me at a café near Constitution Wharf. Hobart was already bearing down towards winter and it was a dim grey day—I clearly remember it. In the café, she sat opposite me, sipping a latte. And she dodged my eyes carefully, furtively.

I had to admit she looked well. Her cheeks were pink, her lips red and full. She was uncomfortable in my presence, but smiles still came to her easily. Somebody was being kind to her, making her feel loved. I didn't remember her looking so self-assured when she lived with me.

'How are you going?' she asked.

She didn't really want to know, so I fed her an appropriate lie. 'I'm fine.'

'I'm sorry about your father,' she said. 'He was a good man. You're like him, the way you hold everything inside.'

I didn't want to be compared to my father. And I didn't want to talk about him. 'I love you, Debbie,' I said. 'We can try again. I'm sorry about Antarctica. It wasn't supposed to work out that way. But we had something before I left. A plan. Things we wanted to do together. I can be the man you want. I'm willing to change.'

'You did try from down there,' she said. 'All those emails you sent me . . . they were lovely. But they didn't help. They emphasised the separation. It was so lonely here. So isolating. Who would think that you could live in a city full of people and feel alone? It felt like you were on another planet. You tried to share Antarctica with me, but it wasn't possible. Only people who've been down there understand what it's like to be there. And only people who've stayed at home understand what it's like to be left behind.'

I reached for her hand, but she had tucked herself safely behind the table. 'Look at you,' she said. 'Antarctica still has a hold on you. It's in your bones. And there's a wild look in your eyes. It frightens me.'

If I looked wild, it had nothing to do with Antarctica. 'I want to come home to you,' I said. 'I haven't stopped loving you. Can't you see that?'

She sipped tidily at her latte and set her cup down again, avoiding my eyes.

'Why did you let things drift so far?' I asked, desperate now. 'You could have warned me our marriage was slipping. I couldn't tell from down there. If I'd known I could have done something about it.'

She smiled sadly and shook her head. 'What could you have done? You were so far away.'

'I would have come back. I would have leaped on the next ship and returned to you.'

She didn't seem to understand. 'What about the job?' she said.

'To hell with the job. We had a marriage to defend.'

For a moment, she looked struck, as if this option had never occurred to her. Then her face shuttered. I knew then I shouldn't have arranged the meeting. I was clinging to the fragile threads of recovery and just seeing her undid me. But there was something more in her eyes, the dark shape of something concealed.

'What is it?' I asked, pressing further. 'There's something, isn't there? Something you should tell me? Please. It might help me understand.'

She hesitated and bowed her head, staring at her lap. 'I didn't want to mention this,' she said. 'And it will only hurt you. It can't change things for us.' She looked away from me, out the window across the wharf where salt-stained fishing boats were moored.

I waited. Her face lost its glow and her eyes became watery with tears. Eventually she looked at me. 'I was pregnant, Tom,' she said. 'I found out two months after you left. I was so sick and lonely. And you were so far away. I don't know, something creeps into relationships when a partner goes to Antarctica. It's like this other love. This ridiculous magical bond with the ice. I could feel it in your letters, in all those beautiful descriptions you were writing to me. You were sharing it with all those other people. People who didn't matter. But you couldn't share it with me—the love of that place that I could feel growing in you . . . And then there was this thing growing in me. A baby we hadn't planned . . . and there was all that distance. The silences. The empty days. I couldn't do it. I couldn't go through with it alone.'

Her face was white and strained. 'I terminated the pregnancy, Tom. It was the best thing for both of us. I couldn't ask you to come back. And by then, I didn't even know whether I wanted you. I felt like I didn't know you anymore. You were so lost to me down there. So lost.'

Her words fell like stones. I hear them now. My mother's death. My father's death. Debbie telling me she destroyed our baby. Death so many times over.

34

The day of the funeral is grey and heavy with clouds. At first, there's only a cluster of us standing mute and tense in the grounds of the crematorium. Then cars begin to arrive, slotting themselves into neat rows in the carpark. People in sombre clothing emerge and approach slowly across the grass. Some faces are familiar to me, but most are not.

Jan, Gary and I stand beside each other as if someone has placed us there, lined up like garden gnomes. My face feels rigid, almost as cold as Mum's. Soon, there are people milling everywhere. Some are crying. I'm hugged by old ladies I've never met before. People reach out to express sympathy. I feel like a rock in a storm, struggling to find stillness within, while waves wash all around.

Jacinta, who was probably closer to Mum than any of us in recent years, stays locked to Alex's arm, her face white and drawn. Judy keeps close to Gary, watching out for Jan. Anyone would think this was Jan's day, the way she pours out grief. She's like a well overflowing. Alex carefully steers Jacinta away from her. The swelling mood of sorrow in the gathering crowd is overwhelming. There are so many people here who knew and admired my mother. People I've never met from parts of her life

I've never known. How little we understand of our parents. How little credit we give for their achievements.

I knew your mum from the opportunity shop. She was a fine lady. A great contributor.

Your mum and I did Meals on Wheels together years ago. We didn't see each other often, but we kept in touch. She was very proud of all her children.

I'll miss Mary terribly. She was a good friend.

We played bowls together till her arthritis became too bad. She still helped out, though. Making cups of tea and serving cakes. That's what she was. A real helper.

She was a community person . . . A strong lady . . . Helpful . . . Unselfish.

I'm from the bridge club and your mother was a fearsome card player. She always thrashed me. I don't know how she did it.

I didn't know Mum had so many friends and admirers. Despite the years of isolation at the cape, she still had a strong community spirit. Seems she must have involved herself in everything when she and Dad moved back to Hobart. I guess she was never one to sit around, until her arthritis incapacitated her.

At one point I notice Leon at the edge of the crowd, waiting to speak to me. He manages a brief smile when our eyes connect, but he looks terrible. We shake hands and he grips my arm firmly. Memories of the last time we saw each other are thick between us; Mum lying dead in the cabin. Now, both of us struggle to speak and Leon's eyes fill with tears. I choke out a thanks for his presence and then the celebrant sweeps us into the crematorium.

Gary presents an excellent eulogy summarising Mum's life, especially her bond with Bruny Island. His observations on Mum and Dad are astute and it's a surprise to realise that he has understood them and known them better than me, despite his distance from Mum in recent years. A demanding spouse can force a degree of distance into family relationships, I suppose. But today, Judy's behaviour is faultless. She's there to stand by

Gary in his role as the male head of our family. Not for the first time, I appreciate being the youngest. Little is expected of me. And I certainly wouldn't have been able to deliver the eulogy with the passion and confidence that Gary manages to muster.

Jacinta somehow holds it together to read from Kahlil Gibran's book *The Prophet*. At the podium she stands, tremulous, and reads with a quavering voice, rich with emotion.

This is when I am reminded how grief can be like a tsunami—how it can rise and rise and then swell and collapse over you, rolling and tumbling you beneath its weight while you struggle to resurface. I'm unable to look at Jacinta as she leaves the podium, and I'm glad she has Alex to give her love and courage, because I'm incapable of anything.

The celebrant moves with polished calm and practised compassion to complete proceedings. Gary has put together a computerised slide-show of Mum's life set to music selected by Jan. It begins after the celebrant's final sympathetic words.

Mum's face, young and fresh, topped with a mass of tousled curls.

Her wedding photos, with Dad. My father tall, straight and serious. Mum is radiant.

Then at the lighthouse. Mum's arms wrapped around Jan and Gary, my siblings squinting in the raw light. Mum is taking it on her face, smiling and unfazed. The tower at the top of the hill behind them.

Mum squatting on the grass with a naked infant me. Chooks pecking beside us. The tails of washing dangling from the clothesline in the background.

Mum beside the lighthouse door with Dad. Their faces closed and unreadable.

Baby Jacinta in Mum's arms, delight dancing in their eyes.

The sequence of photos continues. It's beautiful, but it destroys me.

•

We gather at Jan's house for tea and recollections. Rain crowds us into the lounge room and the air is thick with voices. After initial awkwardness, the stories begin to flow. This, finally, is the celebration of Mum's life.

Leon mingles with the group, and I notice him often, chatting with various old ladies who were Mum's friends. Before he leaves, he comes quietly to my side.

'Thanks for the wake,' he says, smiling kindly. 'I was going to go home straight after the service, but I'm pleased I came.'

I grip his arm. 'I'm glad you're here. She would have been touched.'

'Life on Bruny has changed since she died,' he says. 'There's a new emptiness. I can't drive past the cabin without choking up.'

I nod.

'I've had an idea,' he says. 'I want to do a memorial walk up East Cloudy Head. For her, given that I couldn't take her there. And I'd like you to come. I'd like to share it with you.'

Emotion threatens to overwhelm me, but I hold it together. 'That'd be good,' I say.

We choose a day, and then I watch his bright head disappear among the crowns of grey.

35

After the funeral, I return to work and try to pretend everything's all right again. A week of compassionate leave, a few pats on the back, and you're expected to take up where you left off. They say that keeping busy helps with the grief. Yet, again and again I find myself lying with a tool in one hand, staring unseeing into a truck's undercarriage, or completely distracted by the call of a bird. Often Jess appears in the gloom and licks my face, cleaning away tears I didn't even know were there.

Emma rings a couple of times. When I play the first message, her voice echoes across the lounge room, asking me how my mother is and if I am okay and could I please ring back. I marvel that her voice fails to move me. I don't call her back.

The second time she rings, I answer the phone, thinking it might be Jan or Jacinta.

'Tom,' she says. 'I'm so glad I've caught you.'

Caught me? She caught me long ago.

'How's your mum?'

'She died.'

'I'm so sorry.'

'She was ill. Heart disease.'

'Is there anything I can do?'

For a wry moment I consider the many things she could have done, but most of them are too late now. She could have been straighter with me. She could have sent Nick away.

'No,' I say. 'Everything's done. We had the funeral last week.'

A silence wells between us. From her blanket by the wall, Jess watches me, her eyes shining in the shadows. Outside a cockatoo squawks its way across the sky.

'I'm really sorry, you know,' Emma says. 'About what happened that night with Nick. We were so drunk. And it was all so untimely. I'm embarrassed about it. I didn't know your mum was sick or it'd never have happened. I wish it hadn't.'

'It doesn't matter now.'

'Well, yes, it does. I'd like to see you, Tom. Can we catch up soon?'

The gap in conversation grows heavy.

'Look, I don't want to hassle you when you're feeling down,' she says. 'But I do want to see you. Please will you call when you're feeling better?'

'Sure.'

But *when I'm feeling better* could be a long time away.

She calls again a week later. 'Tom. I have great news. Fredricksen's going to offer you the job. To come south with me. What do you think?'

I sit blankly. This was what I'd hoped for. But I find I can't even contemplate going south.

'Are you okay?' Emma asks.

'I need some time,' I stammer. 'It's too soon after . . .'

She's quiet for a long moment. 'I'm sorry. I was so thrilled, I couldn't wait to tell you. But it wasn't very tactful of me to blurt it out like that. Are you all right?'

'I'm okay,' I lie.

'Look, Tom. I have to go. Take care and we'll speak soon.'

•

The next day Bazza is on the phone. 'I heard Fredricksen offered you a job,' he says.

'I haven't made any decisions.'

'Good. Because I want to offer you a job too—on a better wage than Fredricksen can give you. We're having troubles finding good diesos for the summer. You can winter, if you like. And you can have Mawson Station if that's what you want. So you can see those emperor penguins you're always talking about.'

'I'm not sure I want to go to Mawson.'

'But that's where Fredricksen's job is . . .' There's a pause, and I hope Bazza will give up, but of course he's onto it like a dog at a bone. 'It's because *she's* going there, isn't it? Emma.'

'Maybe.'

'I thought you wanted to go with her . . . ? Ah, well then, if that's the case, I suppose there's something else I should tell you. Then maybe you'll take up my offer at another station. Nick Thompson's going to Mawson too.'

'Great.'

'He's a prick,' Bazza says. 'Emma's not his first antdiv conquest. Look, come and see me, we'll discuss things. How about some remote field work? A traverse? Would you consider that?'

'I don't know.'

'Think about it. These opportunities don't come up very often.'

'Why are you doing this?'

'I need a good dieso. And you're my mate. You need picking up. Don't worry about Nick Thompson. Emma will drop him before the ship leaves, mark my words. He's playing the field, can't help himself.'

'You haven't seen them together.'

'Yes, I have. I work here, remember? His eyes are everywhere.'

'I don't want to talk about him.'

'Neither do I. Come and see me tomorrow lunchtime. I'll buy you a sandwich.'

I meet Bazza in the antdiv cafeteria. We take a table in the back corner and drink awful coffee with flabby sandwiches. Bazza says they have new cafeteria staff, but things haven't improved. He asks me what I think about his proposition, but it's too soon to make decisions. I'm still laden with the burden of Mum's death. And home is no escape. Jan's been calling and leaving messages for me to come and visit. She's rotten with guilt and she wants me to reassure her, to absolve her of her sins. But I can't do it. Neither can Jacinta. We have enough of our own grief to deal with. But Jan keeps finding ways to beg for support. She insists she needs help to go through Mum's things, but I can't face riffling through Mum's wardrobe—all those clothes she'll never wear again. It'll only intensify the emptiness. In the past few days, whenever the phone has rung, Jess and I have left the house and gone for a walk. Every time we hear Jan's voice we need fresh air and wind.

Bazza watches me across the table. 'You're doing it tough,' he observes. 'Shit of a thing, losing a mother. Mine died a decade ago.'

'How long did it take?'

'To get over it?'

I nod.

'I'm still not over it. But you cope, with time.'

'That's about what I thought.'

We sit and chew our sandwiches. I drink the coffee, trying not to grimace at its bitterness. Bazza nods towards the counter and I see Nick there buying his lunch. He's leaning over the counter in intense conversation with one of the staff. I hope he isn't here to meet Emma.

'Look at him, chatting up the cafeteria girls,' Bazza says. 'He's a waste of space. I don't know what Emma sees in him.'

We watch Nick collect his order from the girl behind the

counter. He's smiling at her in an intimate way and shortly afterwards she comes to sit with him.

'See what I mean?' Bazza says. 'He'll be out to dinner with that one tonight. You should forget about him and come south. Have you given any more thought to it?'

'No. I haven't had time to think.'

'You don't *want* to think,' Bazza says.

He's right. I've been avoiding it. Doing anything to distract myself from his offer. And Fredricksen's. I've been walking with Jess. Talking on the phone with Jacinta. I even rang Gary last night.

'Look,' Bazza says. 'Let me tell you about this gig. You won't be able to say no, once I give you the details.'

He outlines the winter program. A tractor traverse out of Mawson to the Prince Charles Mountains. It's an exceptional trip. I'd be mad to say no. While Bazza talks, Nick stands and leaves the room and I watch him go, only half listening to Bazza.

'I'll think about it,' I say, when Bazza has finished. 'When do you need to know?'

'Four weeks.' Bazza reaches out to shake my hand. 'Do the right thing by yourself, will you? Don't turn it down.'

Emma calls on Friday afternoon and leaves a message for me to meet her at Salamanca in one of the pubs. A group of them is going out for a drink. I don't much feel like heading back into town when I've just arrived home. And I'm not sure I'm up to a night of Antarctic reminiscence. But an outing might be good for me. I've been spending too many hours alone. I shower, feed Jess and then drive into town.

Parking is difficult down by the wharves, but eventually I find a space behind Princes Wharf. The orange shadow of the *Aurora* looms behind the sheds, a string of lights along her flank, a spotlight flaring from the trawl deck. I pause to look at her, trying to project into my future. Can I see myself boarding that ship again? Can I imagine myself travelling south? I wait for some clanging bell of intuition, but there isn't one.

I pocket my hands and make my way through traffic across the road to Knopwoods. The doors are open wide and there are people spilling out into the street. Cigarette smoke wafts among laughter and clinking glasses. I edge between groups and slip through the door.

The bar is frantically busy. People are packed shoulder to shoulder, pushing back and forth. Bodies clad in fleece mingle with loosened ties and suits. I smell aftershave, perfume, the stench of spilled beer. I squeeze through to the counter. After waiting several minutes, I buy a drink and move off into the crowd.

Then I see them, a tightknit circle of eight around a table at the back. A knot of laughter and waving hands, sloshing glasses, trivial banter. Just another group among the general drone. I see Emma there, sitting beside Nick. His arm is around her shoulders. Did Emma tell him I was coming? What am I doing here anyway?

I wind my way through the crowd and find a spot along the wall where I can see Emma's profile through the shifting mass of faces and bodies. She won't see me. Neither will Nick. She didn't really expect me to come. It was just a gesture, to cheer me up. Who would want to come to a noisy bar when they have just experienced death? There's no room for loss here.

Watching her, I drink my beer, feeling it warm my stomach. Her face is bright and smiling. She's having fun. She'll go south again and dodge normal life for yet another year. She'll be immersed in the usual summer season—with all its excitement, isolation, gossip and scandal. If I choose not to go, she'll forget me . . . if she hasn't already. She'll be preoccupied with Nick. He'll play with her. Keep her attention.

I watch Nick between all the faces. I see him shift to gulp his drink, his arm still around Emma's shoulders. If he looked straight up, he could look into my eyes. But I know he won't see me. Because I'm the wrong sex. He has his arm around Emma, but he's still taking the opportunity to survey other female talent in the room. I can see him doing it. His eyes are roving up and down, taking in legs, faces, breasts. Poor Emma. I feel sorry for her. She's been so taken in. She might be convenient for now, but a man so busy windowshopping will always be tempted to try other wares. He'll betray her. Secretly, at first. But she'll find out. There are no secrets down south. And he won't last a season. I wish she could see this about him.

A knot of regret twists within me. I have to let go. Emma's a great girl, but she's not for me.

I finish my beer and leave.

36

The following morning, I'm in the kitchen chopping zucchini for soup when there's a knock at the door. I open it, and Laura stands there shyly, arms folded, eyes flicking from my face to Jess and back to me.

'Just thought I'd pop by and see how you were going,' she says.

I shrug. 'Thanks, I'll be okay.'

She gives a small smile. 'It's a hard time. But things will improve. I lost both my parents a few years ago.'

She's stating fact, not looking for sympathy. And her eyes are kind. I suppose her parents' death explains why she looks after Mouse. There's no-one else.

'Mouse is coming home for the afternoon,' she continues. 'Today's his birthday and they're letting him out for a few hours. I was hoping you might come round with Jess. To help celebrate. Mouse loves dogs.'

I draw breath, wondering how to tactfully say no. In my current frame of mind, I'd rather not face company. The agony of stilted conversation. And Jess will be terrified of Mouse after that awful trip to the hospital. I look down at Jess as she pants up at me. 'I don't know. I'm not sure if Jess will let him pat her.'

Laura glances at Jess. 'Mouse is different now,' she says. 'He's on medication. It makes him calmer. I don't think he'll frighten her.'

I hesitate. Laura clearly does not understand the memory of a dog. 'I suppose we can see how it goes . . . If she's frightened, I'll bring her back home.'

Laura's face splits open with delight. 'That'll be wonderful. It'll make Mouse's day. Could you come at four? He should be settled in by then.'

During the afternoon, I try not to watch the clock, but the hands keep moving, and soon it's four o'clock and we wander down the hill and across the road to Laura's house. She flings open the door with frightening exuberance and my anxiety increases. She's excited to see us, desperate to make a success of this occasion for Mouse. Jess and I step tentatively through the door and down the hallway to the lounge.

Mouse is sitting on the couch, his face shadowy. He appears dull and unresponsive, his body large and slack.

'Mouse. Our visitors are here.'

Laura's brightness seems forced, and when Mouse swings his eyes towards us, all I feel from him is disinterest.

'This is Tom, our neighbour.' Laura's voice is high with enthusiasm. 'And this is his dog, Jess.'

Mouse's blank gaze takes me in without reaction, but when he glances down at Jess, sitting very close to my legs, something flickers across his face and I notice the fingers of one of his hands twitching where it lies open, palm up, on the couch.

Jess presses against me and watches Mouse carefully. She isn't entirely at ease, but she's not afraid either.

'Happy Birthday, Mouse,' I say.

Mouse ignores me. I hear him humming to himself and his lips are moving, but I can't make out any words. The fingers of his hand continue to twitch, and I watch them, mesmerised, unsure what to say or do. Then Jess stands up and pads softly across the carpet, sniffs at Mouse's fingers and lowers her head onto his hand. A sigh passes through both of them: Jess and Mouse. I hear it and so does Laura. She stands rapt, watching Mouse's mouth as he mumbles incoherently to Jess, the spark of something in his eyes, the feathery twitching of his fingers beneath Jess's chin.

My dog stands very still, her yellow eyes watching him. Her tail is waving very slightly, and she hasn't shifted her head from his hand.

'He hasn't spoken in weeks,' Laura whispers.

Mouse's muttering doesn't seem to equate with speech, but to Laura it's obviously progress.

'He's been heavily sedated,' she says. Her face is sad. 'They've only just started to back off his dose. I thought Jess might help. Thank you so much for coming.'

She looks at me with tears shimmering in her eyes, and I feel sorry for her. For both of them. My grief is overwhelming, but it's a temporary state, a loss and readjustment that is difficult, but not impossible. This poor man is so lost and so disconnected that he will never see the world as most of us do. Yet he has the security of Laura's love and support. And she will continue to love him even if he never realises it. In that, he is lucky.

Laura has been watching me closely, and I see surprise sweep across her features. Then she gathers herself together, glances at Mouse who is still murmuring to Jess, and smiles warmly.

'I'll just get the cakes,' she says.

While she's in the kitchen, I gaze out the window at my house up the hill. It's strange looking at my place from Laura's; for a moment I almost expect to see myself leaning against the balcony or passing like a shadow behind the windows. It's a shock to realise how much of my life can be seen from here. I hadn't known I was so visible. Laura could sit here and watch me moving in the kitchen, or observe me feeding possums with Jess on the deck. How much does she know about me? How much of my grief has she seen? How much can she tell by watching the movements of a lonely man in his house with his dog?

Then I realise perhaps this is why I am here, in her house for Mouse's birthday. Maybe this is Laura's attempt to help, her way of showing she cares. She can't fix things, but she can offer me company. She understands loneliness.

Then she's back with a plate bearing four cupcakes with a candle stuck in each. 'One candle for each decade,' she says, smiling brightly at Mouse.

He stares at the candles, and the light flickers in his eyes. She sets the plate on a small table in front of him and we sing 'Happy Birthday' in tuneless voices. Laura puffs out the candles then hands a cupcake to Mouse.

'It has pink icing,' she says. 'Your favourite.'

Mouse takes the cake, forgetting Jess for a moment, and eats it. The icing sticks to his lip and Laura wipes it gently away. Then she passes a cupcake to me and also puts one on a plate on the floor for Jess. Jess glances up at me for permission then scoffs the cake quickly. It has been a very happy visit for her. Not at all what either of us expected. Jess pants happily at me, and I'm sure it's because she hopes we'll be invited again.

When we leave, Laura lingers at the door. 'Can we go for a walk tomorrow morning?' she asks. 'I haven't gone for a while—I thought you needed to be alone. But with my new job I'm stuck in an office. And I do like to get out.'

I pause too before nodding. 'What time suits you?'

She smiles. 'How about seven o'clock?'

37

Leon and I arrange to meet at the Cloudy Corner campground. His four-wheel drive is already there when I arrive. I find him sitting near a patch of blackened soil where there's obviously been a large campfire fairly recently.

'She gave a talk to a group of scouts here,' he says, as I join him in the shifting shade. 'Did she tell you? She was a hit.'

'No. She didn't mention it.'

Guilt sweeps across his face. 'Perhaps she didn't tell you because it didn't end so well.'

'What happened?'

'She collapsed. I suppose she fainted.' He flushes. 'She didn't want me to tell anyone. She was worried your sister would take her back to Hobart.'

'Mum had a passionate hatred of nursing homes.'

Leon nods, still flushed. 'Awful places. I'm glad she didn't end up somewhere like that ... It was quick at the end. There wasn't much time for nursing ...'

We pause, each uncertain what to say next. We are two people brought together by circumstance; Mum is our only common denominator.

Leon waves towards East Cloudy Head. 'Let's climb the hill before the weather comes in.'

We pull packs and rain gear from our cars. At the trail head, we sign the logbook and begin the climb. Once we're moving, talk begins to flow. It's easier without eye contact.

'I resented your mum at first,' Leon says, clearly embarrassed. 'She was prickly, and it was a hassle to have to check on her. I was railroaded into it by my boss. And I didn't want extra work. I had enough on at home. Your mum wasn't an easy companion either. She didn't seem to understand I had work to do. Kept trying to corner me into taking her places. Always wanting to go here or there. Asking me intrusive questions and expecting me to stay for cups of tea.'

'Did you take her on trips?' I ask, surprised. 'She didn't tell me about that. She never asked *me* to take her anywhere.'

'She seemed to have an agenda,' Leon said. 'A list of places she wanted to visit. Any opportunity, she'd be bugging me to take her. Not that we did anything when we got there. She just stood looking into space. Like she was living in another time. Maybe she was.'

'Where did you take her?' I ask.

Leon shrugged. 'It was all just local. The campground here. Past the farm. Up towards Mount Mangana. Clennett's Mill. She even asked me to walk her up East Cloudy Head, of all the outrageous things. It was just after she'd fainted and I said no. I took her back to the cabin and tucked her into bed, where she belonged.'

'So she showed you the farm?'

'Just from the road. She didn't say much. Just that she lived there with her relatives. And that she met Jack there—your dad. But she loved this place, I could tell. I can't count the number of times I found her on the couch just staring out the window with a radiant look on her face like she was already in heaven. She didn't get on with your sister though, did she?'

'Mum and Jan have always clashed,' I say. 'Gary and I tend to work around things. To keep the peace.'

Leon laughs. 'Your mum didn't give *me* much peace,' he says. 'I wanted to keep our relationship superficial. But your mum was always probing, seeking out soft spots. I wish her health hadn't deteriorated so quickly—I'd have liked to spend more time with her. I tried to make sure she took her medication. But she probably needed to be in hospital at the end there, with the attention of doctors and nurses. She told me to mind my own business when I mentioned it. She was never one to hold back, was she?' He stops for a moment to look out over Cloudy Bay where the morning light etches shadowy lines in the cliffs.

'What was it like,' I ask, 'at the end . . . ?'

His gaze focuses somewhere out over water, and there's a sense of calm about him when he speaks. 'When the time came, I didn't know if she could feel anything. Her breathing was so slow and weak. But I took her out on the beach beneath the sky, and talked to her. It was peaceful when she went, just beautiful. I think she knew she was in her home.'

We climb again and Leon allows me silence.

'It's amazing really, the way we became friends in such a short time,' he says finally. 'Maybe we could do it because we didn't have any mutual history. And we were both aware it would be short. She was here to die, and I knew it. That meant that we could be honest with each other. Not that she told me anything secret. But we talked openly. She listened to me—that's more than I can say for anyone else in my life.'

He laughs. 'You know, the first time I met your mum she was on a mission to trap me. I was cross and I got away from her on some excuse about checking the campground. But when I came back, there she was going for a walk on the beach. I don't know how she managed to get out there, but she had her head flung back and her nostrils flared, daring me to have a go at her.'

We both laugh at the image and take a rest on the saddle, looking down towards Cloudy Corner and across Cloudy Bay to the distant cliffs. Then we resume the climb, hiking quietly up the last stretch of track until we are on top in the blasting wild breath of the wind, gazing out over the iron grey of the immense rolling ocean. We pull out coats and beanies and sit on rocks sheltered from the worst of the gale. From the depths of my pack, I dig out a plastic container of sultanas and almonds to share. But I have been outdone by Leon, who produces a thermos of hot coffee which he pours into thermal mugs along with a dribble of milk from a plastic bottle. Then he melts dark chocolate into the brew.

'To your mother,' he says, handing me a mug. 'She was a fine woman. The best.'

We clink mugs and stare across the vast landscape of light and sea, wind and cloud. 'This is her home,' I say. 'She's still here.'

'She'd be pleased with me,' Leon says, after a while. 'I'm making a change, and she'd like that. I've applied for a job with National Parks in the Hartz Mountains, and they say there's a good chance I'll get it. I've been here a long time, looking after my folks. But my old man hasn't been too well lately. He's bedridden and going downhill. His liver's shot. Too much grog. Mum's taking care of him now.'

He looks to me for approval and I nod. 'You'll like the Hartz Mountains,' I say. 'It's beautiful there.'

'I'll miss Bruny. But I'll be back to visit Mum.' He lapses to silence and we fix on grey distance where the lighthouse might be visible on a clearer day.

'I'm glad you were with her when she died,' I say. 'I want to thank you for that—the company and friendship you gave her. I wish I could show you how much I appreciate it.'

He glances at me. 'Come and visit if I get this job in the Hartz Mountains. I'd like to keep in touch with someone from your family.' He smiles. 'And I don't think I have much in common with your brother or sister.'

We laugh, and there's a sense of camaraderie between us, an almost-brotherliness.

For a long while we sit, paying private tribute to Mum. When the cold starts to seep in, we pack and wander back down the hill.

38

Jan decides we should scatter Mum's ashes at Cape Bruny—a surprising suggestion given her aversion to the place. Maybe Mum's death has softened her, smoothed her jagged resentful edges. Gary and I quickly agree to the proposal. It will be good for all of us to get some closure.

I suggest we invite Leon along, given his presence at Mum's death. But Jan says she doesn't like the idea of including a stranger. I insist that Leon was Mum's friend, not a stranger, but Jan won't budge, and Gary thinks it'd be an intrusion too.

We make the journey to Cape Bruny in Gary's new car complete with spoiler and shiny mag wheels. He isn't keen to take his pride and joy on the corrugated Bruny roads, but Jan refuses to go in my old car and there's really no other option. I leave Jess at home, whimpering at the gate, and I join my brother and sister in the car. It amazes me siblings can be so dissimilar and feel so disconnected.

The trip is long and quiet. Jan sits rigidly in the passenger seat beside Gary while I relax in the back, savouring the space and the lack of conversation. Even Gary doesn't seem tempted to break the silence. He's probably afraid of sparking Jan off, or setting her going on some tirade about how the past weeks would have been handled differently if she'd had her way.

At the light station, Gary swings his car into the carpark and switches off the engine. It's an average early winter's day, overcast and windy. I feel right at home. We ascend the hill in single file: Jan in the lead, me deferentially just behind, and Gary labouring at the back, undertaking the most exercise he's attempted in years. He hobbles up the hill like a lame old bear, puffing and grunting. I wonder if he remembers the buoyant way he bounded up here when he was young.

By the time we reach the lighthouse, he has dropped back a good fifty metres. Jan and I shelter on the leeside of the tower out of the wind and wait for him.

It's been a long time since I was here—ten years, maybe twelve—and it's good to feel the wind raking over the heath. The tower is pretty much the same, despite a few chips of peeling paint, a few salt stains, a bit of rust on the lock. Back when I was a kid, they were always slapping whitewash on the walls, always cleaning the windows, polishing the brass fittings inside.

Gary arrives, panting. 'Some climb,' he gasps. 'I think I need to join a gym.'

'Not a bad idea,' Jan says. 'You might live longer.'

Gary's face is flushed an unhealthy red and his chest heaves. 'So what do you reckon? Where should we unleash the ashes?'

Jan squints across the hill. 'How about over there, near the new tower.'

Gary shakes his head. 'No, Mum wouldn't want that. She always said Dad detested automation.'

Jan sighs. 'You're right. She'd hate us to do it there. It'd be disrespectful to Dad.' It's the first time I've ever heard Jan admit she was wrong. 'But I don't want to spread her ashes right here,' she says. 'I don't like to think about people walking on her . . .' She trails off, voice quavering.

'We could wander down the hill a little and go off along that grassy track,' I suggest, pointing. 'That'd take us away from the tower and the tourists. I bet most people just follow the path up here and then go straight back down.'

Jan agrees and we walk slowly downhill, each of us meandering somewhere in memory. When I stop halfway across the slope, Jan comes up alongside me. Her face is almost soft. She waits for Gary to join us before handing me the little china urn.

'Here, you do it,' she says. 'You love this place more than any of us.'

'Just be careful to check the wind direction,' Gary cautions. 'I've heard of people wearing ashes all over them.' He laughs stiffly.

'It's a sou'westerly,' I say. 'The wind's almost always from the south-west at this time of year.'

I take the lid off the urn. Honeyeaters dip and flutter over the heath. I wave Gary and Jan behind me, then lift the urn high and trickle Mum's ashes out into the wind. Grey dust catches and drifts and spirals. I toss the rest up as far as I can and stand back to watch the last grey flushes disappear among the bushes.

We stand for a long time, breathing quietly.

'Well, I suppose that's it then,' Gary says after a while.

We start back across the hill to the path, where Jan decides she's going down to talk to the caretaker's wife. Gary wants to sit on the bench seat at the top and look south at the view. I give him my rain jacket as some protection from the wind and then I follow the track down towards Courts Island.

I haven't been this way in years. When I was a child, I used to scramble down here all the time. Each day after lessons, I'd race up past the tower and down the slope to see if the tide was far enough out so I could scoot across the causeway. Back before I was born, they sometimes used to deliver mail in the sheltered area between the island and the cape. Someone from the light station would scrape down to the pebbly cove and grab a few supplies from a dinghy launched from the boat.

Today, I pause as the track steepens. Around the craggy coast, I see coloured buoys floating on the swell, marking craypots.

I climb further down, and the causeway comes into view. Waves run across it from two directions, meeting in the middle, but the rocks are still exposed and it's shallow enough to cross. The track becomes rocky and I pick my way down carefully.

The route has changed since I was young—it's eroded now from use by too many people. Before I was born, people used to flock here during mutton-bird season. They'd park their cars along the road behind the cottages and rush up here to wait for the official opening hour. Then they'd cross to the island, no matter what the tides, to drag chicks from their burrows. Mutton birds were supposed to make good roasts, but Mum said the meat was oily. I never tried it, and then the harvest was banned. So that meant Courts Island was a sanctuary for me, a place to watch birds excavating their burrows at the beginning of each breeding season, their feet scraping, dirt flying. Later in the season the eagles would come, perching on rocks or low scrub, waiting for an opportunity to carry away a fat chick for a feast.

I scrabble down the last precarious section of track onto a stony beach strewn with clumps of kelp and stinking seaweed. After picking my way over rocks, I stride across the causeway through shallow lapping waves. On the other side, I climb the steep track among succulent pig-face and iceplant. The musty smell of bird is thick in my nostrils. Small animal paths crisscross the slope marked by webbed footprints. Dark round holes plunge beneath the vegetation, their openings lined with feathers. As I wander over the spongy ground, a wedge-tailed eagle with a blond mane takes to the air, flapping up slowly from a rock splashed white with guano. I stop to watch him as he rises in a lazy spiral and floats effortlessly higher, cruising over the green dome of the island.

When I was young, I came here once at dusk to be among the mutton birds returning to their nests. I crossed the causeway early, when the tide was out, and waited in the approaching dark until the birds started coming home. Out on the water in the fading light, I saw them floating in large groups, rafting on the tide. When the first bird returned to the colony it came to ground with a thud and scuttled into its burrow, clacking as it reunited with its chick. Then more birds came slamming home, diving out of the darkening sky. Soon the air was thick with them—hundreds of flying projectiles bursting out of the night, crashing awkwardly to the ground and scurrying off into burrows. Some impaled themselves on vegetation as they came in to land. There was blood, cries of pain.

Then the pain was mine. A plummeting bird thumped heavily on my back, raking me with its nails. More birds fell on me, their beaks like spears. I crouched, cowering, arms over my head. When finally there were no more birds cascading from the sky, I struggled downhill, sobbing, and waded across the causeway. The water was up to my thighs, deep enough to be dangerous, and I limped across the beach and then home, facing years of nightmares, of black shrilling birds plunging at me out of the night.

Now, as I sit among the pig-face, remembering, the wedge-tailed eagle rises further above me in ascending circles and disappears to the south of the island. My presence has unsettled him and I should remove myself so he can resume his solitary perch on the rocks. I pick my way back, wandering towards the eastern cliffs.

Finding a sheltered nook, I squat there, watching black waves surging against the cliff walls and shattering themselves on the rocks below. Kelp swirls and kinks, and I sink into the rhythm and movement. The regularity soothes and cleanses me. The roar and drone of the sea.

Beneath my skin contentment settles. My mother is dead, yes. She's gone. But this is her place. She found happiness here, and peace. Her history was written here, her life bending and twisting and folding, like these great lumps of rock—going through a journey of creation, just like the earth and sky and sea and waves. Nature repeating itself over and over.

39

Time passes, maybe two weeks, and Jacinta comes to Coningham to join me for a walk. She comes on a cold grey day and we don coats before strolling down the hill beneath ominous skies. Along the beach track, Jess loops around us, investigating small rustlings in the bush. We pass Laura's house, and she waves to us through the window. Several times recently Laura and I have walked together in the mornings, enjoying the birds.

'Who's that?' Jacinta asks.

'New neighbour.'

'She looks nice.' Jacinta looks at me sideways. 'How's Emma?'

'Not sure.'

'What does that mean? That you're not going out with her anymore?'

'Not since Mum died.'

'You have to keep on living, you know.'

I shove my hands into my pockets and shrug.

'What about going south?' Jacinta asks. 'Did they offer you that job?'

'Yes.' Bazza and Emma have been on the phone at least twice in the past week. 'I'm not sure I want to go.'

Jacinta looks surprised. 'I thought you were keen to go down there.'

'It always seems you want something till you get it.'

'I don't mind looking after Jess, if that's what's worrying you.'

'It's not Jess.'

We step from the sandy track onto the sand. It's chilly on the beach with a cold fresh breeze rippling over the water. The sand is grey to match the light. We sit above the high-tide mark while Jess trots up the beach sniffing at dead Japanese sea stars and other treasures.

'That girl back there,' Jacinta says. 'The one who waved. What's her name?'

'Laura.'

'You should ask her out.'

I shrug again, embarrassed. Perhaps Jacinta can read my thoughts. Inviting Laura to dinner is something I've been contemplating. She's been pleasant company out walking, and we've come to know each other little by little each day.

The tick of a boat's motor trickles across on the wind; it's about a hundred metres out, heading up the channel.

'I've been going through Nana's things with Mum,' Jacinta says.

I picture them working though Mum's wardrobe, pulling out dresses, the fabric swinging. I imagine the clothes laid out on the bed. The coat hangers. The musty smell. 'How's Jan coping?' I ask.

'Better than expected.' A brief smile flickers on Jacinta's lips. 'We've decided to give everything to the Salvos. Mum thought Nana would want someone to use her things rather than throwing them all away.'

I pick up a shell from the sand and toss it into the water. Far out across the channel the small boat is still thrumming.

'Tom, I wanted to bring this to you.' Jacinta bends forward and takes an envelope from the back pocket of her jeans. 'I found it in Nana's suitcase. The one she took to Cloudy Bay. It has your name on it.' She hands the envelope to me and I look at it with vague interest.

'I don't recognise the handwriting,' I say.

'Perhaps you should read it. It might be important.'

I stare at the unfamiliar spidery scrawl. I can't imagine what the letter could be about. The will's been dealt with. I turn the envelope over a couple of times before opening it. Inside is a piece of folded paper. I unfold it, flattening it against my leg. Then I read the uneven writing looping from line to line down the page.

> *Dear Tom,*
>
> *I suspect if you are reading this letter, your mother is dead. Mary was a grand lady in her time, but she was very strong and opinionated. To deliver this letter to you while she was alive would have been too difficult for her. I forgive her for that, even though it means more time lost for me.*
>
> *You see, Mary carried a secret that was important not only to her, but also to me. I met your mother in a park in Hobart when she was sixteen, and over ten days we became close friends. Ten days doesn't seem like long enough to fall in love, but your mother was a passionate person, as you probably know. Our lives were bound together in those few short days in ways neither of us could ever foresee.*
>
> *When your mother's parents found out about me, they sent her to Bruny Island. There she met Jack. I didn't see her for many years. But time does not weaken the strongest of bonds.*
>
> *There was an occasion, when your mother was living with her parents in Hobart, that I met her alone. Her parents and two children were out. Jack was on Bruny Island. And you were not yet*

born. I heard from other people in Hobart that
Mary stayed another six weeks before going back to
Jack. The records of your birthdate indicate that you
must have been conceived during this period when
Mary was away from Bruny Island. This is how I
know you are my son.

> *I don't know what a man should say to a*
son he has never met, but I do know this. If you
are willing, after you have come to terms with this
revelation, I would like to meet you. I will not be
offended if you choose not to contact me. However,
you must know that I start each day with the hope
that it will be the day you call me.
> > *Yours sincerely,*
> > *Adam Singer*

By the time I arrive at the signature I'm shaking. Who is this Adam Singer? My eyes skim blindly over the phone number written at the bottom. I fold the letter and put it away, then pull it out again with quivering hands and read it once more before handing it to Jacinta.

'Read it,' I say, looking out across the water, wondering if the thunder I am hearing is in my ears or my heart.

Presently, I feel Jacinta's hand gripping my arm. 'Perhaps it isn't true.' I turn to look at her. She's pale and stunned. 'Maybe it's some sort of prank,' she says helplessly. She looks so worried and I feel like I'm floating, ethereal and formless.

'I don't know who I am,' I say.

'Yes, you do.' She clutches my arm tighter. 'You're Tom Mason. Nothing changes that. You're the same person you've always been.'

I look at her, blank. 'My roots are gone.' That's how I feel. Like a tree with no roots. A puff of wind could blow me down.

'Perhaps this could be a good thing,' Jacinta says.

'What do you mean?'

'Being without roots,' she says. 'It could be liberating.'

I stare at her, unconvinced. 'How can this man be my father?'

Jacinta frowns. 'Perhaps he isn't.'

I shake my head. 'He must have been. Mum must have known what this letter was about.'

'But it was unopened.'

I stare blindly across the channel. 'She knew. But did she want *me* to know?'

'Does it matter?'

'Yes, it does. If Mum wanted me to know, she'd have given me the letter. Or she'd have told me herself.'

'But the letter says she couldn't have done that.'

'Why not?' I stare at Jacinta in bewilderment.

'It would have been like betraying Grandpa all over again. If she'd already done that once . . . *if* she had . . . maybe she couldn't do it again.'

I look at her without understanding. 'Why didn't she destroy it then?'

'Perhaps she couldn't. Maybe she thought this man— Adam—had a right to know you.' Jacinta pats my arm gently. 'You don't have to decide now,' she says. 'You need time to think. You have to do what's best for you.'

What's best for me is to wind the clock back ten minutes. I shake off Jacinta's hand and kick at the sand, unsure what to do.

'It's all right, Tom,' Jacinta says. 'You won't self-destruct, even if it feels like it right now.'

'I need to run.' I rip off my coat and shove it at her. 'Will you mind Jess?'

'Yes. But be careful, Tom.'

I turn from her and flee, feet stabbing the clinging sand. I run hard towards the end of the beach. My body is tight with adrenalin, my legs pumping, my mind erupting. As I charge along, a pied oystercatcher takes off over the water. Masked lapwings flap into the sky, protesting noisily.

At the end of the beach, I turn up the track and pound through the bush to the road. I pause at the edge of the tarmac, my heart thudding. For a suspended moment, I stare at my house. But I can't go there. The walls would hem me in and I might explode. I have to keep running.

Down the road I sprint, rushing the steep descent and hoofing along the flatter stretches. My breath is coming in tight gasps, but I keep running. I run to obliterate everything. To rub out fear and shock. Where is Mum in all this? Why didn't she give me the letter? There were several opportunities at the cabin, but she let them pass by. Why didn't she do it? Surely it would have been better than this, this overwhelming sense of loss and doubt and confusion. Who is this man who claims he's my father?

The road leads to the water's edge and I hammer along it. A car passes on the narrow stretch and I almost stumble in the ditch. But my feet keep going. I run till I meet the highway. Then I run south up the long hill, cars whizzing past me.

Weather comes in and I pump through it. Rain wetting my face, soaking my clothes, trickling down my back and into my shoes. I thought I knew my mother. And I thought I knew my father too, even though I didn't understand him. Now I have this disorder and upheaval. Do I need to know this man? Do I need to contact him? He's had nothing to do with me. He may call himself my father, but my father is Jack. The lighthouse keeper. The husband of my mother.

I pass the fruit and vegetable shop at Oyster Cove. Cars are parked there, people buying things, thrusting fruit into bags. I run past them up the hill, resenting their normal lives. Just a short time ago, my life was ordinary too. I was Tom Mason, son of Jack Mason, grieving the loss of my mother. But my father is no longer my father. And another man has appeared. A nobody out of nowhere. He hasn't watched me grow up. He hasn't wiped my nose, cleaned my tears, patched bleeding knees. I don't have to invite him into my life. I owe him nothing. Jack is my father.

When I'm close to the top of the hill the rain stops. I run on, past the skeleton of a house under construction, past paddocks where horses and native hens graze side by side, past farm dams reflecting the sullen grey sky. As I run downhill, the rain comes in again. It mingles with the tears on my face. The highway thuds beneath my shoes. The hills push me up and fall away again.

The turn-off to Kettering appears, with signs for the ferry. I keep on running. The road narrows past the marina where the masts of a hundred yachts bristle. Now my breath comes in gasps and sobs. I run to the end of the road, through the carpark, along the waiting lanes, and then I am at the terminal.

There's the ferry, not far out. It has just left for Bruny Island, the white trail of its wash kicking up behind. I watch it pull away, its engines throbbing rhythmically. It feels as if my past is leaving me. As if it is deserting me, and I know it won't come back.

How can I walk bravely into a new and unexpected future? It's not something I've ever been good at.

I kneel on the tarmac, gasping for breath. The ferry rounds the headland. Soon it will be out of sight. When I stand up and walk away from here, I will have to accept that everything is different. Every thought I've ever had will require rethinking.

That night I keep hoping the oblivion of sleep will arrive, but it doesn't. I feel the uncertain texture of the future. I keep thinking about Mum. Adam Singer. My *father*.

Then it is dark.

The sound of the sea is thick around me, rushing somewhere beyond steep cliffs. I'm crouching on the ground, alert, waiting for something. Suddenly I unfurl great wings and surge into a smudged grey sky. The channel is below. I sweep over it, just above the glassy surface of slow waves, flying low and fast, like an albatross.

Near land, I bank upwards, lifting over hills and forests. Cracks of creamy light seep between doleful clouds. I sail out over cliffs, like an eagle now, and the sea falls away beneath me. I drop over the water, skimming through fine spray from the wind-fetched tips of waves. To the west is the dark shape of Cape Bruny. The lighthouse flashes, and streaks of white light shoot across land and sea. I rush towards it on the wind, rising upwards over land, lifting high above the keepers' cottages.

Below, a dark figure approaches the tower. It's the tall shape of my father, Jack the lightkeeper, bent forward in the gale. He stops at the heavy black door, unlocks it, swings the door wide. I sweep in after him and stop at the foot of the stairs. He is on the staircase. I hear the steady clomp of his boots. The hollow ring of his footsteps. I have to hurry. I have to find him before he turns out the light.

I fly up the stairs, swooping around the spirals, ascending towards light. Then I am in the lantern room, the glass windows in a circle around me. The lens is still revolving, still bending scattered rays of light into coherent beams that shoot through grey dawn and lose themselves far out over the heaving sea. All is quiet.

I listen for my father's voice, his cough in the silence, his muffled footsteps on the floor. There's a bang. A rush of wind in the vents. The door to the balcony slams open and a shadow passes through. My father escaping.

I follow him out into the blast of the wind and the airiness of the balcony. The dawn flares red, brightening quickly, the light swirling as I look around.

There is nothing. Just the giddy height of the tower. The wild whip of the gale. And the strangely uplifting sensation of space. The possibility of air.

My father is gone, but the breaking light releases me. In the whirl of wind, I am the calm eye of the storm.

When I wake, the house is still. I've slept in and light slips beneath the curtains and across the floor. Jess is watching me from her basket, her chin resting on her forelegs. As our eyes connect, the fluffy tip of her tail flaps softly three or four times. She's wondering when I'm going to get up. The day has begun. There are things to be done. Dog things, like walks and food.

I roll over beneath the covers and hide from the light. My dream is still pinning me down and I'm not sure what it means. But I can only rest a few minutes before I toss back the covers and slide out. Jess leaps instantly to my side. She pads to the door and looks at me expectantly, wanting out. I open the door for her, feeling the gush of fresh air on my face. After breakfast, I'll go out too. I feel strong. I've resolved something during the night. Maybe it was the dream.

In the kitchen, I make coffee and contemplate my options. My mind is unsettled, but there are ways to move forward. I won't sit around and wallow in sorrow and confusion like I would have in the past. I'm beyond that now. I can be decisive. There are many things I can do, positive things. I could go to the garage and get back on the job, or I could ditch work for the day and see if Laura is home. Maybe we could go for a drive up Mount Wellington, just to feel the wind.

Turning back to the bench to make breakfast, I see the phone and stop. My hand hovers over the handset and I pick it up, feeling its weight in my hand. Then I pick up the piece of paper on the bench, check the number and dial it.

'Hello.'

'Bazza.'

'Tom. I hope you've rung to make me a happy man.'

'I'm sorry, Bazza. I can't do it.'

'Don't tell me you're taking Fredricksen's job.'

'No. But I wanted to tell you first; I'm not going south.'

'Well, that's a bugger. Maybe next year.'

'Maybe. Maybe not. But thanks for the opportunity.'

'No worries, mate. Stay in touch.'

I hang up the phone and lay it on the bench. Then I pick it up again. I ought to ring Fredricksen. But there's someone else I need to ring first. I find the number.

One ring. Two. Three. Four.

My whole body is waiting for the receiver to be picked up. Please answer.

'Hello.'

My hands sweat. I turn the piece of paper over and run my fingertips lightly over the spidery writing. My heart is in my throat.

'. . . Is that Adam Singer?'

'Yes, yes it is.' The voice is gravelly, unfamiliar.

'Hello . . . this is Tom.'

Acknowledgements

The writing of *The Lightkeeper's Wife* has been a challenging but fulfilling journey. For support, encouragement, persistence and good faith, I thank my publisher, Jane Palfreyman, at Allen & Unwin. She pushed me to delve deeper and deliver more, and for this I am grateful. The excellent editing skills and input of Siobhán Cantrill, Catherine Milne and Clara Finlay also helped greatly in the shaping of this book, and A&U designer, Emily O'Neill, has created a stunning cover. Thanks to all of you.

Without the ongoing support and positivity of my agent, Fiona Inglis at Curtis Brown, this book would not have happened. I thank her for guiding me through unexpected squalls along the way. Also, my wonderful husband, David Lindenmayer, had unflinching confidence in me, and read and re-read the manuscript beyond the call of duty. My sister, Fiona Andersen, gave invaluable comments on earlier drafts of the book. Marjorie Lindenmayer provided indispensible help and diligently read the page proofs.

For giving me the opportunity to experience Antarctica and be captivated by this grand wilderness, I thank the Australian Antarctic Division. I went south twice as a volunteer on ANARE projects working on Weddell and crabeater seals (summer of 1995–96 and 1996–97). The caretakers at the Cape Bruny Light

Station, Andy and Beth Gregory, provided a happy and comfortable stay in the assistant lightkeeper's cottage, and I especially thank Andy for answering my many questions. The history room at Alonnah on Bruny Island was also a useful resource.

Where possible I have tried to be consistent with the history of the lighthouse, the region and the era, however deviations from the facts were sometimes necessary to facilitate the telling of the story. Information on lighthouses and the way of life on light stations was gleaned from many books, including: *Guiding Lights: Tasmania's Lighthouses and Lighthousemen* (K.M. Stanley); *From Dusk Till Dawn: A History of Australian Lighthouses* (Gordon Reid); *Romance of Australian Lighthouses* (V. Philips); *Beacons of Hope: An Early History of Cape Otway and King Island Lighthouses* (D. Walker); *Following their Footsteps: Exploring Adventure Bay* (*ed.* C.J. Turnbull); *Stargazing: Memoirs of a Young Lighthouse Keeper* (Peter Hill); *The Lighthouse Stevensons* (Bella Bathurst); *Lighthouses of Australia* (John Ibbotson); and the newsletters and website (www.lighthouses.org.au) of Lighthouses of Australia Inc., a non-profit organisation which aims to create a higher profile for Australian lighthouses within Australia and overseas, to thereby preserve, protect and promote their place within our history. I have also visited many lighthouses both in Australia and eastern Canada, and have had wonderful sojourns at the Cape Bruny Light Station in Tasmania, Green Cape and Point Perpendicular lighthouses, southeastern NSW, and Gabo Island lighthouse in Victoria.

Insights into Antarctica were derived from my time at Davis Station in the Australian Antarctic Territory, from the notes of my friend Raina Plowright, and from several books, including: *The Home of the Blizzard* (Sir Douglas Mawson); *Just Tell Them I Survived* (Dr Robin Burns); *Slicing the Silence: Voyaging to Antarctica* (Tom Griffiths); and *The Silence Calling: Australians in Antarctica 1947–1997* (Tim Bowden). Special thanks also to my lovely friend Mandy McKendrick for sharing her home in

Coningham, and to friend Bryan Ries for elucidating the role of diesel mechanics in Antarctica.

This book is dedicated to my grandmother, Vera Viggers, who is *not* Mary Mason in this story. She was, however, a humble, personable and generous woman who has been a great inspiration in my life. I am sad that she did not see the completed version of this book before she died, but she did enjoy an earlier draft.